MIRAGE

By

Orang Agahi

I would like to dedicate this to my family.
To my adorable wife Susie, my daughter Amy and her husband Nick,
my son Daniel and his significant other, Judith.

Had Susie and I ordered our children from a catalogue,
we could not have got two more wonderful human beings.
Perhaps also a tribute to their mother who raised them and also their strong Faith.

CONTENTS

ACKNOWLEDGMENTS...i
CHAPTER 1 1
CHAPTER 2 8
CHAPTER 3 18
CHAPTER 4 26
CHAPTER 5 33
CHAPTER 6 43
CHAPTER 7 51
CHAPTER 8 56
CHAPTER 9 62
CHAPTER 10 72
CHAPTER 11 85
CHAPTER 12 91
CHAPTER 13 101
CHAPTER 14 105
CHAPTER 15 109
CHAPTER 16 117
CHAPTER 17 127
CHAPTER 18 134
CHAPTER 19 146
CHAPTER 20 159
CHAPTER 21 168
CHAPTER 22 178
CHAPTER 23 182
CHAPTER 24 189
CHAPTER 25 193
CHAPTER 26 197
CHAPTER 27 206
CHAPTER 28 211
CHAPTER 29 216
CHAPTER 30 222
CHAPTER 31 229
CHAPTER 32 239
CHAPTER 33 244
CHAPTER 34 247
CHAPTER 35 251

CHAPTER 36 271
CHAPTER 37 276
CHAPTER 38 292
CHAPTER 39 300
CHAPTER 40 313
CHAPTER 41 318
CHAPTER 42 333
CHAPTER 43 345
CHAPTER 44 364
CHAPTER 45 374
CHAPTER 46 381
CHAPTER 47 396
CHAPTER 48 402
CHAPTER 49 408
CHAPTER 50 419
CHAPTER 51 423
CHAPTER 52 429
CHAPTER 53 435
CHAPTER 54 440
CHAPTER 55 445
CHAPTER 56 448
ABOUT THE AUTHOR 452

ACKNOWLEDGMENTS

I would start with thanking my best friend, Gerry Clarke, for his meticulous proofreading and his encouragement. My close friend Dessie Mullan, another avid reader, spurred me on with his enthusiasm and positive feedback on the story line. Many thanks to Nick Duxbury, my son-in-law, and two favourite (albeit only) children, Amy Agahi and Daniel Agahi, and our dear friend Pat Irvine, for their advice on the publishing front. My greatest gratitude goes to my patient wife, Susie Kelly (Agahi) in her years of forbearance as I tried to combine a demanding medical career with my writing ambition, amongst other things.

CHAPTER 1

The Crime

Jake was awakened by the sound of the key turning in his cell door. The prison guard walked into his cell. He gruffly commanded Jake to get up with a strong and distinct New York accent, beckoning with his hand to show his impatience.

Jake looked around the cell, "Where am I?"

"What, do you have amnesia? Or were you too drunk to remember?"

Jake scratched his head, "No, I don't think I even asked."

"Well next time remember to ask. You are in the New York Metropolitan Correctional Centre." He kicked him on his ankle as he was lying on his bed, "Now get up, I ain't got all day."

Jake asked in a sarcastic tone, "Am I going home then?"

"Going home, my ass! Your fancy-ass lawyers are here to speak to you."

"I don't want to see anybody!"

The guard kicked him harder, "I won't ask you again! My job is to take you to the interview room. Now do you want to go there horizontally or vertically?" He was about to kick Jake again before Jake jumped up.

The guard produced handcuffs. Jake looked at him with an expression of surprise. "Just routine," is all the guard said. Jake put his hands behind him. The guard laughed and turned him round. As he handcuffed his hands in front of him, he said, "You have been watchin' too many movies." He laughed again.

Jake walked behind the uniformed guard through four electrically operated internal prison gates which were each opened by a guard on the other side. He was dressed in a pair of old jeans which looked in need of a wash. He still had the brown T-shirt on from the time he was arrested. He had on a pair of old black shoes in need of a polish. He was unshaven and had a fairly long scruffy beard.

He was shown into a room with a table at the centre of it. It was a basic-looking table with four thin legs. There was one wooden chair at one end of the long side of it and two at the other.

The guard beckoned him to sit down. Jake sat on one of the chairs that was on the side of the table that had two chairs. The guard grunted at him, kicked his ankle again, then hit him on his left shoulder and pointed to the chair on the opposite side. Jake got up and walked across and sat on the chair there. The guard said nothing and stood beside him with his hands crossed in front of his groin area. After a couple of moments, the guard sniffed a couple of times, gave Jake a dirty look and walked a few paces away and stood by the door.

*

There was a knock at the door. Two ladies walked in. One of them said to the uniformed guard, "Thank you very much."

"Welcome Ma'am," was the answer as the guard tipped his head. He stood with his back to Jake and gently waved his hands in front of his nose, then held his nose and let go, "He's all yours, ladies!"

As they turned their attention to the dishevelled man sitting behind the table the younger of the two gasped and whispered, "O my God!"

The slightly older one approached Jake. She was thirty-seven years old, five foot ten, with dark brown hair that was shoulder length and parted on one side. She had a pinstripe skirt with a matching jacket, underneath which she wore a white blouse with the top couple of buttons open. She had a pearl necklace on. She reached her hand over to shake Jake's hand. "Hello my name is Amanda Jackson; I am your defense attorney." Jake reached and shook her hand with a very limp handshake and let go after a second.

Amanda continued, "This is my associate Miss Lucy Walker."

Jake shook Lucy's hand in a similar manner. Lucy was in her late twenties. She was slightly shorter than Amanda at five foot eight inches. She had auburn hair which was fairly thick set and cut just below the ear lobes. She had a plain black skirt on with a beige blouse with a frilly collar buttoned to the top. She had a grey jacket on.

Amanda turned to the guard, "Could I have privacy with my client please?"

The guard was very apologetic, "Sure, I'm sorry." He hastened towards the door.

Amanda's raised her voice slightly, "Excuse me, sir, would you mind removing his handcuffs?"

"But Ma'am, my orders are that he is dangerous and needs to remain cuffed."

Amanda sounded very authoritative, "Please remove his cuffs. I am happy to speak to your senior officer right now if you would like."

"No that is fine, I will remove his cuffs, ma'am, if that is your wish."

"Thank you."

Having removed the cuffs, the guard hooked them on his belt ring and locked them in place. "I will be right outside, give me a shout if you need me." With that he left the room.

Amanda and Lucy sat down opposite Jake. Amanda opened a file that she had in front of her. There were a couple of A4-size lined pages with some handwritten notes on them. She turned to a blank page and wrote the date at the top of the page.

She looked at Jake who seemed to be staring into space. "Mister Chapman." She paused, "Can I call you Jake, I believe you prefer Jake to John?"

Jake shrugged his shoulders without saying anything.

Amanda continued, "Jake I have gone through the statements that you have made to the police; I would like to hear your side to the story."

Jake still avoided eye contact, "I have told all there is to say to the police, I have nothing new to say."

Amanda seemed unperturbed by Jake's lack of cooperation, "Mister Chapman … Jake. Do you realise the gravity of the charges facing you?"

"Yes."

"Do you not care?"

"No."

"Jake you are accused of killing someone, surely you must care. You could spend the rest of your days behind bars!"

"It's a shame they don't just hang me and get it over and done with."

Amanda asked quickly, "Are you telling me that you killed her?"

A few days earlier

The lights of the car bounced off the policeman's NYPD silver badge on his chest and hat, glistening as it was wet with the rain. The policeman raised his hand as the white Mustang coupe approached him, indicating for the car to stop. The driver's window rolled down, allowing the rain into the car. The rotating red light shone on the face of the driver, giving a glimpse of his unshaven face. The driver flipped open his badge. "Detective Sterne, NYPD homicide, this is Detective Johnston with me."

"Good evening detective … Jim … sir! Go ahead," replied the policeman and he waved his left arm to direct the car forward.

The Mustang parked behind the two NYPD police cars with their blue and red lights flashing, parked side by side so as to block the road. Jim looked at his colleague. "Well, Derek are you ready for action?"

Derek replied, "I haven't come out on a Saturday night for the good of my health! You sound as if you are looking forward to this."

They got out of the car. Derek pulled up the collar of his beige full-length raincoat, buttoning up the top button. Jim pulled down his brown leather jacket and seemed impervious to the heavy rain. He was five foot-ten, forty years old, and quite stocky.

"Do you not want your raincoat?" Derek asked Jim. Derek was twenty-nine years old, with jet-black hair, six foot exactly, and very slim.

"Sure, why not, would you get it for me, it's on the back seat."

Derek pushed his seat forward and just managed to squeeze into the back-seat area and had to reach across to get Jim's raincoat. "Would you not get a four-door car in the future, this is not very practical for a police car."

"Maybe when I have kids, which is probably never!"

Jim put on his raincoat and turned the collar up. He approached the policeman standing in front of a white tape. He flashed his badge again, "Detective Sterne, homicide," nodding his head towards Derek he added, "Detective Johnston."

The white tape had been put up between two shrubs and the red writing on the tape read 'NYPD LINE – DO NOT CROSS'. Jim bent down and crossed under the tape. Derek followed him and ran to catch up and whispered, "Why do you always get to flash your badge?" No sooner had he finished the question than he tripped on a small rock and just about managed not to fall forwards.

"That's why, kid!" said Jim quickly. "You have a lot to learn."

Derek put his right hand on his forehead and gave a firm salute befitting of any soldier "Yes sir," he said.

Jim walked to the shrubs by the side of the road and nodded to the policeman. "Detective Sterne, homicide. What do we have here?" The policeman held his cap and tipped it gently, causing the water on top of his cap to pour onto his chin. "That young negro dude says he was cycling home when he saw a shoe by the side of the road. When he stopped to look at it, he noticed a trail of blood and followed it behind the bushes and saw the girl." He paused for a second and looked towards Derek, "It's pretty gruesome, kid."

Derek had a tone of annoyance in his voice, "It's Detective Johnston to you." The policeman shrugged his shoulders.

"I'm only trying to help …"

Derek snapped back, "Just stick to your job."

Jim pointed to the young black man holding on to his bicycle and at the same time leaning on the police car. A policeman had his hand on his shoulder as if trying to console him. Jim continued, "What the hell is someone doing cycling in the month of November when it's pissing down? Make sure you bring him in for questioning."

The policeman replied, "He says he is a waiter and always cycles home. We are getting his details and he is coming in for questioning tomorrow."

Jim stared at the policeman straight in the eyes. "What is your name, officer?"

"Officer Kowalski, sir, 28th Precinct."

Jim replied, "Well, Officer Kowalski, that kid at this precise time is my number one suspect. I want him at thirty-third precinct tonight for questioning. Make sure he is thoroughly searched, and I mean just short of a strip search!"

He then looked at Derek and waved his hand towards the shrub, "Let's go, Derek."

*

Jim stepped into a heap of mud; each time he took a step his shoe made a squelching sound. He walked on totally oblivious to this and after a few paces reached a policeman standing over a body. Derek hesitated, looked at the mud, looked at Jim, and began to look around. He walked a few yards up and then skipped across, trying to avoid the mud. He too arrived at the scene of the body and was obviously not prepared for the scene in front of him.

Jim turned to him. He had to quickly turn back and have a second look at him. "Are you all right, kid? You look as white as a ghost." He couldn't help a wry smile.

"I'm f–" he paused a little bit. "I'm fine."

Jim turned his attention to the body. It was of a young woman. She was naked from the waist up. She was lying face up. Her face was covered with blood, most of which appeared to have come from her nose. The lower part of her left leg was bent at the knee outwards, almost at a right angle. She had a red mini skirt on, pushed up to reveal her red knickers. Her bright red stockings were torn on the left leg, with only remnants of it left. On the right leg the stockings were lowered to knee level. She had one red shoe on the right foot.

Derek walked a few paces away and doubled in two and began heaving. He then vomited a couple of times. Jim walked towards him.

"You okay, kid?"

Derek raised his right hand. "Give me a minute, I'll be fine. It's just …"

"That's okay, Derek, you don't need to explain."

Jim began to survey the scene. It was hard to see much with the heavy rain. Having looked around three hundred and sixty degrees he knelt down besides the body.

Derek stood erect and cleared his throat. "Well how do you read it?

Jim walked a few paces towards some shrubs. He stopped and knelt down and had a closer look. He then walked back and knelt over the dead girl. He pointed to the girl's face. "She looks to be in her twenties. Badly beaten up and her left leg is obviously broken. Possibly attempted rape but certainly very brutal. The bushes up there are somewhat flattened and have blood on them. She was obviously not killed here but dragged and dumped here. With all the rain I'll be surprised if there will be much left here in terms of clues. Let's take a walk around quickly."

Derek replied, "Sure."

Having taken a few minutes to survey the scene Jim walked to Derek, "Let's go and question the kid at the precinct, we won't see much here. We'll see what CSI come up with."

Derek seemed relieved, "I can't say I'm disappointed with that idea."

Jim walked towards the policeman who had stopped them. "Will you take the suspect to the thirty-third precinct? I spoke to the precinct to start the questioning but tell them I will be there soon to also question the suspect."

"Yes detective."

As they were walking towards the car, the second policeman walked to Officer Kowalski. "Acts like a big shot. Who is he?"

"Oh, he is a big shot okay. I've heard of him. Both good and bad."

"I'm only interested in the bad gossip!"

Officer Kowalski kept looking at Jim and Derek as they walked towards Jim's mustang. "Well generally I don't like spreading rumours."

The second policeman smiled, "Yes but in this case you are going to make an exception, aren't you? Seeing we are standing in this shitty weather getting pneumonia."

Officer Kowalski nodded and smiled, "Yes while they go into their heated offices. The boys were saying – and don't quote me on this – they were saying that they heard he planted some evidence in at least one of his cases."

The second officer shook his head. "Shit you have disappointed me! I was expecting something juicy. I don't give a shit if he planted any evidence. I have no doubt the son of a bitch probably deserved it anyway."

Officer Kowalski turned to the other policeman and looked surprised. "That's funny, that's the exact words the detective said when he told me the story."

CHAPTER 2

Pub Stop

Jim and Derek walked back to the car. Jim leaned on the car and turned to Derek, "What time is it?"

"One a.m."

"I need to go to the precinct and question the biker, you can go home."

"No," Derek replied, "I want to be there, anyway this is all new to me and I wouldn't want to miss it."

As Derek opened the car door and was about to go in, he looked at his shoes, "Shit, my shoes are covered in mud!" He scraped his shoes against the footrest under the door of the car, in a futile attempt to get rid of all the mud. "Do you have any tissues on you?"

"'fraid not! And clean your shoes thoroughly; you know how I like to keep my car clean. I only had it valeted last week," said Jim. "In fact, if you get any muck in my car, you'll have to clean it yourself. Try and keep the car clean."

They both got into the car. Derek looked at the soles of both shoes, "I'm afraid I still have a little bit of mud on my shoes!"

Jim sounded annoyed, "Damn it, try and keep your feet in the same place. We'll look for a bar on the way to clean up, I need to take a piss anyway. There is a bar near here, the Mexicano. My father used to go there occasionally years ago."

Derek got into the car and looked very uncomfortable trying to keep his feet on one side of the passenger space. "This wasn't in my job description. I can always take off my shoes."

Jim grinned, "You can always walk, and please don't take off your shoes. Can't stand the smell of sweaty feet."

Derek pressed the button on his door and the window glided down. He put out his right hand, palm up. "The rain has eased, I think I'll take my chances on the road, it will be safer." He smiled and slid the window up.

Jim drove off. There was a sudden silence as if both had gone into deep thought at the same time.

Suddenly Derek spoke, "Mexicano, that sounds like a fast food place."

It was Jim's turn to look at the soles of his shoes and, looking at the mud, he shook his head. "Actually yes, I gather that's actually how it started and the owners then converted it into a bar."

"Well Jim, what do you think?"

"Don't worry I'll get another valet on the car soon."

"No, I was talking about the murder."

"Oh right." Jim rubbed his unshaven chin with his hand a few times. "Not much to go on. I think the Italian job would be good in this case. I have worked with them before on a similar case a few years ago. I'll check them out tomorrow."

Derek looked puzzled. "The Italian job?"

"Yea Rossi and Pasqualli."

"Oh yes, I've heard of them. I hope we are assigned to this case. I have been with you for a couple of months and this would be the first new case we have had."

Jim looked at Derek, "More exciting than traffic duties then?"

"You bet!"

"You did come highly recommended, kid. I heard you were instrumental in nailing the Bronx midnight mugger; he had mugged over a dozen prostitutes. How was is it you got involved?"

"Just fortuitous."

"How's that?"

"Well, I had booked this guy once for parking on double-yellow in a red-light district. I stopped him again a week later after he jumped a red light. He seemed very nervous and shifty this time. I didn't make much of it at the time, thought he was kind of shaky 'cause I had booked him. The next day I discovered that a prostitute had been mugged a block from where I stopped him at almost precisely the same time. When I checked with the detectives investigating the Bronx mugger, I found out that another prostitute had been mugged a short distance from the first place I booked him. The rest is history. Just lucky I guess!"

"I suppose it was not just luck but some detective work too," said Jim with a smile.

Derek smiled as he turned to Jim. "As you always say, sometimes you just need to be lucky to crack a case. What is it you say; there is that one clue? What do you call it?"

"The missing link!"

"That's it, how could I forget?"

Jim pulled the car over and parked it. "This is the Mexicano, this will do nicely."

Derek asked, "Do you usually park on double-yellow lines?"

"Only when I'm in a rush."

"How often would that be?" Derek asked.

"Oh, pretty much all the time."

"Don't tell me you pay a lot of fines!"

Jim looked at Derek with a look of mischief on his face, "I know a good captain. I let him worry about it."

"Well at least the rain has stopped," Jim commented as he got out of the car.

"Are you not taking your raincoat off?" Derek asked him.

"No, I just got the car cleaned and valeted, I want to keep at least the back clean!"

Derek had his raincoat off and had his seat pulled back and was about to throw the raincoat into the back seat. He noticed Jim glaring at him. "I think I'll carry my coat in case it rains in the pub," he told Jim cheekily.

They both scraped as much of the mud as they could on the ledge of the pavement by the side of the road. Jim opened the passenger door and looked at the mud on the mat of the front passenger seat and shook his head, "Oh my

God, you are one messy pup!"

As they walked into the bar Jim instinctively looked around the lounge as if surveying for potential danger. He seemed to visibly relax. He took out a ten-dollar bill and gave it to Derek. "I'll clean my shoes first, dying to take a leak. Get me a coke and get yourself a glass of milk."

"Very funny," Derek replied, not smiling this time. "I'll have a beer!"

"I'm afraid I don't approve of any drinking while we are on duty."

"So you do have some rules that you stick to." As soon as he had said that he looked at Jim sheepishly, "I'm sorry, no offense meant."

"None taken," replied Jim, "you can break all the rules you want, just don't break my rules."

This time Derek held two fingers to his forehead and gave a salute, "Yes sir!"

Jim went into the gents' room and Derek sat on a stool at the bar. "Could I have a coke and a beer –sorry make that a coke and a diet coke."

The bartender eyed Derek up and down and said with a wry smile, "Can't drink while on duty?"

Derek replied without any emotion as he straightened his thin black tie, "I'm on a diet."

The bartender smiled and tilted his head upwards. "Yeah, yeah, whatever!"

Derek started to sip his diet coke when a rather unkempt gentleman sat on a stool beside him. Derek looked at him over his right shoulder. He looked away and suddenly looked back at the man. He took a couple of loud sniffs, flaring his nostrils again. He whispered, "Shit not again, what is it about tonight?"

The man looked Derek in the eye, "Have we met before?"

Derek looked disgusted, he turned his back to the man and looked at him for a few seconds and then said, "I don't think so!"

He picked up the two glasses of drinks and moved to the next seat. The dishevelled man looked at him. He lifted his coat lapel and put his nose under it, "It's not that bad!" His speech was fairly slurred.

Derek raised his glass to the man, "I just like my space."

Derek looked around the lounge. A young man and woman were seated in one corner as if trying to be as inconspicuous as possible. Their shoulders and arms were touching, and they were staring into each other's eyes. He reached across and pushed back her fringe, which was covering her eye. He leant toward her and kissed her neck just below her left ear. She smiled and held his hand, stroking his fingers with hers. He smiled back. Just then Jim sat beside Derek.

Jim looked towards the couple, "Kids in love?"

Derek turned his attention back to the bar. "Not sure if it is love or lust."

"My, aren't we sceptical, and that from a newlywed."

Derek looked at Jim, "Well married for four years. But I'll tell you what, I wouldn't swap it for the world. She is my life and my world, I wouldn't swap her for all the tea in China, or in fact all the money in the world."

"My goodness," Jim said with his eyebrows raised, "it's very nice to hear that, maybe romance isn't dead after all."

Derek changed the subject, "What about you? I suppose you'll never hook up looking this rough. When was the last time you slept? And a shave wouldn't go amiss."

Jim rubbed his hand across his chin and with a grin on his face said, "It's only a three-day stubble. I thought the girls like the rugged look these days."

"You look like shit," said Derek with a smile. "No girl will glance at you looking like this."

Jim was quite for a second then said, "I was forty last week. I am beginning to be happy with the thought of living by myself. Mind you I always liked the idea of being a dad."

Derek quickly said, "Are you still going with that lawyer chick Amanda?"

Jim's facial expression changed suddenly, and the soft smile changed to a frown. "Kid you had better go and clean your shoes, we gotta go."

Derek got up and headed towards the gents. He stopped and turned around and whispered, "At least I can get cleaned up. If you don't wash soon you will end up looking like this guy." He pointed his thumb toward the man at the bar.

The man shouted out loud, "Hey buddy, I might be drunk, but I'm not deaf!"

"O shit, I'm sorry. I ..."

Jim put his hand on Derek's elbow. "Don't worry about it, kid, I'll speak to the man."

The drunken man pointed to Derek's shoes, "There is mud everywhere tonight. Imagine that in the middle of a concrete jungle." He got up.

He stumbled sideways and fell onto the floor. Jim helped him up. "Are you sure you can go home okay?"

The man tried his best to stand fully upright and held up his chin, "Sure I'm okay. I've been a lot worse."

Jim chuckled, "I don't know whether that is good or bad. Look I hope you didn't take offense at my pal; he means no harm."

The man waved the back of his hand, "Listen I've been called a lot worse, but then I just don't give a damn what people think any more."

"Let me buy you a drink," said Jim.

"Since when do policemen buy people drinks?"

Jim raised his eyebrows, "What makes you think I'm a policeman?"

"I don't have a clue. But you see Alfonso behind the bar rarely guesses wrong, he figures your friend is a cop and I wouldn't disagree." He turned to Alfonso, "I'll have another one."

Alfonso reached towards a bottle of Jack Daniels. Jim held the back of Alfonso's wrist. "Make it a beer, in fact make it lite beer."

Alfonso looked at the drunken man as if waiting for confirmation. The man replied, "As a rule I don't drink anything that is low in alcohol, but in this case I will make an exception. But first I must visit the gents." He started to stagger towards the gents.

Derek had just returned, "My goodness the toilet is immaculately clean!"

Alfonso nodded, "The boss is very fussy, in fact he's OCD about clean toilets."

Jim looked at Derek, "Derek could you give this kind gentleman a helping hand to walk to the little boys' room?" Jim leaned his head towards the man and put his hand by the side of his mouth and whispered loudly, "Take it as an apology."

Derek had a look of annoyance and was about to say something when he decided against it. He put his hand under the man's armpit and helped him walk, all the time looking at Jim and shaking his head. Jim's smile just broadened. Jim shouted, "Make sure he doesn't fall into the urinal!" The barman chuckled.

Jim kept watching and seemed to be amused by Derek trying his best to assist the man but keep his distance from him at the same time. He looked at Alfonso, "Remember when I ask you this, it's not as a cop, but just as a pub punter. Do you not have a moral obligation not to serve any more drinks, once someone is intoxicated?"

"You are absolutely right, a moral and legal obligation. However, the guy is harmless and here almost every other night, he is very popular with the locals."

"Well, I'll trust you."

Jim was quiet for a while and looked around the bar. He then focused on the young couple this time. Their gaze was fixed into each other's eyes. She was holding his hand in hers, whilst stroking the back of his hand with her other hand. They seemed totally oblivious of anyone else in the room.

The barman was cleaning a glass with a dishcloth. "I remember when my woman and I used to look at each other like that."

Jim continued to look at the couple, "And I suppose now you hardly speak to each other?"

The barman stopped cleaning the glass and stared into space for a short while, he then resumed the cleaning process, "Oh, there is still plenty of talking, but the silences are okay too. Maybe some of the passion is gone, but I wouldn't change her for the world." He paused for a second. "What about you, copper, does Amanda give you what you are looking for?"

Jim looked at the barman in surprise. "I thought I was the detective here." Just then Derek walked back, assisting the dishevelled man.

"Saved by the bell," said Jim.

Derek led the man to the barstool. He was holding some toilet tissue on the side of his right eye and it had some blood on it. Derek looked at Jim with a look of annoyance and grumbled, "Thanks for all this. I should have listened to you. He stumbled at the urinal and hit his head against the wall. He has a small cut to his forehead. He probably needs to attend ER."

Derek looked at the bartender and said in a rather irritated voice, "Are you not legally obliged to stop serving when a person has had too much to drink?"

The bartender was about to answer when Jim held up his hand and spoke to the bartender, "Hey listen, man, don't worry about it. Let's just forget the whole thing."

Derek then looked at his right hand with some blood on it. "I need to wash my hands, excuse me." He walked back to the gents' room.

The drunken man took the toilet tissue from Derek and pressed it on his bleeding wound for a second. He held it towards the bartender who lifted a small bin and the man put the bloody tissue in the bin. He then used the back of his dirty sleeve to wipe the wound and smeared a bit of blood down his cheek. He looked at his sleeve with a bit of blood on it and shrugged his shoulders.

Alfonso gave him a tea towel which he pressed against the wound. "Hold on. I will put a plaster on that for you. I always keep some here." He applied a plaster over the cut.

The man then took a sip of his lite beer in a half-pint glass. He held up the glass to the light and Alfonso and Jim looked at him quizzically. The man looked at Alfonso. "Are you sure this isn't just water?"

Alfonso laughed out loud. "To you I'm sure it tastes like water!"

Jim chuckled.

After a couple of minutes Derek walked back and saw the three of them chuckling and looked at Jim.

"Don't ask, Derek!"

Derek shrugged his shoulders.

The man at the bar put his glass on the bar and his sleeve knocked the glass of Diet Coke over and some of it spilt off the bar onto Derek's trousers. Derek jumped back quickly and looked at his beige trousers. He stared at the man with a look of annoyance.

The man got up, staggering a little bit. "I'm really sorry, sir," he said, reaching to wipe the spilled coke off Derek's trousers. Derek took a step back. The man reached towards Derek's pocket which had a part of a white tissue protruding slightly out of it and pulled it out. "Let me clean it for you."

Derek held the man's hand and twisted it round to such an extent that he twisted the man's body around. Derek grabbed the tissue from his hand. "Give me that," he shouted and put the tissue back into his pocket. "What the hell are you doing reaching into my pocket?!"

The man looked puzzled. "Sorry I was only trying to help!"

Alfonso reached under the counter and picked up a small towel. "Here you are, sir."

Derek let the man go and took the towel, he wiped his trousers and handed the towel back to Alfonso. "Thanks," he muttered.

The man reached out his hand as if to shake Derek's hand. "I'm really sorry sir …"

Derek help up his right hand. "Just forget it, but I would rather not shake hands as I'll have to wash up again."

The man withdrew his hand. "Okay, whatever."

Jim got up. "Okay let's go before there's any more mishaps." He looked at the man, "No hard feelings, but my friend here is very fussy about cleanliness."

The man replied, "Hey don't worry about it. Matters like that are of no consequence. Now the poor girl that was killed tonight, that is something to be upset about."

Alfonso turned to the drunken man and asked, "Who was killed?"

The man answered, "The young girl that was found dead tonight on the north side of Manhattan. Besides the disused cement site. You know, the girl with the red shoes."

Alfonso said, "Huh. Didn't hear a thing about it!"

Jim looked a bit surprised, "Where did you hear about it?

The man replied, "It was on CNN news. That good-looking girl on CNN mentioned it."

"What girl?" asked Jim.

"I don't know her name, I can just see her face, the good-looking black girl."

Jim looked at Alfonso and looked at the number of televisions around the pub.

Alfonso shrugged his shoulders, "CNN is too up market for me, anyways ... there isn't enough sports news on CNN."

The drunken man tossed back the beer in one swoop and said, "I must be off." And before Jim could ask him any further questions he staggered out the door.

"News travels fast," said Jim. "Okay let's go."

CHAPTER 3

Interrogation at the Precinct

Jim and Derek walked into the precinct. A uniformed officer behind the reception desk nodded. "Good morning Detective Sterne, Detective em …"

Derek snapped, "Johnston, with a T."

"That's it, Johnston." He pointed to Derek's trouser with the stain on it, "Accident, Detective?"

"Very funny," laughed Derek. "Just Coke."

The uniformed looked at Jim. "Do you never sleep, Jim?"

"Sleep is over-rated," said Jim with a straight face. "There was a young kid brought in from the murder scene on Fifty Fourth Street."

"The murder beside the cement production site?"

"That's it, unless there have been two or three murders tonight."

"No," smiled the policeman, "just the one murder. So far! I was told to tell you that he is being questioned in room two."

Jim and Derek walked to the big common room upstairs and took off their coats almost in unison and put them on the coat rack. They both reached for the coffee pot at the same time. "After you," said Jim.

Derek poured coffee into two mugs. "White, no sugar, there you are."

"Thanks," said Jim.

They took their mugs of coffee with them down the corridor. They walked into a room with multiple medium-sized wall-mounted televisions, looking into the various interrogation rooms. They focused on one that had the writing 'Interview Room Two' written under it. There was an officer in plain clothes looking at the TV screen. The screen showed the young black man was on one side of the desk and an officer on the other. The young man had his head covered in his hands and was shaking his head. He said, "It wasn't me; you have to believe me. It wasn't me. I would never do anything like that."

The officer asked him, "Like what?"

"Like killing someone."

The officer in the room beside Jim turned around. "Good morning, Jim, do you ever sleep?"

"Good morning Sid."

Sid turned to Derek. "Hello …"

Derek reached out his hand, "Derek."

Sid gripped Derek's hand quite firmly and shook it, "That's right, I have heard about you. You are that hotshot kid who nicked the Bronx midnight mugger, Johnston isn't it?"

"Yes, with a T."

"So would you be the same guy that performed CPR for one hour on a four-year-old and saved his life?"

Jim turned and looked at Derek with an expression of surprise on his face.

Derek hesitated, "Yes, that was me."

"Carry on," said Jim.

"It was after a multiple house fire and there were so many casualties and so many needed help that the dead were left lying on the ground. There was a young boy who was at the side of the house and seemed to be have been left for dead as well. I wasn't sure if he was breathing or not, but for some reason I had a gut feeling that the kid had a chance and kept going. Then a paramedic arrived and said that he had a pulse, and the rest is history."

Jim looked at Derek with surprise, "You never told me that!"

"Well Jim, you would have done the same."

"You are a good guy to have around in an emergency then."

Jim then pointed to the interrogation room through the glass. "What's the story so far?"

Sid answered pointing to his colleague in the questioning room, "Hugh thinks the kid is caught red-handed. He had a couple of cigarette lighters, two cell phones – a black, and a pink one; the pink one with no SIM card: keys … the usual. But wait for this, he also had a wad of dollar bills. We think he has taken the broad's earnings. His story has changed a couple of times and he has been certainly lying. I think he is guilty."

"Let me give a quick summary. A young guy is riding his bike. He sees a prostitute walking along the road. He gets off is bike, strangles her, drags her into the bushes, robs her, and then calls the police on his cell phone. Does that sum up your analysis so far?" Jim surmised.

Sid raised his eyebrows and scratched his left ear. "Now that you put it that way, it doesn't make a whole lot of sense. He is lying though and has robbed her."

Jim nodded a few times. "You certainly have a point. I will be surprised if one of the cell phones is not hers. Ask Hugh to give me a few minutes with him."

Sid left the room and went into the next room. Jim took a sip his coffee. "Must be fresh, it's nice and hot. Are you still awake, kid?"

"It's only …" Derek paused to look at his watch. "It's only two thirty! Actually, I'd better phone Mary-Beth, she might be worried and waiting up for me. I may give the church a miss tomorrow morning."

"It's nice to know some people are still on the straight and narrow!"

"Well Mary-Beth and I help with fundraising events and the like at the church. I'll call her quickly." He took out his cell phone and went into the corner of the room, whispering quietly.

On the screen they could see Sid whispering into Hugh's ear. The young man looked very anxiously back and forth from one officer to the next.

Hugh said, "Mike, give us a few minutes."

The young man said, "Can I go home now? If not, can I speak to a lawyer?"

Hugh got up, "Sure, sure."

The officers left the room. Jim was watching the young man intently. Again, he held his head in his hands and was shaking his head.

Derek rejoined Jim. The young man in the interrogation room frantically looked all around the room. He quickly reached down and lifted something out of his socks and pushed it down his jeans into the crotch area.

Derek's mouth was open as he looked at Jim. "What just happened there?!"

Jim walked towards the TV screen as if to get a better view. "I don't know, but I reckon the guy thought both the guys were in between rooms and no one was watching."

Hugh and Sid walked into the observation room. Hugh shook Jim's hand, "Thought you would come here tonight."

Jim pointed his hand towards Derek, "This is Detective Derek Johnston, with a T."

Derek chuckled as he shook Hugh's hand.

"What do you think, Hugh?" Jim asked.

"The more I speak to him the more he seems like a harmless type. But he was bullshitting me at the start about holding money for his boss at the restaurant and then for his father. When I told him I was going to phone them, he said he carries his savings with him because he doesn't trust the banks."

"Huh," chuckled Jim. "How well did you search him?"

"All his pockets, and he was frisked good."

Derek jumped in with a degree of excitement in his voice, "He took something from under his socks and shoved it down his trousers."

Hugh looked at Sid, "I wouldn't miss a knife or a gun."

"Don't worry, Hugh, it was quite small, may be a pocketknife." Jim turned to Derek, "You coming in, kid?"

"Wouldn't miss it for the world." Derek jumped up.

Jim and Derek walked into the interview room. The young man looked at them with a surprised expression on his face. He glanced up and noticed a video camera and then looked at the two of them again. He wiped off a few beads of sweat from his upper lip.

Jim grabbed the chair from across the table from the boy and put it on the tableside adjacent to him. He reached to shake his hand. "Detective Jim Sterne, you can call me Jim. This is Detective Derek Johnston."

The young man reached his right hand forward tentatively and held Jim's hand very lightly, withdrawing it quickly after a couple of shakes. Jim rubbed his fingers on his shirt as if to dry them. "Nervous, young man?"

The man did not respond, but there was a nervous twitch from one side of his upper lip.

"What's your name, son?"

"Michael, Mike."

"Mike what?"

"Mike Smith."

"Well Mike, I can't give you a cigarette, but I can give you a nicotine gum?"

"No thanks, I don't smoke."

"Would you like some coffee?"

"Yeah, that would be good, thanks."

Jim looked at the video camera. "Guys could we have a coffee." He put his hand on Mike's shoulder. "White, son?"

"Yes sir, no sugar please."

Jim looked at the camera again, "Extra cream please."

Jim turned to mike, "What are the lighters for?"

Mike hesitated, "Well they are for … for the candles at the restaurant of course."

"Two lighters?"

Mike shrugged his shoulders.

He pulled his seat forward and leaned towards Mike, lowering his voice. "Mike do you watch any police films?"

Mike pulled away from Jim and looked at Derek. "Ye … Yes." He spoke as if he was not sure or happy with the direction of this conversation.

"Well Mike, do you know what those are up there?"

Mike paused and wiped his upper lip again, "Video cameras?"

"That is correct."

Mike was getting more agitated, "I would like to speak to my lawyer now."

"Sure," replied Jim, "but you know I can strip search you right now if necessary. Now you may find yourself in a lot of trouble, and unless you cooperate you could be in some deep shit."

"Look, man, I did not kill her. Why would I call the police if I had killed her?"

"I believe you, Mike, but you see that detective dude, Hugh White, he thinks you are guilty as sin. Now if you cooperate with us and start telling the truth you may just manage to dig yourself out of a big hole. Let me help you, Mike."

He held out his right hand, pointed at Mike's groin area and straightened and flexed his fingers a few times.

Mike hesitated and reached into his trousers. Derek reached for his gun. "Easy does it," he yelled.

"Okay, okay," shouted Mike, slowing his actions into a very careful and deliberate movement. He pulled out a credit card.

Jim held out his hand to take the card. He stopped before his hand reached the card. He had a look toward Mike's groin area. He pulled his hand back and turned to Derek, "Check this out, will you?"

Derek's enthusiasm got the better of him as he reached across and grabbed the card. Immediately afterwards he looked at Mike's groin area. "Shit. Not my night," he whispered.

He wiped the card on Mike's shirt and held it out towards Jim. Jim said, "Go ahead, Detective."

Derek studied the card. "Well, well. Nice to meet you Charlene Mills!"

"Look, man, I refuse to speak until I talk to a lawyer."

Sid opened the door and brought in the cup of coffee. Oblivious to the events in the room he put the coffee down and said, "Extra cream."

Mike looked at Jim. "How did you know I like extra cream?"

Jim smiled, "I know a lot of things, like for example I think you were in the wrong place at the wrong time. Now I will try and help you if you cooperate."

Sid left the room and closed the door behind him.

Mike seemed to be in deep thought for a minute or so, took a sip of the coffee, took a big breath and started to talk, "I guess I have no problem with telling you the whole truth. I finished my shift at the restaurant, I was on the early shift. I was cycling home when I saw this red high heel shoe. I stopped. I noticed the drag marks in the mud and some spots of blood. I followed the marks and came across the body. Her purse was lying open. I took the credit card out and threw the purse down."

Derek interrupted, "And the money?"

Mike shook his head as if to say no.

Jim raised his eyebrows, "Mike make this easier for yourself, will you?"

Mike paused and then changed the shaking of his head to a nod, "Yes and the money."

Derek leant on the table, "And the lighters?"

"Them too," answered Mike.

"Carry on," said Derek.

"I was going to run away. She looked dead. Then I thought I'd better check to see in case she was alive. I couldn't decide if she was breathing or not. I thought I had better call nine-one-one. After I called them, I realised that they had my cell phone number, so I decided to stay. Look, man, I would never kill anyone, I would never steal, and it's just that her purse was lying open."

Derek interrupted again, "And what were you going to do with the credit card?"

"There are guys who will buy … " He stopped in full flow. "I think I've said enough to answer your questions. I would like to speak to a lawyer now."

Jim pushed back his chair, with a loud screeching noise. He stood up. "That is all for now. I'm sorry to have to say that you will be held in custody for theft and suspicion of murder." Jim put both his hands on the table and leaned forward. "I hope what you say is true or I'll nail your ass for sure." Mike's colour seemed to drain from his face. Jim then leaned forward and whispered quietly in Mike's ear, "For what it's worth I believe you. I'll keep my word and try my best to get you off, but you had better not be lying to me, son."

Mike grabbed Jim's right hand with both his hands, "I am NOT … honestly, Detective."

Jim was walking towards the door and turned around. "One more question, Mike. Which cell phone belongs to her?"

Mike hesitated for a short while, "The pink one."

"Well that is certainly a relief that the pink one is not yours," Jim paused, "can I have the SIM card please?"

Mike's demeanour changed suddenly. He smiled, "Certainly, Detective. You can have it in twenty-four to thirty-six hours!"

"Wha … " Jim shook his head. "You didn't swallow it, did you?"

Mike smiled, "Well when I heard the police siren I panicked and thought it was a good idea at the time."

Jim pointed towards the camera again, "Lock him up in a dry cell guys. And give him a bed pan and send the contents to forensics. They will love us! And make sure he gets a call to his lawyer."

As Jim left the room Derek hurried after him. They went into the adjoining room where Hugh and Sid were waiting. They all watched Mike without saying anything.

Mike began to look anxious again. He rested his head on the table and his shoulders were heaving slightly, suggesting he might be crying.

Hugh was the first to speak. "Well Jim, do you think he is telling the truth?"

Jim rubbed his stubble again, "More or less. I don't think he did it. Doesn't make sense."

He paused, "It's time for bed. Make sure he gets his phone call."

He turned to Derek, "Your car is here?"

"Yep."

Jim walked out, "See you guys tomorrow."

Derek ran after Jim. "I'm dying to know the answer to one question."

"Shoot."

"How did you know he took extra cream?"

Jim smiled. "I didn't. I just didn't want to get hot coffee poured over me in case he lost the plot!"

Derek smiled. "Good night. And yes, I am learning something new every day! See you tomorrow."

CHAPTER 4

Meeting with the Captain

As the suited black gentleman walked into the thirty-third precinct he was greeted with a salute by the officer at the desk. "Good morning Captain."

"Good morning Sally."

He went into the elevator, took off his sunglasses, wiped his eyes, and put them back on. He got out of the elevator and went into the general open office area.

A young policewoman winked at him, "Happy birthday sir."

"Good God! Does Jim keep anything to himself? I mean, thank you Maria."

He made his way down the corridor and stood outside a door, he read the engraved name facing him. 'Captain Will Jones.' He used the cuff of his jacket and wiped the sign. He opened the door and walked in.

"Good morning Captain."

"Holy shit, Jim, I nearly crapped myself," said Will. Will looked at his hand on his gun, "Sorry, reflex. Are you looking to get yourself killed? What time did you come in anyway, it's not even seven?"

Jim smiled, "Sorry to scare you, Captain. You know I can't sleep when I am engrossed in a case."

Will put up his hand, "Give me a couple of minutes till I have a coffee then you can fill me in with this murder case I was told about downstairs."

"Sure, I left word for the Italian job to come here too, hope you are okay with that."

Will said, "That's fine, but coffee first."

Jim pointed his index finger at him with his thumb up as if pointing a gun. "You're the boss, after all it was your birthday yesterday."

"I didn't hear anything on the news this morning." Will shook his hand, "But coffee first."

"Well, Captain, how was your birthday celebration? Did you have a good sixtieth?"

"I don't want to talk about it."

"It must have been good, Captain, if you have your dark sunglasses on indoors."

There was a knock at the door and Maria walked in with a mug of coffee which had steam coming out of it. "Thanks Maria."

"You're welcome, sir. Do you need some aspirin too?"

Will answered, "Very funny. Not too many of these youngsters will be able to keep up with me. Thanks, and dismissed."

Maria left the room laughing out loud.

*

After she left the room Jim turned to Will, "Well Captain, what is it with the glasses? Let me guess you were out drinking all night and your eyes are red from the hash you smoked after."

"Very funny, Jim." He walked towards his window. "Okay the dinner was cancelled. The opera was cancelled, and before you ask, there was no romance on my sixtieth night."

"What? You had been looking forward to the night for weeks. Romantic dinner for two—"

Will interrupted "I know, I know, you don't have to remind me."

"Oh no Captain, did you have a fight with Michelle?"

"No, certainly not! We never fight!"

"Now you have me intrigued. You know I won't stop until you give me all the gory details!"

"Some other time, Jim."

Jim leant back on Will's black leather swivel chair and put his feet on the desk. "I'm not moving till I hear everything."

Will walked over and pushed Jim's feet off the table. "Okay but off my chair."

"Yes sir!"

Will sank into his chair as he prepared to tell all. "Here goes. I got up in the morning and Michelle had a few presents for me. Among them was a pair of sunglasses for golf. She had already booked me in for an early round with Leo. I started the round with Leo, who by the way I have beaten in the last three rounds. Well, I was going well and three up with four to play when my eyes began to get sore, they got worse and worse. Lost the next three holes and could hardly see anything on the eighteenth. Missed a four-foot putt on the last to lose by one. My eyes were red and sore as fuck!"

Will took off his glasses to reveal two very bloodshot eyes. "I took off my glasses and my eyes were red as cherries. When I got home Michelle couldn't stop laughing. She told me that the glasses were special glasses to improve visibility by brightening the light. It's to help you find your golf balls when you lose them in the trees or dark areas. I spent the night putting drops into my eyes feeling sorry for myself. Michelle spent the night giggling. She must have phoned all her friends to tell them the story!"

Jim couldn't stop laughing.

There was a knock at the door and two men walked in.

"Good morning Captain."

"Good morning Captain, what's the joke?"

Will put on his glasses in a hurry and answered quickly, "Oh nothing, it's too intellectual for you gigolos."

Jim eyed the two arrivals up and down. "Well if it isn't the Italian job. Have you two arrived for police duty or are you about to go onto a catwalk?"

Paolo Rossi was the taller of the two at six foot two. He was very slim, dressed in a pinstripe navy Armani three-piece suit with a dark blue shirt and a slim maroon tie held back at the collar with a tie pin. His hair was cut short and jet black, with a parting on the side. Geno Pasqualli was shorter than Paolo. He was five foot eleven. Also very trim, dressed in tight blue jeans with a dark cashmere pullover and a black leather jacket. His hair was shoulder length, dark brown with gold streaks through it. He had a stud earring on his left ear.

Will waved a hand as if to say hello, "I think you guys missed a career on the catwalk."

Geno pushed his leather jacket back by placing his left hand on his hip. He then wiggled his hips and smiled, "Maybe I chose the wrong profession."

Will nodded, "I think you have. I'm fed up with the girls constantly walking past when you two are here."

Paolo brushed some imaginary dust off Will's suit collar, "I think the girls are just stalking you, Captain. Especially because you look so dashing with your cool sunglasses on … indoors."

Jim chuckled, "Well actually his wife handcuffed him and beat him up last night for his sixtieth birthday. He has two black eyes."

Paolo and Geno laughed.

Will did not look amused, "Very funny."

Jim continued, "Actually he was crying all night because he missed a two-foot putt which cost him fifty bucks."

Will was disgruntled, "It was a four-foot putt, and I told you not to tell anyone."

Jim was on a roll and could not stop, "Sorry captain I thought you meant for me not to mention that you wore your new golf-ball-finding glasses instead of sunglasses."

Paolo and Geno could not stop laughing. Geno was doubled in two.

Will saw the funnier side of things "Okay, okay, very funny, now let's get down to business." He sat on his swivel chair and put his hands on top of his desk and his demeanour changed, at once the mood in the room changed. Jim sat up and Paolo sat on the second chair and Geno stopped, leaning on the desk and stood a few paces back and crossed his arms. Everyone's expression changed to a serious one. "Right boys what have you got. By the way, where's Derek?" He looked at Jim.

Jim looked at his watch, "It's not nine yet. He is not like the old school! We left the questioning room after three."

Will responded, "Well I'm glad you got to bed early, now shoot."

"Homicide on east fifty fourth street. Right beside a disused cement factory. Young girl, late twenties, maybe a hooker, found half naked, waist up. Possible strangling. Definitely badly beaten up. Obvious sexual overtones but not obvious if she was raped. Young black waiter was caught on the scene. He actually dialled nine-one-one. He was lying during the questioning. He had taken her money, cell phone, and card. Nervous kid, Mike Smith, haven't checked for previous convictions, but I'll be very surprised if he actually killed her."

Derek walked into the room at that moment.

"Good afternoon," said Jim.

"I don't know where you've been all morning, Jim, but I've been doing my homework!" Derek said as he held up a sheet of paper in his hand. "Mike Smith, born nineteenth of the third, nineteen ninety-three. He has nothing on him, completely clean." He looked at Jim, "What's wrong?"

Jim responded, "Nothing, good job, kid. It's just that I don't often get surprised."

Will held out his hand and Derek handed him the sheet of paper. He perused through it quickly.

Jim introduced Derek to Paolo and Geno.

Will continued, "Well what do you think, Jim?"

"I think we have some work ahead of us. Mike's not our guy. We can question him again later, no doubt he will have his legal representation, but I think we have to fish somewhere else."

Will turned to Derek, "What do you think, Derek?"

"I don't think he killed her."

Will nodded, "I agree, it doesn't look like this guy, whatever his crime, had anything to do with her death. If he hadn't dialled nine-one-one, it certainly would have been more suspicious, but I don't think he would have killed her and then brought the police to the scene."

They all nodded almost in unison.

There was a knock at the door.

"Come in," shouted Jim absentmindedly.

Will looked at him, "Would you like to take my seat as well?"

"Sorry Captain, was on auto pilot!"

Will smiled, "Just kidding." He looked up at Maria, "What is it Maria?"

"It's the press on the phone, Captain. They have heard reports of the murder and want to speak to someone."

Will looked at Jim, "Maybe I'd better speak to the press so you can keep a lower profile for now."

"Sure Captain."

Will got up. Jim suddenly grabbed his arm. "Hold on a second." He turned to Maria, "Maria, have you had any other approaches from the press about this case?"

Maria shook her head, "No Jim, I mean the murder only happened last night, and no one on the night shift was asked about it."

He clicked his fingers looking at Derek. "That drunkard last night. He talked about this girl dying, and said it was on the news. God I'm stupid!" He stood up, pushing his hair back on both sides with his hands. "How the hell did he know about the murder?!"

Derek said, "Perhaps it was some other case he had heard about. He was drunk, it could have been from a different night."

Jim shook his head, "No! He said it was that night, in fact he even said that she had red shoes!"

Derek hit his forehead with his hand, "Good God! You are right. In all the annoyance with him spilling a drink on me I got distracted."

Paolo and Geno looked in amazement, whilst Will raised his hand, "Hold on boys, what the fuck are you talking about?"

Jim answered, "We stopped in a bar on the way over to get rid of the mud on our shoes and chanced upon this drunk man, who for all the world looked like a tramp. Just before he left, he said that he heard about the murder on the news. I believe he said it was on ... what channel was it? Oh yes, he said it was on CNN."

Derek nodded and there was a tone of excitement in his voice, "He said it was a girl on CNN news." He paused, "To be precise, he said it was a young good-looking black girl."

Will shook his head, "Well, I'll be damned! What are the chances of that?"

Jim looked at the Captain, "As you always say in golf, Captain, better to be lucky than to be good."

Will replied, "Why are you still sitting down? Jim and Derek, you go to the bar and bring this guy in – whatever you need to do. Paolo, Geno, you guys phone CNN and find out what news they have and have broadcast … " He paused, "Be careful in case they don't have any info. I'll deal with the press for now."

Will got up. "Well I am not paying you to sit down all day. Off and get me the culprit!"

With that they all jumped up like spring rabbits and left the room quickly.

Will followed Maria.

CHAPTER 5

Arrest of Jake

Jim and Derek walked into the pub. Jim stood at the entrance and looked from one side of the pub to the other. They then walked to the bar. Alfonso nodded to them. "Good afternoon gentlemen." He looked at his watch. "What's your poison?"

Jim brought out his badge, "NYPD, Detective Sterne and Detective Johnston."

Alfonso nodded, "Oh yes! You are the two coppers that were here the other night. I knew you were cops."

Jim continued. "I want to ask you about the chap we saw the other day, you know the drunk guy."

"Hey, a lot of guys come here to drink, can you be a bit more specific?"

Derek leaned forward, "The ignorant one who spilt drink on me."

"Oh yes, you mean the oracle."

"Who?" Jim said with a slightly bemused look.

"Jake, although I believe his name is John." He looked at Derek, "Ignorant is not a word I would have chosen."

Jim put his badge on the inside pocket of his brown tweed jacket. "Perhaps there was a misunderstanding. Never mind that." Although he was looking at Alfonso, he was more directly addressing Derek. "What is his surname?"

"I believe it is John Chapman. He is generally known as Jake. What is this about anyway?"

Derek followed the questioning, "What else can you tell us about him, for example do you know what he does for a living – apart from drinking?"

Alfonso smiled. "Have you read the book on how not to win friends and influence people?"

Derek smiled suddenly, "I am sorry, I suppose he had been drinking when he spilt his drink on me. It's just that he was in my face."

"Don't worry about it, buddy, I understand. I see it all here. Not a bad guy. I think he was some sort of shrink. Doesn't say much, keeps himself to himself generally. Occasionally he would get into a conversation. I gather his wife died a year ago and since then he is not working and drinks most days. He would be here every second day or so."

Derek continued, "Do you know where he lives?"

Alfonso smiled, as he picked up a pint glass and looked at it against the light, "As a matter of fact I do."

Jim looked very surprised, "Did you say yes?"

"I suppose you were expecting me to say no."

Derek said, "Naturally we wouldn't have expected a yes answer, do you know him personally?"

"You could say that. On a couple of occasions, I have had to help him to walk home. He was very inebriated."

"Do you provide this personal service for all your customers?" asked Derek somewhat sarcastically.

"No," said Alfonso. He lifted the tea cloth that was resting over his left shoulder and started to clean the pint glass and was now speaking with no emotion. "But I don't mind helping Jake."

"And how is that?" asked Derek.

"Well he has helped us … me with some betting tips."

Jim sounded surprised, "What, horse racing?"

Alfonso nodded, "Yep." He put down the pint glass and lifted another.

It was Jim's turn to sound sarcastic, "Let me get this right, you get tips on horse racing from a drunkard?"

Alfonso looked at the glass against the light again, twirling it. He started to clean it with the cloth, "You know what they say; the proof of the pudding is in the eating!"

"Whatever," said Jim, "it's your money, all the same I'd rather keep my money in my pocket."

Derek sounded a bit impatient, "Back to the point, can you give us his address?"

Alfonso put down the second glass and leaned on the counter. "Can I ask you what you want to question him for?"

Derek answered, "Yes you could, but you wouldn't get an answer right now."

"That's what I thought you would say." He paused and threw the cloth back over his left shoulder. "He lives in one of the apartments on Madison Avenue and east Fifty Seventh Street. I think they are called Paradise Homes. He is in apartment five on the second floor."

Two men walked in and sat at the counter of the bar. One of them smiled at Alfonso, "How you doing, Alfie." He pointed to the television at the back of the counter, "Can you switch to the Knicks game?"

"Yes, Charlie, but not if you call me Alfie again!"

The other man laughed, "You know he is only pulling your leg, Alfonso!"

"Yes Matt, but I hate Alfie, my neighbor's dog was called Alfie, and my school friends reminded me of this frequently!"

Charlie pointed to the remote sitting behind the counter. "So long as you have the remote control you are the boss."

"Now you are talking," said Alfonso as he picked up the remote control and changed the channel to the basketball game and then turned up the volume, "Is that loud enough?"

Matt gave a thumbs-up.

"Two pints, the usual?" Alfonso asked.

Matt gave the thumbs up again.

Alfonso started to pull the beer into a pint glass.

Alfonso turned to Jim, "Anything else, gentlemen?"

Jim reached out his hand in an offer to shake Alfonso's hand. "No that's all for now, Alfonso."

Alfonso shook his hand. "Don't mention it."

Derek and Jim walked out.

Matt looked at Alfonso, "They look formal!"

Alfonso nodded. "Yep, coppers."

"What did they want?"

"Looking for Jake."

"Not Jake?"

"Yep, him."

Charlie asked, "What for?"

Alfonso shrugged, "Beats me, but I'm sure it wouldn't be much, I'm sure it's not DIC, I don't think he's driven a car in about a year."

Matt laughed, "It's probably for pissing on the street or something like that. Anyway, all they need to do is hang around here, he will be here sooner rather than later."

Alfonso served the two pints of beer. He picked up another glass and looked at it against the light. "Somehow I don't think the cops would be out here looking for him unless it was something more serious."

Matt looked in both directions and then leaned close to Alfonso and whispered, "Any new racing tips?"

Alfonso shook his head, "No, nothing for two months unfortunately."

Matt leaned back, "Pity, my wife would love a holiday, and I could certainly do with one." He shrugged. "So, do you think the Knicks will beat the Bucks? Who's playing point guard?"

*

Jim and Derek got into the car and Jim started it up. He gave his cell phone to Derek. "Get the Captain for me."

Derek called the Captain and handed the phone to Jim. "Captain, I have his name and address. Can you get me a warrant for his arrest and to search his house?" He nodded. "Great, Captain, that's what I like to hear."

*

Twenty minutes later Jim phoned Will whilst he was driving. "Well, Captain, any news?"

Will answered, "The judge says he needs a lot more information."

Jim nodded, "I was just thinking he may say that. We'll go ahead and bring him in for questioning and the search of his apartment can be done later."

"Go ahead," Will replied, "I'll see what info we have after the questioning."

Few minutes later Derek pointed, "There it is, Paradise Homes."

Jim parked a few yards up the road. The 'r' from the paradise sign was missing and the 'm' was upside down.

They got out of the car and went to the steps of the apartments. Jim stopped and looked at both sides and then walked up the steps. At the doors to the apartments they looked at the various buzzers. There were five sets of buzzers in two columns, numbered one to ten. Some had names against them. The number five one did not have a name.

Derek looked at Jim. "What do you think, should we ring?"

Jim shook his head, "I would rather catch him off guard, let's try one of the ground floors."

Jim rang the number one apartment buzzer a couple of times, there was no answer after a few seconds. He pressed it again and waited, again there was no answer.

Derek held his finger against the number two and looked at Jim. Jim nodded, "You learn fast, kid."

Derek pressed the buzzer. After a few seconds, they heard the intercom. "Who is it?"

Jim shouted, "Pizza delivery."

They could hear the man shouting, "Honey did you order pizza? Guys you have the wrong address, on-one here ordered pizza."

Derek answered, "That's the address we have, apartment two Paradise homes."

"But we didn't order pizza."

Jim shouted, "Sorry I can't hear you, is that apartment two?"

"Hold on," the man said. They heard him shouting, "Honey I'm going to the door, this damn intercom system is useless! Why do people always interrupt during the Knicks games?"

A few seconds later a man in his fifties walked hastily to the doors. He was wearing faded jean shorts and an undersized Knicks basketball top which just about reached his shorts due to his oversized belly.

He looked somewhat hesitant as he reached for the door handle and seemed to slow down his movements. He opened the door very slightly and put his head against the gap so just his nose and part of his mouth had room to poke through. "I don't see no pizza!" He looked a bit apprehensive.

Jim had his badge in his hand and opened it. "NYPD. Detective Sterne. I'm going to need your cooperation, sir. We need access to one of the apartments above."

"Can I see your badge more closely?"

Jim took his badge close to the gap in the doors. The man squinted his eyes and looked at the badge carefully. He nodded and opened the door and stood back. "That's fine, Detectives. You scared the crap out of me!" He paused for a second. "It wouldn't be apartment five by any chance, would it?"

"Why do you ask?" said Derek.

"I knew it," said the man rather excitedly. "I always told my wife that man is up to no good. He should be ejected. He is lowering the whole status of these apartments. I told her it wouldn't surprise me if he was a murderer or something!"

Derek asked quickly, "Who mentioned murder?"

"Holy shit!" said the man. "That is it, he has killed someone, hasn't he?"

Jim held up his hand, "Now calm down and keep your voice down. We just want to ask him a few questions. Do you know him at all?"

"No way," said the man, whilst trying to tuck his Knicks top into his shorts. This failed because as soon as he straightened up, his big belly pushed out the top. "There is no way I would associate with a slob like that."

Jim put his hand on the man's shoulder. "What's your name, sir?"

"Zachary. Zach Davis."

"Look Zach, just go back in and watch the Knicks. We are going to go upstairs and ask a few questions and then go away. Nothing more exciting than that."

Zach nodded. "Sure thing, Detective. You'll have to walk up the stairs, the elevator is broken again. Paradise my ass!"

He went in and slammed his door. They could hear him shouting. "Honey what did I tell you. The fuzz are here to get the guy in number five. I knew it. I think he has killed somebody!"

Jim shook his head. "Everyone is a God damn detective these days!"

They walked up two flights of stairs. They waited outside apartment five and Derek put his head against the door. A black lady opened the door of number six across the hall. The number six had a screw missing and was upside down and looked like a 9. She looked at the two detectives. She had a baby in her arms. Jim put his finger to his lips and pulled out his badge. He pointed to the inside of her apartment. A small boy ran to the side of his mother and stood beside her. When he saw the two men he walked back and hid behind his mother's leg, peeping his head out to look at the men again. His mother pushed him back and walked backwards and quietly closed her door.

Jim nodded at Derek. Derek rapped the door of apartment five. After a few seconds he rapped the door again. A woman from the floor below looked up at them from the bottom of the stairs. She quickly went back into her apartment.

The door suddenly opened. "Come in, Detectives."

Jim showed his badge, "Are you expecting us?"

"Yes, I'm psychic!"

Jim sounded stunned. "How exactly did you know?"

The man laughed, "No, actually Alfonso just phoned me."

Derek asked, "Are you John Chapman?"

"Yes Detectives, and I'm called Jake."

The curtains were drawn and it was dark in the room. Jake switched the light on. Jim looked at Jake. He was very unkempt. His dishevelled hair was shoulder length and looked very dirty. He was wearing a dressing gown over a dirty brown T-shirt and as he opened and adjusted his gown, he could see his black boxer shorts. He had a moustache and beard that were long and very unkempt and dirty. He still wore the band aid that Alfonso had placed over the small cut over his left eyebrow. The dressing gown had stains and food material on the front of it. There was an empty vodka bottle on the sofa and one on the floor. There were a few empty beer bottles on the coffee table and sofa. As he turned to lift a pizza box off his couch Derek looked at Jim and pinched his nose with one hand and waved the other in front of his nose.

Jake stumbled and nearly fell. He held on to the sofa armrest which prevented him from falling. He sat down on the sofa. "Clear yourself a seat and sit down, gentlemen. I just woke up five minutes ago when Alfonso phoned me. It will take me a few minutes to surface properly." He burped and Derek turned his face away. "Sorry Detective, I haven't eaten in over a day and the acid builds up. How can I be of assistance to you?"

Jim looked at the sofa chair that had a number of items of clothing on it. Jake got up and stumbled across the room, holding on to the arm of the sofa. He lifted the clothes off the sofa chair and pointed to it and walked back and sat on the sofa.

Jim sat down. "Thank you."

Jake lifted some more clothing off another chair and threw it on the floor. "Please sit down, Detective."

Derek looked around the room. There were clothes all over the floor. There were a few pizza boxes and some Chinese takeaway boxes scattered around the room. There were some newspapers in areas of the floor that looked like they had been placed there to cover vomit material. "I'm happy to stand."

"Mister Chapman–"

Jim was interrupted, "Please call me Jake."

Jim continued, "Okay Jake. We would like you to come downtown with us, to the police precinct for questioning."

"Why would you interested in me about anything?"

"There was a young girl killed a few days ago and we think you may be able to help us with our enquiries."

"I'm not sure how I can help you with anything, but I am certainly happy to cooperate with the police in any way I can."

"That's good, Jake."

"When exactly would you like me to come there?"

"Now would be good."

Jake looked at his watch. "What, at four thirty on a Saturday morning?"

Derek interrupted, "Mister Chapman, it is four thirty in the afternoon, and it's Sunday."

"Oh!" Jake looked genuinely surprised. He stood up, staggering as he did. Derek jumped forward to stop Jake from falling. Jake put up his hand. "I don't need help, it's not as if I am drunk. Well not too much anyway." He laughed a little. He went over to the window and pulled back the curtains and was blinded by the light. He quickly pulled the curtains shut. "I'll get dressed."

Jake walked into the bedroom and was about to close the door.

Jim followed him towards the room, "Do you mind leaving the door open, I get nervous when doors are closed."

Jake laughed, "I don't mind if you don't mind."

Jim stood up and positioned himself so he could see Jake. Jake threw a few items of clothing off the bed and chose a pair of trousers. He held it against his nose and screwed up his face. He picked up a pair of trousers and held it against his nose, he smelt it again. "This will have to do," he said quietly to himself.

He walked in a wavy line to his chest of drawers. Jim walked quickly to the door of the bedroom and said rather loudly. "Gently there, friend."

Jake smiled as he pulled out a sweater. "Be careful, Detective, I may shoot you with my sweater."

Jim looked very serious, "Somehow I don't find that funny."

Jake chuckled, "Well one of us does." He put on the jumper on top of his dirty brown T-shirt and walked out, again staggering as he did. Jim tried to hold his arm. Jake put up his hand. "What is it with you detectives? I can walk by myself."

He took another step and fell to the floor. He looked up rather sheepishly.

"Can I have a helping hand please, Detective?"

Jim and Derek held one of Jake's arms each as they walked down the stairs. The lady on the floor below opened her door slightly and looked at them as they walked Jake down the stairs.

On the ground floor Zach came out with his keys and walked to his letter box. "Just checking for letters."

Jim pointed to Zach's door, "Later Zach, later!"

"Sure thing," said Zach as he eyed Jake up and down and shook his head. As he was closing his apartment door he shouted, "Honey…"

CHAPTER 6

Second Meeting at the Precinct

It was seven thirty a.m. on Monday morning when Paolo arrived at the precinct. He went straight to Jim's room. Through the glass in the door Paolo could see him working. He knocked at the door.

"Come in, Paolo," Jim said without looking up.

Paolo came in and took off his long beige cashmere coat. "Good morning Jim. How did you know it was me without looking?"

Jim looked up with a hint of a smile, "The same reason you knew I was going to be in here early."

"Touché!"

"Oh please, we are beginning to sound like a married couple. On to more pressing matters, Paolo."

Paolo walked over to Jim's desk and leaned over. He saw the picture of the young girl who had been murdered along with various pictures of the murder scene that had been taken that night and the next morning. "Well, anything?"

Jim shook his head, "You can see the track where Charlene's body was dragged and some blood stains on the way, but nothing we didn't know. Not a damn thing to go on."

"I presume you don't suspect this Mike fella either."

"No, and you?"

"Not one bit. More importantly Geno doesn't either."

Jim looked puzzled, "I always thought you were the brains of the operation."

"Let me tell you something, Jim. A lot of people make this mistake. In reality

Geno has the most amazing insight and wonderful intuition. He rarely gets it wrong. He is just happy taking the back seat and letting on he is a bit dim, but don't underestimate him."

"I'll remember that."

Jim turned his attention to the picture in his hands, rotating it to look at it from different angles. "No it would have been very implausible that he had killed her. He certainly would not have called the police if he had killed her for her money. Derek is double-checking his background. So far as we know no previous major convictions to his name. Has worked in that restaurant for a few years, lives with his girlfriend who is pregnant. Seems like he turned up at the wrong place at the wrong time. That leaves us with no hard evidence to go on." He threw the picture onto his desk. "What about the case you and Geno were on last year?"

Just then there was a knock at the door and Geno walked in.

"Speak of the devil." Jim waved Geno in.

"Anything?" Geno asked in a tone as if he was expecting to hear no for an answer.

Jim shook his head just once, enough for Geno to get the message. Jim looked at Paolo again. "We'll be questioning Jake later. So what can you guys tell me about Chapman's wife's murder?"

Paolo sat down and Geno followed suit. Geno looked at Paolo who nodded, "Her name was Tracey, Tracey Chapman."

"Like the singer?" asked Jim.

Paolo continued, "Yes. She was in her thirties, thirty-five to be precise. She was a social worker and did most of her work with underprivileged girls. She was married to the guy you arrested, John Chapman, otherwise known as Jake, for six years. It seems that they were in financial difficulties. She worked all the hours that God sent for next to nothing and he was a psychologist but must not have been making a whole lot. She was found dead in a park one day. It turned out that her husband was in the same park at precisely the same time. He was the prime suspect. He told the police that he had a premonition or something that she was in danger. They were both quite heavily insured for life cover and he stood to make a lot of money. There were some thoughts that he may have been involved with another girl. Eventually the prosecution had to drop the case because there was insufficient evidence to convict him, but I had strong suspicions that he was guilty. Geno was not so sure. In any case, we had to drop the case, we just ran dry in terms of hard evidence. Get this: He had even texted her that day saying that she was going to die."

Jim interrupted, "Any clues about the other girl?"

"I presume you mean the girl Jake may have had an affair with?"

Jim nodded.

"Yes, seems like Tracey Chapman had insisted on confidentiality and had not told anybody else any details, and if her husband, Jake, knew anything we could not get any info from him. Her name was Sarah Miller, Geno can fill you in on her."

Geno leaned forward, "Now you will be interested in this. This girl was not a regular street walker, but the classy kind. She was a law student but was working for a high-class escort agency. She mysteriously disappeared just before Tracey Chapman was whacked. Her cell phone went missing but we traced the numbers called from the cell phone. The only calls made from it that day were to Tracey Chapman a few hours before she was last seen. She received two calls from an anonymous caller. We think she is dead and that her hidden body may be the missing link to solving this case. There were a few contact numbers on her cell phone bill. This phone was not her personal cell phone, let's call it a business phone, but all numbers were followed up and, well… nothing."

Paolo interrupted, "And nothing on this Jake guy."

"Nothing could be traced to him. He was a bit whacky. I don't think anyone thought he was innocent, but we just couldn't get the evidence to nail him."

"Well I have heard that before. How was this Tracey girl killed?" Jim enquired.

Paolo answered, "One bullet from a handgun. Smack in the middle of her forehead from close range, actually from point-blank range. No signs of struggle. Reckon she must have known the person and was chatting to him … or her. Forensic say a silencer was used, which is not surprising, considering no-one heard anything in broad daylight. The body was found a few hours later behind shrubs. Bloodstains were found on a bench nearby. No witnesses, nothing else, except her husband seems to have been in the same park at around the same time. His story seems a bit far-fetched. He admitted texting her telling her she may die that day, but says he had a premonition. There was no CCTV surveillance in the vicinity."

"What about the gun?" Jim asked.

Paolo continued, "Point four five bullet from a handgun. And yes, no trace of it."

"Did Jake have a handgun?"

Geno shook his head, "No record of this. But as you know anyone can get a hold a gun these days."

"What about Tracey's phone record?"

"She had the text and also a couple of missed calls from Jake's mobile. She had called Sarah Miller earlier that day. There was an incoming call maybe a couple of hours before her death. It was recorded as an unknown number; the person must have withheld the number."

Jim leaned back and clasped his hands together on top of his tummy "So what is your theory?"

Paolo was first to respond, "I think Tracey and Jake were having financial difficulties. They could not have any children either. It is possible that Jake was having an affair with this Sarah girl and Tracey found out. He calls Tracey and arranges to meet her in an area of the park that he knows is going to be quiet. He whacks her. He either kills Sarah and gets rid of the body, never to be found again, or she may have possibly left the state to start a new life. I reckon she is dead." He stopped and turned to Geno, "How would you sum it up?"

Geno thought for a few seconds, "Well I agree that Sarah must be dead. It is possible that someone else might be involved in Sarah's death, but it's hard to see who would have killed Tracey. As you know in the majority of cases the murderer is known to the victim. But I just am not sure if Jake is the type of guy that may kill someone, I am on the fence with that one. However, Jake certainly would have a lot to gain from Tracey's death. He would have killed her to collect the insurance money or because he was having an affair and she found out. But it's hard to figure he did it for both reasons. And by the way the insurance money was not collected."

Paolo added, "Although that could have been due to the heat on him."

Geno and Jim nodded.

Jim asked, "Well guys do you see any connection between those two cases and Charlene's death?"

Paolo shook his head, "On the face of it I don't see any connection." He looked at Geno.

Geno shook his head, "Well they were both in the … let's call it hospitality business. It wouldn't be the first time someone killed call girls."

Jim stood up, "Yes that's what I was thinking. The only thing connecting the two cases is John Chapman. I will speak to the Captain, but I am sure you are happy that Derek and I pursue this case."

Just then Derek arrived and knocked at the door and walked in, "Hi guys, sorry I am not a morning person."

Jim's phone rang. "Hello? Yes Captain … That was quick, Captain! … Great, Captain, yes they are all here."

Jim put the phone down. "He is coming here. We have the autopsy report."

"That was quick," said Geno.

Jim nodded.

It seemed like an eternity, but eventually Will arrived with a cup of coffee in his hand and an A4 sheet of paper in the other. "My goodness this is some party. Now that I have my coffee I can talk. Ready for the autopsy report?"

"Go on, Captain," Derek said eagerly. The others all nodded.

Will referred to the report before speaking again. "Twenty-two-year-old brunette."

Derek interrupted, "Surely she was a blond."

Will looked at Derek and raised his eyebrows, "You are a bit naive, how many of the blonds you see do you think are natural blonds?"

Derek looked a bit sheepish, "Open mouth and insert foot, carry on."

Paolo leaned over a bit more to try and read the paper. Will pulled the paper towards his chest "Be patient." Paolo leaned back.

Will continued. "Twenty-two-year-old brunette, hair dyed blond." He looked at Derek and smiled. "She had a broken nose, a fractured right cheekbone, broken right fifth rib with a punctured lung. She had some of her hair pulled out at the back, in fact a whole area of about two inches diameter. Cause of death was a depressed fracture of her skull and a bleed in her brain. This was in the back of her head, may have been as a result of falling onto her head, but more likely a blow to the back of her head with a blunt object, possibly a hammer." He paused, it seemed just for dramatic effect. "As you know she was topless. She had an intrauterine contraceptive device inserted. There was some sperm present in her vagina, but there were no signs of forced sexual entry, so it is not clear whether the sperm may have been there from earlier or from the previous day. Certainly her clothes from her lower body were not removed. Time of death was about six to seven p.m. She was killed elsewhere and her body was dragged to the site." He stopped and flicked the paper with one of his fingers. "That's about all. It looks like it was not a rape case."

Derek was the first to ask, "Well what is the theory?"

Will instinctively turned to Geno, "Well, Detective, what is your hypothesis?"

Geno scratched the top of his head furiously in a very comical manner, moving his lips from one side of his mouth to the other as he stared at the ceiling.

"What do you think, Jim?"

Jim looked at Geno, "No Geno, let's hear you."

Will repeated the same, "You go on, Geno, we will hear from Jim in a second."

Geno became quite animated. "Guy picks up the hooker. He negotiates the price, starts his business. She becomes uncomfortable and asks him to stop. He gets angry and starts to hit her. Rage takes over and before he knows it, he has hit her on the head as she turned around or perhaps knocked her to the ground and she dies. He panics and takes the body and dumps it. That's about it."

Will turned to Jim, "What is your take on this?"

Derek and Paolo turned from looking at Geno to looking at Jim.

Jim nodded, "Very good, Geno. No doubt you suspect the guy is left-handed."

Geno nodded without much emotion, "Of course."

Derek looked a bit puzzled, "What makes you think …" He stopped before he had finished the sentence. "Of course, all the blows were to the right side of her body, making him more than likely left-handed."

"That's right," Jim continued, "The only other thing I would add is that he may have gone on his rampage with intent."

Derek looked puzzled again, "How is that?"

Will interrupted, "Yes that did cross my mind."

Derek was getting impatient, "Would one of you guys explain what you mean?"

Jim looked at Will, "Captain."

Will smiled at Jim and gestured with his hand, "Go ahead, Jim."

"Well her cause of death is a little worrying. A blow to the head from a fall would resemble a fracture from a blow. So if someone was angry and lost his temper where would he find an object to hit her with?"

Derek interrupted, "I suppose he may have found something in her room. Assuming of course they went to her room."

Will turned to Derek, "Now you are getting warm. The forensics are going through her room at this minute with a fine-tooth comb. Carry on, Jim."

"Well we just have to consider that he may have had his deadly weapon with him before picking up the girl," Jim replied.

Derek looked at Jim with some surprise, "It is strange to carry a hammer on him, isn't it."

Jim replied, "Strange and worrying." He paused for a second or two and then continued. "Worrying if the person was carrying a hammer, a gun, or other object. But he may have picked up anything blunt and delivered the blow."

Geno and Paolo nodded.

Will pointed to Jim and then Derek. "I want you two to go to the dead girl's room, Charlene that is, and look for any clues. After that do what you need to do to get us some leads. I believe the doc said this guy Chapman will be ready to be interviewed at fourteen hundred hours today."

Jim and Derek nodded.

Will then turned to Paolo as if giving Paolo his expected authority, "I want you two to start looking at any similar cases over the recent past. In fact, look at every prostitute that has been killed in the past two to three years or so."

Will stood up and walked towards the door. He stopped at the door and turned around. "Guys I hope I am not over-reacting." He paused. That pause had the desired effect, he got everyone's undivided attention. "I don't want to see a serial killer on the loose. There are aspects of this case that worry me. Don't waste any time eating or sleeping. In fact, don't even take a shit if it is going to take too long. We need some answers soon."

Geno answered, "Yes boss."

Will walked out of the room and came back in after one second, "What the fuck are you guys doing standing around, get to work!"

With that Geno and Paolo left the room and Jim and Derek grabbed their coats and left in a haste, "We are on it, Captain," Jim shouted.

Will gave him the report he had in his hand. "Here's her address."

Jim stood up, "Derek and I will go over a few things before we question Jake."

Will got a little closer to Jim and whispered loudly, "Jim I don't want this guy on the loose."

Jim nodded, "I understand, Captain."

CHAPTER 7

Questioning of Jake

Jim and Derek arrived at the custody suite about quarter to two in the afternoon. Jim nodded to the sergeant on duty, "Well, Serg, is Mister Chapman fit for an interview?"

The sergeant laughed, "He was pissed as a fart last night, Jim, he was seen by the doc again half an hour ago and is now fit for interview."

"Did he ask for a lawyer?"

"No, he declined, said he didn't need one. In fact, his exact words were 'what the hell would I need a lawyer for?'"

*

A police officer unlocked the cell door and walked into the cell. The officer shook John, "John wake up! John wake up!" Jake opened his eyes and looked at the police officer leaning over him. He looked at the blanket that was over him and then at the integrated plastic bed with a thin mattress on top of it. He looked at the door of the custody cell with another officer standing at the door. His eyes veered downwards towards the officer's belt and he looked at his Taser.

He felt a hand shaking his shoulder, "John, John, are you with us?"

He looked up at the officer. "If you mean physically, yes, of course I'm here, but if you mean …"

The officer interrupted him, "Let's not get philosophical 'bout this, the doc says you will be sober enough for an interview now."

Jake nodded and stood up. He steadied himself and followed the officers. "I was sober enough last night."

The police officer smiled, "That's what they all say. We need to get your fingerprints prior to questioning."

Jake nodded.

He was fingerprinted in an off room and then had his picture taken. "Follow me, John, you are going to be interviewed."

Jake nodded his head.

"Are you still sure you don't want a lawyer with you?"

"Yes, I don't need one!"

Jake walked to the interview room and sat down. He looked at his wrist and then held it before realizing that his watch was not there. He looked at the clock high up on the wall. It was two o'clock. He looked at the video camera attached to the ceiling.

Jim looked at Derek outside the interview room, "Here goes. Are you ready, kid?"

"Sure thing, Jim."

Jim and Derek walked into the interview room. They sat across the table from Jake.

"Would you like a coffee, Jake?"

"No thanks, Detective … what was your names again?"

"I'm Detective Jim Sterne, this is Detective Derek Johnston."

"Thank you, Detective Sterne, I don't drink coffee, all that caffeine couldn't be good for the body!"

Jim raised his eyebrows, "Hmm … Jake … Can I call you Jake?"

Jake nodded. "That is what most people call me, except for my mother, she never liked …" He paused, "Yes Jake is fine."

Jim continued, "I have to read you your rights before I ask you anything. You know you have the right to remain silent …"

Jake interrupted, "I know my rights, Detective Sterne, and I have no need for a solicitor either so carry on quickly so I can get home!"

Jim opened a notebook and Derek similarly opened his. Jim started the questioning, "Jake can I ask you first of all, are you left-handed?"

"All my life!"

Jim continued, "You are thirty-two years old, is that right?"

"That's a yes."

"Okay Jake. Do you know a girl named Charlene Mills?"

Jake shook his head. "Never heard of her."

"Where were you on the night of Saturday November the sixteenth?"

"Probably either at home or the Mexicano."

Jim continued, "Probably is not good enough, I need you to be more precise."

"I'm afraid one day often blends in to the next for me and I often don't know what day of the week it is, for example I don't even know whether it is now two a.m. or two p.m. Judging by the fact that you two are here I presume it is two p.m."

Derek continued the questioning, "Were you in the vicinity of Fifty Fourth street in Manhattan on Saturday night?"

Jake smiled, "I thought one of you has to be the good cop and one of you the bad one, just my luck I got two bad cops!" Jake chuckled to himself.

Derek's expression did not change, "Please answer the question, were you in the vicinity of Fifty Fourth street on the night of sixteenth November?"

Jake stopped smiling, "As I said, I can't remember."

"Mister Chapman do you remember meeting us previously, that is before today?" Jim was leaning back and looked relaxed.

"Do you mean earlier this afternoon, or yesterday or whenever it was, I am not sure. If you are talking about a former life, no and I don't believe in re-incarnation."

Jim looked at Derek and looked back at Jake, "Jake I do ask you to take this seriously as this is a murder case."

"I thought I was taking it seriously. So, what have I missed?"

Derek sat forward a little bit, "Do you remember meeting us in the Mexicano bar two nights ago, Saturday night to be precise?"

"I'm sorry, Detectives, I may have had one or two drinks in me, so my focus may not have been so sharp."

"You may remember you spilt our drink on me," Derek said.

Jake looked at Derek, "O gosh I vaguely remember something. I am so sorry; I hope I wasn't rude to you or anything. Surely you don't arrest people nowadays for that sort of thing."

"No Jake, Detective Johnston is not worried about that." Jim leaned forward and stared at Jake straight in his eyes. "Do you remember what you told us about a young girl being killed that night?"

Jake shook his head. "You must have me mistaken for someone else. I wouldn't have any such knowledge. I'm sure you are mixed up. Now please can I go home? I think I will need a drink soon." He held his right hand up and there was a slight tremor in it. "I may go into alcohol withdrawal!"

Jim looked towards the camera for a second. He looked at Jake again. "Mister Chapman, I am going to ask you once again. I would like you to pay close attention to what I am saying. You told Detective Johnston and me that … " Jim paused and looked at a small notebook in front of him, "it was awful that a young girl had been killed that night." He looked up at Jake. "You said that you had heard it on CNN news."

Jake suddenly sat up. "Well that probably explains it. I don't remember anything about this incident. But I must have heard it on the news. So, I don't understand what the deal is here."

Derek spoke with a hint of anger in his voice, "The deal is that we don't believe you."

"And why not, Detective Johnston?"

"Because Mister Chapman, this item of news was not broadcast on the news until the day after we saw you."

"Detectives I am sure there is an easy explanation to this …" His expression changed to one of bewilderment. "Wait a minute, why did you want to know if I am left-handed? I am not a suspect here am I, because that would be totally ludicrous."

Jim stood up, "Mister Chapman, you are under arrest for the murder of

Charlene Mills. I would advise you to call your attorney. You will be detained in a secure place until your hearing." Derek got up as well.

Jake laughed out loud.

Derek was walking towards the door and turned back, "What is so funny, Mister Chapman?"

"Well for the past year I haven't cared whether I lived or died. And now I am arrested for murder. Something incongruous about that to me."

Derek looked a bit angry, "I don't think this a laughing matter. A young girl has been killed."

Jake looked serious all of a sudden. "In any case, I don't want an attorney. Que sera sera."

Jim spoke as he stood by the door, "If you do not want to choose an attorney, the state will provide one for you."

"I don't want one!"

"Well the procedure is that the attorney will speak to you, and if you still don't want one, you can defend yourself." Jim opened the door, "Do you understand this?"

Jake said in a sarcastic tone, "God forbid if I get in the way of procedure."

Derek shook his head, "Mister Chapman, do you realise the gravity of the charges that are facing you? You do realise that because of this you will be detained in a secure place until your hearing? That is, you will be kept in prison in the meantime."

Jake shrugged his shoulders.

Derek looked at Jim. They walked towards the door. As they opened the door Jake suddenly asked, "By the way, Detectives, who was the young girl?"

Derek looked at Jake, "Why don't you tell us?

They walked out and closed the door. A police officer came in to usher Jake away.

CHAPTER 8

Jake Meets His Attorneys

Back to present time

Jake was awakened by the sound of the key turning in his cell door. The prison guard walked into his cell. He beckoned with his hand for Jake to get up and spoke with a strong New York accent. "Get up John!"

Jake looked around the cell, "Where am I?"

"What, do you have amnesia? Or were you too drunk to remember?"

Jake scratched his head, "No, I don't think I even asked."

"Well next time remember to ask. You are in the New York Metropolitan Correctional Centre." He kicked him on his ankle as he was lying on his bed, "Now get up, I ain't got all day."

Jake asked in a sarcastic tone, "Am I going home then?"

"Going home, MY ASS! Your fancy-ass lawyers are here to speak to you."

"I don't want to see anybody!"

The guard kicked him harder, "I won't ask you again! My job is to take you to the interview room. Now do you want to go there horizontally or vertically?" He was about to kick Jake again when Jake jumped up.

The guard produced handcuffs. Jake looked at him with an expression of surprise. "Just routine." is all the guard said. Jake put his hands behind him. The guard laughed and turned him round. As he handcuffed his hands in front of him he said, "You have been watchin' too many movies." He laughed again.

Jake walked behind the uniformed guard, through four electrically operated internal prison gates which were each opened by a guard on the other side. He was dressed in a pair of old jeans which looked in need of a wash. He still had the brown T-shirt on from the time he was arrested. He had on a pair of old black shoes in need of a polish. He was unshaven and had a fairly long scruffy beard.

He was shown into a room with a table at the centre of it. It was a basic looking table with four thin legs. There was one wooden chair at one end of the long side of it and two at the other.

The guard beckoned him to sit down. Jake sat on one of the chairs that was on the side of the table that had two chairs. The guard grunted at him, kicked his ankle again, then hit him on his left shoulder and pointed to the chair on the opposite side. Jake got up and walked across and sat on the chair there. The guard said nothing and stood beside him with his hands crossed in front of his groin area. After a couple of moments the guard sniffed a couple of times, gave Jake a dirty look and walked a few paces away and stood by the door.

There was a knock at the door. Two ladies walked in. One of them said to the uniformed guard, "Thank you very much."

"Welcome Ma'am." was the answer as the guard tipped his head. He stood with his back to Jake and gently waved his hands in front of his nose, then held his nose and let go, "He's all yours ladies!"

As they turned their attention to the disheveled man sitting behind the table the younger of the two gasped and whispered, "O my God!"

The slightly older one approached Jake. She was thirty-seven years old, five foot ten, with dark brown hair that was shoulder length and parted on one side. She had a pinstripe skirt with a matching jacket, underneath which she wore a white blouse with the top couple of buttons open. She had a pearl necklace on. She reached her hand over to shake Jake's hand, "Hello my name is Amanda Jackson, I am your defense attorney." Jake reached and shook her hand with a very limp handshake and let go after a second.

Amanda continued, "This is my associate Miss Lucy Walker."

Jake shook Lucy's hand in a similar manner. Lucy was in her late twenties. She was slightly shorter than Amanda at five foot eight inches. She had auburn hair which was fairly thick set and cut just below the ear lobes. She had a plain black skirt on with a beige blouse with a frilly collar buttoned to the top. She had a grey jacket on.

Amanda turned to the guard, "Could I have privacy with my client please."

The guard was very apologetic, "Sure, I'm sorry." And he hastened towards the door.

Amanda's raised her voice slightly, "Excuse me sir, would you mind removing his handcuffs?"

"But Ma'am, my orders are that he is dangerous and needs to remain cuffed."

Amanda sounded very authoritative, "Please remove his cuffs. I am happy to speak to your senior officer right now if you would like."

"No that is fine, I will remove his cuffs ma'am if that is your wish."

"Thank you."

Having removed the cuffs the guard hooked them on his belt ring and locked them in place. "I will be right outside, give me a shout if you need me." With that he left the room.

Amanda and Lucy sat down opposite Jake. Amanda opened a file that she had in front of her. There were a couple of A4-size lined pages with some handwritten notes on them. She turned to a blank page and wrote the date at the top of the page.

She looked at Jake who seemed to be staring into space. "Mister Chapman." She paused, "Can I call you Jake, I believe you prefer Jake to John?"

Jake shrugged his shoulders without saying anything.

Amanda continued, "Jake I have gone through the statements that you have made to the police; I would like to hear your side to the story."

Jake still avoided eye contact, "I have told all there is to say to the police, I have nothing new to say."

Amanda seemed unperturbed by Jake's lack of cooperation, "Mister Chapman… Jake. Do you realise the gravity of the charges facing you?"

"Yes."

"Do you not care?"

"No."

"Jake you are accused of killing someone, surely you must care. You could spend the rest of your days behind bars!"

"It's a shame they don't just hang me and get it over and done with."

Amanda asked quickly, "Are you telling me that you killed her?"

Jake looked up at Amanda for the first time, "I have already told the police I didn't kill her or anyone else for that matter!"

Lucy sat forward a little bit, "Mister Chapman, we are trying to help you, we are on your side you know."

Jake looked at Lucy for a few seconds. Lucy became noticeably uncomfortable and looked away. Jake looked down again. "Thanks but I don't need any help. I can defend myself."

"Look, Jake, it is in your best interest to cooperate with us." Amanda was getting visibly irate and her tone had changed slightly.

"My best interest does not exist anymore. I stopped living a year ago."

Amanda's tone softened again, "Are you referring to your wife's death?"

"Yes, and she was murdered. As if that wasn't bad enough, the police thought … think, I killed her too."

Amanda was very direct, "And did you?"

Jake shot Amanda a look of disgust, "I thought you said you were on my side."

"I am," replied Amanda, "but part of my job is to ask probing questions."

Jake smirked. Amanda looked a bit annoyed, "May I ask you what you find funny?"

"Oh nothing. Just watching your faces trying to psycho-analyse me."

Amanda responded quickly, "I must say, that's not something I have ever heard before quoted to me."

"Well, psychology is my profession don't forget."

Amanda felt that Jake was beginning to communicate with her, "Well, do you know who killed your wife?"

Jake suddenly lost the softness in his face and became very impassive again. "No one believes me, and I doubt whether you will either."

Lucy spoke, "Mister Chapman, why don't you let us be the judge of that. Why don't you tell us your part of the story, it can't do any harm?"

"You mean about my wife?"

Amanda interrupted, "Why don't we start with the present tense."

Jake seemed to be studying his fingernails very intently as he casually said, "What part do you want to know?"

Amanda got to the point, "How did you know about the murder of Charlene Mills?"

"I told the police that I heard it on CNN news."

Amanda checked her notes, "Oh yes, the black girl. That's right. You mentioned to the detectives that she said something about a young girl who was killed at the old cement production site and that her shoe was found on the road which led to her being found."

Jake shrugged his shoulders.

Amanda turned over the top page of her notes and read some notes on the second page. She tapped the middle of the page a few times, "You see, Jake, there are a couple of problems here. Firstly, CNN did not break the news until after you spoke to the policemen in the bar that same night. The second problem is that at this moment in time CNN do not have any black women news announcers."

Jake looked up in amazement, "But I heard it myself. She seemed very upset when she was reading it, she said …" He paused for a while. "Unless…" He stopped.

Lucy asked, "Unless what?"

"Doesn't matter."

"Come on, Mister Chapman, you need to give us something to go on."

"Well … maybe I dreamt it."

Amanda could not control her emotions and showed a little bit of anger, "Come on, you can't expect me to believe that, now why don't you tell me the truth?"

"You may choose to believe what you like, but I can only tell what I believe to be the truth."

Amanda tried to control her anger by lowering her tone, "You know if we don't come up with a better explanation to how you knew about this girl's death, we will be hung out to dry."

Jake looked at Amanda and noticed she was squeezing hard on the pen she was holding in both her hands. He looked at her and had a hint of a smile. "You know I am the one who will be hung to dry, why are YOU so tense?"

Amanda's voice was slightly raised again, "I am not tense." No sooner had she uttered those words that she squeezed the pen so hard that it broke.

Jake smiled, "They don't make pens like they used to!"

Amanda took a big breath, "Look Jake, maybe I am a bit worked up, but you have to give me something to go on, perhaps you heard the news somewhere else. Maybe you were drunk and got mixed up."

Jake raised his right hand. "No that is my story and I will not change it. Listen Miss … "

"It's Jackson, and you can call me Amanda, I don't like formalities."

"Miss Jackson, Amanda, I do appreciate that you are trying to help me, but I have nothing to live for, I simply do not care what any judge or jury may think or indeed what will happen to me. In fact, I have told you all I know about that night. I would like to be by myself now."

Lucy spoke in a quiet voice and with a very soft tone, "Jake, do you not want us to help you?"

"I appreciate your efforts, but I have nothing more to tell you."

Amanda put the papers back into the makeshift folder and closed it. "Why don't you go back to your cell and think about where this is all going and whether you want to spend the rest of your life behind bars and we will come back to see you tomorrow."

She took the two pieces of the broken pen and put them in the pocket of her jacket. "I have to mention this. If you plead guilty you will get a reduced sentence. Perhaps we can plead that you were intoxicated or depressed and not in full control of your actions. Perhaps you may get away with only five to ten years."

Jake was about to speak but Amanda continued, "You don't need to say anything now, just think about it and we will see you again tomorrow, okay?"

Jake's unshaven face remained expressionless. "Okay, but you already know what I am going to say tomorrow."

Amanda got up. "Just think about it."

CHAPTER 9

District Attorney Meeting

The young black personal assistant knocked at the door. On the door it read:

'Andy Gomez

Deputy District Attorney'

"Come in," said a voice from inside the room.

The girl walked in.

"Hi Sandra, does Peter want me?"

"Yes sir, he wants a quick word before the case meeting."

"Do you have all the witness statements of the Chapman case printed yet?"

"It's nearly finished, there were a lot of pages."

"No problem Sandra, bring them to the board room when they are ready."

"Yes sir."

"Okay then. Wish me luck, this is a big case for me." He looked very anxious.

"I know, sir. We have heard the rumours."

"What rumours exactly have your heard?"

"About Mister North possibly retiring soon."

"How would you have heard about those when I have only heard about it a couple of days ago?"

"Well Mister Gomez," she paused and then said with a slight smile, "You could say that if you want to know anything that is going on ask the attorneys, and if you want to know anything that is going to happen ask the PA's."

Andy laughed. "I must remember that! And please call me Andy." Andy got up and picked up a few pieces of papers.

"Don't forget the photos." Sandra handed him some photos from the desk.

"Shit! I nearly forgot them, thanks Sandra." He looked up, "Sorry Sandra, didn't mean to curse."

"I've heard a lot worse, Mister Gomez."

He looked up at her and smiled, "I guess so. And call me Andy please, Sandra."

She smiled, "Okay … Andy. It sounds strange!"

"Maybe, but it sounds nice!" Andy was about to go out the door and stopped and tried to see his reflection on the glass between his room and the hall. "Can't see. Do I look okay?"

He was wearing a silver-grey pinstriped suit with a brilliant white shirt and a grey tie. Sandra walked up to him and fixed the knot on his tie, which was a bit loose. She then fixed the lapel of his jacket by running her index finger under the lapel and straightening the edges with her thumbs. She patted him on the lapel of his jacket and said, "You look perfect, Andy."

"Oh, thank you." His face was slightly red.

As Sandra walked out Andy looked at her. She had a white dress on. It was quite short and covered half of her thighs. It had a black ring around the bottom of it, a couple of inches above the bottom of the dress. This was matched by a similar black ring at the neck area. She was not wearing any stockings and he stared at her long black legs. She had a gold charm bracelet with a number of items hanging from it.

His eyes seemed to be focusing on her bottom when she suddenly turned around. "Did you say something, sir?"

Andy blushed and looked up towards her face. "N… No. I was just thinking."

"What about, Andy?"

"Oh nothing."

Sandra turned around.

"In fact Sandra I was thinking … never mind, I have to run."

"Yes sir." She turned around and walked away but had a big smile on her face.

Andy suddenly hears a voice. "What's keeping you?"

Andy seemed to jump out of a daydream. "Oh Peter. Yes, I was just coming to your room."

"I just wanted to make sure you have everything in order before the case meeting."

"I think so, Peter, I am just waiting for the copies of the witness statements. Sandra should have them soon."

"That's fine, we can start then. I'll let you take the lead in most of the proceedings. So, you can also do the introductions."

"Sure Peter, let's go then." He paused for a second and looked towards the direction of Sandra's table. "Peter did you notice anything different about Sandra today?"

Peter pursed his lips. "Nope, looks exactly the same to me! Why do you ask?"

"Oh nothing much, I just thought she looked different today. Okay, let's go."

Peter and Andy walked into the boardroom. There was a very large oval table with twenty high back, swivel leather chairs. Eight of the seats were taken. On one side there were three men and one woman and on the other two men and two women. The men were all dressed in suits and the women likewise had skirts with matching jackets.

As they walked into the room everyone stopped talking. Andy walked to one of the seats on one side of the table and put his papers down. Peter walked to Andy and pointed to the head of the table. "That's your seat, Mister Gomez."

Andy smiled, "Yes sir." He picked up his papers and took them to the seat at the top of the table. He then walked to a side table and poured himself a cup of coffee and brought it to the seat. He sat down and organized his papers in front of him.

He then took a sip of coffee and placed his cup on the saucer. He seemed to take a deep breath. "Okay gentlemen … Sorry and ladies … Not a good start was it?"

Everyone laughed.

Andy seemed to relax. "Okay guys you are all welcome. Let me go through the introductions. No doubt you all know our District Attorney, Mister Peter North."

Peter nodded.

"On my right we have four of our top attorneys. Our two most senior attorneys, Mister Rafael Dominguez and Miss Patricia Crawford." The two of them nodded in turn. "Alongside them, two of our experienced attorneys Miss Shirin Jamal and Mister Des Hammond." They nodded in turn.

He turned to his left-hand side. "On my left we have Mister Justin Hunter and Mister Rupert Lampard of the Swift Private Eye Agency." They nodded. "Those of you who do not know Mister Hunter, he is Hunter by name and hunter by reputation." They laughed and Rupert patted Justin on the back.

Andy continued, "And last but not least, we have Anita Sheehan and William Mackenzie from our research department. Anita and William will research any background information, previous cases, criminal records, medical history – anything we can get our hands on; psychiatric history, dental history, shoe size, etcetera, etcetera. In fact, anything that you think might be of use in the case.

"Ladies and gentlemen, as you can see, we are not leaving any stone unturned here. But let me first go over the facts as we know them. Any questions before I start?"

He looked around the room, some stayed motionless whilst others shook their heads.

Andy continued, "Okay, good. Twenty-two-year-old prostitute Miss Charlene Mills was murdered on Saturday sixteenth November perhaps at six or seven p.m."

Just then there was a quiet knock on the door and Sandra walked in. "I have the files, Mister Gomez."

"Come on in, Sandra."

Sandra came in and quietly walked around and put a file in front of each person starting with Peter. Finally, she put a file in front of Andy and placed one to the side. She said quietly, "I always like to have a spare one in case."

Andy grazed her right elbow very gently with the tips of his fingers. "That's very thoughtful of you, Sandra."

Sandra smiled, "You're welcome sir, will there be anything else?"

Andy pointed to the cups of coffee in front of those around the table, "Anyone like more coffee?" There were general shakes of the head from everyone.

"No Sandra, many thanks, that will be all."

Sandra walked out.

Andy continued, "Okay guys, I hope you are not squeamish, but if you open your files you will see the photos of Charlene Mills as she was found at the scene of the murder. Her body was discovered on Saturday night, November the sixteenth about eleven pm p.m. adjacent a disused cement factory on Fifty-Fourth street in Manhattan. Please turn to page two of your folder for the autopsy report. The summary is of multiple facial injuries. Cause of death was most probably a blow to the skull resulting in a depressed skull fracture and haemorrhage of her brain. She had some sperm cells in her vagina, but this may have been from earlier in the day, certainly no signs of forced sexual intercourse. There were some abrasions on her legs and arms, suggesting she may have been killed elsewhere and dragged to the murder scene. Examination of the shrubbery around the murder scene confirmed that the body was dragged to the final site."

Justin Hunter put up his hand.

"Yes Justin?" Andy smiled.

"I am sure you have considered why she would have sperm inside her?"

Andy smiled again, "Yes Justin I thought you may ask this question. She was still wearing her underwear and there were no signs of external injury to her genital area, so the sperm is unlikely to be from her killer. And as you are no doubt thinking, she would almost certainly use barrier method of contraception with a client. She had positive levels of the contraceptive pill in her blood, so perhaps it was from a boyfriend, but this is an area we would like your help in."

Justin wrote something on his notepad and nodded.

"In short, Justin, I would like to know if she has a pimp, if she had any regular customers, her friends, family, acquaintances. Basically, anything you can dig up.

"Now we turn to the accused. A Mister John Chapman, generally called Jake Chapman. A psychologist by profession. By some quirk of fate on the same night that she was murdered and only a few miles away Mister Chapman volunteered information to two detectives about the murder of Charlene Mills, before the news had hit the media. He seemed to have very specific information about her as well, for example he knew she was beside a disused cement factory and even that she had red shoes. His story was that he heard this on the news on CNN, when in fact the media had no knowledge of this murder at the time the detectives spoke to Mister Chapman. This man is an alcoholic and one must presume that in his drunken stupor he spilled the beans."

Peter interrupted. "How long after the murder did the detectives meet Mister Chapman?"

Andy answered, "Perhaps three to four hours, certainly sufficient time for Mister Chapman to have killed her, gone to the bar on Fifty Seventh street, had a few drinks, and got drunk by the time he met the detectives."

Peter was rubbing his chin. "Okay, but the story is a bit odd. Check the background of the detectives, see if they are straight."

Andy nodded, "I already have." He went through some of the papers in front of him, looking for a specific one.

Peter smiled, "Pay attention folks, this is why he is the Deputy DPP."

There were smiles around the room.

Andy looked a bit uneasy and continued, "I have spoken to one of our contacts in the precinct. A very reputable and reliable source. One of the detective, James Sterne, sails a bit close to the wind at times; our source suggests that he has been suspected of planting evidence on one occasion, but was not proven, and the source was quick to say that the person more than deserved to be behind bars. The story of them meeting Mister Chapman was corroborated by Mister Hunter from the bartender who was actually a witness to the conversation between the detectives and Mister Chapman. The bartender is, by all accounts, friendly with Mister Chapman, so I think everything is above board."

Peter gave Andy the thumbs up, "Good job, Andy. Continue."

Andy sat back and paused for a second. "Ladies and gentlemen, the plot thickens. Almost exactly a year ago Mister Chapman was accused of murdering his wife. Mister North was the Deputy District Attorney in charge of the case. The state postulated that Mister Chapman was having an affair with a Miss Sarah Miller. Miss Miller went missing, presumed murdered. Missus Chapman was then shot dead. The state believed that Mister Chapman was having an affair with Miss Miller, his wife found this out and he killed her. We think he has also killed Miss Miller and disposed of the body. However, the case had to be dropped due to lack of evidence."

Andy looked at Peter, "Would you like to add something at this stage?"

Peter nodded, "I will not get into the details of the case at this point in time, suffice to say that the District Attorney was very unhappy with the judge's decision not to proceed with the murder case. On later reflection, we were highly critical of our own efforts to put a killer behind bars. There was a significant introspection. This case led to the District Attorney's close association with Swift Private Eye Agency and a determination to endeavor not to be in a similar situation again."

He looked at Andy and nodded, "Please continue."

Andy nodded back. "Thanks Peter. Continuing on. Mister Chapman's wife, Tracey Chapman, was found dead in a park close to the vicinity of their home and a short distance from where her husband was. She was a social worker and it is evident that she had been in touch with Sarah Miller. The file that Tracey Chapman had on Sarah Miller was never found and social services say they had not received any specific info about Sarah Miller as Tracey Chapman was sworn to privacy. Again, it is likely that if any files were there, they could have been accessed by her husband and destroyed. Both females went missing at the same time. Jake Chapman had texted Tracey a short while before her death and I quote: 'I saw you dying today.' There was certainly motive, and some evidence. However, the judge called it circumstantial evidence and the case was eventually dropped.

"Sarah Millar was a law student. She had joined an agency called the Elite Club, a formal escort company. A company that is apparently registered and paying taxes. This company stroke club provides escorts, both male and female, usually to high-class customers, generally but not exclusively for one night. It's not what it sounds like. The idea is that high-class business folks and the like have someone on their arm for the night to impress clients. Other than that is not clear whether there is any – bluntly putting it – sex involved. No doubt Anita and William will fill us in. Next …"

Anita had put up her hand. She spoke with a strong Irish accent, "Yes Andy I had looked up the blurb you sent to me this morning and I have some information for you."

Andy looked at Peter and looked back at Anita. "I just emailed you the contents of the meeting this morning."

Anita picked up a notebook and opened it, "Yes Mister Gomez, but that was forty-five minutes ago."

Andy sat back and smiled, "Go ahead, Anita."

"I phoned the Elite Agency. I sold them a story about being a model and trying to make my way to the top. I got through to recruiting and have an audition next week."

Peter clapped a few times. "Bravo Miss Sheehan, all that in forty-five minutes!"

"Actually, Mister North, that was the first ten minutes. The rest was more difficult. I was able to actually speak to one of the escorts that work for them."

Peter's eyebrows visibly rose.

Anita looked at her notebook. "Quote; 'they don't tell you to sleep or not to sleep with your clients. But they do re-iterate that you can get more money from tips than from your regular pay. They only have one strict rule. If you snitch on your clients, you are out on your ass.'"

Andy was silent for a couple of seconds. "Wow. I can say that I am truly stunned. Thank you, Anita. Is that an Irish accent?"

"Yes, Mister Gomez, Dublin to be precise. I haven't lost it in ten years!"

"Whatever you do don't lose it. It's melodic."

"I'll take it as a complement."

Andy smiled, "That's exactly what it was … Now, where was I? Yes, okay. The hearing is set for Monday of next week. I understand that John Chapman had turned down his rights to an attorney so he will be represented by legal aid. Rafael, Patricia, I want you to find out as soon as humanly possible who will represent him. Get the background on the attorney and some of the significant cases he would have represented."

"Or she," said Patricia Crawford.

Everyone laughed.

"I have to apologise again," Andy put up his hand. "However, this time it was just a figure of speech."

Patricia nodded, "Okay Andy, we'll let you away with this one."

Andy stood up. "Right LADIES and gentlemen." Everyone laughed again. "Let's go. We'll meet up again on Friday. That gives us four days to put some more facts together before the hearing on Monday."

They all got up and started to leave the room with the exception of Andy and Peter.

Peter waited until all the others had left the room. He sat back and rocked on his chair for a short time. "Very impressive, Andy."

"Thank you, Peter."

"I will stay in the background. I will step forward if you ask me, or …" He paused.

Andy finished his sentence, "Or if I make a balls-up of this."

Peter laughed, "I couldn't have put it better myself. Okay let's go. Have a look at the evidence and your opening statement to the Judge and run it by me when you are ready. Make no mistake, it is never straightforward, and always expect some bumps and some surprises, good and bad. And always expect the…" He paused.

"The unexpected," finished Andy.

Peter nodded.

"Sure thing, Peter."

They both left the room. Peter went to his room.

Andy stopped at Sandra's desk. Sandra was talking to one of the other secretaries on the desk beside her.

"Thanks a lot, Sandra. The files were prefect. Good job."

"Thank you, Andy." Suddenly a couple of girls stopped working and looked up. "How did the meeting go, did you do all right?"

"Yes Sandra, everything went well. In fact, couldn't be better. I'll see you later then."

"Sure Andy."

Andy took a couple of steps towards his office and walked back and spoke rather quieter, "Is there something different about you today, Sandra?"

A few of the girls now seemed to get interested in the conversation.

Andy continued, "Is your hair different?"

"Did you notice, Andy, yes just had it trimmed." She touched her medium short Afro-style hair.

"I thought so!" said Andy looking pleased with himself.

As he got into his office the girl behind the desk next to Andy turned to Sandra. "Hi Andy, how are you Andy, do you think I'm sexy Andy. When did all the Andy shit start?"

"Oh just today," said Sandra as she looked towards Andy's office.

"And you have never had your hair trimmed, girl, have you?"

"No but I put special conditioner on it." Sandra said as she turned to the other girl and patted her own hair.

The girl smiled, "Girl, you may have black skin, but I can see you blushing through it."

A few of the girls laughed. "Shut up you," said Sandra as she laughed too.

CHAPTER 10

Second Questioning of Jake by Amanda and Lucy

Amanda and Lucy were waiting for Jake as he entered the room. As he turned around momentarily to sit on his chair Lucy turned to Amanda and pinched her nose with one hand and waved the other hand in front of her nose. She put her hands by her sides quickly as Jake turned around.

Amanda took the lead again, "Good morning Jake, did you sleep well?"

"Yes thanks. Good morning Lucy!"

"Oh!" Lucy seemed to be taken aback. "Good morning."

Amanda continued, "Well Jake, have you thought much about what we discussed yesterday?"

"Nope. In fact, not at all."

Amanda shook her head once as if in annoyance and then flicked through the few pages of the file in her hand. Jake looked at her and turned his focus on the file. He squinted his eyes and stretched his neck forwards slightly in an attempt to get closer to the writing. He saw his name: John Chapman. He made a chuckling sound.

Amanda pursed her lips together and suddenly lifted the file and slammed it on the table. "I'm glad you are amused because I sure as hell am not. Would you mind sharing with me what you find so funny so we can all have a laugh!"

Jake looked very impassive again as he swirled the hair at the end of his beard over and over again, "This is what my life has come to; a name of a file. A no one, soon to be forgotten about."

"Well it doesn't have to be like this, Jake, we can help you to try and make something of your life, but you will have to cooperate with us."

Jake began to look at his fingers again and rub the tips of his fingers as if brushing some dust off them. The end of the nails were black due to the dirt under them.

Lucy got up from her chair and started to pace up and down in a very agitated state. Amanda softened her tone a little bit. "Look, we are trying to help you. Now we can't help you unless you start to communicate with us and give us something to go on."

Jake's expression did not change. He shrugged his shoulders, as he seemed to look right through Amanda at the space behind her.

Amanda looked at Jake, "Jake, I have been giving this a lot of thought, I think it may be in your best interest to plead guilty, with diminished responsibility … "

Jake interrupted, "To be honest I really don't give a damn. I'd much rather be left alone."

Amanda raised both her hands up and gave out a sigh. "I don't know!"

All of a sudden Lucy stopped. She walked straight towards Jake, lifted her right arm and slapped him so hard across his right cheek that his face was jolted backwards. Lucy shouted at him, "Will you stop being such an asshole and a miserable jerk and tell us something of use? If not for yourself, then for your wife, Tracey's sake."

Jake looked at her in disbelief. Amanda was leaning forward on the table and seemed to be frozen in her position. Jake pushed his chair back, causing a screech on the wooden floor.

He got up and said in a quiet voice, "I wonder if you could excuse me for a few minutes." Amanda nodded; her body still frozen in a stooped position.

As the door closed behind Jake, Lucy looked at Amanda, "I am so sorry I don't know what got into me." She began to pace again, "Do you think he will complain? Oh, dear, he will probably ask for another attorney. I am so sorry, Amanda; I have never done anything like this before."

Amanda still seemed dazed, "Well I don't know if I have ever seen anything like this before. It certainly is not in any 'how to treat your client' manual that I have read. You do have a habit of acting before you think, don't you? You must learn to control your temper. This is not going to look good for me."

Amanda got up and sat on the edge of the desk and noticed the anxious look on Lucy's face "Don't worry about it, kid, anyway even if he decides to opt for another attorney, at least he would have had to make some sort of decision or movement from his stalemate position." She flicked through the few pages in the file very quickly and then closed it. "Anyway we have nothing at all to go on. I have never been so frustrated in my life. If it was not for pride, I would have given up on him myself."

Lucy looked at Amanda very sheepishly, "Will you tell the bosses about this?"

Amanda afforded a small smile, "Look Lucy, don't worry about it. You only did what I felt like doing. I don't give a shit what he does. I'd much rather deal with someone who appreciates our efforts."

Amanda stood up and started to walk towards a painting on the wall, which looked rather out of place. "Anyway, I am now stuck in this hell-hole with a … " she paused and looked at Lucy. She wiggled the index and middle fingers of both hands to indicate quotation "an asshole, who is probably guilty as hell. I suppose I may kiss my reputation goodbye right now. With any luck, he will want rid of us."

She walked towards the painting of a seaside on the wall. She seemed to go into deep thought for a few seconds and said softly "At times like this I wonder."

Lucy asked, "What about?"

Amanda seemed to be studying the painting in some detail. She was silent for a second as Lucy looked at her expectantly. Finally, Amanda broke the silence, "Have you heard of Whyte and Kidd Associates Attorneys?"

"Well who hasn't? Actually, they turned my application down a while back."

Amanda continued, "They head hunted me about eighteen months ago and offered me a huge contract with bonuses. I turned them down to work for legal aid in order to help the ordinary folk. I was also engaged to Stephen at the time and we were talking about starting a family. Stephen was a lecturer at the law school that I also lectured at." Her eyes seemed focused on two children playing with their buckets and spades on the beach alongside a couple resting on deck chairs.

Lucy waited for a few moments and as Amanda did not say anything else could not hold back the question. "What happened to Stephen?"

"Oh nothing much. A few months later I dropped into his apartment on his birthday with a birthday present and a bottle of champagne. The surprise present was some Victoria's Secret sexy lingerie. As it happened it was not needed. The surprise was on me. I found him in bed with a girl. Found out later it was a call girl. He had the cheek to say that it was not what it seemed. I said to him, while he was still on top of the girl, 'Please Stephen I'd love to know what it is in reality!'. He later told me that he really loved me, but that there was something missing. And that was the end of Stephen and look at where I am now."

She looked at Lucy, "You are single, aren't you?"

Lucy held out her left hand and shook her ring finger, "No man is going to put a chain around my neck."

There was a knock at the door. The guard opened the door and held it open. "Your client is back." He announced with a surprised look on his face.

Jake walked in. Lucy gasped. Amanda had to focus for a second to recognise him. He had shaved off his mustache and beard, his hair was slightly wet and was shiny as he had obviously had a shower and washed his hair. He had a clean grey T-shirt on and was wearing the standard grey bottoms. As he walked in, he asked the guard, "Could I have a cup of coffee?"

The guard looked at Amanda who asked, "Is that okay?"

He nodded.

Jake said, "White two sugars. In fact, can you make it very strong."

The guard had a wry smile, "Sir in here there is only one type of coffee, it's called take it or leave it coffee!"

Jake answered immediately, "That will do fine, I'll take it."

The guard left the room.

Jake sat on the chair he had previously occupied. He turned to Lucy, "I would like to thank you for making me realise that I have a responsibility to my wife's memory."

Amanda sat down and opened her file. She was rummaging through her bag for a pen. She asked Jake, "What do you mean?"

Jake thought for a few seconds, "Perhaps I should start at the beginning." He paused again as if not sure as to where to start. He finally turned to Amanda, "Do you ever have dreams?"

Amanda replied, "Never remember them, what is the point exactly?" She seemed a little impatient and put the pen down on top of the file with enough force to make a loud noise.

Jake seemed oblivious to her impatience. He turned to Lucy, "Do you?"

Lucy smiled. "I presume you are not referring to dreams after cheese and wine?" She noticed that Amanda was looking at her sternly. Her smile quickly disappeared and she said in a more serious voice, "Yes, what is your point?"

Jake paused and wiped a tear that was rolling down his cheek. "I killed my wife."

Lucy looked at Amanda whose eyes seemed to be transfixed on Jake. It was as if Amanda was studying every move of Jake. Realising perhaps that Amanda was studying Jake's body language she turned her focus on Jake.

Jake had to wipe off a few tears again and seemed to be unable to go on.

Amanda reached into her handbag again and got a tissue and handed it to Jake. "How did you do it?"

Jake looked up, "I don't mean I physically killed her. God, I could never do that. She was all I lived for. I loved her more than anything in the world."

Amanda lifted her pen and leaned forward and seemed to be getting interested, "Can you explain what you mean?"

Jake took a deep breath again, "I mean that I caused her death."

Amanda put her pen down again and could not hide her frustration, "Look could you be a little bit more direct, maybe a bit more specific?"

Realising that her impatience was obvious she spoke in a softer tone, "Look Jake, I'm sorry. It's just that the case starts on Monday and we just have a few days left and I have nothing to go on. I'm here to help you, but you need to give me some information that I can use."

Jake nodded, "Okay. I'll try and give you a concise version."

Amanda interrupted, "The longevity is not a problem, so long as it is to the point."

Jake nodded again, "Okay. Let's see. Okay. You know that Tracey was a social worker,"

Amanda nodded, "Yes I have heard that."

"No doubt you know that I was accused of killing her."

Amanda nodded. Lucy grabbed a seat and sat down, looking very interested. Amanda started to write something on a blank sheet.

Jake continued, "Well over the course of my life I would have had the odd dream, you know the sort of dream where you would see something that would happen to you in the future."

Amanda looked blankly back at him.

"Well anyway that's not important now, but one night, oh about two years after we had been married, I had a dream that Tracey was holding a baby in her arms. I woke up and was quite excited, because we had been trying for a baby for about two years. Tracey really wanted a baby."

Jake paused and he smiled for the first time. "Anyway, she, we, couldn't conceive. We had put all our money into getting fertility tests carried out, without any luck. So, I thought, I hoped, my dream meant that we may have a child. At first, I didn't mention the dream to Tracey. A couple of nights later I had a dream that Tracey was holding a baby, but there were some dogs trying to bite the baby and Tracey held the baby in her bosom and it was as if the dogs were not able to touch the baby, as if Tracey had a protective shield around her. I was a bit preoccupied and over breakfast Tracey asked me what was on my mind. I mentioned my dream to her, and she laughed at me. She didn't generally pay a lot of attention to my dreams and used to tease me and ask why I didn't dream the numbers of the lottery so we can be rid of all our debts. Well actually we were never worried about any financial issues, even though the police made a big fuss of it when they arrested me after her death, after she was murdered." He stopped again and the tears fell down his cheeks.

Lucy reached to put her hands on his shoulder and Jake lifted his left hand. "It's okay, I'm okay. I'm fine. I have had a lot of time to think about it, in fact I have thought of nothing else in the past year or so."

He sat upright again and continued, "Where was I? Yes, that same night she came home and told me that the strangest thing happened to her. Late that morning her office got a call from a girl who was very distressed. Tracey was assigned to meet her. Tracey found out that she was pregnant. She was being pressurised by the father to have an abortion. Tracey had a busy workload and didn't want to take on the case when she suddenly remembered my dream. To cut it short she took on the case, but the girl begged that Tracey would not tell her co-workers that she was pregnant. Tracey promised this to her. So the girl had got pregnant by some guy who didn't want her to have the baby. He had offered her money to have an abortion and when she didn't agree he threatened to kill her. The girl was scared and called for help …"

Lucy interrupted Jake, "What was the name of the girl?"

Jake shook his head. "Tracey was very discrete. She would sometimes talk about situations, but she never broke anyone's confidentiality. When the girl phoned Tracey's office, she was quite scared and would not give any details. During the police enquiries later, I found out that she was called Sarah, Sarah Miller. She was, funny enough, a law student."

Amanda was flicking thought some of her notes, "I am really sorry to interrupt, Jake, but there was no mention of pregnancy in your previous statements to the police last year."

Jake nodded, "Yes, that is right. But I only disclose this to you in confidence and I do not want it repeated anywhere. That was information that Sarah would have given to Tracey in strictest confidence and she may have relatives that are alive and I would not want this information disclosed in any other forum."

Amanda continued, "But Jake you do realise we are in a sticky situation and we need to use anything we can to help you."

Jake shook his head, "Anything but this information!"

Amanda nodded, "Okay for now I give you my word, but perhaps we can come back to it later if needed. So, do continue."

Jake continued, "Sarah had to supplement her scholarship by working for a high-class escort agency. She got involved with some married guy. He saw her on occasions and she got careless and got pregnant."

Lucy interrupted, "I would have thought that a law student would have enough intelligence to know how not to get pregnant!"

Jake smiled, "I asked my wife nearly the same question, how would a girl now-a-days not know how to prevent pregnancy. She mentioned that she wore belts and braces ..."

"Pardon me?" Lucy interrupted.

"She took the pill and insisted on condoms, but she had slight diarrhoea for a couple of days, and unbeknownst to her the guy took the condom off during sex, pardon me, during intercourse."

The guard walked in with the cup of coffee. Jake said, "Thanks."

The guard said, "No problem, what about you ladies?"

Amanda and Lucy answered simultaneously and almost impatiently, "No thanks."

Jake took a couple of sips of the coffee. He shook his head vigorously from side to side a few times. "Oh that feels good."

Amanda and Lucy were sitting forward in their seats with anticipation. He took another couple of sips before continuing. "Sarah eventually decided to carry on with the pregnancy and give the baby up for adoption. She went to a different State, unknown destination, except to Tracey, and few weeks after she gave the baby for adoption. Tracey was ... she was murdered a few days later and Sarah was also never seen again."

There was a short silence. Amanda was taking notes. Lucy broke the silence, "So you think you are responsible for getting her involved in the case?"

Jake nodded, "Yes but that was not all. I slowly began to have the inkling that there was a danger ahead. A few months after she started to help Sarah, I dreamt that I walked into our bathroom to brush my teeth. We had a glass that sits on top of the bathroom sink and we had both our toothbrushes in it, my blue one and her pink one. When I reached for my brush, I noticed that there was only one blue brush in there. I didn't take much heed of this. The next night I dreamt that I put on my bathrobe in the morning and when I reached for mine, hers wasn't there. The very next night I woke up in bed and Tracey wasn't there in bed with me. Just then I woke up and realised that I had dreamt it. You know one of those dreams when you wake up, but you are really dreaming that you have woken up and are still sleeping."

Lucy nodded, but Amanda shook her head and said, "No. But carry on."

"It was a Sunday and I was very anxious, so I went to a nearby park and was ruminating on the dream all day when it suddenly occurred to me that her life was in danger. I got home in a rush and saw a note from Tracey to say that she was going to meet someone about Sarah's case. I phoned her but she was not answering. I left a message for her that she was in danger. But it must have been too late. The irony is that Tracey was killed in the same park I was in."

Amanda asked, "Did you keep the note?"

Jake shook his head. "I have no idea what happened to it. With the shock of having to identify …" he paused and wiped a tear, "to identify her body, so much of what happened in that day became a blur."

Amanda asked, "Did you have any witnesses in the park?"

Jake looked at Amanda, "I have been through all this with the police several times last year. I saw a few people walking, one or two with dogs. I saw a lady with her Great Dane that I recalled. I spoke to her for a brief period. But apparently, she walks down that stretch every day and speaks to so many people that she had no recollection of meeting me."

Jake got up and walked towards the glass in the door that looked towards the corridor. "I didn't see Tracey again. Well not alive. The next time I saw her was to identify her body. She looked so different, yet somewhat peaceful. I see her face every day. And the dreams." Jake stared into space.

Lucy interrupted, "What dreams?"

Jake sat down again and buried his head in his hands. "It started a couple of months after her death … after she was murdered. The first time I dreamt that I was sitting in the park and she was suddenly standing in front of me. She seemed very upset and asked me why I hadn't gone after her. I dream of her over and over in different situations and she keeps asking me why I hadn't gone after her."

He shook his head whilst holding it very firmly. "That's when I started to drink. I really did not have much of a liking for alcohol, mainly because Tracey didn't like to kiss me when I had been drinking. I started drinking ten months ago and only stopped a few days ago. It's the only thing that makes the pain go away. I'm not sure why I have these dreams, I wish they would go away."

He looked up at Amanda and then at Lucy, "You don't believe a word of all this, do you?"

Lucy was about to say something, but Amanda was first to speak, "Let's say I have a healthy scepticism."

She put her pen down. "Irrespective of whether all this is believable or not, I don't know if there is anything I can use here to help your case. I'm not sure how much a jury is going to believe any of this."

She crossed the fingers of her two hands, rotating her thumbs around each other. She spoke so softly it was as if she was thinking aloud, "In fact I don't even know whether any of this should be mentioned in court. Let's go back to the girl, Sarah. Can you tell me anything else about her?"

"As I said, Tracey didn't give much confidential information, she talked about the scenarios and dilemmas. They never found her body. I never knew whether Tracey knew the identity of Sarah's lover. I think that over the time preceding her pregnancy she spent a lot of time with the guy. When she got pregnant, he changed completely. I also understood that he had been violent as well."

Amanda interrupted, "You mean after the pregnancy?"

"Not exclusively, but Tracey certainly thought he was fuming that Sarah would not have a termination of her pregnancy. Tracey mentioned once that she had had a black eye. Something about getting violent during intercourse. But again, she just mentioned it in passing, but I didn't pursue this, I generally just listened whilst she talked over aspects of the case. I think somehow when she talked out loud, she was better able to analyse the case. Very rarely I would give her some ideas … "

Amanda interrupted again, "Jake you do realise that if the whereabouts of the baby can be discovered, DNA samples from the baby may help in locating the father and therefore may help in knowing if Sarah was murdered and who the culprit might be."

"Yes I realise that, but this is not my decision. I have to be true to Tracey. I will be breaking her oath and not mine."

Amanda nodded, "Okay let's park this point again for now." Amanda finished writing some notes. She put her pen down and sat back. She looked at

Jake, "It will take me a bit of time to digest this information."

Jake interrupted her, "Very diplomatic. I don't mind if you go ahead and say you don't believe a word of what I have said."

Amanda carried on as if she had not been interrupted, "Can I change the topic? Now you need to tell me about Charlene Mills."

Jake shrugged his shoulders.

Amanda said, "Jake can I have an agreement with you?" She paused. "I will stop breaking pens if you stop shrugging your shoulders. Let's face it, for a psychologist it is not a very communicative action."

Jake smiled, "Okay Amanda, we have a deal." He leaned back, "But I am sorry, I have never met her, and only heard her name for the first time when I was arrested."

Lucy interrupted, she flicked through the pages in front of Amanda. "Jake as we discussed with you yesterday, you told some detectives about Charlene's death before anyone had knowledge of the case. How can you explain this?"

"As I said I heard it on the news."

Lucy carried on, "Do you not remember our discussions yesterday? Let me remind you – you said you had heard of her death on CNN news. CNN had not announced her death for about twenty-four hours after you had mentioned her death. Also, you had specifically mentioned that a black girl had read the news." Lucy paused, "There are no black newsreaders on CNN."

Jake started to shrug his shoulders and stopped. He looked at Amanda and smiled, "Sorry." He turned to Lucy again. "I must have dreamt it then."

Lucy shook her head, "You can't expect a court of law to believe that, do you?"

Amanda made some notes again. "I have to agree that it does sound suspicious. However, we can worry about that later, perhaps it is only circumstantial evidence, we will have to wait to see if the prosecutors have any hard evidence, I don't think this would be enough for a hearing."

Lucy looked at Amanda, a bit surprised, "It would be a damn good start, would it not?"

"Let me worry about that." She turned to Jake. "Are you telling me categorically that you did not kill Charlene Mills?"

"I can tell you categorically that I have never met her that I know of!"

Amanda stood up quickly, "Well I think that it is as much as we need for now. I need to meet with the prosecutors to see what else they have."

Lucy looked a bit surprised and got up slowly. "Okay … "

Amanda reached her hand over in a gesture to shake Jake's hand, which he did. "Don't go far, we will probably see you tomorrow."

Jake smiled, "Don't worry, I'll be here."

He reached out towards Lucy. Lucy reached out her hand, somewhat reluctantly, and shook his hand briefly. Amanda opened the interview room door.

A prison guard came in and took out the cuffs and handcuffed Jake. He was taken away.

Amanda closed her file.

Lucy was silent for a while before speaking, "Well what do you think of him? Do you think he did it?"

Amanda did not respond for a few seconds. "I'll tell you this, a jury may have some sympathy for him with that story, but when it comes to his knowledge of Charlene Mills' murder and with respect to any cross-examination I think he will be crucified!"

Lucy asked, "So you think he is guilty?"

Amanda looked at Lucy, "How often do you think you actually know the truth? I sometimes think that the truth is like a mirage. You think you know what it was until time passes and realise that your perception of what you saw earlier was distorted and now everything looks different."

"Hmm, that is interesting, I see exactly what you mean, I will remember that."

Amanda continued, "Our job is to see what charges there are against our clients and to defend them to the best of our ability. The truth may never come to the fore. I don't lose any sleep worrying about the truth. Well … very rarely."

"There is something else bothering me though."

"Are you talking about the fact that he hasn't mentioned the pregnancy to the police?"

Lucy nodded. "Yes and the thought that he will not disclose the information because the DNA testing may match his."

"Yes, that's the exact thought that went through my mind as he was talking."

CHAPTER 11

Lucy Questioning Jake by Herself

Jake walked into the room. Lucy was seated behind the desk.

"Hello," she said quietly.

Jake looked a little surprised, "Is Amanda not here?"

"No, she had some other business to take care of."

"That's okay. She doesn't believe a word I've said anyway so I suppose it doesn't matter whether she's here or not."

Lucy seemed to be searching for the right words and was unable to find them. Jake put her out of her misery. "Don't worry, you don't have to answer that." Lucy seemed relieved until Jake spoke again, "Do you believe me?"

"I want to believe you, but you need to give us some more information to help us understand. You must agree that you story is a little farfetched."

"Yes." Jake sat down and looked Lucy in the eyes. "You know I have no control over what I dream of, at least not that I know of." He paused for a couple of seconds, "Sometimes I think it is a curse. Do you think I am crazy? Do you not have any dreams?"

"Jake, I feel more comfortable not talking about my personal life–"

Jake interrupted, "I'm sorry I didn't mean to pry."

"No that's okay." She paused for a second and put her pen down. "Actually, my mother died suddenly five years ago. Oh, I loved her so much; my father was always busy with work and not a very emotional man, and me being the only child, my mom and I had got very close. Anyway, a few weeks before she died, I dreamt that I was sitting on the porch of our house in Rochester, Minnesota. She came out of the house and kissed me on the forehead. She then walked towards the horizon and walked straight into the sunset. She died a few weeks later of a cancer. I was so sorry I hadn't spent more time with her during that week. After a few years my dad passed away too and the town reminded me of my folks too much, so I decided to come to New York to start a new life. Anyway, that day when you asked if I had any dreams, I suddenly remembered that dream. So, you see I am open to the possibility of prophetic dreams."

Jake seemed very empathetic, "I am sorry about your mom."

"Thanks, I pray for her every night. For my dad too."

"I think of them as a refraction."

Lucy looked puzzled "I am sorry, I don't follow you."

"Dreams. They are like a refraction. When you see things through water you get a distorted view of what they are and their size, shape, and so on. Dreams to me are the same; you get a distorted view of what is to come, nonetheless it is a glimpse of what is to come. I have found over the years that they have been a guide to me."

"In what way?"

"Let me see what example to use." Jake looked upward towards the ceiling for a few seconds. "For example, my sister used to drive her car and hated to wear her seat belt. I dreamt that she was driving her car and she drove into a wall. I phoned her the next day and made her promise to wear her seat belt. A few days later she was hit by a truck. Her car rolled a few times. The paramedics had to cut her out of her car. She had a broken leg and multiple bruises. But the doctors told her that her seat belt saved her life. There are other stories, but I think you get the picture."

"But she didn't run into a wall."

"Yes, hence why I call it a refraction. To me it is a distorted glimpse of the future. Does any of this make sense to you?"

Lucy smiled "Yes, in a way. And no, I don't think you are crazy. But I need to try and understand. Tell me a little bit more about your dreams of Tracey, what was it she was telling you?"

"Well she said something like I didn't go after her."

Lucy leant forward slightly, "Can you remember exactly what she said?"

Jake thought for a few seconds. "It was something like 'why did you not follow my trail?'"

"What do you think that means?"

Jake shrugged his shoulders, "Not a day has gone by without hearing Tracey's words in my head. Why I didn't go after her trail. I sort of think that I had dreams about her and should have been able to stop her from being killed."

"Well Jake, I'm a bit confused, did she ask you in the past tense or in the present?"

Jake looked at Lucy quizzically, "What is the difference?"

"Well did she mean you should have gone after her before she died or does she mean to go after her trail now?"

"You are confusing me, Lucy. Why would I be going after her trail now?"

"Well you tell me, Jake, perhaps she wants you to help find her killer!"

Lucy got up out of her chair and walked a few steps towards the door. "God I don't believe I am talking as if she was still alive." She turned to Jake. "Well, do you think that maybe she is trying to help you find her killer?"

Jake sat back in his chair, "My God! All this time I have felt so guilty about not alerting her of the danger that I never thought that she would be referring to the present."

"Is there anything else she said that might help?"

"I don't know. I never looked at it from this angle so I will have to think for a while."

"Can I ask you something?" Lucy asked timidly.

"Sure go ahead."

"Are you psychic or something?"

"O yes," said Jake, reaching his hand forward. "Give me your hand and I will be able to tell you something about you."

Lucy looked at him suspiciously, and after a little hesitation reached out with her left hand.

Jake took her hand in his left hand, turned it round and looked at the back of her hand and then turned it palm up and studied the palm of her hand. He then closed his eye and rubbed her hand for a few seconds. "Yes, it's coming to me now. You love cats, in fact you have a cat, in fact you have two cats, one has dark hair and the other one has light hair."

Lucy pulled her hand back very swiftly, "I am sorry. How did you know that? I, I …" She put her hand in front of her mouth and could not hide her anxiety.

Jake laughed out loud.

Lucy seemed a little annoyed, "I am glad you are amused!"

"I am sorry. You see the scratch marks on your arms, those are typical of cat owners, a lot of my clients were cat owners. You also have cat hair on your clothes, two different colours, none of which match your red hair."

"You had me spooked for a second." Lucy breathed a sigh of relief.

"So, no! I am not a psychic! My mother was a very spiritual person and had a profound effect on me and taught me to be aware of my … let's call it higher self. In turn, I always tried to encourage my patients to trust their instincts. We often get vibes from people. Occasionally very positive or negative vibes. I have just learnt over the years to trust these vibes. I have heard that we only use something like ten percent of our brains. I think what we see and appreciate with our senses is only a part of our awareness of this world. Our instincts, our intuition, our dreams are an extension of the world around us. Most children have instincts and as they get older we teach them to ignore their intuition and dreams, and they become a product of our material world." Jake paused for a second. "We are surrounded by spiritual forces that most of us are heedless of."

"Do you not find that spooky?"

"Oh no. Perhaps this world is just a mirage and the reality comes hereafter. To be honest with you I have spent the past year or so longing for my departure from this plain of existence."

"Did you say a mirage?"

"Yes."

"Huh! So you think your dreams are a way of guiding you?"

"I am just an ordinary guy. Everyone has dreams, most of the dreams are probably meaningless, but some aren't; but people just either forget them or don't pay any attention to them. At certain times in my life, generally before major events, I seem to get a lot of dreams, and they seem to build up to a crescendo before some sort of cataclysmic occurrence, and then I seem to go back to my normal life. I just wished I had acted more decisively on my dreams about Tracey."

Jake paused and looked at Lucy, "You probably think I am a nut case, don't you?"

"Oh no," Lucy exclaimed, "I just think it must be some sort of special person who could have dreams about futuristic events."

"No actually it could be considered a curse."

Lucy looked surprised at Jake's comment.

Jake explained, "It is not something you wish, it just happens. But it can be quite a burden being warned about things, occasionally events that happen across the world to people you have no connection with. Well no apparent connection. Sometimes I think I should have been born in the old days in a native Indian community when you could sit around the fire in the open air and talk about your dreams."

Lucy laughed, "Yes but they also sometimes smoked some heavy stuff before their hallucinations!"

Jake laughed, "True enough."

Lucy started to rub her upper arms with her hands and was rather quiet.

Jake must have realised she was feeling a little uncomfortable. "Well I haven't given you much that will be useful in a court of law, have I?"

Lucy smiled. "Perhaps not, but it has been very interesting. You are a very unusual man; Tracey must have been a special sort of person to you."

Jake whole expression changed as he began to look into the distance. A warm smile lit his face. "When I held her in my arms I was transported to a different place. I wished time would stand still so I could hold her forever."

"And what is your destiny, Jake?"

Jake's expression changed suddenly. "What did you say?"

"You are a young man. You had better get used to not seeing her for a while. You have to get on with your life now and fulfil your own destiny.

What is your destiny?"

"Are you always this frank?" asked Jake, he looked a little perturbed.

"It sometimes gets me into trouble, but sometimes things come out of my mouth before common sense has time to intercept it. I hope I didn't offend you."

"No, it's just that … never mind."

"Go ahead Jake, why hold back now!"

"Well in one my recent dreams Tracey said, 'And what is your destiny, Jake?'"

Lucy laughed, "Great minds think alike."

Jake got up. "Do you mind if I leave now, I am a little tired?"

Lucy seemed hesitant, "I was hoping I would have something concrete to present to Amanda tomorrow."

Jake was up and was looking at the floor. "I am sorry I have to go."

"Sure." Lucy was going to finish her sentence, but by this time Jake was at the door and knocked. The prison officer opened the door and let Jake out. "Good–" Jake was out of the room, "bye," she finished softly.

She looked a little bemused. She shrugged her shoulders, picked up her handbag and notes, and left.

CHAPTER 12

Second Meeting of District Attorneys

Peter and Andy walked into the boardroom. Peter again sat on one side of the table and Andy sat at the head of the table.

Rafael Dominguez, Patricia Crawford, Shirin Jamal, and Des Hammond were seated to his right again. On the left of the table were Justin Hunter and William Mackenzie.

Andy arranged some papers in front of him. "Good morning LADIES and gentlemen!" They all laughed. "Can I ask before we start, Justin, will Rupert be attending?"

Justin shook his head, "No Mister Gomez–"

Andy interrupted, "Please call me Andy." He looked around the room, "Unless we are in an official setting, please you can all call me Andy."

"Sure thing Andy. Rupert is looking into a matter at present. We've only had four days since Monday."

"Fair enough. And William, will Anita be here?"

William shrugged his shoulders, "Your guess is as good as mine, Andy. I have a new name for her. I call her the whirlwind. She is constantly on the go. It wouldn't surprise me if she storms in here any second. Nor would it surprise me if she phoned me from Houston with some information."

"Why Houston?"

"Sorry Andy, it was just a figure of speech."

Andy nodded. "Okay let's proceed. Justin, why don't you kick off."

Justin flicked through the pages of his notebook. "Well I guess–"

Just then the door was flung open and Anita walked in at a brisk pace. She slipped into her chair and said very quietly, "Sorry!"

Andy smiled, "Better late than never."

Anita tried her best to tidy her jet-black hair with her hands. She pushed her fringe to the side, exposing her dark green eyes.

Andy turned to Justin, "Carry on."

"I'll start with Charlene Mills. A Romanian pimp called Petre Lupescu emigrated here in the early 2000s, 2001 to be precise. Started trading in groceries. Seems to opportunistically pounce on young girls who had financial or family difficulties. He lends them money and occasionally gives them drugs, and then gives them a way out of their debt and misfortunes by working them on the streets as prostitutes. By all accounts he looks after them well, if that is not a contradiction in terms. He gets them biannual health checks for sexually transmitted infections, gets them apartments, good security, well obviously, not in this case. If they have children, they are catered for very well. Unfortunately, the girls tend to get trapped into this way of life, and as they get older they are abandoned. In the meantime, he makes a fortune. One of his girls certainly seemed to have no qualms about giving me a lot of information for a couple of hundred dollars. On the face of it, it is a legal escort agency. He pays his taxes, and always on time. Get this; in the last financial year his tax bill was a quarter of a million bucks. And please don't ask me how I got that info.

"Charlene Mills was one of his girls. She had a few regular customers. We have done background checks on the most regular customers. I won't bore you with the details, but nothing of note. She had one recent regular customer which she told one of her friends, scared her. But no more details on him. On the night in question she had not arrived to her usual designated pick up area. There are agreed areas between the various pimps and the girls stay in those areas. Charlene Mills usually walks about four blocks from her apartment to sixtieth street. She preferred not to take her customers to her apartment, so this obviously increased the risk to herself. On the ill-fated night, she left her apartment on the Saturday night at the usual time of six p.m. and did not arrive on fifty fourth street. She was later found dead. We have no clues as to the identity of the killer. The murder time is estimated at between six and seven p.m. I would assume that for some reason she got into a car with someone, perhaps she knew him. Her aforementioned friend said that Charlene was very apprehensive before going out that night but said this guy paid very well but behaved a bit weird. She had the feeling he could get violent."

Andy interrupted, "Violent in what way? Was alcohol involved?"

"That's the exact question I asked her, Andy. Charlene's friend couldn't fully elaborate, but got the impression that when the person had some drink on him, he became a bit violent."

"Thanks Justin, continue."

"I have spoken to the police who had interviewed her boyfriend, a Kyle Sanders, and I spoke to him. He says he didn't know she was a hooker. The sperm in her vagina matched his DNA. He had spent a couple of days of fifteenth and sixteenth November at his parent's house in Boston so he is out of the picture. A young man found her body and phoned the police. He is not a suspect. After the SIM card of her phone went through his gastrointestinal tract the numbers on it were followed up. Zilch. So, her killer is unknown."

Peter interrupted, "Perhaps that night she was lured by a financial offer she could not refuse."

Justin nodded, "Yes that would be the other strong possibility, or she would not have deviated from her routine. The sad part is that they usually go out in pairs, for security, and more often than not a bodyguard would follow them and generally watch over them on their walks. However, for whatever reasons she was alone that night."

Andy was jotting down some notes, "Thanks Justin, any background information?"

"No Andy. Both her parents died at the same time from being poisoned by a contaminated batch of heroin. She was thirteen at the time. She was handled by social services and moved from one foster home to another. Petre Lupsecu got his claws on her when she was sixteen. I believe one of her friends enticed her to working for Lupescu as she had her own apartment and money to spare."

Andy pursed his lips tightly together and shook his head. "I've lost count of how many times I have heard that generic story. Anyway, let's focus on our immediate problem. William what do you have for us from the legal aspect?"

"There have been a number of cases where the judge has ordered a trial based on specific knowledge of the crime by the accused. However, there was the case of State versus Hamill. In this case, in October 2008, the judge deemed that although the accused had very specific information about the murder, there was enough information by the media and that the accused could have, and I quote, 'postulated or extrapolated the events at the murder scene.' The accused in fact inadvertently said that the victim had had his windpipe cut open. This was not known by the media. The judge decreed that more evidence was needed and the trial never went ahead. Several months later the accused went to court for another murder and confessed to the first murder."

"Thanks William." Andy then looked at Anita, "Anita what do you have for us?"

"I have looked through the Tracey Chapman case, or perhaps a case that never was. I was able to look at her social services case load prior to her murder. There were no notable names. I obviously was not permitted to look at the specifics of her cases due to confidentiality. I can tell you, off the record, that I looked at all her files she dealt with in the year prior to her death."

Justin interrupted, "Wait a minute, Anita, do you mean you looked at the confidential social services notes?"

Anita reached in her handbag. "Sorry did you call me Anita? Perhaps you didn't read the name right, I am Joan Perkins, representing social services review body set up earlier this year for internal monitoring of caseloads of social workers, in order to assist in increasing the resources allocated to this department!"

Justin smiled. "In all my years I have never been able to access social services records."

Anita continued without seeming to take any delight in her accomplishment. She put her fake ID card away. She continued, "Tracey Chapman was working on one confidential case that she had not put anything in writing. No names, no numbers. However, as Mister North's investigations had shown previously, she had phoned Sarah Miller's number on a few occasions. The initial contact dated back exactly a year prior to Tracey's murder. There were no texts between the two. All conversations were short. I assume they were only to arrange meetings.

"Looking at Sarah Miller's lifestyle, as you know, she was a law student. I have as yet not had time to trace down her background." She looked at Justin, "I don't quite have your skills."

Justin smiled. "You are not doing too bad!"

Anita referred to her notes, "As you know she worked for the Elite Escort Agency. She had a number of regular customers. I am informed that she never went to bed with her clients, but not sure if that is true. She mainly went to big functions with sophisticated clients and was told to keep quiet and look pretty, but a couple of her customers actually took her to functions because she was so intelligent that she dominated the conversations. I do believe that at least one of her clients proposed to her!"

Peter was rubbing his chin, "Miss Sheehan, you seem to have a lot of detailed info. How did you manage to get such delicate information?"

"Oh, I have registered as an escort with the Elite Agency. Some I got from other girls in the agency."

"And other details?"

"I dated a couple of her regular clients. One of them was totally infatuated by her and proposed to her three times."

Andy scratched his head, "Let me see, in four days you have been employed by the Elite Agency, and been on a couple of dates with clients? Have you had much sleep?"

"No, we only had four days!" said Anita, "But make up comes in handy."

They all laughed.

Anita looked very businesslike. "We are not here to talk about me." She carried straight on with her presentation. "It seems like Sarah Miller went missing for a few months and stopped attending her college. One of the girls in the agency thought her mood was a bit low and she was putting on weight. Sarah apparently confided to her that she was going to be admitted to a clinic for counselling and that she had contacted her college to say that she was going to be off for a few months. She seemed to come back fit and healthy and full of the joys of spring, and then she suddenly disappeared a couple of months later. I have limited info on her regular clients. I am working on it. I couldn't ask for any specifics or I would raise too much suspicion."

Anita paused and was doodling on her notebook. Everyone looking intently at her. "My thoughts were …" she paused again, "well, I suppose I am not paid for my hypothesis."

Andy sat forward, "Anita, you are paid to do research work into cases. If you had stuck to your job description, we would not have had any of this information. I believe you are entitled to your opinion!"

Peter nodded, "Carry on Miss Sheehan."

Anita took a deep breath and then proceeded to give her opinion as quickly as possible. "I think that Jake Chapman got Sarah Miller pregnant. Tracey stepped in. She may have had an abortion, however, if so, she would not have been off that long. I believe Sarah Miller was pregnant, was putting on weight and at about five to six months of pregnancy lay low, perhaps went to a different state and gave the child up for adoption. She then came back. However, Jake Chapman was in love with her and wanted to leave Tracey. Tracey at some stage found out that they were having an affair and wouldn't budge so Jake knocked her off – I'm sorry that's awful; he murdered her. Sarah then either left and changed her name with the promise that Jake will join her at some stage, or more likely Jake had to kill her too as she was going to spill the beans on him." Anita then inhaled deeply, and suddenly did not seem as confident. "Hope I have not overstepped the mark."

The room was silent. Peter was flicking through the notes of the Tracey Chapman file and was also looking at some hand-written notes he had on the side of the manuscript. "Carry on, Andy. I will review my facts later on."

Andy nodded, "Thank you Anita, and I would like to see you in my office later. Whatever we are paying you I am sure it is not enough."

"Certainly, Mister Gomez. Yes, to your first point and definitely YES to your second!"

Everyone laughed.

Andy turned to his senior solicitors. "Rafael and Patricia, what are your opinions of how our chances look for the hearing and whether the judge will go ahead with the case?"

"Well firstly there is little doubt to me that he is guilty, based on the conversation he had with the detectives. Secondly, I think there is sufficient incriminating evidence to go ahead with a case. What do you think, Rafael?" Patricia said.

"I am not sure. I think our chances are good, but I don't have a good feeling about it."

Andy nodded, "Yes I have some reservations too, but I am quietly confident." He turned to Peter, "What do you think, Peter?"

Peter took a big breath. He paused for a second. "I am worried that this won't even get to a hearing! I think unless we come up with some more concrete evidence, we may come short."

They all looked stunned.

Peter smiled, "But ignore me. I am a born pessimist."

Andy turned to Rafael. "I have heard about their defense. Fill me in."

Rafael turned the pages of his notebook back and forth. "Ah yes. Miss Amanda Jackson."

Peter interrupted, "That is partly why I have reservations."

"Fill me in, Rafael."

"Miss Jackson was a late starter and came out of Harvard law school some four years ago. She attended a lecture in Manhattan by Stephen Jackson and ended up in New York in love with him. She lectured at Columbia Law University with him. It didn't work out between them, but she stayed and started her work in New York. She apparently took the scene by storm the first couple of years. She doesn't know the meaning of giving up and hates losing. She was approached by Whyte and Kidd Associates and offered a six-figure contract but turned it down to work for legal aid. Essentially to help the downtrodden. This Stephen guy she was in love with turned out to be some sort of a playboy. Looks like she lost out twice. However, she is very good and seems to always find a way around obstructions. Worse still, she is even better at creating obstacles when they are needed to proceed with a case."

Sandra walked into the room quietly and handed Andy a note. Andy smiled and mimed, "Thank you." Sandra walked out.

Peter nodded, "Thanks Rafael, I have asked around about Amanda Jackson. The advice I was given was to be ready for a fight!"

Andy looked at Rafael, "I am going to ask you a question, not because I expect you to make the final decision but because I trust you so much, do you think we should ask for a postponement?"

"I don't think so, Andy. Unless we have any strong leads I think any delay will lead to more publicity and work in Mister Chapman's favour."

Andy nodded. "Peter, what do you think?"

Peter thought for a second, "It is your call, Andy. I will remain silent."

Andy nodded again. "I agree with Rafael, we will go ahead." He looked at the note that Sandra had given him. "By the way Peter, Judge North wants to see us this afternoon, what do you think this is about?"

Peter frowned, "It's about Miss Jackson. Don't like it." He stopped abruptly.

Andy tidied the pile of papers in front of him. "Right guys I know we have not had a lot of time, but keep digging up whatever you can, anything else we can use in the hearing would be welcome. If Mister North is wary about what the judge may do, well then so am I. Anita get some sleep and see me in my office next week. We will discuss your salary. Okay meeting is over, let's go."

Justin passed a note to Anita as she got up. Anita read it and nodded. Justin then went over to Andy and whispered something to him. Andy nodded.

Andy looked at Peter, "Peter I will see you in your office shortly."

"Okay." Peter left the room, as did everyone else except for Andy and Justin.

"I'll be to the point, Andy."

"Go ahead, Justin, I can take it, whatever it is you want to say."

"It's about Anita. It seems a bit unprofessional of me to poach her when I am working on a case in your office, but I think she is in the wrong business and I was going to offer her a senior post in my detective company."

"Ordinarily it is not something I would take too kindly to. However, I do think that the detective line of work is what she is best suited to. I can't see us being able to keep her in our research department in any case. So be my guest. But you owe me one!"

"Thanks Andy. And yes; I DO owe you big time!" He cleared his throat. "Do you mind if I use this room here to speak to her?"

"You don't waste any time, do you?"

"No. She reminds me of me when I was her age. I don't want to lose her!"

"Sure thing, Justin, go ahead."

Andy left the room and nodded to Anita who was waiting outside the room.

Anita looked a bit apprehensive as she nodded back. She pointed to the boardroom.

Andy smiled and nodded.

Anita seemed unsure as she walked towards the boardroom.

Justin was seated on the side of the oval table and beckoned with his hand for Anita to sit down.

Anita seemed a bit hesitant. She sat down and immediately began to talk. "Look Mister Hunter, I am sorry if I stepped into your area of expertise. I am sorry if I overstepped the mark. I just got a thread and didn't seem able to let it go. I had to keep going until I saw where the thread led me to."

"Go on, explain yourself."

"Well I come up with these theories now and then, I guess I just enjoy detective work. I guess I should have kept my peace!"

"Did you enjoy it?"

Anita looked very excited. "I have never had such a thrill. It's better than sex! Oops, ignore that last remark. Detective work is so exciting! I have only had about two hours sleep a night and could go on for another few days like this. I can't compare anything I have done in the past to this."

"Well Anita how much do you get paid here?"

Anita hesitated for a few seconds, "Thirty-five thousand dollars a year, plus expenses."

"I'll double your salary, pay for your expenses, including travel and hotel accommodation and offer you a senior position at Swift Private Eye Agency."

"Wait a minute, Justin, do you mean you were going to offer me a job and you watched me squirm all this time?"

"Yes Anita, I was rather enjoying it. You see I think you'll go far in this agency and I don't think I'll get the opportunity to see you apologetic!"

"My salary just went up. I want two and a half times my salary."

"Sorry Anita, no can do. But you will have a solid pension, and your salary will be reviewed after six months."

Anita was hesitant.

"I'm sorry, Anita, I am already pushing out the boat with this offer. I have a partner that I have not spoken to yet."

"It's not that, Justin. I am worried about being unprofessional leaving my firm to work for you."

"Don't worry, Anita. I have spoken to Andy and he has given me his blessing."

"Well I would like to speak to Andy myself, but pending that I accept your offer, and I will resign my post here with the usual three-month notice period. But I have a pre-condition."

"Here we go again," said Justin, throwing up his hands. "What else do you want?"

"It's simple, Justin. I do not want a senior sedentary post. I want to be on the action front."

"Don't you worry about that. I have no intention of putting you behind a desk. However, I have a precondition as well. Well in fact two."

"Now it's your turn to bargain."

"I'm not sure how to put this, Anita. So, I'll be direct. Firstly, you'll have to lose that Irish accent. It's beautiful, but too noticeable. And you'll have to de-beautify yourself, certainly when you are working. They both make you very prominent."

Anita smiled and spoke in a strong New York accent, "You won't need to ask me again!"

CHAPTER 13

Truth is a Mirage

Amanda and Lucy were in the queue at Starbucks cafe.

"May I help you?" asked the young girl behind the counter with a seemingly very genuine smile.

"I'll have a small skinny latte please," said Amanda.

"I'll have a small Americano please; black," said Lucy, returning the smile.

"Are you sitting in?"

"Yes," replied Lucy.

"If you would like to sit down, I will bring your drinks to your table."

"Thank you," replied Lucy.

They chose a table by a window, taking off their overcoats before sitting down.

"It's cold out there," said Lucy.

"It's nearly December. It's hard to believe that Christmas is around the corner."

"It's a shame I have no nieces or nephews – in fact, anybody – to buy for," said Lucy in a pitiful way.

"Do you not have any family at all?" asked Amanda.

"Well an older aunt in St Paul's, and a couple of second cousins I haven't seen in years."

Amanda was staring at a couple of children running around and playing on the pavement outside, oblivious to the cold.

Lucy looked at Amanda. "Are you getting broody?"

"Well I am just getting worried that I will get too old to have kids."

"What about Jim? How is that going."

"You tell me. Every time we seem to get close to each other we seem to get busy and not see each other for a couple of weeks at a time. I have also lost count how many times he has had to cancel our dates."

Lucy looked at her knowingly. "I know, it's awful being stood up."

Amanda was quick to answer, "Well I don't know if I would call it being stood up. I have had to cancel on occasions as well. I suppose we are both so committed to our professions. Maybe we are just used to being on our own for so long we are worried about having to change our ways." She paused for a second, "Gosh! I just psycho-analysed myself!"

The girl arrived with the drinks and placed them on the table. "Enjoy."

"Thank you very much," replied Lucy.

Amanda took a sip of her latte before asking the question, "Well what about your meeting with Jake yesterday?"

"You first."

Amanda shook her head a couple of times, "Nothing much unfortunately. I met a couple of interesting cops at Jim's precinct, a Paolo Rossi and Geno Pasqualli. Charming characters they were. At least one of them felt strongly that Jake was guilty of his wife's murder. Not that he said it; just reading between the lines his suspicions did not dissipate after the charges were dropped. Charges were dropped due to insufficient evidence. He was not happy. They feel that the disappearance of Sarah Miller is at the centre of the whole saga. They seem pretty sure she had been murdered and will probably never be found, although there is a possibility that she may be living somewhere else with an alias. They think it is possible that she may have left the area, especially as she would find it impossible to practice law anywhere near here. That is the long and short of it really, nothing much we didn't know."

Amanda paused to drink some of her latte. "What about your meeting with Jake?"

Lucy put her coffee down and sat forward and looked very excited, "Well Amanda, you probably think I am gullible, but I believe him."

"Believe what exactly?"

"Well I think what he says about having premonition dreams makes sense to me. I think it is possible that he may have had a dream warning him about Tracey's death. I suppose you think this is all silly. You know he thinks you don't believe a word of what he says."

"Well Lucy, as I always say, I have a healthy scepticism of anything out of the ordinary. As I have said, the truth is a mirage. But as you know it is not just a matter of what you and I believe, it's a matter of what any jury would make of a story like his. Was there anything that we can use for our defense?"

"The honest answer is no, not really. I also double-checked and CNN do not have a black female newsreader, nor did they broadcast the news of the murder until the morning after Jim met Jake. The girl in CNN seemed very bemused by the question and said I was the fifth person to ask her that question. When she found out I was an attorney she put me directly through to the head of Personnel. She in turn was very defensive, gave me a speech about their equal opportunity policies!"

Amanda confirmed, "So not much to go on."

Lucy still had a tone of excitement in her voice, "What are the chances of that do you think? Is it not strange that Jim should be involved in the case and you should be defending the accused?"

"Yes, but in this line of work you do see a lot of strange things."

"I suppose this will not help your relationship any."

"Well it will certainly curtail courting during this time, if you excuse the pun."

Lucy laughed, "That's very clever actually!"

Amanda continued, "Assuming in the first instance that there is a relationship worth commenting on," said Amanda. "Anyway, I have some possible good news."

Amanda looked over both shoulders, leaned forward, and lowered her voice. "I saw the judge yesterday and asked for the case to be dropped. I suggested to him that there was insufficient evidence and that Jake was drunk at the time and he may have got confused about another murdered girl he may have heard on the news some other day. I suggested that unless any new evidence is forthcoming, he should drop the case. I also requested to release him on bail."

Lucy looked excited, "And?"

"Well Judge Temple is very strict, but very fair. He is going to put the case to the prosecution team and let me know later today. But he was very sympathetic to my viewpoint."

Lucy asked rather apologetically, "Can I ask you a question?"

"Go ahead."

"You asked for the case to be dropped even though you think he might be guilty?"

"Well, to be honest with you I haven't quite made up my mind about Jake." Amanda looked over her shoulders again. "However, if I was pushed, I would say I have strong doubts about his innocence. But for now, I hope we don't need to cross that bridge. The way I figure, we rarely know or discover half the truth, never mind the whole truth."

"And does it bother your conscience if he were to be guilty?"

"My job is not to collect evidence and prosecute people, that is up to others. If they don't have enough evidence, that is their problem."

"Fair enough," said Lucy.

"Now drink up." It was Amanda's turn to sound a little excited. "We have to see Judge Temple at twelve thirty. The more I think about it the more positive I am that the judge may drop the case."

CHAPTER 14

Amanda and Lucy meet the Judge

Amanda and Lucy arrived at the courthouse and were greeted by a young girl behind the counter.

Amanda greeted her, "Good morning I am–"

The young girl interrupted her, "Miss Jackson, good morning!" she said enthusiastically.

Amanda blushed a little bit. "I am sorry have we met before?"

"Yes, I mean no. I mean I know you well, but you don't know me. I am a law student and am working here for experience. My lecturer Stephen Jackson advised me to follow your case in the Lorenzo trial. I thought you were brilliant."

The young girl reached out her hand eagerly to shake Amanda's hand.

"Pleased to meet you," said Amanda, "This is my colleague Miss Lucy Walker."

The girl shook Lucy's hand. "My name is HEATHER WILLIAMS." She seemed to be stressing her name, as if to make sure Amanda remembered it.

Amanda seemed almost embarrassed by the attention and continued, "Judge Temple is expecting us I believe."

"Yes Miss Jackson. He advised me to ask you to wait in the library. He will see you as soon as he is finished his meeting with the deputy of public prosecution."

"Thank you," said Amanda.

She had taken a few steps with Lucy and suddenly stopped and said, "Can you wait here for a minute please?"

"Sure!"

Amanda walked back to the reception desk, "Heather how old are you?"

Heather looked quite excited about being involved in a conversation, "Twenty-two, Miss Jackson."

"Have you gone to bed with him yet?"

"Sorry what do you mean?"

"Has Stephen taken you for a midnight walk in central park, a show on Broadway, and an early morning breakfast in a diner?"

"How did you … ?" She did not finish her sentence.

"Heather you seem like a nice girl. Stephen is a nice guy, enjoy your time with him, but don't give your heart to him, that's all." With that Amanda spun on her heels and walked away, leaving Heather open mouthed, standing there, following Amanda with her eyes.

Lucy had to run slightly to keep up with Amanda. "What was all that about?"

Amanda smiled, "Oh nothing. Just making sure there is one less broken heart in this world."

Lucy looked back at Heather and it looked to her like she still hadn't moved an eyelid. She turned around and Amanda was a few paces ahead of her. She ran to keep up.

They both sat down on plush dark brown leather armchairs. Lucy looked around the very large room in admiration.

Amanda whispered, "Although nominally the library, solicitors often sit in areas of the library and discuss their cases, and though not totally silent, the conversations are kept at a quiet level."

Lucy kept looking around the room and eventually turned her attention to Amanda who was looking through her notes. "I am not aware of the Lorenzo case."

"Antonio Lorenzo was a thirty-five-year-old cloth merchant. He was tracked by the feds for two years and arrested and charged with money laundering. They confiscated his accounts book and claimed it showed thousands of dollars that were recorded in the ledger were laundered money and could not possibly be obtained from selling cloth.

"I eventually managed to get him off by arguing that he had business in Egypt and Brussels. We were also able to show that he had paid his tax bills and had declared all his money."

Lucy looked surprised. "You would have thought the feds would have discovered all that!"

Amanda looked at Lucy. "Don't be naïve! You don't really think he was a cloth merchant, do you?"

"But… " Lucy stopped talking suddenly. "I see, it's up to the DPP to produce the evidence!"

"Now you got it!"

The judge walked into the library and walked up to Amanda and Lucy. They both got up.

"Good morning Judge Temple, this is my associate Miss Lucy Walker," said Amanda.

"Good morning Judge," said Lucy. She tentatively reached out her hand but withdrew it quickly as the judge had already turned around. "Good morning ladies," he said as he started to walk back out of the library. "Follow me!"

Lucy and Amanda looked at each other. Amanda put out her two hands palms upwards and shrugged her shoulders and whispered to Lucy, "Don't know."

They followed the judge to his office. As they walked into the room, the look on the face of the prosecution brought a smile to Amanda's face. They could not look glummer.

The judge pointed to the two attorneys and turned to Amanda and Lucy. "I am sure you know each other, but just in case." He pointed his hand towards the older of the two, a man in his late fifties. He had a stereotypical dark navy pinstripe suit with a bright white shirt and a thin navy tie. "This is Mister Peter North DPP." The judge then pointed to the other gentleman, "Andy Gomez, deputy DPP."

He then turned to the ladies, "Peter, Andy, this is Amanda Jackson, and Miss Lucy Walker."

The judge sat behind his desk. "Right folks I will get to the point. I have looked at the evidence. I agree that there are some facts which appear to be compelling, however I am very much swayed with Miss Jackson's argument that there is very little hard evidence to incriminate Mister Chapman."

Peter jumped in, "But Judge—"

The judge held up his hand, "Please, please, you have told me all you had to say." He turned to Amanda, "However, in view of what I see before me, Miss Jackson, you will not have it all your way. I am going to allow two week's extension."

This time Amanda tried to object, "But Judge they have had ample time to present their case."

"My decision is made, new evidence in two weeks or else no case." Judge Temple then added, "And I have also decided to let the accused out on bail effective immediately."

Peter North raised his hand akin to a child in a classroom, "But he is a dangerous man, Your Honour!"

"Well Mister North, get me the proof!"

Peter North dropped his hand.

Judge Temple then opened a file in front of him and began to read. "Any questions?" Before anyone could speak, he said, "Good!"

He didn't look up again. Everyone got up quickly and left after saying goodbye. Judge Temple continued reading.

CHAPTER 15

Back to the Drawing Board

It was late Friday afternoon. Derek was in Jim's room chatting when the phone rang.

Jim answered the phone, "Jim speaking."

Jim was silent for a few moments, "Yes Captain. Yes, Derek is with me here." Jim listened briefly, "Yes Captain, we'll be there right away!"

Derek asked, "What's the news?"

Jim stood up, "Not sure, but I don't think it's good news. The Captain wants us in his room straight away. Paolo and Geno should be there too."

Jim and Derek arrived at the Captain's office. Jim knocked and walked in. "Good evening Captain."

Derek walked in, "Good evening Captain, what's up?"

Will pointed to the seats, "Sit down you two. Paolo and Geno are out. I will speak to them later."

Jim was impatient, "Well Captain, is it bad news?"

"I'm afraid the news is not good. The prosecution attorney was just on the phone to me. The judge has decided that there is insufficient evidence to prosecute John Chapman."

Derek interrupted, "But Captain that is impossible, he knew about the death of the young girl before it was on the news."

Will put up his hand. "You don't need to remind me, I know all the arguments, but at the end of the day the judge is the judge and we can't argue with him."

Derek continued, "Surely this can't be true."

"I'm afraid it is, Derek."

Jim was very pensive, "I presume you are asking us for more evidence."

"Got it in one, Jim. The prosecution wants something more that we can pin on this character. I am a bit baffled myself. It seems like an open and shut case on the face of it, but our job now is to get some hard evidence and leave the legal arguments to the attorneys."

"How much time do we have, Captain?" Jim asked.

"They have given us two weeks. If we have nothing new in the next two weeks the case will be dropped."

Jim and Derek sat expectantly.

Will finally broke the silence. "Well what are you waiting for? You've already wasted a few minutes. Cancel all your plans for the weekend. I want something soon, don't make me sweat it for the whole two weeks. Get me something quick! Don't disappoint me, men, I don't want this guy getting away. And by the way, he will be out on bail as of today, just to irritate us even more."

Jim jumped up first, "Yes captain, we're on it. I'll contact Paolo."

Will answered, "Figured that, now get on with it."

Derek looked a bit deflated. He got up and followed Jim. They walked towards Jim's office.

"Right Derek, we'll have to go through the evidence piece by piece and see if there is anything new, any new angle we can pin something on."

"I thought we had already done all that."

"Yes, but we'll have to do it again and again until we nail the son of a bitch. I am not about to let him get away with this. He is guilty as sin and I am going to nail him."

They arrived at Jim's office. Jim got behind the desk and sat down. He leaned back on his swivel leather chair and stared at the ceiling.

Derek sat on the chair facing Jim. "You seem to be taking this personally."

"With me it's always personal when it comes to someone who is so obviously guilty walking the streets and laughing at us."

"If you don't mind me asking, is it not your girlfriend who is defending this Jake character?"

"Firstly, I don't know if I will regard her as my girlfriend, or I suppose the main question is whether she regards me as her boyfriend as you would put it. Secondly, yes, it is Amanda and I am not altogether surprised that she has managed to sway the judge. She is damn good at what she does. Most importantly for you and me, our job is to find hard evidence, one that is irrefutable."

Jim sat forward and picked up the phone. "I'll get in touch with the Italian job. Can you get us two coffees? We'll be here for a few hours. I hope you don't have any plans for the weekend."

"Well, actually Jim, you know that Mary-Beth and I help the church on Sundays. Mary-Beth is in the choir and I help out with the collections. It's our small contribution to the church."

"When am I going to get to see this lovely wife of yours anyway?"

"Mary-Beth is the shy type you know, maybe sometime in the near future."

"How long are you married now?"

"Four years."

"Still in your honeymoon phase then?"

"As I have already told you, I am so lucky to have Mary-Beth, I sometimes think she is too good to be true. She is the most caring, considerate person I have met."

"All I can say, Derek, is hold on to what you have tight. Good relationships are hard to find. Anyway, we can hopefully make some inroads tomorrow and you can join me on Sunday lunch time or whenever you finish. I dare say the Italian job will be here too. If I am out anywhere, I will text you. If I can work the damn cell phone!"

Jim started to dial on his phone. "Now will you get the coffee and I'll get Paolo and Geno."

Derek left the room.

Jim waited for a few seconds before he spoke. "Hey Paolo, wherever you are, whatever you and Geno are doing, drop it and contact me at once. News from DA's office. Not good. Phone me soon."

He put down the phone and took out his cell phone and began to text. He looked rather clumsy texting, looking for the letters on the phone screen slowly and meticulously. Once he finished, he brought out a file and put it on top of his desk. He stared at the file for a few seconds. The writing on the cover of the file read 'Charlene Mills" and below it read 'John Chapman'.

He opened the file and took out the picture in it, looking at it for a few seconds. He tried to place the picture on his desk and looked around the table, looking for an empty space on his desk. He looked round his desk a couple of times. He placed the picture back in the file, closed the file, and stood up. He started to pile up all the papers and files on top of each other and threw them on the floor beside his leather chair. He continued this with all the paper and files on his desk until there was only one file left – the Charlene Mills one.

He took out the pictures and spread them over the table and then began to look at them one by one.

His phone rang. Jim picked up the phone. "Hey Paolo, I'm afraid the news is not too good."

"Ah. Well I suppose Will explained the time restrictions as well?"

Jim listened for a few seconds, "Okay I will see you boys here later on."

Derek walked in with two mugs of coffee. He put the mugs on Jim's desk. "I have never seen your desk so tidy," he commented.

Jim pointed to the pile on the office floor, "Acme instant filing system."

Derek laughed, "Maybe the captain has use for this system too. Was that the Italian job, as you call it?"

"Yep. Paolo's 'mama' has prepared a meal for the two of them. They will be over as soon as."

"So, what next? We have been over the facts a number of times. I have no idea where we go from here."

"Well kid, there are always little things that are overlooked. They may not lead to anything, but sometimes a little oversight, a little clue, a little something may open an avenue of investigation. Now where this case is, we are not even near exhausting our investigation."

"We are short of time though, Jim, aren't we?"

"Yes and no. Time span is rather short, but sometimes we have had a lot less time and come up with a lot more."

Jim began to spread the pictures on his desk. He then walked to a brown display notice board and put a pin through the picture of Charlene. He put four pictures of her in one corner. He then placed up an old picture of Sarah Miller, one that had been taken a few years earlier. Besides that, he put a picture of Tracey Chapman. He took a post it pad and wrote 'Married man X' on it. Underneath that he wrote 'Jake'. He put this piece of paper between pictures of Tracey and Sarah. He drew an arrow from each side of this paper towards one of the two pictures. He took another piece of paper and wrote 'Mike Smith' on it. He put this beside Charlene's pictures. He then took another piece of paper and wrote 'complete stranger' and drew an arrow beside this and pinned it beside Tracey's picture. He then wrote 'boyfriend' and put it under Charlene's photo.

He looked at Derek. "As you say, we do not have a lot of new clues, do we?"

He looked back and forth for a couple of minutes. Derek spent most of this time looking at Jim wondering as to what he was going to say.

Jim smiled and looked at Derek. "I suppose you are expecting some wonderful insight into the case?"

"I wouldn't say expecting, maybe hoping."

"Right let's look at the facts that we do know." Jim held his chin in his thumb and index finger and rubbed his chin. "What about the waiter Mike Smith? It is a bit of a textbook name, isn't it? What did you uncover on him?"

"Well nothing."

"No records, no previous misdemeanours, petty theft, anything?"

"Well, actually, I mean nothing at all. I needed to cross reference his date of birth. There were plenty of Mike Smith's, but I could not find a match. I left it with Sid to look into."

"Sorry Derek, what do you mean you left it with Sid?" There was a hint of annoyance in Jim's voice.

"Well when we started to get hot on the trail of Jake, I thought this guy was small fish. I am sorry, in the excitement I didn't follow this lead up, although I did think that Sid would let me know if there was anything of note."

"That's okay, Derek. I have just learned from experience to follow every lead up and put it to bed. Once something is left in the air, I have found that it may be forgotten about at a cost."

He picked up his phone. "Let me see if Sid is in."

"Don't worry, Jim, I will go to his office and check."

"You sure?"

"Yes, you focus on the clues and see if you can come up with something."

Derek left the room. Jim picked up the notes, he started to read through them and some of the interviews with various witnesses.

Derek walked in. "I just contacted Sid on his cell phone. There was a mix up and he hadn't pursued this point. I will get on it."

"Hold on," said Jim as he opened a drawer in his desk. He shuffled around and shifted items back and forth until he found a card. "This is Nick Munroe of the FBI. Fax him a picture of Mike Smith and his other details, see what he can come up with. He's a workaholic. Odds on he will be at his office. If there is no answer on his direct line, phone the main switchboard and ask them to page him. Tell him I am looking for it and I need it yesterday. It will be a lot quicker."

"Sure Jim. I will go to my own room."

"You can use my phone here."

"I need to phone home too. I won't be too long."

"Sure, see you soon."

Jim was staring into the distance when there was a knock at the door. Paolo and Geno walked in.

"You were miles away," said Paolo.

Jim responded, "Sorry I was just thinking that – to put it bluntly – we are stuffed."

"Come up with nothing new?" asked Paolo.

"Nope!" said Jim very bluntly.

"No developments with the judge then I take it?" Geno enquired.

"Not good boys," said Jim as he pursed his lips together. "The judge has said categorically that unless we have some further evidence the case will not go ahead in court."

"Surely not!" Geno exclaimed. "Surely there is enough to take the case to court."

"I would have thought so," said Jim, "but let's not spend time making legal arguments, we only have two weeks to come up with something new."

"How many times have you looked at these photos, Jim?" Paolo asked.

"Too many." He paused, "Not enough."

Geno tapped one of the photos, "You know the answer is not in these pictures."

"Yes Geno, but I am drawing a blank everywhere else."

Derek walked into the room. He stopped very suddenly, "Oh hi guys, didn't realise you guys were here." He waved a piece of paper. "Just got a fax from the FBI. Mike Smith's name has an alias, before he changed his name it was Mark James."

"Mama Mia," exclaimed Paolo.

Geno and Jim looked very surprised too.

Paolo continued, "What took so long to discover this?"

"Exactly," said Geno, "this was an elementary task, why was it not done sooner?"

Derek put up his hand. "I will take responsibility. I passed it on to Sid, and–"

Jim interrupted, "Let's not worry about that now, what do you have on this James, what's his other name?"

Derek continued, "Mark James. And it gets better. He was arrested for armed robbery in Boston six years ago. He served four years for being an accomplice, but the judge was lenient on him as he stood at the door of the shop during the robbery and was not involved in the planning or carrying a weapon. By all accounts he became a Christian in prison and has worked as a waiter for three years and lives with his partner in a rented house in the outskirts of Manhattan. After getting out of prison he changed his name to Mike Smith. Nothing in the past few years."

Jim shook his head. "Okay guys. We are not going to come up with anything sitting here. Paolo and Geno, you guys go to the street where Charlene worked and see if you can come up with anything else. I will stay here and go over the statements of everyone. Derek you go home and come in bright and early tomorrow. You and I may need to go and see Joe soon."

"Who's Joe?" Derek asked.

"A contact of mine. I will explain later."

With that the others nodded and left.

CHAPTER 16

Look Under the Surface

It was Saturday morning; Derek arrived at the precinct and left his coat in his room. As per usual he went to Jim's room. He knocked and walked in.

"Good morning Jim," he said rather cheerfully, "I thought I would come in early for a change."

Jim smiled. "Half past seven is hardly early, I've been in for an hour."

"Yes Jim, but normal people go to bed and get some sleep."

Jim chuckled, "That is true."

"Anything new?"

Jim shook his head, "Sweet nothing!"

Jim walked towards the notice board with the pictures when his phone rang. He walked back to his phone whilst still looking at the pictures, "Jim speaking."

The police operator spoke, "There is an anonymous call for you, Detective Sterne."

Jim sounded impatient, "Please take a message and tell him I will phone him back."

"Detective, he says he had information about the whereabouts of Sarah Miller's body!"

Jim bolted upright and snapped his fingers at Derek and pointed to the phone, "Listen Maria, please delay the transfer for about twenty seconds, but no longer as he may get suspicious, but get the IT team to trace the call."

"Sure Detective."

Jim paced back and forth with the phone in his hand. He then stopped,

"Hello, Detective Sterne here … Who are you? … No please don't hang up. I am happy to listen." Jim kept nodding. "You are sure it was John Chapman?" He listened again. "Okay, and where did you say he buried the body?" Jim nodded again. "No, I'm afraid there is no reward … Who is speaking anyway? … Listen … Hello … Hello!"

He put the phone down and looked at Derek.

Derek asked, "What was all that about?"

"Well I don't know how to take this. Maria says he asked for me by name. His voice was a little bit muffled. He said he was a drinking buddy of Jake but wouldn't leave his name. He had heard about the murder and saw John Chapman named as the suspect. He said that Jake told him once that he had killed a girl and that he had buried her body in a disused cement production site. He was very specific. He said that he had buried the body behind a disused shed. What made him ring was that Jack had got out on bail and they were drinking together and Jack told him he was worried about the body being discovered and was going to dig it up again."

Derek looked surprised. "But surely the police went through that place with a fine-tooth comb and didn't find anything."

"Yes, they did." Jim was staring into space.

"Did he say anything else?"

"No," said Jim, "except he asked if there was a reward and when I said no he hung up abruptly!"

"Do you think it's a hoax?"

"Don't know. Let's go and check it out anyway. We have nothing else to go on and definitely nothing to lose!"

Jim's phone rang again. "Hello Maria … Didn't trace the call then? … Okay thought so, I think the guy knew we were tracing the call and that's why he cut off abruptly. Thanks anyway, Maria."

*

Jim drove the car to the disused car park at the old cement production site. As they got out of the car, they had to walk through the weeds that had sprouted copiously through the gravel that had been laid down. They stood by the car and looked around over the one acre or so. The large gates were open. There was a twenty-foot-high wire fence around the whole area with a number of areas where it had been cut through at the lower section of the fence pushed inwards to make entrance points. There were a number of sand mounds about twenty feet high with areas of pitting where kids had obviously been playing and jumped into the sand. There were two areas where there were burnt-out remains of small logs and branches with a dozen or so empty beer cans near each of them.

Derek laughed. "See the youngsters have been partying here."

"Yep," said Jim as he picked up some of the ashes from the site of the used log fire. "This may be since the forensics were last here. There are so many shoe print marks that it may be impossible to get any clue from any of them."

Derek looked around again. "Don't remember a shed being mentioned anywhere in the police report."

Jim looked around again. There were three large metal cylindrical containers used for mixing cement. There was a large portacabin on an elevated site with a rusty metal staircase leading up to it. "Let's go up there and see what we can see."

Jim shook the metal staircase. It swayed a little and creaked as they climbed up the horizontal stairs.

"Derek why don't you wait here, the stairway is not very secure, I'll go up."

"Four eyes are better than two, I'll follow behind."

"Okay but be careful, I don't want to be explaining to Mary-Beth why you have a broken neck."

Derek laughed. "So long as you promise to visit me in hospital, I will be happy."

Jim climbed up the stairs gingerly. Derek followed a few steps behind.

When they got up to the top they stood there and looked around.

Jim put up his collar as the wind was much stronger in the exposed area. He was about thirty feet above ground level. He could see the early sun rising on the horizon. "This is a spectacular sunrise; under different circumstances I could stand here and enjoy this scene."

Derek did not seem to be quite in the same frame of mind. "This was a good vantage point to make sure all the workers were doing their job."

Jim slowly scanned the fenced area until he had covered the one-hundred-and-eighty degrees or so that was in front of him.

Derek followed suit. "Do you see anything?"

"Not yet, but it's damn cold up here. The wind would cut you in two!"

He looked at the entrance door to the portacabin. A sign on it said 'Police investigation scene. Do not enter.' Jim chuckled, "If this is not an invitation for anyone to go and look around I don't know what is."

The lock had been forced open. Jim walked into the room. It was very dark in there. He took a torch out of his coat pocket and turned it on. There was an old wooden desk and a basic wooden chair. There were some papers on the desk. The room was otherwise bare. He noticed a small window at the back of the room. Jim looked out and all he could see was bushes. He walked to the door again as Derek went to the window.

Jim stopped for a second. He turned around and looked at the window. "Now, Derek, if you were going to put a window in a small room like this where, would you put it?"

Derek thought for a second. "Well I suppose at the front so I can see the sun and look out over the work area."

Jim stood there with his hands on his hips. "Exactly. So, the only reason why you would have a window at the back is either for the view." He paused for a few seconds. "Or… "

Derek continued, "Or because you want to watch over something else at the back."

"Exactly," said Jim.

Jim went over to the window. "Do you mind, Derek?"

"Oh sure," said Derek as he stepped aside.

Jim looked out the window again. Something caught his eye. He was straining to see. He pointed the torch at the window but only got the reflection of the light so turned it off and handed it to Derek who put it in his pocket. He pulled his head back away from the window and with the sleeve of his coat wiped the window. He pressed his nose against the window.

"Bingo!" He shouted. "Look, Derek, there is something glistening through the bushes. I think it may be the flashing of a shed roof. Look there." Jim stood back and pointed with his finger on the glass.

Derek pressed his nose against the window and looked down. "Yes, I see something shining down there and I think you are right I can see a corner of a small roofing canvas."

Jim headed towards the door. "Let's go."

They hurried down the stairs so fast that the metal staircase swayed from side to side. As they reached the bottom Jim frantically ran back and forth to see a way into the back of the mound that the raised room was built on, but all he could see was thick bushes.

Derek went further down. "It looks like this was an old pathway."

Jim rushed down towards Derek. "So it is," Jim said.

They followed the path some forty yards or so and the path seemed to be heading into the bushes. Derek was about to head in that direction.

Jim put his hand in front of Derek's chest. "Hold on a second, kid."

Jim reached and held a small branch of the bush at ankle level in his hand. "See this?"

"What is it?" Derek asked, crouching low.

"This is a broken branch. The only thing is that the bit hanging off is still green and thriving. Someone has been here in the past day or two. Let's take is slow so we do not disturb any possible evidence."

Jim lead the way. As soon as they went past the first few feet of thick shrub they came into a clearing and an old walkway was evident by the gravel, which had plenty of weeds growing through it. They followed the path around to the left and saw a large shed.

Jim walked towards the door of the shed and took out his handkerchief. He saw a padlock on the ground. It was broken and rusted. "Look, the padlock has been broken. Someone has certainly been here before us."

He held the doorknob with his handkerchief and pushed the door open. "Can you shine the torch, Derek?"

Derek switched the torch on. It lit up the shed.

"Thanks," Jim said as he took the torch from Derek.

He shone it around the shed. There were a number of spades, a couple of sledgehammers, a couple of pickaxes, some green hosing, and a number of shelves that had containers on them. Jim carefully tilted one of the containers and shone the torch inside. He quickly dropped it back, showing little interest in it.

Derek turned around and suddenly noticed a spider suspended from the ceiling of the shed. He jumped back. Jim laughed, "Are you scared of a small spider?"

Derek looked stern. "Don't you dare mention this to anyone in the precinct."

"My lips are sealed!"

"Why would anyone want to watch over this shed?" Derek asked inquisitively.

"I suppose they kept some equipment in here and wanted it hidden so at nights youngsters would not steal it or use it to damage the property," Jim replied.

"Makes sense," Derek responded.

Jim shone the light around the shed. He walked towards one the spades and knelt down. "Well, well. What do you know? I think we are onto something."

Derek squatted besides him. "What is it?"

"Nothing but mud, good clean muck. But it is fresh. Look."

He pointed to the bottom of the spade that had some mud on it. Derek was about to touch it.

Jim put out his hand. "Don't do that, leave that for forensics. Look, the pickaxe also has fresh mud on it. Let's go outside."

They went out and went to a side of the shed, but it was overgrown with shrubs. They walked to the other side and there was a narrow gap. Jim stepped through the narrow gap and Derek followed him. As Derek went through the gap, he bumped into Jim who had stopped only a foot into the gap.

Jim shook his head. "Son of a bitch was right, I think we have found the body, well probably a body."

The two of them stood there and looked at the raised heap of mud, which covered about a six foot by three-foot area.

"Holy smoke!" exclaimed Derek. "What now?"

Jim pushed some of the soil back with his hand. He continued this for a while until he suddenly stopped.

"What is it, Jim?"

"I think this is a hand!"

He pushed some more soil away and tugged at something under the earth and suddenly pulled out two fingers of a hand. He stopped.

"Well, kid, I have a strong suspicion that this is Sarah's body. I don't quite understand it, but I am fairly certain this is going to be her body."

"Should we dig some more do you think?"

"No, we'll call in the experts, I think our job is done for now. Can I use your phone kid? I think mine is in the car."

"Sure thing," replied Derek.

Jim dialled a number. After a few seconds, he spoke. "Captain, it's Jim. We have found a body." He listened for a short while. "Well I am not sure if it's Sarah Miller's but I have strong suspicions."

Jim listened for a few seconds again. "Well I can't be sure it is Sarah's; but I got an anonymous call this morning saying that Sarah's body was in the disused cement mixing place and Derek and I have just discovered a body in a grave."

Jim listened again. "Okay Captain. It's the Ceylon Cement Factory. We will go to the parking lot and wait for the CSI. I will see you here and I will fill in the details." Jim gave some details of the address on the phone. He handed the cell phone back to Derek. "Now we wait. Let's get in the car and get warmed up, kid."

They walked back to the car. Just as Derek was about to get into the car Jim pointed to Derek's shoes. "Shoes off please. Soil is bad enough, but the cement mixed in the soil makes such a mess. I don't want my car dirty again!"

"Honestly!" said Derek as he shook his head. "You are worse than Howard Hughes, and he was pretty OCD about cleanliness."

Jim took off his own shoes and held them in his hands as he got into the car, as did Derek.

*

Jim pulled his coat collar on both sides so they met at the front. He looked up at the sky. The sun was now fully hidden behind the clouds and there were a few spots of rain. He looked around at the eight police cars and two police vans, most of which had their lights flashing. A couple of policemen were chatting near him and they burst out laughing.

He turned to Will who was leaning on the car beside him. "I hate the rain."

Will replied, "I thought you liked the rain because it clears the air and the smog."

"It does, but it also interferes with forensic evidence."

Will smiled, "Always a cop, aren't you?"

"Yes Will, I am very sad, aren't I?"

"Not from where I'm standing, Jim. You are my mister dependable."

"O God! I was right! I am a sad case."

Will laughed out loud. He took off his sunglasses. "What do my eyes look like, Jim?"

"Still red, Captain."

Will shook his head and put his sunglasses on again. "Yes and still dry as fuck, should come okay soon."

A voice interrupted them. "Right Captain, here is the body."

They both jumped up and walked towards the stretcher that the body was carried on.

Derek was on his mobile and as soon as he saw the stretcher he walked towards it. "I'll see you later, Mary-Beth … Right honey. See you tonight."

A white body cover that was zipped at the top covered the body. Jim and Will got to the stretcher just before Derek.

The two men pushing the stretcher both were wearing all white overalls, head covers, masks, and had blue gloves on.

One of them acknowledged Will. "Captain Jones."

"Good morning," said Will, "do you mind if I eyeball the body?"

"Sure Captain, but there is a fair bit of mud covering it."

"Thanks," replied Will.

Will unzipped the cover and pushed the two edges aside. Jim and Derek peeked over his two shoulders. Will turned to Jim, "It's fairly well decomposed, isn't it?" He then turned to the man in the white overall, "That's all right, son, we have seen enough."

A man in his forties, also dressed in all white overalls, walked up to Will. "Good morning Captain Jones."

"Good morning Luke," Will replied.

Will pointed his hand to Jim. "Luke you may know Detective Sterne of the NYPD."

Luke nodded, "I believe I have had the pleasure." He reached and shook Jim's hand.

"Nice to meet you again, Luke."

Will pointed his hand at Derek, "Luke this is the newest detective in our precinct, Derek Johnston. Derek this is Luke Adams of the CSI unit."

"Derek." Luke nodded.

"Morning Luke."

Luke looked skyward, "The rain won't help." He turned to Will, "The rest of the team will arrive soon. I take it you are looking for someone specific in mind."

Jim nodded, "It may be a Sarah Miller. She went missing a year ago. Look I know you haven't had long, but is there anything you can say about the body that can help us?"

"Well Jim, you are right, it is early days. I can say that she was fully clothed, although her blouse was unbuttoned. Maybe facial injuries, but that's all I can commit to at the moment."

"Thanks, Luke, I appreciate it."

"Pleasure."

Will reached to shake Luke's hand, "Thanks Luke, I will speak to you this evening."

"Oh, by the way, Captain. There is something that is odd that I should mention."

Will raised his eyebrows, "What on earth could it be?"

Jim and Derek were fixated on Luke.

"Well," Luke hesitated, "I don't know whether I have personally come across this ever before, but it looks to me like the grave has been dug twice."

Will leaned his head slightly forward. "Come again?"

"Well it looks to me like the grave was dug quite a while ago, one third of the soil is tightly packed. The other two thirds have been dug again, and my guess is within the past few days, and maybe in a hurry. I'll explain later, for now I have to go and make use of the daylight."

"Well," Will remarked. "Let's get to work, boys. Thanks again Luke. Phone me if you come up with any other info. Speak to you later."

"Captain. Jim. Derek." He nodded in turn to each of them and walked away quickly.

As they were getting into the car Jim pointed to Derek's feet, "Shoes off please!"

CHAPTER 17

All News is Not Good News

Jim and Derek walked through the automatic sliding double-doors. A young blonde-haired girl was seated behind the large circular reception desk. She greeted them with a broad smile. "Good morning gentleman, how may I help you?"

Jim smiled back, "With a smile like that you have cheered me up already."

"Gee that's very nice of you to say," she said with an even broader smile.

"Don't mention it," Jim replied.

Derek grinned, "Would you like me to leave now while you two finish flirting?"

The girl laughed. "Well gentlemen, how can I help you?"

Jim answered, "We are here to see Miss Amanda Jackson."

"May I ask your names please?"

"Yes, you may," Jim replied.

The girl smiled, "Okay, and what are your names?"

Jim seemed to be enjoying himself. "Just say Jim is here, Jim Sterne."

"Would that be Detective Sterne?"

"That would be right."

"Yes sir, hold on and I will check with her PA."

She picked up the phone and dialled a number, looking at Jim rather flirtatiously. Jim smiled back.

As she looked away Derek rolled his eyes. Jim looked at Derek quizzically and said quietly, "What?"

Derek shook his head, "Still a teenager, are we?"

Jim tried to look very innocent, "Just chatting."

"Yeah, yeah!" said Derek, still shaking his head.

The girl turned around again. "Sorry gentlemen she is with a client."

Jim leaned over, resting his elbows on the table. "Listen darling. Would you mind telling Amanda that this is vitally urgent? I am sure whatever she is doing can wait a few minutes."

The young girl seemed a bit breathless. "Yes darling … I mean, yes sir; I will go and check with her."

"Thank you, darling," Jim smiled.

The girl walked down the corridor.

Jim followed her with his eyes. Derek stared at Jim. Jim looked all around the reception hall, avoiding Derek's eyes. Derek kept staring at Jim. Jim finally looked at Derek. "What?"

"I can't believe you are flirting in Amanda's office."

"I was not flirting. I was just being civil."

"Civil? She was nearly panting," Derek responded.

"I have this effect on girls you know," Jim replied.

"All I can say is hungry eyes!"

"Am I disturbing your bonding time gentlemen?" A female voice said over Derek's shoulder.

Derek jumped around. "Oh I am sorry."

"Good morning Amanda," said Jim.

"Good morning Jim. I wasn't sure it was you here. Betty here said you were very good looking."

Jim smiled at the receptionist who was now blushing. "You must choose your staff for their good taste."

Amanda sounded very business-like. "Okay gentlemen I am with an important client who is in my office. I just have a few minutes. Betty, is one of the interview rooms free?"

Betty looked at a diary on the desk. "Yes Miss Jackson. Interview room three is free until three p.m."

"That's good, we'll use that. Will you see to it that Mister Holmes gets served some coffee in my office? And please ask Lucy to meet us in the board room. Right now!"

"Sure thing, Miss Jackson, I will see to it straight away."

Amanda then turned to Jim and Derek, "Would you gentlemen like something to drink?"

Jim turned to the receptionist and said quickly, "Gin and tonic with a twist of lemon please!"

She looked quizzically at Amanda.

Jim said, "Just kidding, no we won't be having any drinks, we won't be long."

The receptionist laughed out loud.

Amanda turned around quickly, "Please follow me, gentlemen."

Derek and Jim followed Amanda. Jim waved to Betty as he was walking away, and she blushed again. Derek looked at Jim and shook his head again. Jim turned both his hands outwards and whispered, "What? I am just saying goodbye."

"Yeah, yeah," said Derek.

Amanda turned around, "Did you say anything?"

"Oh, nothing!" said Jim.

Amanda walked down the long corridor and opened the interview room door. She leaned her head forwards and peeped into the room. In the centre of the room was a small oval mahogany table. She sat on one of the broad sides of the long table and pointed to the two chairs facing her without saying anything. She took out a small notebook and went to lift a pen out of the spring part of the notebook and realized she didn't have a pen with her. She looked towards the coffee table across the room.

Jim reached into coat pocket and took out a pen. He reached across the table, "Here you are, darli– I mean, Amanda."

Amanda took the pen without looking at Jim and then began to look through the notebook, flicking back and forward, seemingly looking for the right page.

Jim broke the silence; in a very soft voice he said, "Amanda you are very pre-occupied!"

Amanda stopped what she was doing. She seemed to break out of her official voice and behaviour. "I'm sorry Jim, you must think of me as rude, I was in a middle of an important meeting and …" she put down her notebook, "I'm sure you wouldn't disturb me if it were not important."

Jim sat forward, "Yes Amanda, I'm afraid that we are about to make your life a lot busier."

Amanda looked at Jim, then at Derek and then at Jim again, "How is that, Jim?" she seemed almost hesitant to say those words.

"Should we wait for Lucy?" Jim asked.

"No, I am not sure how busy she is and I am in a rush and now I am rather curious."

"Amanda." He paused for a few seconds. "Amanda, we have found Sarah's body."

"Sarah …"

"Sarah Miller."

Amanda interrupted, "You mean the law student who had gone missing?"

Jim continued, "Yes, her. We were tipped off to her body's whereabouts–"

Amanda interrupted again, "Tipped off by whom?"

Derek Leaned forward as if to be involved in the conversation, "Well we got an anonymous phone call …"

Jim looked at Derek and raised his hand "That's all right, Derek, we can fill in the details later."

Jim took out a couple of photos from his pocket. "This is a picture of her."

Amanda looked at the picture and became very pale, "Oh my God!"

"What's wrong? You look dreadful. Do you know her?"

Amanda nodded. "The last time I saw this girl she was naked?"

Jim looked astonished. "What did you say?"

Amanda seemed to recover a bit, "Perhaps this will explain it. She was naked lying under my fiancé at the time, Jim! A girl doesn't forget a face in a situation like that."

Jim was struggling to speak, "Amanda I am so sorry–"

Amanda composed herself and interrupted, "Gentlemen I am very busy, so what brings you here?"

Derek spoke, "What we need now is buccal samples from your client."

"I presume you are talking about DNA samples?"

"Yes Amanda."

Amanda thought for a second. She nodded, "That's okay, I don't think there is any point delaying matters as eventually he will need to provide a sample. I will contact him and see if he will cooperate. I am sure he will."

"Fine. This is the number of the office you can phone for the samples; our forensic team will obtain the specimen from him; they may also need blood samples; is that okay?"

Amanda looked at the piece of paper. There was a name on it with a phone number, underneath that in capital letters were the words, 'Dinner together?'

Jim looked at Amanda, "Well?"

Amanda answered, "The answer is yes and maybe."

Jim looked at Derek, "Derek could you give me a minute with Amanda please?"

"Sure Jim." Derek stood up and pushed his chair under the table. "Pleasure to meet you, Miss Jackson."

"Goodbye Derek, no doubt our paths will cross again soon."

Jim looked at Derek until he had walked out of the room and closed the door. He turned to Amanda, "Mandy, it's been quite a while since we did anything together." He paused, "It's strange, I would like to think of you as my close friend, as my ally …"

Amanda interrupted, "That doesn't sound very romantic, I would prefer girlfriend or lover perhaps."

"Well I didn't want to be presumptuous. It's just when we came here you seemed so distant, I felt like I could have been any copper walking in!"

"I'm sorry Jim, my only hesitation is that I am working on this case and I may have to even question you on the stand, now how will it look if we were going to bed one night and I was questioning you the next day?"

Jim smiled, "That will be a first! I only asked you to dinner, you have just raised the stakes!"

"It was a figure of speech!"

"I'm disappointed. I thought you would have inadvertently given away your secret thoughts. I know the thought has crossed my mind one or twice, or maybe fifty times!"

Amanda's demeanour changed suddenly, and she spoke very officially. She sat up straight, "Jim I'm afraid we cannot socialise until after this case is resolved."

Jim sat back, "I guess that is non-negotiable?"

"That's correct," she said very firmly.

Jim got up. "In that case I'll see myself out. Goodbye Amanda." He got up and walked towards the door.

As he opened the door Amanda suddenly said, "Just a second, Jim, there is something I have forgotten."

"That's all right, you can keep the pen."

"It's not the pen, Jim."

Jim looked back as Amanda picked up her notebook and walked towards him, "You've already kicked me in the groin, I am not sure what else is left!"

Amanda reached over and kissed him on the cheek. "See you soon."

She was walking out of the room when Jim held her hand and pulled her back into the room, "Mandy, you know I don't always play things by the book." He hesitated, "We think that this Jake character got out of prison and tried to dig up her body but for some reason was disturbed or interrupted. He told someone that he had killed Sarah and this guy phoned us. I am giving you info that you will get in due course but thought I would give you a heads up."

"Thanks Jim. I have to return to my client now."

Jim nodded.

Amanda walked out. Jim stood there holding on to the door handle. He watched her as she walked down the corridor. He walked out with a broad smile.

Derek met him at reception, "Is everything okay with you two?"

"Never been better, never been better!"

Amanda met Lucy on her way to her office. Lucy looked surprised, "I thought you wanted me for a meeting!"

"I did Lucy, but it's over."

"What was it and who was it?"

"Jim … Jim and Derek, were here. The police have found Sarah Miller's body. They want DNA samples from Jake Chapman."

"Do you think they have got blood stains or something?"

"That's what I was thinking. I did not ask them, but I have a bad feeling about this one. The police apparently got a tip off about the whereabouts of the body. I have a feeling things are going to get bumpy from here on."

"Do you want me to contact Jake?"

"Yes, would you? I believe he is staying back at his apartment. You have his cell phone number in any case. I have a client waiting and I may have to give the case to someone else. I have handled a case for Mister Holmes before and he will not be happy!"

"All right, Amanda, I will speak to Jake."

Amanda gave the piece of paper to Lucy, "Here you are, that is the number of forensics he needs to phone?"

Lucy had a look at the piece of paper, "Well, what is going to be?"

"What do you mean?"

"Did you say yes to Jim?" she showed Amanda the piece of paper that said 'dinner tonight?'

Amanda took the piece of paper from Lucy and tore off the bottom. "Business first; as the saying goes, can't mix business and pleasure!"

CHAPTER 18

Sarah's Post Mortem

It was about eleven a.m. and Jim was sitting at this desk. He kept looking at his phone. He got up and started to pace the room. There was a knock at his door.

"Come in."

Derek walked in. "Any word of the autopsy yet?"

Jim shook his head, still pacing.

There was a knock at the door again.

"Come in," Jim shouted this time.

Paolo and Geno walked in.

"Before you ask," Jim said, "No word yet."

"Maybe we'll come back later," Paolo said as he grabbed the door handle.

"You might as well wait here," Jim said. "It's hard to get any work done with the anticipation."

Paolo stood there fidgeting and looking nervous and Jim continued to pace. Derek sat on the edge of Jim's desk, looking a little more composed.

Geno laughed, "I've never had to wait outside a delivery suite, but I expect it will be something like this!"

They all laughed.

Just then the phone rang. Jim jumped across the room and lifted the phone. "Jim here."

He listened for a few seconds. "Yes Captain, right away." He listened again. "Yes sir, we'll be there ASAP."

He put the phone down. "Grab you coats, boys. We will meet the captain at the pathologist's office. Derek you come with me. We'll meet you guys there."

*

Jim parked the car outside the mortuary. A security officer approached the car and looked inside. Jim put down his window.

"I am sorry sir, this is a no parking zone," said the security officer.

Jim pulled out his badge, "Detective Sterne, NYPD homicide."

"My apologies, Detective," said the security officer.

"That's okay, is Captain Jones here?" asked Jim.

"Yes Detective, he arrived 'bout an hour ago. Do you know where to go?"

"That I do. Detectives Pasqualii and Rossi will also be here soon."

"Oh! they are already here, Detectives!"

Derek asked, "When do I get to flash my badge?"

Jim answered, "When you stop dirtying my car!"

They got out of the car hastily and walked into the mortuary. Jim stopped at the small desk in the reception area. There was a middle-aged man sitting behind the desk. He was bald and fairly overweight. There was a small specimen jar at his right hand filled with some sort of fluid. Within the fluid was something floating.

The man was reading a book and eating a sandwich. He put his sandwich down beside the specimen jar and sat up in his seat. "May I help you, gentlemen?" he asked.

Jim reached towards his coat pocket. As he put his hand inside the pocket to pull out his badge he stopped. He looked at Derek and nodded his head and pointed towards the man with his head. Derek looked puzzled for a second. Jim pointed towards the man with his head again.

Derek suddenly said "Oh!" He reached into his coat pocket and pulled out his badge. "Detective Johnston, NYPD homicide, this is Detective Sterne."

"Sure thing," the man behind the desk said, "the pathologist is in the autopsy room, but I believe he has company at the minute."

Derek looked pleased with himself. He continued, "That will be Captain

Jones, and the other detectives, they are expecting us."

"Sure thing," the man continued and pointed with his hand. "It's down that corridor, last door on the left. It says autopsy room four on the door."

"Many thanks," said Derek as they began to walk away.

Derek stopped and looked back. Derek pointed at the specimen jar. "Do you mind if I ask you what is in that?"

"Not at all," said the man continuing to eat his sandwich as a couple of small bits of chicken fell out of the sandwich onto his table. "You can ask if you want," the man said, continuing to chew his sandwich.

Derek looked at the man and after a few seconds said, "Well what is it?"

The man put down his sandwich and picked up the jar. "It's a piece of liver Doctor Morrow would like get an electron microscopy on." With that he picked up the jar and brought it close to Derek's face and turned it round. Derek pulled his head back. The man continued, "It's just routine here." He put down the jar. He had to lift it again as it was leaning to one side. It was resting against a piece of chicken that had fallen out of his sandwich. He put the jar beside it and picked up the piece of chicken and put it in his mouth. "Is that all, gentleman?"

Derek said, "Yes … thank you very much."

"Sure thing," said the man as he sat down, picked up the rest of his sandwich with one hand and his book with the other.

Derek walked on and whispered, "I am sorry I asked!"

At the bottom of the corridor was a door with 'Autopsy Room Four' written on it. Jim knocked at the door a couple of times. After a few seconds he could hear footsteps coming to the door. A man opened the door. He looked to be in his early sixties. He had a head of neatly combed thick hair which almost was white with a few dark streaks through it. He wore light green scrub bottoms with a short-sleeved scrub top which was slightly darker green. He wore a badge which was suspended from the top pocket of his shirt. It read 'Senior Pathologist' and underneath it the words 'Doctor JJ Morrow'. It had a picture of him which must have been at least fifteen to twenty years old.

Jim reached out his hand, "Doctor Morrow, Jim Sterne, homicide."

The doctor smiled, "Yes Jim we have met, please call me JJ, everyone does, except my wife when she's angry."

They all laughed.

"Yes JJ, it's been a year or so since I was last here. Please meet Detective Derek Johnston."

JJ nodded, "Detectives let's skip the formalities. Please come in."

They walked into the room. The room was bigger than it looked from the outside. On the right as they walked in were low and high cupboards. The low cupboards had a worktop surface which had a number of empty specimen jars of different sizes. On the left was a large aluminium sink and adjacent to the sink was a corrugated aluminium surface designed to drain into the sink. There were a number of instruments on this part. Most prominent was a circular saw which had white debris on it. There were a number of different size retractors which had black tissue on them. In the middle of the room was an operating-room-style metal table with a narrow base. There was a sheet on top of it, which was obviously covering the frame of a small human body. There was a tray on a high stand beside the table. It contained a couple of scalpels, some probing instruments, and some other equipment. Will was standing at the head of the table. Jim's eyes went from the table to Will.

He nodded, "Captain."

Will replied, "Hi Jim."

"Captain," Derek said.

"Derek."

Derek and Jim nodded to Geno and Paolo who nodded back.

Will turned to Doctor Morrow, "Gentlemen as you probably know Doctor Morrow is the senior pathologist. Doctor Morrow, will you repeat your comments of the last five minutes."

"Sure Will. I don't usually have the pleasure of so many live bodies in this room!"

They all laughed briefly.

"Yes doc, I guess we are all anxious to get something to go on."

"Sure, I understand, it makes me feel part of the investigation … Gentlemen please come closer." He pulled away the sheet that was covering the body.

Derek jumped back. Most of the body tissues were decomposed.

Doctor Morrow exclaimed, "Not the first time you've seen a dead body?"

"No doc. Just forgot what a body looks like a year after death. In my mind I had a different picture."

"Sometimes I forget, Detective, that I deal with dead bodies and others are not so used to it. Happy to go on?"

Derek nodded, "Sure thing, just caught off guard."

Doctor Morrow continued, "Naturally please ignore the central partition of the sternum. This is routine to cut the sternum and gain access to the thoracic cavity. There are also incisions in the central abdominal wall, or what's left of it, for accessing the abdominal cavity and the coronal incision around the skull to gain access to the brain cavity. Excuse me for a second."

He went across the room and put on a pair of gloves and picked up small metal forceps. He came back to the table. He pulled the end of the gloves away from his hands, causing them to make a loud snapping noise as they made contact with his skin.

"Now if you look at the face here, however, you can see the displacement of the maxillary, sorry, of the cheekbone. The bone is displaced medially, that is towards her nose. The tripod of the cheekbone shows fracture of all three posts. The displacement of the maxilla is highly suggestive that she was hit with a left hand–"

Will interrupted, "Sorry JJ, how is that?"

JJ replied, "Well you see if I were to punch you with my left hand, your cheekbone," he swung his right hand in slow motion towards Will's right cheekbone, "your zygoma would probably be displaced to the right, or you may get a depressed fracture downwards. But the significant displacement of the cheekbone medially, that is toward the nose, although not conclusive, suggests that she was punched with the left hand. But there is more. As you can see …" he pressed against the both sides of the chest wall, the right side caved in a bit.

JJ continued, "You can see that there is a bit of give on the right chest wall. Internal examination in fact shows fractured sixth, seventh and eighth ribs on the right chest wall. She also has a fractured eleventh rib on the right-hand side with the rib bent back on itself. I suspect this perforated her liver and caused internal bleeding."

Jim interrupted, "Are you suggesting that the killer was left-handed?"

"No Jim, I didn't say that. I am just stating that she was hit a few times with the left fist. You are right, however, the clear implication is that the person was probably left-hand dominant."

Will looked at Jim, "Is this Jake fella left-handed?"

Jim nodded, "I believe so, Captain. He was observed via video in the cell of the custody suite and he definitely seemed to favour eating and drinking with his left hand."

Geno stepped forward from behind Derek, "Doctor Morrow, was the liver damage the cause of death?"

Doctor Morrow hesitated, "Well no son, I don't think so. If she had died from the liver damage this would have taken a few hours or even a day or two. She would have certainly had time to get help."

Will asked the obvious question, "Well JJ, what exactly killed her?"

"If you examine the occipital area, here at the back of her head, she has a fractured skull. She also has a fracture of her first and second cervical vertebrae. I believe the fracture of her neck is what killed her; however it could also have been the skull fracture and cerebral haemorrhage." He looked at his notes. "I should add some other findings at this point. Her blouse was partially open, and she had remains of her skirt and stockings on. The stockings were actually the best preserved of everything, probably because they are made of nylon and will take another hundred years to disintegrate!"

Jim interrupted, "Meaning that she was probably not raped?"

"Yes Jim, exactly. Not many rapists replace people's stockings! Sorry … Maybe that was a bit callous. Anyway, there are no signs of other major injuries." He paused and scratched his head with the part of his forearm that was not covered by gloves. "You'll find this hard to believe, 'cause it's a first for me. I was looking for possible clues in the pelvic area, and what did I find? I could hardly believe my eyes." He raised a small sealed plastic bag. "I saw a glistening. At first, I thought she had had a coil inserted or some sort of piercing in her labia. But no! There was a cell phone SIM card in the pelvic area. I mean, I am open minded, but this is stretching the boundaries."

Will asked, "Do you mean she had swallowed this?"

"Good thought, Will. Actually, that did cross my mind. I suppose she may have swallowed it and it may have tracked down to her pelvis. But it is likely that if she had swallowed it near the time of her death, it would still be sitting in her stomach proper. By the time the internal organs would have disintegrated she would have been lying in a prone position underground. So, it would be unlikely to have got all the way to the pelvis."

"JJ, what exactly are you telling us?"

Geno interrupted, "She put it in her …" He motioned with his fingers in an upward direction.

"Yes Detective, inside her vagina."

Geno screwed up his face, "I hate that word!"

"Well if she had sufficient time, she may have put her SIM card inside her," he looked at Geno and said loudly, "VAGINA," Geno screwed up his face again, "to ensure some sort of information is withheld from the assailant."

"Or," said Geno, "ensured that information was kept for the police."

"Now that would be speculation," JJ smiled.

Will held JJ's elbow very lightly, "Can I push you for your initial assessment?"

JJ raised his eyebrows, "You know, Will, I never do that."

Will looked at Jim.

Jim thought for a second. He suddenly smiled. "Doctor Morrow, I realise that you need a day or so to prepare your official report."

"Yes …" Doctor Morrow seemed hesitant, "where exactly is this going?"

"Well," said Jim, "there is nothing to stop us from speculating, is there?"

"I suppose not …" said Doctor Morrow, still suspicious sounding.

"Well," said Jim, "we can speculate, and you can tell us if our hypothesis is off the mark completely."

Doctor Morrow looked at Will and then at Jim. "Look Will, I realise you guys are under pressure of time, and I don't want any of this quoted, but I am happy to listen to your speculations."

Will looked at Jim in anticipation. Jim carried on. "Would it be right to assume that she either fell to the ground or was hit on the head and died as a result of a broken neck?"

Doctor Morrow paused for a few seconds, "The blow to the head was from a blunt object or secondary to falling backwards."

"So exactly what are you saying?" asked Will.

Doctor Morrow smiled, "I am not saying anything."

Jim interrupted, "Okay JJ, just listen up for a couple more minutes. Let us say," he stopped and turned to Geno, "Geno do you want to do a sum up?"

Geno talked without hesitation, "This is spookily similar to Charlene Mill's death. Let us say, Doctor Morrow, that she was with a guy, maybe a client, he got angry for some reason. He lost his temper and hit her. She fell down and in doing so broke her skull and her neck. She died instantly. He maybe didn't mean to kill her but on finding her dead panicked, or perhaps he hit her a few times and then hit her on the back of the head with a blunt object, causing her death. Or there may be another theory …" He looked at Jim.

"Yes …" Jim started to walk back and forth, "if indeed she had hidden her SIM card in …" He looked at Geno, "in a delicate area," Geno smiled, "then she must have been expecting trouble. Therefore, the meeting with the killer would have been arranged. She hid the SIM card because she was anxious, perhaps she was meeting John Chapman and that's why she phoned Tracey Chapman. She met him, he killed her as pre-planned, perhaps beating her to death and hitting her on the head with a hammer or such like …"

JJ interrupted, "Far be it for me to get involved in any speculation; but what about her torn blouse?"

Jim nodded to Geno, "If you are thinking as I am thinking, Jim, the clothes were torn to give the impression of a random attack, but there was no sexual attack. It was in case the body was discovered. That would give the impression that the killer may not have known her. Sort of clever idea one would expect from a psychologist."

There were nods around the room. JJ chuckled, "That's why you guys are detectives. I think in my next life I will come back as a detective."

Others chuckled. Will looked at JJ, "Doc, don't deceive yourself. You have been responsible for putting over a hundred killers behind bars by your astute diagnoses."

Doctor Morrow smiled. "Now you flatter me. I will leave the rest of the speculation to you clever detectives. I will not argue with your hypothesis. But don't quote me."

Will reached to shake Doctor Morrow's hands and Doctor Morrow raised his gloved hands, wiggling his fingers. He took off his gloves to shake Will's hand.

Derek suddenly approached the body. He pointed as he walked toward the body. "What is this, doc?"

Everyone followed the direction Derek's finger was pointing towards. It was pointing to the body's right hand.

Doctor Morrow walked towards the body. "What exactly are you talking about?" he asked, sounding a little bit apprehensive.

"This," Derek said with some excitement in his voice.

Doctor Morrow stooped down until his face was only a few inches from the body's right hand. "Oh yes she has plenty of mud under her nails, more than likely due to when she was buried. She has false nails on as well may have helped to preserve her nails. We may analyse that at a later stage, after our initial main histology reports."

"Is this hair under her nail?"

Everyone stepped closer to the body and there was a bit of frenzy as they competed for head space to get closer to the hand.

Doctor Morrow looked a bit embarrassed. "Well I'll be damned!" he said. "It looks to be the same colour as remnants of her hair." He lifted the body's arm up, holding it with the sheet. Everyone's head followed the hand in tandem.

Derek reached to touch the hair. Doctor Morrow reached with his other hand and grabbed Derek's wrist and looked at him sternly.

"Sorry!" Derek said. "It was involuntary, I just wanted to check the thickness of the hair."

"Yes," commented Jim. "It does look rather thick."

Doctor Morrow let go of Derek's hand and pointed to the corner of the room. "Will one of you boys get me the large magnifying glass on the stand with light on it?"

Geno walked across the room swiftly and wheeled the magnifying glass over.

Doctor Morrow put on a fresh set of gloves and held the body's hand in his left hand, he placed the magnifying glass on top of the right hand and pressed a switch, turning on a light within the glass. He then held the middle finger of the hand and moved the magnifying glass closer to the finger.

He studied it for a few seconds, staying silent. Will's eyes went from the hand to Doctor Morrow's face, back and forth.

Finally, Doctor Morrow broke his silence. "Well I'll be damned."

Will sounded impatient, "What is it?"

Doctor Morrow held up his right hand as if requesting patience. He then looked at the thumb, index, and ring fingers closely, taking a few seconds with each. He then held the little finger between his thumb and index finger and moved it close to the magnifying glass. He moved the magnifying glass back and forth a couple of times. He pointed the little finger of the body so that he could look right under the nail bed, tugging at the pulp of the finger a few times. The false nail fell off onto the floor. He left it there.

All eyes were now fixed on him.

He looked at Geno and snapped his fingers and pointed to a package. Geno handed this to JJ who tore it open and pulled out a small tweezer.

Doctor Morrow pointed to the tray. "White swab please."

Geno picked up the swab which was wrapped in a packaging that was transparent on one side. He was about to open it.

"No son, you'll contaminate the sample and destroy the evidence. Everyone step back."

Doctor Morrow went back to the middle finger and with the tweezers slowly grabbed a piece of hair. He brought it across so it was on top of the swab. He studied it for a few seconds and then looked at Will. "Have a look."

Derek moved back to allow Will to position himself over the magnifying glass.

Will looked at hair for a few seconds. "Well JJ, do you want to enlighten me?"

Doctor Morrow pointed to the piece of hair with his free hand. "You should be able to see that the hair is very dark, probably black. Her hair is brown."

Will put his face closer to the magnifying glass. "I'll take your word for it, JJ."

Doctor Morrow continued, "More significantly the hair is very thick and coarse, her hair is very fine."

Will replied, "Yeah I think I can see that." He did not sound very convincing.

"I'll have that analysed and DNA tested. I'll put them in these specimen bags." He then looked at Geno. "I once had to get on all fours to find a piece of hair from the floor. It was very embarrassing when the DNA report from two pieces of hair came back, one of which matched my DNA! Thankfully the blood stains matched the accused, or he may have got away with it because of the mishap!"

Doctor Morrow placed the piece of hair in the bag. He then let go of the body's hand which dropped down. He took the small bag from Paolo and ran his finger and thumb across the top of it, sealing it. He then took a pen out of his top pocket and wrote on a label 'hair sample – right middle finger, nail' He placed the bag on the tray.

He used the same tweezer and picked up the false nail from the floor and bagged it separately.

He then went back to the body and lifted the body's right hand again and this time placed the little finger under the light of the magnifying glass. With the tweezers he lifted another piece of hair. He looked at it under the magnifying glass, rotating the tweezers a few times to look at the hair from different angles. "Well I'll be damned!" He said again. "I do believe we have hit the jackpot here!"

"What is it, JJ?" Will asked.

"Well, this hair is very short and it is certainly curly," Doctor Morrow answered.

Will raised his eyebrows, "Pubic hair?!"

"Sure looks like it, Will," he replied. He looked at Paolo. "Another bag please, son."

Doctor Morrow put the hair in another specimen bag. He took his pen out again and wrote on the bag 'hair sample – right hand little finger, nail.'

He took off his gloves and turned to Derek and shook his hand. "Well spotted, son. I don't often miss something like that, but I suppose the dark nail varnish camouflaged the hair."

"No problem, doc," Derek said, "glad to be of help."

Doctor Morrow looked at Will. "If you boys don't mind, I'll finish my report and send the samples off to the various labs.

"Sure JJ," Will said. "Right boys, let's get back to base. Thanks JJ."

CHAPTER 19

Golf Match

Geno and Paolo were in the Captain's room going over the Sarah Miller case.

Will put the papers in his hand down. "Right guys this will have to wait. I have a golf match with the captain in the fifty-second precinct Sunday morning. This is a grudge match. We are one match all and the loser will have to buy drinks at the annual ball."

Geno looked at his watch, "Don't tell me you are going to bed at this time to get ready for the match?!"

The captain shook his head. "No, sleep is not the problem. I am going to the driving range to practice. There is only one problem!" He took off the sunglasses, showing the white of his eyes were still slightly red. "My eyes have not fully recovered from the other day. The doc told me the corneas have dried up a bit, but with the use of drops they should be okay in another few days. I can see the ball to hit, but I can't see the damn pin far away, so I have no idea of distances."

Paolo asked, "Can you not call it off?"

Will shook his head. "That is like admitting defeat. I'll just have to wing it."

"Well boss," said Geno, "I have an idea."

"Go on," responded Will.

"I can caddy for you."

Will stroked his chin, looking pensive. "I suppose there is no rule against having a caddy. The question is how well do you play, and have you caddied before."

Geno blew on the tips of his fingers and rubbed them against the lapel of his leather jacket. "Well my handicap is twelve and I won the club's Captain's Day tournament two years ago. Anyway, caddying is easy, just look up the yardage and the wind direction."

Will paused for a second. "Okay, although something tells me I am going to regret this."

Geno put his arm around Will's shoulder, "Boss, you have nothing to worry about, the game is as good as won."

Will looked at Geno and then looked at the arm that was draped over his shoulder. Geno slowly retracted his arm and dusted Will's collar with the same hand.

Will shook his head. "Yes I am definitely going to regret this! Be at the Pelham Bay Golf Course at 9 a.m. sharp on Sunday morning. Don't be late, and for God's sake wear proper attire or they won't let you in. That means no jeans!"

"No problem, boss, you can rely on me."

Will grunted and shook his head, "I am going to regret this. Now off you go, you two, I have to go to the driving range. I don't want to lose this one."

"Right boss, see you Sunday."

Paolo also got up, "Ciao boss, and good luck on Sunday."

*

It was Sunday morning. Will pulled up his large brown Chevy into the golf club car park. He looked at his watch and looked around the car park. "Shit I hope he isn't going to be late."

He took his golf clubs out of the boot of his car and changed into his golf shoes. He took out two brand new golf balls from a new box and marked them with a big W with a permanent marker. He placed one ball in each pocket and looked up. Geno was standing next to him, smiling, "Good morning boss."

Will looked up and down at Geno. "What the fuck!" he exclaimed. Geno had a pair of pink trousers on with black checks. He had a bright yellow shirt on which was just about visible over his bright pink pullover. His golf shoes were white with a brown trim. "Are you dressed for a gay party, or are you here for golf?"

Geno seemed unperturbed by Will's sarcasm. He put his arm around Will and said, "Boss, your golf clothes are very smart but you gotta loosen up and move forward with the times."

Will looked at Geno's arm around his shoulder. Geno lifted his hand off Will's shoulder, made a fist and covered his mouth with it whilst giving a nervous cough.

Will shook his head, "I'm already regretting this!"

He then gave Geno a small booklet. "This is the course shot saver, it gives you the yardage to the green from various landmarks. There is no wind today and it's a beautiful mild sunny November day. You just have one job. Calculate the yardage for me. Ninety yards and less is a sand wedge. One hundred yards is a pitching wedge, one hundred and ten yards is a nine iron, etc. Do you get it?"

"Yes boss."

"So, if the yardage is one hundred and twenty yards, which do iron do you give me?"

Geno spend a few seconds counting with his fingers, "That will be an eight iron, boss."

"Good, and you don't have to call me boss here!"

"Yes boss."

"Oh, what's the use?" Will said, waving his hand. "Just remember, you only have to hand me the right club, leave everything else to me."

"Yes boss."

Just then a smart-looking gentleman approached them and put his clubs down. "Good morning Will."

Will shook his hand, "Good morning Adam."

Adam pointed at Geno, "Is there anything you want to tell me? I see you have brought your boyfriend along. Does Michelle know about this?"

"Haha," Will remarked. He pointed to Geno. "This is Officer Geno Pasqualli from the precinct. As I have already told you my eyes are still a bit of a problem. So Geno is caddying for me today." He turned to Geno, "Geno this is Captain Adam Smiley."

Geno shook Adam's hand. "Good morning Captain. I hope you are playing well, cause boss here is on a hot streak at the minute."

Adam tipped his head towards Geno. "Geno, don't hustle a hustler."

Geno looked very meek and responded quickly, "Yes Captain."

Adam looked at Will. "I suppose you can have a caddy." He picked up his clubs and walked towards the clubhouse. "I have booked us one buggy; we should be able to get a second."

Will tapped the course booklet in Geno's hand and whispered, "Remember, just stick to giving me the right club."

"Yes boss."

Will whispered, "And stop calling me boss!"

Geno made a salute, "Certainly boss!"

Geno looked at Will. "Can I say, boss, you look a bit tense. You need to loosen up. I think what you need is a joke."

"You are kidding me, right?"

Geno was unperturbed. "Fellow goes to his doctor. He says, 'Doctor, I have a sore chest, a sore tummy, sore legs, in fact I am sore everywhere.' The doctor examines him thoroughly and then stands there scratching his head. He tells the guy, 'Look I have made a careful examination and I can't find anything. It must be the drink.' The guy gets up to leave, 'That's okay, Doctor, I'll come back tomorrow when you are sober!'"

"Stick to caddying, Geno!"

"Sure boss."

Will shook his head and walked on. They got a buggy each and Geno put Will's clubs in the holder.

*

The match was all square going to the par four eighteenth green. Adam was first to his shot to the green and landed his ball to within twelve feet of the flag. Will's ball was closer to the hole, just six feet away.

Adam was lining up his putt on the green. Will tried his best to increase the pressure on his opponent. "Well Adam, no pressure. You were two up with three to play and I've won the last two holes; but if you don't make this, you know I am not going to miss."

Adam ignored him and having walked to the other side of the hole to line it up and back again he took his putt and it landed in the centre of the hole. It was his turn to make a fist pump. "Yes! Now the best you can do is a draw."

"Shit," Will said involuntarily.

He walked up and down, sizing up his putt. He looked at Geno, "It looks like it's right to left putt, but my gut feeling is that it is straight."

Geno scratched his head, he walked up and lined himself so he could see the ball and the hole in one line. He then looked to his right. He shook his head. "Hmm, quiet word, boss." He walked a couple of steps away.

Will looked at Adam and shrugged his shoulders. "Whatever!" He followed Geno.

"I have to disagree with you, boss. You see the stream there on the right? The ball nearly always goes towards the water, so I think this will be a left to right putt. I would give it just two inches outside the hole. Trust it." Geno walked away, leaving Will looking at where he had been standing.

Will shrugged his shoulders again and walked up to the ball. Without much hesitation he got behind the ball and putted. It went at quite a pace at the left-hand side of the hole and in the last foot turned two inches and went straight into the hole. He punched the air and shouted "Yes, yes!"

He came over and lifted Geno into the air. He suddenly realised what he was doing. He put Geno down and composed himself. He came over and shook Adam's hand. "Good game. Honours even and probably a fair result."

"Yes good match." Adam shook Will's hand firmly. As Will was ready to pull his hand away, Adam held on to it tight. "Next time I am bringing my caddy with me; Jack Nicklaus."

"Sure, sure," laughed Will.

"See you at the annual ball, Will."

"Are not joining us at the nineteenth hole?"

"I'd love a drink, Will, but after this round of golf, it's payback time, I have to go shopping with Nancy. That was the pre-condition, seeing I work all hours that God has sent."

"Okay Adam. What about you, Geno? Are you joining me for a drink?"

"You paying?" responded Geno quickly.

"Consider it as your caddy's fee."

Geno smiled, "Well it's not quite fifteen percent of your winnings, but I accept the offer." Geno then shook hands with Adam. "A pleasure to have met you, sir."

"Nothing personal, I wish I hadn't met you! I would have nailed Will's ass otherwise."

Geno laughed.

"Dream on," shouted back Will.

*

Will and Geno walked up to the bar after they had put the clubs away and changed their shoes.

They walked into the bar and were approached by a waitress wearing black trousers and a frilly white shirt with a waist coat. "Hi, my name is Gabriella, please have a seat, I will be with you shortly," she said as she eyed Geno up and down.

Will looked at Geno and then turned to Gabriella, "Sorry about the fancy dress!"

"Oh, not at all, sir, I was admiring his sense of self-confidence."

Will looked at Geno and shook his head, "Whatever!" He then asked Geno, "Is a window seat okay for you?"

"Sure thing, Captain," replied Geno.

Will sat down so he was facing the window. No sooner had they sat down Gabriella came to the table holding an i-Pad in her hand. "Would you gentlemen like something to eat?"

"No just drinks please," answered Will. "I'll have a Martini, dry."

"Do you have any Chianti red wine, from Tuscany area in Italy?"

The young girl looked somewhat puzzled and embarrassed.

Will rescued her. "Do you have cheap red wine, the ten-dollars-a-bottle job?"

The girl smiled, "We have plenty of that sort, sir!"

"A glass of your cheapest will do, miss," Will said smiling.

"No problem, sir."

"I guess it will have to do," remarked Geno.

Will looked out the window. "I love the view of a golf course. In the middle of a concrete jungle, it is like a taste of paradise."

"You are not going to break into a poem or anything like that, are you Captain?"

"No, and you can call me Will here."

"Yes Captain."

"Oh, what's the use?" Will exclaimed.

"You played well, Captain, you should have won."

"He finished well. But I enjoyed it. I look forward to my retirement, I can see me playing three or four days a week."

"That's of course if you are not out shopping every day."

"No Geno, I may do a lot of things, but shopping is not on the list. I just hate it. I like to go to a shop and buy exactly what I want and get the hell out. Whether I pay a bit more for it, or can get a different colour or style down the road, is not relevant to me."

Geno leant across the table and looked Will up and down. "Captain, you are wearing dark brown trousers, sky-blue sweater with black shirt, white socks and black shoes, I suggest next time you go shopping you take your time and perhaps take your missus along."

Will slid his chair back and put out his foot and looked at his socks and shoes. "I thought I look rather smart when I dressed this morning."

Just then the waitress arrived with their drinks.

Geno looked at her, "Gabriella, can you give us your honest opinion, do you think my boss here looks smartly dressed?"

Without looking at Will Gabriella said, "Are you talking about the brown trousers and blue sweater, or the white socks?"

Before Geno could say anything Will asked with a surprised tone "Hold on a second, you can't even see my socks from where you are."

"Yes sir, but I could hardly miss them from across the room."

Geno laughed out loud. "You are busted, Captain! Well Gabriella, what is your verdict then?"

Gabriella thought for a couple of seconds and looked at Will and then at Geno. "Well sir, I like it. It reminds me of my dad."

Will laughed, "Diplomatic answer! That's good enough for me, thank you Gabriella. You just increased your tip by one hundred percent."

Gabriella smiled and turned around to leave. Will held her forearm very gently, "Just one more question. Give me your honest opinion, what do you make of this man dressed in pink?"

Gabriella eyed Geno up and down. She then put her hand on his hair and ruffled it a bit, running her hand up and down his scalp. "I will surely take him home to mamma."

She turned around and walked away.

Geno was open mouthed for a second and looked at her as she walked away.

Will looked at Geno, "Geno you are blushing!"

"No Captain. It's just all the walking and then coming into the heat from the cold."

"Aha!" muttered Will.

Geno looked at Gabriella as she was standing at the bar, "Nice ass, would you say, Captain?"

"Yes, it is very nice, not that I was looking."

"Certainly not."

"Anyway, are you and Paolo not meant to be gay or something like that?"

"What exactly is 'something like that', you mean we might be just half gay?"

"You know what I mean. There are plenty of rumours about the two of you, especially since you are very pally and neither of you have had a girlfriend or even look at any of the girls in the office."

"Would it matter to you if we were gay?"

"Hell Geno! I don't give a shit who you are or what you are or what you do in your spare time, so long as you don't break the law and turn up in time for work in the mornings."

"Paolo and I had an agreement that we wouldn't talk about this matter, but I suppose you have forced my hand."

"Look Geno, I am no agony aunt, perhaps you should keep certain things to yourself."

"No Captain, but promise this won't go beyond you."

"When did you ever hear me mentioning other colleagues' matters to you?"

"Good point, boss. Anyway, this is not quite what you might think. It's like this; when we were in the Bronx precinct Paolo went out with this police officer. She was a real good-looking girl, and they were dating for a couple of months and everything was rosy – she was apparently very hot. To give you a short version of the story she invited Paolo to her parents' house after two months. He was given the fifth degree by her father – who had been a major in the navy – and asked him what the marriage arrangements were. He tried to break up with her, and she wouldn't let go. She was totally obsessed with him." Geno stopped and scratched his chin. "I suppose on reflection it may have been the coward's way out, but he told her that he was gay and I played along as his friend. Rumours soon flew around the precinct that we were gay, and actually it suited both of us. She left him alone, and it actually stopped any advances by female colleagues. So, we just kept the rumour going when we got here. Anyway, you know the saying 'you don't shit in your own backyard'. Well we were happy to play away from home ground, i.e. not date girls in our own precinct."

Will nodded. "I suppose it makes sense. It's just that you are both just so well dressed that it made sense that you were gay."

"Captain, you forget, we are Italian."

"Sorry, forgot! So, you are dating anyone at the minute?"

"I have had a couple of girlfriends. They were nice, but American."

"What does that mean?"

"Well American girls are nice, but …"

"But what Geno?"

"Well they are nice, but they are not Italian."

Will raised his eyebrows. "You mean American girls are nice to date and fuck, but not good enough to marry!"

"I wouldn't put it like that. You just want to take an Italian girl to mamma's house." With that he looked towards Gabriella.

Will shook his head. "You are a hypocrite, you know that, don't you?"

"I can see what it looks like, but I have my own ideas of a family."

"I give up on you, Geno." With that Will finished his drink. "I have to get going, you coming?"

"You go on ahead, Captain," said Geno, "I have something to attend to."

Will looked at Gabriella. "Sure; and I am sure it is an Italian matter."

Geno stopped looking at Gabriella and turned to Will. "Wha … What? No, I just have to go the ladies … I mean the Gents."

Gabriella was walking towards their table. Will nodded, "I think you got it right the first time. Just don't tell her you are gay!"

Gabriella had just arrived at the table and paused. "Am I interrupting something?"

Will was about to speak when Geno raised his right hand. "I am working under cover, it's a long story."

"Are you gentlemen finished with your drinks?"

"The Captain has finished and was leaving."

"I can come back," said Gabriella, turning around.

"No!" exclaimed Geno. "If you want to wait a minute I will be finished."

"Okay …" she said, as if unsure what to do.

Geno looked at Will and gestured towards the door with his head.

"Right Geno. See you soon. And I won't tell your boyfriend about any of this."

"Very funny, Captain."

Will looked at the bill and put a twenty-dollar note on the tray, and after a second put down ten dollars and smiled at Gabriella. "Keep the change honey, you earned it."

"Thank you, sir."

"You're welcome."

"See you tomorrow, Geno."

"Yes Captain."

Will walked away.

Geno took a sip of his drink. "Would you like to sit down for a minute?"

Gabriella looked very relaxed, leant on the table and lowered her voice slightly, "I would like to, but I may be looking for a new job."

"Surely this is just a temporary job."

"Yes, I am applying for a job with NYPD, like my pappa, but the next round of intake isn't until May."

"What a coincidence, I am with NYPD."

Gabriella raised her eyebrows. "Do they accept gay officers too?"

"Do you have anything against gay people?"

"No problem at all. Only I wouldn't be taking one home to mamma."

"I could give you a few pointers."

Gabriella got a bit closer to Geno and lowered her voice even more, "Pointers about what?"

Geno swallowed, "About the NYPD application and induction."

"Is that all your intentions are?"

Will arrived back and walked to the table. He looked over Gabriella. "I'm sorry, I must have dropped my keys."

Neither of them took any notice of him.

Geno stopped looking into Gabriella's eyes and looked all the way down to her feet and back up again. "I could tell you about my other intentions, but I have a feeling I will have to keep those intentions locked up until after I see your mamma."

Will tried to walk past Gabriella but she had her eyes fixed on Geno and didn't budge.

"I'll take up your offer."

"You don't think it's too early to go to your mamma's house?"

Gabriella shook her head. "No, I mean the offer to help me with the application."

Will tried to reach around Gabriella. "Do you mind, guys?"

Geno stood up and looked at the seat Will had been sitting on. He picked up a set of keys and without looking at him handed them to Will. "There you go, Captain."

Will took the keys and walked backwards. "Don't bother to say goodbye or anything."

Gabriella and Geno were staring into each other's eyes.

"Is this where we exchange numbers?" asked Geno.

"I finish at five today and will be very hungry," said Gabriella. "Where should we eat?"

Geno looked at his watch. "I can be here for five. I generally don't eat Italian out, can't compare to home-made cooking."

Gabriella smiled, "My sentiments exactly."

"You like steak?"

"Love steak."

Geno stood up, "I know a nice place downtown, I will book us a table."

Gabriella picked up the two glasses and put them on her tray. "See you at five, and don't be late."

"I won't, Gabriella."

Geno turned to leave the same time as Gabriella stood up from her crouched position and as Gabriella turned her face around, she was within a couple of inches of Geno's face. They were both silent.

Geno then slowly moved his face towards Gabriella. Gabriella looked into Geno's eyes.

"You are blushing," she said.

"Ahem," He cleared his throat. "It's the wine."

"Obviously. A real man would never blush!" She smiled. "By the way, are you not forgetting something?"

Geno looked surprise. "I thought I don't need your number."

"No, you don't, but I need your name."

"Oh. It's Geno."

"Nice to meet you, Geno."

"My pleasure, Gabriella."

"Ciao."

"Ciao," said Geno, composing himself. "See you tonight."

"Don't be late."

"I won't."

CHAPTER 20

First Date

Gabriella had just finished her work in the restaurant and walked outside through the back door. She pulled up the collar of her large beige coat to protect her from the drizzle. She was tapping her foot and looking at her watch every few seconds. She paced back and forth for a few seconds and looked at her watch again. As she turned back, she nearly bumped into Geno.

She slapped him on his chest. "You are late, and you have kept me waiting in the rain!"

Geno smiled, he had both of his hands behind his back.

Gabriella looked annoyed. "Give me one reason why I shouldn't walk away!"

"I'll give you two."

Gabriella was standing with her arms folded and was moving her fingers as if she was playing a piano. "Well, I'm waiting!"

Geno brought out his left hand from behind his back. He had a flower in his hand. A single dark, almost purple, rose.

"Just one rose!"

"Some deep matters are sometimes best understated."

Gabriella took the rose and smelled it, "It is beautiful. But you are not off the hook yet."

Geno brought out his right hand from behind his back and held out a bottle of wine and spoke in a very Italian accent, "Brunello di Montalcino Altero, from Tuscany!"

"Where did you get that?"

"I had to go all the way to Queens to a supplier. That's why I am a couple of minutes late."

"You were four minutes late," she kissed him on the cheek, "but I forgive you Geno."

"Okay Gabriella, let's go before we get soaked."

"Please call me Gabby."

"All right Gabby, you don't have a car I take it?"

"I don't. I am learning to drive but never seem to have the time to, I prefer the subway anyway."

They sprinted towards Geno's car.

Gabriella shook her head to get rid of some water in it. "Oh, I'm sorry, Geno, I am making a mess of your car."

"That's only a problem for Jim."

"Huh, that doesn't make any sense to me."

"Jim is our senior detective. He is so fussy about his car. I think he'll throw you out of his car if you fart in it."

Gabriella laughed. "Well I don't plan to do anything like that!"

Geno gave the bottle to Gabriella. "Hold on to this for dear life, I may throw you out if you break it."

"Keep on talking like that and I'll break it over your head!"

They both laughed aloud.

Gabriella looked at the wine bottle. "What sort of restaurant are we going to that you need to bring in your own wine, don't be disillusioning me now."

Geno smiled. "Now it's going to be a surprise."

"Oh good. I like surprises." Gabby looked excited.

Geno drove off and they were silent for a couple of minutes.

Gabriella broke the silence. "Well Geno tell me about yourself. I was standing there in the rain waiting for you and suddenly realized that I knew next to nothing about you. In fact, being a cop, you can start by telling me about your partner, I know from my dad, you can be at times closer to your partner than your spouse."

"You are right, that is a cop saying. Where do I start?" He turned around suddenly and looked at Gabriella. "I'll tell you what, Gabby, I'll arrange a get together, between the three of us."

"That sounds romantic," said Gabriella, not sounding convincing.

"It'll be great, trust me, you'll love him."

"So you want me to meet your partner before I meet your mama?"

"What can I say, Gabby, I'm a cop."

"Figures." Gabriella pointed to the windscreen. "You can turn off your wipers, it has stopped raining, I hate the noise of wipers on a dry windscreen, it's like fingernails on a blackboard."

"I know what you mean." Geno turned off the wipers.

Gabriella looked at the road. "You are crossing the Queens Bridge, where exactly are we going?"

"It's a surprise!"

Geno seemed to back up on his direction and drove to a car park that was close to the bank of the Hudson River.

Gabriella looked around her in every direction. "I'm sure there are no restaurants around here."

Geno pointed to the back seat, there was a large picnic basket on the backseat. "Oh yes there is. Chez Pasqualli's! I figured steak is a bit boring. We have olive bread with pure virgin olive oil and balsamic vinegar first, a pasta and tuna salad, followed by homemade lasagne, which I had to pick up from Luigi's restaurant as late as possible. If you have any problem swallowing some beautiful Tuscany Rose wine to lubricate your gullet."

"Oh my!" Gabriella looked excited, "That's why I like surprises."

Gabriella pointed to the basket. "Are you sure the olive oil is virgin olive oil?"

"Extra virgin."

"That's good, Geno, at least we have one virgin in the car!"

There was a momentary silence. Geno then burst into laughter. "Gabby you are so funny!" He reached over towards her and kissed her very softly on her cheek. "Gabby I don't think there is anything you can tell me about yourself that can either shock me or make me dislike you."

Gabby looked a bit stunned. "Oh my!" is all she could say.

"Well do you think it's dry enough for you, I like to sit on that bench and look at the lights of Manhattan shimmering on the surface of the Hudson, it's hypnotizing."

"That is so romantic," Gabriella said very softly.

Geno and Gabriella carried the basket to the bench. As they got closer they reached over to put the basket on the bench when something moved. Gabriella let out a yelp and nearly dropped the basket. The wine bottle fell off the top of the basket, but Geno put his foot out to catch it and the bottle landed on the footpath and rolled towards the railing beside the walkway and stopped.

Someone sat up on the bench and Gabriella let out another yelp. The man was very dishevelled, with a long dirty beard, a very dirty overcoat. "What is going on?" His speech was very slurred, he looked somewhat confused as he looked at Geno and Gabriella.

Geno had his hand on his gun in the back of his trouser, he let go of the grip. "Sorry to startle you, sir, we were just coming out here for a bite to eat."

The tramp rubbed his hands together. "Great I'm hungry, what are we eating?"

"No sir, we were going to have a romantic dinner, I wonder if there is anywhere else you can lie down?"

The man looked indignant. "Well SIR, this is my bed for the night, so why don't I suggest that you romance somewhere else! There are some seats further along. I am rather attached to this spot, this is my bed, and you are actually now in my bedroom, so please leave." He lay down on the bench.

Geno raised his voice, "Listen buddy, I hate to say this but I'm with NYPD."

The tramp held up his two wrists together. "Please arrest me, I could do with sleeping in a warm cell on a cold night like this."

Gabriella smiled and spoke very gently, "Well, sir, maybe NYPD couldn't convince you but I'm sure President Andrew Jackson could convince you to vacate your bed for the night."

The tramp sat up, "I thought Obama was the president?"

"He is, but he doesn't have his face on a twenty-dollar bill."

The tramp lay down again. "No Jackson won't convince me, but now if President Ulysses Grant was to talk to me, I would surely listen to him!"

Gabriella shook her head. "You drive a hard bargain," she took out a fifty-dollar bill and gave it to the tramp. "Here you are."

The tramp got up. "You can have my room for the night."

Gabriella said, "Thank you."

"You're welcome." The man burped. "Pardon me."

Gabriella seemed curious. "Say, you seem to know your dollar bills very well."

"I should! I used to be a banker. Used to make multi-million-dollar decisions."

Gabby sounded sympathetic. "What went wrong?"

"Well I gambled with people's pensions once too many. The rest is history. Enjoy your romantic dinner." He staggered off.

Geno shouted after him, "Excuse me sir, what is your name?"

"It is Balance, Rick Balance." Rick pointed to the bottle of wine on the ground. "Will you be needing that by any chance?"

Gabby shook her head. "That is not negotiable, Rick."

"Okay, but no harm in asking." He started to stagger away. "I'm off!"

"Nice to meet you, Mister Balance," Geno said as he waved.

"Man, you are not the sharpest, are you? It is not Balance, its BAA-LAAnce! I thought cops used to be smart!"

"I get it Rick, it's BAA-LAAnce."

Geno and Gabriella sat down. Gabriella opened the basket and saw two blankets on top of the food. "Oh you brought blankets as well, you think of everything."

"Well I figured we could be here for a few hours, so we may as well be comfortable. Should we start with you telling me about your family?"

Gabriella nodded, "Sure …"

Geno looked at the river and then looked at her. "I am almost scared to ask; do you have a boyfriend?"

Gabby shook her head. "No."

"I find that hard to believe!"

"Well I just got tired of the dating game, meeting men who were drifting in life. Over the past year I decided to grab the bull by the horns, learn to drive, and apply for NYPD, and stop talking about doing these things. My mamma really did not want me to join the force, she used to worry about my pappa so much. But I guess now she is resigned to this. So, I've been quite happy with things and away from the stress that seems to inevitably follow my relationships." She paused. "Funny, I am anxious about asking you if you have a girlfriend. If you have a girlfriend, I would be very disappointed if you were dating me behind her back. If you didn't have one, I would think there must be something wrong with you."

Geno laughed. "It's funny 'cause people say all the good guys are taken, but that doesn't make sense. I guess if someone is meant for you, you will eventually meet."

Gabby smiled. "That's exactly what I believe. But I note that you didn't answer my question."

"Yes. I mean yes I didn't answer your question and the answer is no. And yes, if I had a girlfriend, I would not be sitting here with you on a romantic date." Geno pointed to the basket. "Are you ready for the starters?"

Gabby clapped her hands. "Definitely! Starving; have not eaten since breakfast. The golf club is so busy on Sundays, my feet are killing me."

"Well now I have a cure for that. Take your shoes off."

Gabby looked reluctant. "It's a cold night to take my shoes off."

"You won't regret it!"

Gabby took off her shoes and Geno massaged her feet through her stockings.

Gabby started to eat and Geno ate in between massaging her feet.

"So Gabby, where does your father work?"

"He is stationed in Queens. He always wanted to be a detective, but mamma didn't like that. He finally got a chance for promotion ten years ago, but suddenly decided that he was happy to be on the beat as he calls it. He loves chatting to people and really enjoyed his work. He worked a lot in the

Ridgewood and Middle Village area of Queens, and actually started to ditch the police car and walk around. After a few years everyone in the area knew him. He chats to all the youth; he has a way of communicating with young people that breaks down barriers. The NYPD noted that the crime rate in that that vicinity was very low as everyone had great respect for the police, especially notable in the youth."

Geno poured some wine for both of them as Gabby was talking. "Wow, that's amazing. It must be nice to retire and know that you have made some sort of difference."

Gabby nodded. "Yes, he's my inspiration. That's why I want to join the force. Although I love my mamma to bits. You only have one mother. She always loved staying and keeping the home, and with my three sisters and two brothers she had her hands full."

"So you had a small family then?"

Gabby poured some olive oil on the bread. "Haha." She gave him a cheeky grin. "What about your family, Geno?"

"Well I have a small family. My parents got married when they were eighteen and have been together since. My father owns my grandfather's bakery which has been in the family for four generations. Mamma helps him out. Pretty ordinary really, but they seem to be so in love. They fight now and then, but always bounce back. I have one sister. She is an accountant and works in Brooklyn. She has two children and I adore them. Whenever I get a chance, I take them to the park near their home. Her husband is an accountant too and at the end of the tax year between January and April both of them are very busy. I help out a lot. I adore Michaela and Brian and they seem to enjoy me being there. Nothing to do with the fact that I always let them stay up late and break all the rules. Well actually not all of them, I can be quite strict but just little things that makes them feel they are being naughty without actually doing anything major."

"I'm sure they love you," said Gabby. She clapped her hands again. "Ready for some more food."

They talked for a few hours, drinking the wine slowly and every so often there were periods of silence when they looked at the lights of Manhattan across the river.

Geno asked Gabriella, "Are you working tomorrow, or should I say later today?"

"Yes, I start at midday, so I am not too bad."

Geno looked at his watch. "I have to be in early in the morning. We are usually at the precinct about eight. It's now three a.m."

Gabby put her arm through his so their arms were locked. "I wish we could stay here all night."

"So do I," said Geno, looking her in the eyes, "but we will be too tired to meet up tomorrow night."

"Not tomorrow, unfortunately I am working late."

"I'll call you tomorrow to arrange to meet soon. I also want you to meet my partner, Paolo."

"Paolo who?"

"Paolo Rossi."

"Paolo … Ross-ssi?" Gabriella said very slowly.

"Yeah, you know him?"

"I th … think so," Gabby said somewhat reluctantly.

"And how is that?"

Gabby thought for a couple of seconds. "My father is a big Italian soccer fan – although he still calls it football. All he would do when Italy were in the world cup is go around the house repeating the names of the players. First it was Paolo Rossi, then it was Salvatore Schillachi. Paolo Rossi was the soccer player for Italy who scored a lot of goals in the one of the World Cup Finals, wasn't he? I suppose it is a common name."

"You know your soccer as well."

"So tell me a bit me about Paolo."

"The rest is for later!"

"In that case we had better be off then."

Gabriella was about to stand up when Geno held her forearm and pulled her down. "Not so quick, Gabby!"

He kissed her on the lips very passionately. It seemed to go on for a long time. When they stopped Gabriella said, "Oh my!"

Geno was about to get up and this time Gabriella held his forearm. "Would you mind biting me on my forearm?"

"I beg your pardon?" Geno's frown of surprise could be seen in the dim light.

"Just bite me gently on my forearm."

Geno shrugged his shoulders. "Whatever turns you on!"

Geno bit her forearm quite gently.

"No that's too gentle, slightly harder!"

Geno obliged.

"Ouch!"

"I'm sorry, but you did ask!"

"Yes Geno, I just wanted to make sure I'm not dreaming."

Geno kissed her forehead. "If you are dreaming, well, so am I!"

They got up and tidied up. Gabby was putting the plastic dishes and cutlery into the basket. Geno picked up the blankets, "Give me a minute." He walked up the walkway for a while and saw the tramp. "Here you are, sir, these should help you over the winter."

"Many thanks, sir; much obliged." He burped again, "If you need any financial advice, just see me in my office."

Geno pointed to the bench. "At the bench there?"

"You are a bit slow, aren't you? That is my bedroom, this is my office right here!"

Geno laughed. "I'll remember that advice!"

Geno drove Gabriella home and kissed her again in the car before she went up the stairs to her house. He watched her as she ran up the stairs. She stood at the door and blew him a kiss and went in. Geno drove home.

CHAPTER 21

Detectives Question Jake

Jim walked into the Captain's room. "Good morning Captain. Are you well rested after the weekend?"

"To be honest with you, I'm a bit exhausted after a round of golf on Sunday."

"Oh yes, how did that go, did you beat Adam?"

"No, it was an honourable half, but I was pleased with my game."

"Did you wear your special golf sunglasses?"

Will laughed, "I'll never live that down, will I?"

Jim shook his head.

"I should have known better than to tell you."

"What about Geno, was he a good caddy?"

"He was great." Will paused for a few seconds. "I am going to ask you a question Jim, and I want you to be very honest with me."

"If it's to do with golf, Captain, I know nothing about the sport, except that I know Tiger Woods earns more in one week than I do in one year, or is it ten years, and that is if he doesn't hit a ball in anger."

"No Jim, it's not about golf."

"Well if its marital advice you want you are again asking the wrong person."

"Will you shut up and listen, Jim!"

"Sorry sir, I am talking when I should be listening."

Will hesitated, "Jim do you think I dress badly?

"Wow, that came out of left field! Okay stand up." Jim looked at Will for a few seconds, eyeing him up and down. "Well sir, for a man of your age, you always look prim and proper, but I am sure you can jazz things up a little bit. Why do you ask?"

"Oh nothing. And not a word to anyone."

"I presume you didn't want to see me because of that."

Will sat down and picked up a sheet of paper. "The Forensics had a look at the list of numbers on the SIM card found in Sarah Miller's body. The District Attorney insisted on being present, as the finger has been pointed at Jake Chapman for this murder. In fact, there were only nine numbers on it."

He pointed to the paper, "Now, I'm a dinosaur, but I checked the contact list on my phone, and I have seventy-two names on mine, so it does seem a bit odd."

"Hmm," Jim was in thought for a second, "do you think it might be her work cell phone, like a business phone as compared to her personal cell phone?"

Will nodded. "Yes Jim, it has to be, that's all I could come up with."

Jim reached towards Will. "Okay boss I'll look into those straight away."

"Who are you going to put on it?"

"I was thinking the Italian job."

"Thought so!"

*

Jim and Derek were in Jim's office.

Derek pointed at the sheet of paper with the phone numbers on it. "Do you want me to check these numbers?"

"Thanks Derek, but I think Paolo and Geno would be best to look into this one."

Derek looked at the numbers. "One of the numbers seems a bit odd."

Geno and Paolo walked into Jim's office.

Jim nodded. "Yes I noticed that." He looked up. "Good morning boys, have a seat."

Geno and Paolo sat down.

Jim handed the paper to Paolo. Geno leant over to peep. "These are the

169

numbers on the SIM card in Sarah Miller's, em, body. I want you boys to go through these numbers with a fine-tooth comb. Don't leave any stone unturned."

Geno took the paper from Paolo and the two of them looked at the numbers for a brief period.

Paolo pointed to one of the numbers, "This one isn't right."

Geno nodded. "Yes it has nine rather than ten numbers."

Paolo reached into the inside pocket of his leather jacket and brought out a small notebook. "We were checking out the file on Sarah Miller." He flicked through a few pages until he found the page he was looking for. "Yes, here it is. Sarah Miller had two cell phones registered to her name. One was her personal one, and the other seems to have been her, let's call it, work phone. Her contacts were explored in detail after she went missing. The phone was last used on twelfth of October 2012. Interestingly the last day that Tracey Chapman was seen alive."

Jim nodded, "Good work guys. It stands to reason why at the time Jake Chapman was suspected as taking them both out."

Derek smiled and looked at Jim. "I can see why you wanted Paolo and Geno to pursue this line!"

Jim nodded.

Paolo continued. "If you give me a minute we will just try and match the numbers to what we have on the records."

Geno and Paolo checked the numbers on the Sarah Miller file and put a tick beside the number on the sheet that Jim had given to them. After a couple of minutes Paolo nodded, "Yes the numbers tally with her cell phone bills, except for this nine number one. We'll look into it."

Jim got up. "Right Derek, we have a far more interesting task. We will go interview Jake Chapman."

"I shall look forward to that. I presume we'll have to contact his attorney."

"Yes, I'll do that. I'll see if we can get that done today."

Derek smiled. "I'm sure your girlfriend will do you a favour."

"I can assure you that Amanda will not be doing any favours for anyone other than her client. One step out of line and she will pounce, so beware!"

Derek nodded. "Il be sure to remember that."

Jim looked at Geno. "Can we meet up early tomorrow morning to go over our findings?"

"Sure thing."

*

Jim was talking to Amanda quietly in the corner of the interview room in the prison. Derek and Lucy were making small talk when the door opened and Jake was brought into the room.

Amanda pointed to a chair and Jake sat down. Lucy and Amanda sat on either side of him. Jim and Derek sat on the opposite side of the table.

Amanda spoke first, "Did you provide the forensic samples?"

Jake nodded. "The swab tastes rotten on the inside of the mouth! I'd rather give the blood sample any day."

Amanda spoke softly, "Jake you realise that you do not have to answer anything you don't want to."

"Yes, I know."

"And if I ask you to stop, please do stop!"

"Sure thing, Amanda, but I do not have anything to hide. And yes, I understand what you are saying."

Amanda looked at Jim. "Go ahead."

Jim brought out a small notebook and at the same time Derek, Amanda, and Lucy almost simultaneously brought out small notebooks.

"Good morning Jake, do you remember Detective Derek Johnston, and myself, Jim Sterne?"

"Yes I do, Detective. Nice to see you again."

"Oh yes. Em, good morning. I would like to remind you of your rights."

Jake held up his hand. "That's okay, I know them well."

"You do realise that you are accused of the murders of Charlene Mills and Sarah Miller?"

"So I've been told."

"Can you tell me where you were on the night of Saturday, sixteenth of November?"

"I am sorry I can't remember."

"Do you recall meeting us in the Mexicano bar that night?"

"I have a vague recollection. But to be honest, I think it's because you told me this at our last interview."

"If you remember you spilt a drink on me," added Derek.

"Oh yes I remember that bit, I think, or again is it because you reminded me of that during your last questioning?"

Derek continued, "Do you remember telling us that you had heard of the young girl being killed earlier that night, and in fact you described the colour of her shoes?"

"I am sorry I do not remember any or that."

"How very convenient," Derek said sarcastically.

Amanda raised her voice, "If you continue that line of comments, I will simply have to ask my client not to answer any further questions."

"I am sorry." Derek looked a bit sheepish.

Jim seemed very calm and asked in a very quiet voice, "Do you remember meeting a girl in a red dress, wearing red shoes?"

"No, I didn't meet her."

"Do you mean you don't remember meeting anyone, or you didn't meet her?"

"I think I would have remembered if …"

Amanda put her hand on Jake's arm, "Detective Sterne, I think we have established that on the night of Saturday November sixteenth, my client was intoxicated and does not remember any of the events of that night. Now do you have any other questions you would like to ask?"

"Yes, Mister Chapman. Did you ever know or meet a girl called Sarah Miller?"

"I knew of her, but never met her."

Jim wrote down a few words. "Can you clarify what you mean?"

"I know that my wife was dealing with her case, but I never met her. I mean at the time I did not know who her client was, but subsequently I found out that Tracey was dealing with her case and deduced she was helping Sarah Miller."

"Your wife was a social worker?"

"Yes, that's right."

"What did you wife tell you about her?"

"Not a lot really, she did not discuss her cases, as they were confidential. In fact, I rarely knew their names either. She sometimes discussed the characteristics of her case and would occasionally ask me my professional opinion."

"As a psychologist?"

"Yes."

Derek asked, "So how did you know her name?"

"Tracey, my wife, found the case very taxing and she would occasionally say she was going to see Sarah. After Tracey was …" Jake went silent for a few seconds and seemed to compose himself. "After Tracey was murdered, I was questioned about the missing girl Sarah Miller, and I gathered that it was who Tracey was dealing with."

Jim stopped taking notes and looked up. "What did Tracey say about Sarah?"

"I am sorry, Detective, what little I knew was confidential information and I cannot under any circumstances reveal them to you."

Amanda held up her hand. "Detectives can you give us a few moments alone with our client?"

Jim got up, "Sure thing, Amanda, we'll be waiting outside. Call us when you are ready." The two of them left the room.

Amanda looked at Jake. "Listen, are you sure you don't want to tell them what you know? Any information you have may be useful in proving your innocence. I mean what is it that is so confidential that you can't tell them?"

"I am sorry, firstly other people's lives are in concern, and I am not happy to disclose info about them. Secondly I am innocent and have no worries."

Lucy looked very concerned. "Jake I don't think you realise the gravity of what is facing you."

"I do, but I will be fine. They will not be able to find any evidence, because there can be none."

Lucy seemed somewhat perturbed. "Look Jake, I'm not sure how you see things, but from where I stand you could do with all the help you can get. I don't think you should hold anything back."

"I'm sorry I have nothing else to say on this matter." Jake turned his back to Lucy.

Amanda looked at Lucy and shrugged. She went to the door and opened it and just looked at Jim and Derek who walked in and sat down again.

Amanda walked towards her seat and as she passed Lucy she gently put her hand on Lucy's shoulder.

Amanda sat down and looked at Jim. "My client does not wish to say anything further with respect to your last question."

Jim looked at his notes. "So you have some information about what Tracey and Sarah talked about and you do not wish to discuss it."

Jake was about to speak when Amanda held up her hand in front of Jake. "Detective Sterne, are there any other questions you wish to ask?"

Jim looked at Jake straight in his eyes. "Did you kill Sarah Miller?"

Jake laughed.

Jim sounded annoyed, "You find that funny?"

"Well Detective, would you not find it funny if you had never met someone and you were asked if you killed them?"

"Please answer the question," Jim said rather authoritatively.

Amanda turned to Jake, "Are you happy to answer the question?"

"Sure, I have never met Sarah Miller and I sure as hell didn't kill her."

Jim sat forward. "Can I ask you another question?"

"Sure."

"Do you believe in hell?"

Jake seemed to stumble on his words, "Well, actually … No!"

Jim continued, "So you are not sure?"

Jake paused and raised his voice slightly, "I did not kill her."

Jim leant forward, "Jake, did you kill Charlene Mills?"

Jake raised his voice, "NO, definitely not!"

Derek leaned forward, "Can you say with confidence that you did not kill Charlene Mills?"

Amanda got up. "Gentlemen, I think you have asked all your questions, I will now ask that you leave my client alone."

Derek put up his hand. "I would just like to ask one more question."

Jim folded up his notebook. "That's all right, ladies, we will leave you with your client, I believe we have covered most of the main points."

As they got up Jim looked at Amanda, "Can I have a quick word outside?"

Amanda shook her head. "I have to spend time with my client, I will see you in court."

Jim looked very disappointed.

Jake looked at Jim and then at Amanda and smiled.

Jim was by the door and had reached for the door handle when he turned back and looked at Amanda. "Goodbye." Amanda just waved a hand.

Amanda looked at Jake. "Well that went so-so!"

Lucy said, "I suppose it could have been worse."

Amanda shook her head. "I don't like it. Something is up. I don't like it at all. I know Jim, they have something up their sleeve."

"Like what?" Lucy seemed concerned.

"I don't know, but I am worried."

Jake got up. "You have nothing to worry about."

Amanda looked at Jake. "Can you put your hand on your heart and say for sure that you did not meet Charlene Mills that night?"

"I was probably in a drunken stupor that night, as in fact most of the past year. So my recollection of events are a bit blurry as you can understand. But there is no way I would have hurt someone and not remember it. Anyway, I would have no reason to."

"Jake sit down." Amanda pointed to the seat that Jake had occupied. Jake looked at her somewhat quizzically and after a momentary hesitation sat on the chair.

Amanda leaned over so her face was very close to Jake's. "Right Jake, this is the court, you are sworn in and are in the hot seat. I am the district attorney. Remember you are sworn in. Right?"

Jake nodded. "Right."

Amanda started to pace up and down. "Mister Chapman, do you remember the events of Saturday November sixteenth?"

"Well most of that year …"

"Mister Chapman, please answer the question!"

"I was just saying …" Jake hesitated. "No I don't remember the events of that night."

"Do you remember meeting anyone that night? Accepting the fact that Detectives Sterne and Johnston had reminded you of meeting them that night?"

"Well most nights I go to the bar and then go home …"

"Mister Chapman, please answer the question!"

"I am sorry what was the question?"

"Mister Chapman I will ask so you can hear me clearly. Do … you … remember … meeting … anyone … that … night? Apart from the detectives?"

"No, I do not."

"Mister Chapman, is it possible that you would have met Miss Charlene Mills and not remember it?

"I … g … guess so."

"That is all, Mister Chapman. Now that you have given me the rope, I will hang you with it!"

Jake slammed his fist on the table. "But that is bullshit, that has nothing to do with truth!"

Amanda leaned over Jake again. "Jake we all have different versions of the truth, but you have to have respect for the way the court of law is conducted. And for God's sake, make you sure you don't lose your temper or slam the table ever again, the judge would not take too kindly to that, nor indeed any jury."

Jake got up. "I am tired now; can I be dismissed?"

"Yes Jake. You can go. We'll see you soon."

"Thanks ladies." Jake walked quickly to the door and walked out, escorted by the guard.

Lucy looked at Amanda. "So, what is it you think they have up their sleeve?"

"I don't know, Lucy, but I have a very, very bad feeling about this one!"

"I was thinking that they don't have a lot of concrete evidence."

"Lucy I can feel it in my bones, I don't like it one bit!"

CHAPTER 22

SIM Card Numbers

Paolo's desk was in the big common office. He wheeled his chair across the narrow walkway and finished up beside Geno's chair. Geno was sitting behind his desk and held up his index finger as he was on the phone, "Yes Mister Jackson, I do realise that the police interviewed you extensively last year, but the case has re-opened … Yes Sarah Miller has turned up as you put it, but unfortunately she is dead … Yes her body has been found … Look Mister Jackson, if it is all right can you come to the station for some questioning … Yes I see … well perhaps if you have about twenty minutes between lectures tomorrow at lunch time, we can come over to ask you a few questions? … That will be great … Good, oh and Mister Jackson, it will be myself, that's Geno Pasquali, or Detective James Sterne … Okay, goodbye."

Geno put down the phone. "Anyone interesting?" Paolo asked.

"A guy called Stephen Jackson, a lecturer at the Columbia Law School that Sarah Miller was at. He was one of the numbers. The old records say that he told the detectives that he tutored her on a couple of occasions and that was all. What about you, come up with anything?"

"Of the five I have, four were dead numbers, I assume after the police investigations they all changed their numbers, or perhaps their wives made sure they did. Let me see, there were two businessmen, one neurologist, one electronic consultant, and then we have this cell phone number with only nine digits."

Geno flicked his notebook to a previous page. "Apart from Stephen Jackson, three of the numbers were dead, and one was for the Elite Agency. The three dead numbers from the records were from one businessman, one civil servant, and one was a principal of a school. They were all interviewed by the police,

178

nothing notable in any of the interview records, but I will contact them individually and interview them myself. It will probably take a few days to track them all, maybe a couple of days will do it." He closed the notebook and leaned back on his chair and stretched his arms and then his whole body.

Paolo smiled. "Bit tedious, isn't it?"

"Yep, it's the part of police work that's the most laborious, but as you know it takes only one breakthrough. What about the nine-digit number?"

Paolo pointed to his desk that was about three meters away. "Would you like to step into my office?"

"Sure thing!"

Paolo wheeled his chair across the narrow walkway to his desk and Geno followed suit.

Paolo looked back at Geno's desk. "I think I much prefer my office to yours."

Geno pointed to the small plant that was on his own desk. "No; the Feng shui in my office is much better."

Paolo looked at Geno's plant. "Okay you win by a small margin."

"So, what do you have?"

"Not much. I added numbers zero to nine at the end of the nine digits. With the two-one-two area code we can safely assume that it is a New York number. Two were dead-end lines. Three were elderly couples that had the same number for donkeys' years. Two were business numbers that likewise were longstanding businesses. One I have left a message on twice to call me back. Let me see, that leaves two. One was a chap called David. When I told him I was calling on behalf of Sarah he got agitated, I thought I was onto something. Turns out he is a war veteran with below-knee amputation of both legs. He had a sister in Australia called Sarah and thought she was dead. So that leaves one, which would not accept incoming calls. I'll look into them further. We need to catch a break!"

Just as he said that Jim arrived with Derek walking behind him. "You can have a break when the case is shut, meanwhile into my office!"

Jim sat at his desk. "Well guys give me the good news first."

Geno looked at his notes. "This guy Stephen Jackson is the most prominent one. He is a law lecturer at Columbia University Law School, New York City.

He has been interviewed by the police previously."

"Did you say Stephen Jackson?"

Geno looked up from his notes. "Yes, why do you ask?"

"I shouldn't be surprised. He is the asshole who cheated on Amanda. In fact, when I showed Amanda Sarah Miller's picture, she said that she went home and found him in bed with Sarah Miller! The son of a bitch!"

"Yes we are due to meet him at twelve thirty tomorrow."

"Guys do you mind if Derek and I go to see him?"

"Sure thing," Paolo said, "The scumbag is all yours. I suppose that moves him up the suspects' list."

Geno nodded. "By a few notches."

Geno and Paolo filled in Jim and Derek with the rest of the information about the numbers on the SIM card. Likewise, Derek reported back from their meeting with Jake.

Jim looked at his watch. "It's nearly eight p.m. Why don't you guys call it a night, I will stay here for a while longer to review our findings. Derek, I'll see you here tomorrow."

'Sure," said Geno.

Paolo nodded.

The three of them left the room. Jim took out his cell phone and went through his contacts, speaking quietly to himself. "Why the hell is Amanda not there anymore?" He scrolled up and down the contact list. "Oh, for God's sake!" He scrolled down to the M's and saw her name under 'Mandy'. He waited while her phone was ringing, "Come on, come on."

"O good, Mandy, it's me here."

"Who's me?"

"Me, Jim!"

"I know you dummy, cell phones have number recognition you know."

"Silly me. Mandy what is the name of your boyfriend?"

"Is this a trick question? Okay I'll say James Sterne. Is that the answer you were looking for?"

Jim was taken aback. "I mean who is the guy you dumped before I got lucky while you were on the rebound, was is Stephen Jackson who lectures at Columbia Law School?"

"Firstly Jim, you are not a rebound. Well maybe initially, but that was a long time ago. Secondly unless there are two Stephen Jacksons lecturing at Columbia Law School, that would be him. Why do you ask?"

"Look Mandy, I can't tell you right now, but I promise to tell you as soon as I have some more info."

"Now you've got me intrigued. You know that if you don't disclose sensitive information, I can requisition it?"

"Yes honey, you can trust me."

"I can tell you once and for all, if I ever lose your trust, that will be the last time I speak to you. I have been there before and never want to face it again."

"I have no reason to hide anything from you."

"Okay Jim, I'll hear from you soon then."

"Bye now." As he pressed the red button on his phone he seemed to be in deep thought. He looked at the phone and shook his head. He pressed Mandy's number again, looked at it for a second and cut it off before Mandy's phone had rung. He thought for a couple of seconds, looked at his watch, and put his phone away.

He then began to flick through the documentation in front of him. He whispered to himself, "Just one clue could solve this, just one missing link!"

CHAPTER 23

Stephen Jackson: Right Side of the Law?

Jim and Derek were waiting outside lecture room two. They heard very loud laughter, followed by very enthusiastic applause and some whistling from inside.

Derek looked at Jim, "This guy must be shit hot, I can't imagine that sort of applause after every lecture."

The lecture room door opened and the students walked out. The buzz in the room could be heard, and a number of them were laughing.

After the last few left a rather short man opened the door. He was very slim. He was wearing light blue jeans with a worn-out patch over his right knee and faded patches on his thighs. He wore a black shirt with vertical grey stripes. The top three buttons were open, exposing a rather hairy chest with bulging pecs and biceps. He skin was tanned, and he had a trim very dark moustache. He head was shaven with just the outline of his dark hair on the sides of his head.

He reached out his hand. "Good afternoon gentlemen, which one of you is Geno Pasqualli?"

Jim shook his hand. "Mister Stephen Jackson?"

"Please call me Stephen."

"Stephen, I'm Detective Jim Sterne, this is Detective Derek Johnston."

Derek showed his badge.

Stephen looked up and down the corridor. "For God's sake put that away, I may get a bad reputation quickly."

Derek obligingly put his badge away. "Sure thing, Stephen."

"No harm done, please come in, gentlemen." Stephen pointed to the seats in the front row. "Please take a seat."

"Thanks, but we'll stand if that's all right." Jim walked around slightly so he could see the door.

"Suit yourself, but if it's okay I will rest myself. I tend to walk during most of my lectures."

He sat on the edge of the desk at the front of the lecture theatre.

Derek pulled out a notebook and was flicking through it, Jim commented, "Nice tan, Stephen, it's good going for November in New York."

"I have a second home in Phoenix, tend to spend as much time as possible there. I love the sun, and if I wasn't for this great job, I would spend the whole year in Arizona. I think I am the only person in Phoenix who sunbathes."

Derek got straight to the point, "Stephen I gather Detective Pasqualli told you that Sarah Miller's body was discovered?"

"Yes, I was very sorry to hear that. She was a top student, even though I gather her extracurricular activities were somewhat unorthodox."

"Yes, that is one way of putting it. Can I ask you when you last saw her?"

"You are aware that the police have already interviewed me about a year ago about Sarah?"

"Yes indeed, but the case has re-opened with the discovery of her body, so we will be questioning all witnesses again."

"Well I have nothing to add in addition to what I told the police a year ago. She was my student, an exceptional one I may add, and I talked to her a couple of times with regards to her academic work. That's all really."

Jim sat on the armrest of one of the seats, "Stephen what was your exact relationship with Sarah?"

"As I said, a professional one, as a lecturer and student. I gave her some additional tutoring."

"Stephen, are you aware what the extracurricular activities of Sarah were?"

"Yes. She was a … well, an escort."

"That's right. Did she ever go out with you as a date?"

"Certainly not. I keep my relationship with my students strictly on a professional basis."

Jim stood up and walked towards Stephen. "I bet you are quite a lady's man, aren't you, Stephen?"

"What do you mean?"

"Come on, Stephen, don't play dumb with me, it doesn't suit you. You are quite a playboy, aren't you?"

"Well there isn't a law against that, is there?"

Derek shook his head. "There sure isn't, nor is there a law against dating your student, but there is one against giving false information to the police."

"Look guys I don't know what you are talking about. I have given all the info to the police before and if you'll excuse me, I'll have to prepare for the next lecture."

Derek tapped his finger on his notebook. "Stephen, you are aware that your name was on Sarah Miller's cell phone?"

"Yes, the police told me that."

Jim raised his voice slightly, "There is only one problem. The cell phone in question was her business phone, if you catch the drift. She only used it for her escort clients."

"You must have got that wrong, I was her tutor, I met her a couple of times to discuss her dissertation."

Derek asked, "Stephen you told me, let me see …" He turned the page of his small notebook back, "Ah, that's it. 'She was a top student'. So why did she need tutorials?"

Stephen sounded a bit unsure of himself for the first time, "Well, I guess she wanted to be better."

Jim suddenly said, "That's fine, Stephen, why don't you come downtown and we can question you at the precinct? You may want to speak to your solicitor beforehand."

Just then an oriental young girl walked into the room. She had a very short jean skirt on that was just below her crotch level. She wore a sky-blue blouse with a low neckline that revealed a very prominent cleavage. She had a book in her right hand. She looked startled as she had walked a couple of steps into the room. "Oh, I'm sorry Mister Jackson. You … You asked to come over today for a quick tutorial on patent law."

"Yes, Miss …?"

"Lo, Jacqui Lo."

"Yes Jacqui, would you mind waiting outside for five minutes or so, my relatives from out of town just dropped in."

Jacqui looked at Derek up and down and then Jim. "Sure." She walked out.

"Right gentlemen, I'll be straight with you. Look, I work hard and play hard. I have two loves, my work and women. I go out with a girl for a while, have a good time, she has a good time and then I move on. I treat them well, but never give them promises I can't keep."

"And Sarah?" asked Jim.

"She was falling behind in her studies, and I knew she was a straight-A student in her high school. I met with her a couple of times to see why she was not performing well in her essays. She broke down and explained what she was doing. So, I made a deal with her in exchange for tutoring her."

"That's a bit low, isn't it, taking advantage of a girl?"

"Oh no, it wasn't like that. We never slept together–"

Jim interrupted, "Come on, Stephen, if you persist in lying to us you will make life difficult for yourself."

"Okay Detectives, whether I slept with her once or twice is neither here nor there. Our relationship changed after an incident. She provided me with a valuable service. When I went out with a girl for a while, well, I get bored. So, Sarah would dress real sexy and we would go to where I knew my then-girlfriend was and we would be quite amorous, kissing and cuddling. My girlfriend would walk in and see us. That way she would ditch me, so I didn't need to ditch her. It was best for everybody."

Jim had a tone of anger in his voice. "Is that what you did to Amanda Jackson?"

Stephen was taken aback. "Yes … I'm sorry, do you know Amanda?"

Jim composed himself. "Never mind that for now."

Derek shook his head. "By everybody you mean it was best for you? I thought you said you treated them well."

"Look Detective, please don't moralise. The girls know that I am after a good time and I never make any commitment to them."

"When is the last time you saw Sarah?" Jim asked.

"I saw her a week or so before she disappeared. She looked really well. She had previously put on a bit of weight and seemed depressed. She confided to me that she was going to a private psychiatric unit for therapy and was away for a few weeks to a few months, but then was great when she came back. In a way it makes sense that she was killed; 'cause some people said that she upped and went to a different state to live. I didn't understand why she would do that."

There was a momentary silence. Stephen looked at his watch. "Gentlemen if you don't mind, I have a private tutorial before my next lecture."

Jim nodded. "Sure, but you know the ritual, don't leave town and no doubt we will see you again."

"Thank you, gentlemen."

Derek and Jim walked towards the door. Jim reached for the door handle and stopped and turned around. "Mister Jackson, what is your specialty, I mean your area of expertise in law?"

"Commercial law."

"What do you know about patent law?"

"Jack shit! But I know there is a girl here who is lonely and needs to be shown the town and American customs."

Jim shook his head. "Please don't flatter yourself, treating women like you do is very un-American."

"Whatever Detective, to each their own!"

As Jim opened the door Jacqui was leaning against the door and was propelled forwards and nearly fell. "Oh … I was about to knock the door."

Jim nodded to her as he walked out.

Stephen reached over to shake hands, "Well, Miss …?"

"Lo, Jacqui Lo." She held his hand very lightly with the tip of her fingers.

"Your English is very good."

"Most Chinese learn English. We feel it is an investment into our future."

"Yes Miss Lo. Jacqui. So, we were going to talk about patent law?" He sat behind his desk. "Exactly how long were you listening behind the door?"

Jacqui pushed a book out of the way and sat on the edge of Stephen's desk. She then crossed her legs and swivelled around so Stephen was looking at her legs. "I heard everything, Mister, em, I heard everything, Stephen. Shall we cut to the chase, how about dinner and a tour of Manhattan?"

Stephen smiled. "Tonight all right?"

"Pick me up at seven thirty, for some strange reason I had my address and phone number written on this piece of paper." She took out a piece of paper from a small pocket of her jean skirt.

Stephen took the piece of paper and put it in his shirt pocket, "See at you at seven thirty, don't worry if I'm a few minutes late, I am a bit disorganized."

"Listen, I've always been a straight-A student, but I if I don't get top grades here it will bring shame to my family." She stroked his chin with her index finger, "I suppose it's not asking too much to help me with my grades?"

"What, do you think I'm the sort of man that would cheat?"

"No Stephen, I would never want to cheat, but I would like some help."

"Miss Lo! You have read me just right! I will be able to help you."

Jacqui walked towards the door. Stephen brought out his cell phone and opened Google. Jacqui peeped her head around the door. "By the way, Stephen, what should I wear?"

"I am tempted to say wear what you are wearing now, but a nice long dress would be nice."

Jacqui pointed to his cell phone. "And what exactly are you doing now, cancelling a date with one of you other girlfriends?"

"Certainly not, I am looking up nice restaurants for tonight."

"Oh, I'm flattered. But please don't insult me by taking me to a Chinese restaurant."

"The thought never crossed my mind!" He beckoned her to go away with his hands. "Now I'm busy, go away."

Jacqui waved her hand. "See you later."

Stephen looked at his cell phone, the Google heading read 'Emerald City Chinese Restaurant'. He ran his hand across his forehead. He spoke to himself, "Phew that was a close one, nearly blew it before it started."

CHAPTER 24

Stephen Dines with Jacqui

Stephen tooted the car horn outside Jacqui's apartment. Jacqui opened her first-floor window and looked out. Stephen rolled down his window and waved at her. Jacqui squinted to see who it was. Stephen got out of the car and waved at her. Jacqui shouted, "Oh, it's you. I thought … I'll be down in one minute."

A short while later Jacqui came out of the building. Stephen was standing beside his car. He looked at Jacqui, "WOW!" is all he could say.

Jacqui had on a long silk dress which was a deep purple colour with a slit on one side of it to her mid-thigh area. She was wearing black high heel shoes and carried a small black bag. She had a purple flower in her jet-black hair which was parted on one side.

Jacqui went to the passenger side of the car and waited. Stephen had got into the car and had re-started the car when he noticed that Jacqui was still waiting at the car door.

"Oh!" he exclaimed. He jumped out of the car and ran to the passenger door. He opened the door for Jacqui to get in. When she was in the passenger seat he ran to the other side and got into the car. "I thought women wanted equality," he teased.

Jacqui crossed her legs which exposed her very shapely leg. She then elegantly lifted the parted skirt and brought it across so that her bare leg was hidden. "Well you see sir, women want their equality, but that doesn't mean sameness as men! Where I come from men don't toot the horn for ladies to come out and gentlemen open the doors for the ladies!"

"Emm, I see." Stephen looked a bit sheepish.

There were a few moments of silence. "Where exactly are we going, Stephen?"

Stephen looked at her clothes and again sounded hesitant. "I tried to book a couple of places and had no luck so I thought a nice pizza place would be cheerful and fairly quick."

Jacqui turned to him, "Fairly quick? Do you have another appointment tonight?"

"No, I just thought that …"

Jacqui thought for a couple of seconds, "Oh yes, of course you thought that you and I would go together and …"

"Yes Jacqui, that's what I'm trying to say, go together and …" He paused.

Jacqui smiled, "God, I am silly, of course. We need to chat about patent law."

Stephen looked at her before looking at the road and looked at her again. He laughed, "Of course, patent law."

Stephen indicated and stopped the car. Jacqui looked at the restaurant. "Is this where we are going? Pizza Hut?!"

Stephen looked at her, "If you don't like pizza there is a nice Italian restaurant down the road."

Jacqui looked at the restaurant again, "No I love pizzas."

"That's good." Stephen seemed relieved and got out of the car and closed his door.

Stephen started to walk towards Pizza Hut. Jacqui waited in the car. Stephen looked back and saw her sitting. He ran to the passenger door and opened it for her. "I'm sorry, I'm not used to this."

"Used to what, Stephen?"

"Just the formality."

Jacqui followed him to the restaurant. They waited to be seated. Stephen addressed the waiter at the door, "Table for two, booked for Stephen Jackson."

"Certainly sir, please follow me." They followed him. Heads turned around as the customers saw Jacqui.

The waiter stopped. "Is this table okay?"

"Yes, this will do," said Stephen.

"Please sit down, here are two menus. Someone will be along to take your drink orders."

Jacqui asked Stephen, "Do you eat here regularly?"

"Only when I'm in a rush."

"And are you in a rush tonight?"

Stephen became very fidgety. "Not exactly."

"So, does that mean you are in a bit of a rush?'

"Well not exactly, Jacqui."

"For someone who is trained in law, your answers are very vague."

Stephen sat upright. "Look Jacqui, you and I both know why we are here, don't we?"

"Tell me, Stephen, why is that?"

"Come on, Jacqui, you told me you overheard the conversation with the cops earlier today. Did you think we were getting together for a lasting romantic relationship, or for mutual gain?"

"I see the picture. So, you thought you would give me food, show me around New York, give me some tutorial about law, and in return you would get some pussy?"

"Well yes! Minus the tutorial."

The waitress came to the table. "Good evening, my name is Phyllis, I will be looking after you tonight. May I first ask what you would like to drink?"

Stephen seemed relieved. "Yes I will have a large coke."

Jacqui looked at the waiter and smiled, "I will not be staying long enough for a drink, so no thanks."

The waitress looked at Stephen and looked at Jacqui. "Oh right … sure. I'll be right back with your coke, sir."

The waitress turned around and walked towards the bar but could not hold back the smile.

Stephen looked at Jacqui. "I don't understand. Is it the restaurant you don't like?"

Jacqui was very calm. "Stephen, I was thinking if my father and mother could see their little girl, who they have worked so hard for, sitting here with a man who has no respect for her."

Stephen looked around at the next table and leaned forward and lowered his voice, "Look Jacqui, I am really sorry. We can go to a different restaurant."

Jacqui leaned forward. "Stephen you are dressed in the same clothes that you were wearing all day, you are probably carrying with you all of today's sweat and you have brought me out to a fast food joint and then want to get me into bed after."

"No, I mean …"

The waitress brought the coke and said with a smirk, "Will we be ordering tonight?"

Stephen looked at her. "Young lady there is no need for sarcasm, now please leave us."

Phyllis nodded, "Certainly sir." She walked away, again smiling.

Stephen seemed to be struggling to find his words. "What I am trying to say is that … By the way you look stunning."

Jacqui got up and leaned forward and said quietly, "Mister Jackson, you have no class. You have no respect for women, but that is not the main reason I am leaving. It's because you have no respect for yourself as a human being. I am sorry I wasted your time. Enjoy your pizza."

She walked a few paces and came back. She looked around the room and she said quietly again, "You know when my parents took me to the most expensive restaurants in Beijing, we went past a couple of pizza huts, I always wondered what they look like from the inside." She looked around, "I am taking a good look, because I will never be going inside another one again."

She turned around and walked out. A lot of the customers stopped talking and stared at her as she went past them.

Stephen sat there and again all he said was, "Wow! That is one classy broad!"

The waitress came back, "Will you be ordering, sir?"

"Oh yes, I am starving."

CHAPTER 25

Never Know Who You Meet in Red Light District

Geno was standing on the pavement and looking up and down the street, observing passers-by. He then focused on a girl with a mini skirt, barely below her crotch level. She had black fishnet stockings and as her beige shiny coat was pushed back over her shoulders it revealed her bright yellow sleeveless top. She wore boots that extended above her knees. As she lifted her right leg to pull up her boots, he got a glimpse of her white panties. He walked towards her. She became aware of him and nervously looked over her shoulders up and down the street. She then looked at a man standing at the corner of the street. He had tweed brown trousers and matching jacket and a white shirt. He had a matching tweed hat on. He looked back at her for a couple of seconds and then nodded. She relaxed slightly.

Geno stopped very close to her. "You must be cold, young lady."

"Young lady? I haven't been called that since my daddy … Anyways, you are a cop, aren't you?"

"Is it that obvious?" Geno raised his eyebrows.

"You stick out like a sore thumb, mister. Is this a bust? If so just get on with it."

"No don't worry, I am just trying to get justice for a call girl that was killed few weeks ago. Did you know Charlene Mills?" He showed her a picture.

The girl looked nervously at the man in the corner who was standing behind where Geno was.

Without turning around Geno asked, "I suppose your man in the tweed suit in the corner has noticed me as well."

"Yes, my man, as you call him, will get very anxious if I talk too long."

"I won't keep you long."

The girl looked very anxious.

Geno asked in a very soft tone, "What is your name, honey?"

"Honey?" She smiled. "You certainly have a way with words." She paused, "You can call me Lily."

"Well, Lily, or whoever you really are. I have been up and down this street and no-one seems to know anyone or anything. Let me put it to you this way. If let's say, something was to happen to you, would you like the world to pass on by, or would you like someone like me to care and try to get some justice?"

Lily thought for a second. She smiled, "You certainly do have a way with words. Just give me a minute."

She walked to the man in the tweed suit and hat. She said something to him and he looked at Geno. He said something back and Lily walked back to Geno.

"He says you have five minutes and then I have to get to work."

"That is generous of him," Geno said sarcastically.

"No, he thinks it will give his workers a feeling of security with you enquiring. So, it is just selfish."

"Well, Lily. Our time is short. What do you know about Charlene?" He showed her the picture again.

Lily looked at the picture for a few seconds. "I can't say I knew her personally, I would have seen her occasionally, and had the usual chat."

"The usual chat?" Geno asked inquisitively.

Lily nodded. "Yes about the weather and sore body parts."

"Body parts, hmm. Maybe I shouldn't ask." Geno was rubbing his chin.

Lily had a twinkle in her eye. "Did you not hear about the call girls standing outside a hotel door?"

Geno had a dubious look on his face.

"The first prostitute asked the second one, 'How is business?', the second one said, 'If I've been up those stairs once, I've been up there a hundred times.'

The first one replied, 'Poor you, your feet must be aching!'"

Geno burst out laughing. Some people passing by stopped and watched him and then continued. It took him a while to stop laughing. The man in the tweed suit raised his head as if to take a better look at what was going on between Geno and Lily. He lifted his hat, scratched his head and looked away, putting his hat back on.

"That is very funny," said Geno, still sniggering. "So; time is running out, tell me about Charlene."

"Well we were all shocked. You know this sort of thing happens, but when it happens in your patch, it brings it home. I don't know anything definite. There is just a rumour."

"A rumour?" Geno raised his eyebrows again.

"I don't feel comfortable saying this." She looked at the man in the tweed suit, the relaxed look on her face was replaced by a look of anxiety again.

Geno turned around and saw the man getting close to them.

"Come on, Lily, you have got to give me something to go on!"

Lily looked at the man coming towards them and looked at Geno. "You've been very nice, not many people, especially cops, talk to me as if I am a human being. The rumour is there is a cop frequenting this area."

The man arrived and held Lily by the elbow. "Come on now, we have work to do."

Geno raised his hands. "Just a minute, sir, I just want to ask a couple of more questions."

Lily started to walk away. "There is no need, I really have nothing else to add. I must go!"

With that they both walked away, and Geno was left standing there, feeling very frustrated.

Geno stood there for a minute. He then shrugged his shoulders and started to walk away. He stopped for a second. He looked at a doorway in front of him.

He saw Jim walking out of the doorway. A few seconds later a young girl stepped out onto the doorway. She reached over and kissed him on his cheek.

He stroked her on the cheek and said goodbye. She stood there for a few seconds watching him and smiling before she went in.

Jim had walked a few steps when he suddenly saw Geno who seemed to be frozen in the spot.

"Oh, Geno. What in the heavens are you doing here?"

"I could ask you the same question, Jim. Not sure what I just saw here."

"Geno, it's complicated, best not to ask. Just trust me, Geno."

"O-kay Jim."

"Well?" asked Jim.

"Well what?" Geno looked a little dazed.

"You didn't tell me what you are doing here."

"Oh, just asking a few questions from call girls in the area to see if they know anything about Charlene."

"Well?"

"Well, what?"

"Well," said Jim a bit impatiently, "Did you get any useful info?"

"Just one girl who said …" He paused. "Actually, nothing of any use."

"Okay Geno. I'll see you tomorrow. I have to pick up Derek to follow up a lead. See you tomorrow."

"Yes," said Geno quietly. "See you tomorrow."

CHAPTER 26

Dining with the Enemy?

Amanda arrived at the restaurant and walked in. She stood at the top of the few steps that led onto the main serving room. She scanned the room quickly to see if she could see Jim.

A waitress was standing behind a menu stand and put up her hand to get Amanda's attention. "Excuse me, ma'am, do you have a reservation?"

Amanda was still looking around the room. "Yes I have, we have a reservation for two under the name of Mister Sterne, I don't expect he will be here …" She suddenly stopped. "That's okay, I see him there." She noticed Jim sitting at a table for two. He was looking at his watch and looking towards the entrance but did not seem to notice her there.

"That's fine, ma'am, go on ahead."

Amanda walked down the stairs and nearly tripped on the last one. She quickly composed herself but still looked rather nervous. She took a couple of deep breaths and moved forward.

As she walked to the table Jim stood up, "Hi Jim, do you always sit in a corner?"

"Occupational hazard. Like to see everyone. Don't like anyone creeping up behind me."

Jim then eyed Amanda up and down and let out a low whistle. "You look stunning."

Amanda was wearing a red dress which stopped four inches above her knees. It was tapered, showing off her narrow waist. It was low cut at the neck, just enough to show some of her cleavage. She had bare legs with a black pair of high heels which brought her to a height of just over six feet, making her legs look even taller.

"Thanks Jim, and you can stop staring at my breasts!"

"Oops, sorry, I didn't realise I was staring."

As Amanda sat down the skirt rolled up to reveal the upper part of her legs.

Jim sat down and leaned towards her and whispered, "I suppose staring at your legs is out of the question."

Amanda blushed slightly and smiled, "Shoosh, now you're embarrassing me."

Jim kissed her lightly on her cheek. "And you love it. Thanks for meeting up, I couldn't wait until the case is finished. I wanted to see you."

Amanda didn't answer. She picked up the menu. "Do you bring all you girlfriends here?"

"Oh no! On Monday I went to the disco with Emily, on Tuesday I took Deborah to a ball game—"

Amanda butted in. She looked at her watch. "Don't take too long, I have to meet Bill in two hours."

"Very good. Touché," Jim laughed.

Amanda pointed to the menu. "What is good here?"

"You know me. I am a steak man. They have nice fish, very fresh. The shrimps are nice for starters."

"Oh no," exclaimed Amanda. "Too much cholesterol in shrimps. In my line of work, I have to watch my figure. I have to look good on stage."

"Is that what the court is to you?"

"No, it's not just that, but there is an element of that. The judge and jury are very much affected by the delivery of the presentation as well as the contents."

"Well I give you ten out of ten."

Amanda laughed, "Yes darling but you are biased."

"That I am."

A waiter approached the table. "Are you ready to order?"

"Could we have a couple of more minutes, Amanda has just arrived," Jim said.

"No that's okay, I know what I want, have you made your mind up, Jim?"

"Yes, I'll have the shrimps for starters and a rib eye steak, well done please, with the pepper sauce."

"And I'll have the melon for starters and the sole with lemon, I take it it's fresh."

"Yes madam. The fish is delivered here fresh every day. Will there be any side orders?"

Amanda looked at Jim. "Would you like to share a portion of mixed vegetables?"

"Yes that would be very good."

Amanda looked at the waiter. "A portion of mixed vegetables please."

"Yes madam." The waiter turned to Jim. "What would you like to drink?"

Jim looked at Amanda. "Can you drink some wine or are you going to be working late?"

Amanda looked straight into his eyes. "Whatever I am doing late into the night tonight does not involve my paperwork. I would like some wine to relax me."

Jim looked at Amanda suspiciously. He looked like he was about to ask her what she meant but then decided not to.

Amanda continued, "Is white wine okay with you?"

Jim seemed to be tongue tied. He turned his hand palm up to indicate it was okay.

Amanda turned to the waiter. "A bottle of your best white wine please."

As the waiter left, she turned to Jim. "And it's my turn to pay this time."

"Oh no, you don't need to do that."

Amanda was adamant, "I don't need to, I want to."

"Well, if you insist."

Jim finally plucked up his courage, "What exactly did you mean about tonight?"

"Patience is a virtue," Amanda said dismissively. Jim decided not to pursue this any further.

In any case Amanda changed the subject, "When did we last eat out?"

"Just after the Lorenzo case. We had several cancellations." Jim held up one hand. "Mainly on my account."

"Saving the world, are we?"

"That's me."

"You try and catch them, and I try and release them. I wonder would a computer match us up as an ideal couple?"

Jim laughed, "Somehow I don't think it would." He paused for a second. "Do you think we are a good couple?"

Amanda returned the question, "Do you think we are good together?"

Jim held her hand. "I think we are a match made in heaven."

Amanda stroked his hand and smiled with affection. "That is a beautiful thing to say."

Jim held Amanda's hand with both hands. "I think what we have is very special. In fact …"

The waiter arrived with the wine. He showed the wine's label to Jim and asked, "Would you like to taste it first, sir?"

"No, no," Jim said very impatiently. "Just pour it please."

The waiter uncorked the bottle and poured the wine slowly into two glasses, oblivious to the impatient body language of Jim and the fact that he had disturbed a dramatic moment. Jim started to tap the table with one finger and was visibly irritated, desperate not to lose the moment and the mood that was there.

Just then another waitress approached the waiter at their table. She spoke to him in a quiet voice, pointing at a young couple a few tables away. "You see that guy there, he is going to propose to his girlfriend tonight here. He wants this ring to be placed in her ice cream."

"No problem, I will sort it out." With that they both left Jim and Amanda's table.

Jim looked towards the couple the waiters were talking about. "That is a lot of fuss, isn't it? I would have thought the girl would prefer a quiet moment on their own when he could pop the question."

"Well Jim, maybe you don't know women that well. Some women like to be asked in a very dramatic way."

"Is that the way you would like to be asked?"

"Maybe," she said as she put her hand to the back of her head and straightened her hair.

"So, where were we?" Jim said suddenly, "Yes we were talking about us. Before we go on, let's have a toast to us." He raised his glass.

"I'll drink to that." Amanda raised her glass. She had just taken a sip of her wine when a waiter going past knocked her elbow and some of wine spilt on her lap.

"I am sorry, madam." He looked very embarrassed.

Jim looked very annoyed, but Amanda quickly replied. "Don't worry, accidents happen." She looked at Jim and smiled. "Nothing is going to annoy me tonight."

Jim smiled back.

Amanda wiped her dress with her napkin. She addressed the waiter, "Carry on before you attract any more attention. Don't worry about it."

The waiter looked somewhat relieved. "I can speak to the manager. I am sure he won't charge you."

Amanda was adamant, "No forget about it, these things happen."

The waiter walked away.

Amanda continued wiping her dress with a napkin, "Just give me a few minutes, I'll go to the ladies and try and clean it with some water."

"Are you sure you don't want me to speak to the manager?"

"No darling, tonight is our night, I don't want any hassle."

"I am sure you don't need my help in cleaning up."

Amanda reached over and kissed him gently on his lips. "You can help me undress when we get to my place."

Jim raised his eyebrows in surprise and became suddenly speechless. Amanda got up and walked away and Jim was left at the table with an ear-to-ear smile, watching her every step until she went around the corner.

Amanda walked into the ladies and turned on the cold-water tap. She cupped her hand and poured some water liberally over the area at the bottom of her dress that had the spillage on it. She did this several times. She suddenly became aware that there was a girl standing at the sink beside her.

The girl was looking at Amanda with amusement. "Wine is it?" she asked Amanda.

Amanda smiled. "Yes, a waiter bumped into me when I had a glass in my hand."

"That is white wine I presume?"

"Thankfully yes," replied Amanda.

"You are lucky, red wine would be more disastrous, even on a red dress."

Amanda looked at the girl and had to take a second look. "You are the girl sitting at the table with the young guy who–" she stopped suddenly.

The girl laughed. "Don't worry, I know he is going to propose to me tonight. He is very loving, not very good with secrets. I had lost one of my rings four weeks ago and he mysteriously found it in his car. I realized he used it to measure my ring size. He thinks I have no idea about his plans, and I will let him think that way. I just feel so lucky to have such a wonderful person. I thought he would never get around to asking me to marry him."

Amanda looked inquisitive. "Do you mind if I ask you, was it a big decision to marry him?"

The girl thought for a second. "Not really. It's like the first time I decided to go to bed with him. I just knew it was the right time and the right guy."

Amanda smiled. "Well just girl to girl, I am at that stage with my man."

"What, are you getting married?"

"No, just at the other stage you were talking about."

The girl smiled. "Oh I see, tonight is the night, is it?"

"Tonight is the night!"

The girl laughed out loud. "I remember our first night. It all ended so quickly. But that was only the first time, by the end of the night, or should I say morning, well that was a different story."

Amanda went to the hand dryer. "I had better dry this or it will look like I wet myself."

The girl laughed again. "Well good luck tonight."

"Thanks."

The girl left as Amanda turned on the hand dryer and held her skirt under the blast of hot air.

Amanda walked back to the table and despite the ordeal she was very cheerful and was singing under her breath, "Love is all you need; love is all you need."

She sat at the table and continued to wipe her dress with her napkin.

"You are in a good mood," said Jim. He sounded very chirpy too.

"Yes I am. Tell me something nice."

"Well you are gorgeous, and I can't keep my eyes off you tonight."

"That's nice, tell me more."

"Well as I was telling Cindy the other day, I have never felt like this about anybody. I don't ever remember feeling–"

"Sorry Jim, who's Cindy?"

Jim paused for a second. "Well it's not important now, what I was going to say is the I have never–"

"Why do I get the impression you are being cagey?"

Jim sounded a little agitated. "I don't think that's very important now. I want to discuss something very important with you; we have all night to talk about other matters."

Amanda's voice could not hide her irritation. "Jim who is Cindy? It sounds like you are trying to hide something."

"It's a girl I see now and then. Well actually Cindy is not her real name."

Amanda interrupted, "Why does she have an alias, is she an FBI spy?"

"Well no," he hesitated, "actually she's a ..." He fidgeted on his chair uncomfortably.

Amanda looked very cross. "Go on Jim, the suspense is killing me."

"Well … she is a prostitute."

"Sorry what did you say?" Amanda looked white as a ghost all of a sudden.

"Well don't get worked up, it's not what it sounds like."

"Yes, go ahead and explain why you see a prostitute occasionally."

Jim sounded irritated. "Well I've known her for a long time."

"Oh, that's very touching. When was the last time you saw her?"

"Last night, but–"

Amanda interrupted again, "Was this at the precinct?"

"No, at her place, but …"

Amanda voice was getting louder. "Please answer me this, Jim, during the past week that we have been talking about our future, you visited a prostitute? And you have been telling her things that you have not told me?" The couple at the next table turned around and looked at Amanda and then at Jim, as if waiting for his answer.

"Well yes, but …" He hesitated.

"Go ahead, explain to me. I am dying to hear this. In fact, how often do you see her?"

"Listen darling, this is being taken out of context. I see her generally weekly but I feel as if you are questioning me in a court of law."

Amanda's voice was very loud now. "Stop calling me darling! You know when Stephen cheated on me, I thought he was just a jerk and I was able to put it behind me. But now you as well. And I am dying to know why you are seeing a prostitute once a week and discussing your private affairs with her, our affairs to be precise!"

Jim looked around the room. The waitress was looking at him. She had a frown on her face and almost seemed to be shaking her head, slightly disapprovingly. He looked around the room and everyone had stopped talking and were looking at them.

He whispered, "Darl… Amanda, can you please keep your voice down and I can explain everything!"

Amanda pushed her chair back and in the process her chair fell onto the ground. The waiter arrived with the starters and stood beside Amanda, not knowing what to do.

Amanda threw her napkin at Jim. "How could you?" Tears began to our down her face "This is déjà vu. I can't believe this is happening to me again. How could you?"

"But Amanda let me explain."

"There is nothing to explain, Jim. I will see you in court tomorrow, and hopefully that will be the last time I ever see you again. Don't bother getting up." With that Amanda turned around and walked out of the restaurant.

After she walked out, all the eyes of the customers that had followed her out turned to Jim.

The waiter asked hesitantly, "Will you be eating, sir?"

"No, I just lost my appetite. Just get me the bill will you."

As the waiter went to get the bill Jim looked over his shoulder. The couple sitting beside them were quite elderly. The lady looked at him and shook her head, tutting quite loudly. Jim looked away. He looked at the table on the other side and the lady leaned over and whispered something to the man she was eating with. Jim pulled at his collar, giving the impression that he was hot and sweaty.

Jim took his wallet out and walked towards the cashier near the door. The cashier looked at him with a sheepish smile. She said, "The manager has instructed me to just charge you for the wine and not the rest of the food, as the waiter spilled wine on your friend's dress."

Jim nodded and took out his credit card. He took his credit card back and put it in his wallet. He took out a fifty-dollar bill and dropped it on the checkout counter and walked out.

CHAPTER 27

Jake Meets Big Al in Prison

Jake left his cell and walked to the large dining hall. He stood in the queue for his lunchtime meal. He noticed one of the inmates nudging another and pointing at him and whispering something in the inmate's ear. He looked away impassively.

He picked up a plastic plate and held it out for his ration of food. The person behind the counter had a pristine white top and brilliant white trousers with a tall chef hat. His name badge said 'James'. He would have looked good in any top-class restaurant. He lifted his large ladle and filled it with a mixture of spaghetti and meat sauce and ungracefully slapped it on to Jake's plate. Jake paused for a second, half expecting some more. The server was looking at the next inmate in the queue and beckoned him forward. Jake moved on.

Another person who was equally well dressed took a piece of brown bread that seemed to be cut up very crudely, as if it had been divided piecemeal by hand, and put it on Jake's plate. He quickly pointed Jake to move forward and said with a wry smile, "If you would like to take a seat sir, your steak and mange tout will be served to you soon."

It took Jake a second to register that the person was being sarcastic. He heard the sniggering of the inmates who were queued behind him. He noticed that he was holding up the queue. He grabbed a transparent plastic glass with water in it, picked up a plastic knife and fork, and walked towards the tables.

He stood for a few moments, looking around the room trying to decide where to sit. He was aware that a lot of the inmates were watching him, he scanned the room as quickly as he could. There were fifty or so tables, with benches on each side, each bench large enough to cater for three or four people.

He noticed a number of single empty seats on various tables and tried not to stare at those seated at the tables whilst trying to decide where to sit beside. He suddenly noticed a table situated in the far side of the room and right down the centre of the row of tables was completely empty. Elated, but somewhat surprised, he walked towards the empty table. He put his plate right in the middle of the table on one side and sat down.

As he sat down, he couldn't help noticing a slight flurry of activity at the other tables. There seemed to be a lot of nudging and smirking and chuckling as the heads of the inmates at one table turned one by one to look at him, the bobbing of their heads so closely timed that it was akin to a synchronized swimming team. The sniggers became louder and he noticed those sat at other tables turning to look at him. He became a little uneasy and began to look quite uncomfortable as he kept looking around him to try and figure out what the amusement was about. He finally decided to ignore the goings on and started eating his meal. He placed the first bolus of food in his mouth and after chewing on it a couple of times pushed his lips together and made a face which seemed to indicate his approval of the food. He was just about to place a second spoonful into his mouth when he became aware of a large shadow appearing on the table. As he looked around, he saw someone standing behind him. He had to take a second look. He was looking at the man's mid-rift and had to look up and up to see his face. The man standing behind him was about six foot four and his chest size was fifty plus. His head was shaven, revealing three scars on his scalp. One on the left side of his forehead which extended from top to bottom, one on the right side of his forehead, similarly top to bottom, and a diagonal across his forehead which tangentially joined the two, almost forming the letter N. For good measure, he also had one scar under his left eye, one above his left eyebrow and one above his right eyebrow. He had a vest on which showed his muscular upper body. The veins on his upper arms were very prominent and the outline of his biceps and pectoral muscles suggested many hours in the gym.

The man just grunted. Jake tried to speak but found out that his throat was suddenly very dry. He swallowed hard before he could speak. "Good afternoon," Jake said, trying to smile, "would you like to join me?" Jake didn't sound very convincing.

There was laughter from the next table followed by more nudging with elbows and further sniggers.

The man grunted again. Jake seemed frozen. A deep voice said, "You are sitting in my seat!" His voice was loud enough to stop most small conversations that were going on the tables nearby. In a matter of seconds all conversations at all the other fifty or so tables stopped, and all eyes were turned towards Jake's table.

Jake was now looking visibly nervous. "I am sorry I have never been in prison before. I didn't realise you can book tables." With that he slid to the edge of the bench and moved his plate there. The man grunted and sat down beside him.

Jake looked around the room nervously and decided the best thing to do was to eat so he grabbed his fork. He was about to put a spoonful of spaghetti and sauce in his mouth when someone knocked into his elbow, causing his food to fall onto his lap. Jake shouted out, "Hey!" However, as he looked up he shut up quickly.

"Holy shit," Jake said before he realised he had said out loud.

The man standing beside him was about six foot eight and made the previous guy look average size. His physique was even leaner and a thin white T-shirt showed the outline of his upper body muscles. He too had a shaven head with a couple of scars to give an indication of his past. He too grunted.

The first man who was seated behind him talked, "You are in Atlas' seat."

Jake decided not to make any more wise comments. "Sorry," he said as he got up, picked up his plate and walked across and sat on the bench across the table. He heard another burst of laughter and further sniggers. He looked around again and could see the amused faces around the room.

The second man called Atlas spoke this time, "You are in big Al's seat."

Jake looked at the first guy and then at Atlas. "I dread to think how big Big Al is," he said nervously and laughed quietly but stopped quickly as the men looked at him with no emotions.

He was searching for the right words to come out but seemed unable to say anything and thought the better of any further wisecracks. As Jake sat there trying to decide his next course of action, he became aware of someone who had just brushed against his left shoulder. He slowly and apprehensively turned to his left, looking towards the ceiling. He had to gradually lower his gaze. He kept looking downwards until he finally saw a face of a man standing next to him and he was barely above Jake's shoulder height whilst he was seated. He breathed a sigh of relief.

"Are you Big Al by any chance?"

The short man nodded and just stood there. Even though he was no more than five foot he seemed to have a certain presence about him. Jake knew not to hang around any further. "Sorry I didn't realise this is your seat." He picked up his plate and got up. The sniggers around the room turned to laughter which got louder as he stood up apologetically.

Big Al put his own plate down. Jake noticeably sniffed the air and looked at Big Al's plate with two pieces of chicken, and a mixed salad with some cauliflower cheese. "Is that garlic I smell, and is that chicken Kiev?"

Big Al sat down without looking at Jake. Atlas looked at Jake and motioned with his head for him to go.

Jake walked towards another table and sat down at an empty place. The level of noise in the room increased all of a sudden as everyone started to have conversations again.

There was a young black man seated beside Jake. He reached out his hand. "Hi my name in Ben."

Jake just nodded and put his head down, trying his best to ignore the guy.

Ben pointed to Jake's plate. "I know this is a classical line, but are you going to eat your bread?"

Jake pushed his plate across towards Ben. "Here you go, I've lost my appetite."

Ben talked with the enthusiasm of someone who could be chatting to a friend at a party. "I am in for armed robbery, but I was just driving my friends to buy some liquor, I had no idea they was going to rob the place, let alone kill someone." Ben paused, "Well what are you in for?"

Jake looked at Ben. "I know this is a classical line too, but I haven't done anything."

"They all say that at first, but you'll come around."

"Well I haven't had my trial yet, so technically I am innocent until proven otherwise."

Ben raised his eyebrows. "Wow, you must be dangerous if they have put you in here before your trial."

"Look Ben, can we talk about something else?"

"Sure, what do you want to talk about? Do you think the Giants will make the play offs?"

Jake pointed to the table he had just come from. "Who is Big Al? Is he the gofer for Atlas or the other guy?"

Ben laughed out loud. He got a couple of glaring stares from others at the table. He leaned toward Jake and whispered. "Atlas and Nigel are Big Al's bodyguards. Don't be fooled by his size. Big Al has been in here for about fifteen years. He has got to the top of the chain here by fighting his way up. He is tough as nails. You see the scar on Nigel's head? Big Al cut a big N on his head to show him who is boss. Since then Nigel and Atlas have guarded Big Al. Don't mess with him whatever you do."

"I have no intention of messing with anyone. I hope to have my trial soon and will no doubt walk out a free man."

"Yeah, yeah. I have heard that before. I have been in for five years. I hope to be out next year. My attorney thinks I should be out by next fall. I have a wife and a seven-year-old boy." He reached into the top pocket of his inmate uniform. "Here look, his name is Benjamin Junior, after me of course. He will be eight soon." He pointed to the girl in the picture beside the boy. "This is Letitia, isn't she gorgeous?"

Jake tried to look interested. "Yes, very pretty."

Ben put the picture back in his pocket. "I just needs to keep my nose clean and I will be out soon." He pointed to Jake's plate, "Do you mind if I eats your spaghetti as well?"

Jake pushed his plate toward Ben. "Be my guest."

CHAPTER 28

First Day in Court

Jake was brought into the court handcuffed. His handcuffs were taken off and he was shown to his seat beside Amanda and Lucy. Lucy had not seen him and turned around. She said, "Wow!"

Jake had a grey suit on with a brilliant white shirt and a blue tie. He was clean shaven, and his hair had been trimmed and was combed back very neatly.

"You clean up well," said Lucy.

"Thank you," smiled Jake, "you do tend to say the first thing that comes to your mind, don't you?"

Lucy looked a bit embarrassed. "That was meant to be a compliment."

"Indeed Lucy, that's the way I took it."

Jake shook hands with Amanda and they both said good morning.

"Please be upstanding for the honourable Judge John Temple."

All in the court stood up. Jake, however, seemed to be in a daze, staring straight ahead and in deep thought. The judge walked in and out of the corner of his eye saw Jake. Lucy nudged Jake who suddenly stood up.

The judge sat down.

"Please be seated."

The judge poured himself a glass of water and read from a sheet of paper. "This is the case of state versus John Chapman. The charges are of two counts of first-degree murder. That of Miss Sarah Miller and Miss Charlene Mills. Mister Chapman, please state your plea in reference to the murder of Miss Sarah Miller."

Jake started to speak, "Your honour—"

The judge interrupted Jake, "Please be standing when you address the court."

Jake stood up. "Sorry your honour … not guilty."

"And what is your plea with reference to the murder of Miss Charlene Mills?"

"Not guilty, your honour."

The judge wrote on a piece of paper. "Please let it be known the pleas are not guilty to both charges. Please be seated, Mister Chapman."

He put down his pen. He looked at the District Attorney table. "Would the district attorney present the case for the prosecution."

Andy Gomez sat for a few seconds, perhaps getting his thoughts together.

He slowly walked to the front of the court room. He walked across the length of the judge's table which was just above his head height. He stopped and turned around. "Your honour, ladies and gentlemen of the jury. The prosecution is going to prove to you beyond a shadow of a doubt that the man seated in that seat" (he pointed to Jake from across the room) "Mister John Chapman, known as Jake Chapman, killed Miss Sarah Mills in cold blood and buried her and left her to rot in a disused cement yard." Andy walked towards the jury and leaned on the armrest across the front of the jury seating area. "He also killed Miss Charlene Mills in cold blood. Why did he kill poor Charlene? Perhaps because he was denied his sexual gratification." He lowered his tone and spoke much more gently, "Why did he kill Sarah Mills, a young girl who was a law student and had her future ahead of her? Perhaps because his wife found out he was having an affair with Sarah. His wife mysteriously disappeared at the same time." He walked towards the judge and stopped and turned around. "But ladies and gentlemen of the jury, we are not here to understand how the twisted mind of a murderer works, or the reasons why someone would take another human's life and stifle out her light. No, ladies and gentlemen, we are here for one thing and one thing only, to decide whether," he suddenly raised his voice and pointed to Jake, "That man there murdered these two young girls in cold blood."

He walked to his table. "Ladies and gentlemen, during the course of the next few days, you will see how Mister Chapman not only killed young Charlene Mills, but also was cocky enough to brag about it in a bar a few hours later.

Furthermore, we will also be able to show that he killed Sarah Mills, whilst probably trying to force himself on her. We will also be able to show that samples of his pubic hair were under the nails of Sarah Mills. That will be all, your honour!" There was a murmur amongst the jury members with a few of them whispering to each other.

Lucy looked at Amanda. Amanda looked very pale and seemed to be in shock.

Judge Temple looked at Amanda. "Would the defense attorneys like to present their case."

Amanda whispered something in Lucy's ear. Lucy shrugged her shoulders.

Amanda looked up. "Your honour, may I approach your bench."

"Please do, Miss Jackson."

Amanda walked towards the judge who held his hand over his microphone.

Amanda's tone showed some anger. "Your honour, there is no mention of any pubic hair in the disclosure documents, this is highly irregular and totally unacceptable. I request a short recess to discuss this in private."

"Okay I grant you that."

He looked at Andy and Peter. "I have never had a recess at this early stage of the proceedings, I hope this is not a bad omen of things to come. Will the prosecution and defense attorneys please meet me in my chamber. The court will take a fifteen-minute recess." He hammered his gavel and walked out.

Amanda and Lucy arrived outside the judge's chamber. Amanda walked up to Andy. "What the heck is going on? This is very back-handed and I would say immoral! I don't know where to start!"

The judge opened the door of his room and asked them to come in. Amanda, Lucy, Andy, and Peter walked in. The judge took off his robe.

Amanda was like a dog with a bone. "Your honour, the disclosure documents did not mention any genetic material. I cannot allow this evidence to be presented."

Judge Temple seemed very calm. "Everyone please sit down."

They all did. "Now Miss Jackson, as no doubt you have read the documentation from the prosecution, they have reserved the right to present late evidence on the count of new genetic material. Now; I met with the prosecution this morning and I can assure you that the evidence was only finalized this morning. So, I allowed this to be presented. You were given notification of this early in the morning."

"Your honour, the office contacted me early and asked me to phone them, but as yet I have not had a chance."

"Well your office was contacted in the early hours, and under the circumstances I will have to allow the evidence. I can assure you that there is no intent from the prosecution for obfuscation of the facts or evidence. It would be a travesty to the course of justice to allow this vital evidence not to be presented."

Amanda seemed very irate and was finding it difficult to elucidate her sentences properly. "But your honour!"

Judge Temple raised his hand. "Miss Jackson, in the interest of justice I have no choice but to allow the evidence to be presented. I suggest you gather your thoughts and decide how you are going to proceed with this case. But I have to allow this evidence."

Amanda blew out a big puff. "In that case, your honour, I will need about a week to look at the evidence."

The judge thought for a few seconds. "I have never come across this scenario before. This is very irregular. That is fine, we will go back to the courtroom, but I will allow you two weeks."

*

They were all gathered in the courtroom.

The judge asked everyone to become silent. "In view of evidence that has only been disclosed by the prosecution this morning, the court will have a recess of two weeks to allow the defense attorneys to examine the evidence. The court will resume next Monday week at ten a.m."

Most had left the courtroom. Lucy was sitting down. Amanda was chatting to two men who then left, leaving only Amanda and Lucy in the courtroom.

Lucy looked stunned. "Was that Mister Huston?"

Amanda nodded. "Yes, the senior lawyers in legal aid more often than not stay silent during cases and let you get on with it, unless you ask them for help. I asked them to look at the forensic evidence and get one of the senior pathologists or geneticists to scrutinize the evidence."

Amanda sat down and looked at Lucy, her shoulders were slumped. "You look very dejected."

Lucy let out a sigh. "I feel totally deflated. I feel like such a fool."

Amanda sat back and waited.

After a few seconds Lucy continued, "I really believed him. Shows you how gullible I am. I actually thought he was innocent, and now we have his genetic samples on Sarah from a year ago."

Amanda put her hand on Lucy's shoulder. "Lucy, don't worry about it. As I always say, the truth is a mirage, as you get closer and closer, it begins to look different! Now come on, we have to start our damage limitation process."

CHAPTER 29

Mi-chelle Ma Belle

Later that evening Will was getting dressed. He had put on his brown trousers and a cream-coloured shirt with a thin vertical brown stripe in it.

He looked downwards and said, "You are going down, down, down baby."

Michelle looked at him with surprise, "Will are you talking to your ..." she hesitated and pointed to his privates, "To your penis?!"

Will laughed briefly. "No silly, I am talking to my belly, it's time I lost it."

"Your tummy is fine, anyway it has never bothered you before."

Will didn't seem to notice her. He sat on the edge of his bed and started to polish his dark brown shoes.

"Do you have to go to this meeting?" His wife asked him.

"Yes Michelle, you know as the captain I am expected to attend these regional meetings. As boring as these meetings are, analyzing staff expenditure, other expenses, overtime comparison, allocation of other resources etcetera, etcetera, but if I don't go there and go through the motions of justifying our expenditure, our budget may be cut for next year."

"You sure are dressing up for a regional meeting."

Will didn't seem to pay any attention to her. He looked at his polished shoes from different angles. "Perfect!" he said.

He walked over to his chest of drawers and opened the top drawer. He looked through his socks, lifting the ones at the top and putting them on top of the chest of drawers.

Michelle was standing in front of the mirror and was wearing only a silk slip.

"What are you looking for, honey?"

"I don't see any brown socks," he said, almost as if talking to himself.

"Are those ones at the top not brown?"

"What, these ones?"

"Yes Will, those are brown!"

"Yes, they are, but they don't quite match the shade of the shoes."

"Oh!"

"Here we are. Perfect!" He picked up another pair of lighter brown socks and threw them on the bed.

He then walked over to the wardrobe and pulled out his tie rack. "Now let's see." He picked two ties and held them in front of his shirt alternately, looking in the wardrobe mirror. "Let me see, what do you think, honey? Will I wear this brown one, or will I go for a slight contrast and wear this maroon one?"

"Either is good."

"Hmm, I will go for the maroon one."

Will put the brown tie back on the tie rack and walked to the bed and put the maroon tie on with a very neat knot which he tightened. Michelle walked towards the mirror and stood in front of it with her side towards the mirror. She held her hand on her tummy, looking at the mirror. "Do you think I've put on weight?"

Will looked up very briefly at her and reached for the socks and started to put them on and again absentmindedly said, "No honey you look fine."

Michelle then pulled up her slip, exposing her long fairly slim legs and her black thongs. "Do you think my legs are a bit chubby?"

Will again looked up quickly and then turned around and reached for his tie, "You look fine, honey."

He then moved to the mirror. "Excuse me, darling, I need to see what I am doing." He gently pushed her to the side with his hip so he was standing in front of the mirror and adjusting his tie again.

Michelle walked over and sat on the edge of the bed. Will was whistling to himself. He suddenly became aware of a murmur from Michelle. He turned around and noticed that her shoulders were bobbing up and down slightly. He then heard her snuffling.

"Are you crying?"

"No, I'm not," Michelle said sniffing. She then began to sob loudly.

"What is wrong, honey? Are you sick?"

"Who is she, Will?"

Will looked very surprised. "I didn't know you cared so much, honey."

"Of course I care. Now please put me out of my misery."

"Okay honey, if you really want to know."

"Yes, I do!" said Michelle between sobs.

"Well she was a law student. She also worked for an exclusive escort agency. It looks like this psychologist guy, Jake, killed her because …"

"Not her, Will. I mean who are you having an affair with?!"

"What the hell are you talking about?"

"You don't think I am that stupid, do you? You have never paid any attention to the colour of your ties, and now you are even matching up your socks. You must be going out with a young thing."

"You can't be serious, honey."

"Don't you honey me! All those late nights and overtime, and I thought you were working hard."

"Whatever are you talking about, Michelle?!"

"I am practically parading around naked in the room and you didn't even notice me."

"Well … I." Will paused. "Well I just wanted to wear matching clothes for a change."

"And what is the name of this young floosy you are getting dressed for?"

"Well if you really want to know, the name is Geno."

"Is that not a man's name?!"

"Yes, my secret is out, it is a man's name."

"What exactly are you telling me?"

"Michelle, will you get real. I am not having an affair. I was playing golf the other Sunday and Geno told me that my dress sense is appalling. So, I decided to listen to him."

"But I've been telling you that for years and you never paid attention."

"I know, honey, but somehow he got through to me."

Michelle wiped some tears from her face with the back of her hand. "So you are not having an affair?"

"Come on, what man in his right mind would go out to eat a burger when he can eat prime steak at home."

"Are you calling me a piece of meat?"

"Come on, honey–"

Michelle interrupted, "I know, maybe a different analogy would be better next time, but I appreciate the sentiment."

He sat down on the bed beside her. "If I ever decided to have an affair, first off she would have to be a sister …"

"What?!" Michelle exclaimed with a big frown on her face.

"Hear me out, girl. She would have to be a sister. She would have to be gorgeous like you." He then ran his finger slowly down her nose. "She would have to have a cute nose like yours."

"Aha!" Michelle raised her eyebrows.

"She would have to have beautiful hair like yours and she would have to tuck her hair behind her ears just the way you do."

"And which way is that? And how is that different from anyone else stroking her hair?"

"Well you just do it differently!"

"Tell me some more about this sister."

"Well she would have to be just as sexy as you."

"How sexy is that?"

"Well now you would not get a girl that sexy anywhere in New York."

"Just in New York?'

Will put his hand on his chin. "Let me think, in fact you couldn't get a girl this sexy this side of Paris, France."

"Paris is long enough away for me. So how are you going to find a gorgeous girl like that?"

Will smiled. "Right here, honey." He kissed her forehead. "I don't ever need to look anywhere else, baby."

Michelle had a tear trickling down her face. "I feel so stupid. How could I think you could cheat on me?"

Will stroked her hair. "I suppose I have been very busy. It's a conveyor belt. One case goes out, another one comes in. And all the admin and paperwork. Maybe I should be thinking of retiring soon."

"No chance, Will! You will just get in my way. You love what you do, and you are very good at it. You worked very hard to get there. But a bit of attention now and then would not hurt."

"Sure honey." He leaned over, kissed her on the forehead again and stood up.

"What time does your meeting start?"

Will looked at his watch "At eight. I have plenty of time."

Michelle slowly took off her bra and threw it on the floor. She crossed her legs. She was sitting in her thongs. She sat upright, which made her bare breasts more noticeable. "Would they mind if you are a few minutes late?"

Will smiled. "No they wouldn't. But they will be pretty pissed off when I arrive one hour late."

"And what exactly are we going to do that is going to take one hour?"

"Turn over."

"What for?"

Will put his finger on her lips. "Shut up and turn over."

Michelle rolled onto her front on the bed.

Will pulled her hair back. "Well I would start by kissing your neck for a couple of minutes." He held her hair back and kissed her very gently on the back of her neck, going from one side to the other.

"Then I would kiss your back a few minutes."

Will sat up.

"Aa-aa!" said Michelle.

"What's wrong?" Will looked surprised.

"Your two minutes is not up yet!"

"Okay." Will laughed. He kissed her neck for a while longer. "Then I would go on to your back." He kissed her very gently, going down her back very slowly.

"Aa- aa!"

"What's wrong now?" said Will, leaning up on his elbow.

Michelle lifted her head off the pillow and turned around to look over her shoulder. She pointed to the middle of her back. "You missed a spot, honey."

Will laughed quietly. "I better attend to it immediately." He kissed her again in the middle of her back and again slowly progressed kissing down her back.

Michelle looked over her shoulders. "What happens after the back?"

"You need to turn around for that."

Michelle turned around and propped herself up on the pillows. "Come here, you big hunk." She grabbed him by his tie and pulled him over. She kissed him on the lips for quite a long time.

When they stopped, he licked his lips. "That was delicious."

"Get your clothes off, Will!"

Will pointed to her breasts. "But honey there are a few spots I haven't got to yet."

"Honey tonight you have hit all the right spots in more ways than you can think. Now get your clothes off. We only have fifty-five minutes left!"

CHAPTER 30

Jake Sees Big Al's Sharp Side

It was the third day in prison. Jake was finishing off his evening meal and Ben was seated on the table beside him.

Jake pointed to Big Al's table. "I see Big Al and company must be dining out today!"

Ben shrugged his shoulders. "It's never a good sign when he is not at the table; everyone gets nervous. He must be up to something. Maybe he is just receiving his incoming stock."

"What, you mean like cigarettes and grass?"

Ben nodded. "Or perhaps cocaine, liquor, Playboy magazine, you name it, he can get it."

"I suppose he has no problem getting them past the guards."

"Every man has his price."

Jake looked around the room. "Hmm, I wonder ..."

"What Jake?"

"I dreamt last night ... Never mind." He looked at Ben again.

Ben paused. "Go on Jake, tell me what you are charged with, I promise not to tell anyone. Have you killed someone?"

"Ben ask me something else."

"Do you have a family?"

Jake hesitated for a second. "My wife is dead."

"When did she die?"

"About one year ago."

Ben's eyes lit up, "O my God, you have killed your wife!"

Jake looked irritated. "I take it you are not known for your tact."

Ben looked a little embarrassed "Sorry, I didn't mean to cause offense."

"Can I ask you a question, Ben? Do people take advantage of you?"

"That's what Letitia keeps telling me. She says I am a little bit naïve and that's how come I ended up in here. To be honest I know I am a little bit simple, but I suppose I can't help being the way I am." He paused and asked, "Hey you are not a shrink, are you?"

"Not quite; I am a clinical psychologist."

"What is the difference?"

Jake smiled. "About a hundred thousand dollars a year!"

Ben laughed.

Jake asked Ben, "So how have you been able to survive in here for five years without everyone taking advantage of you?" He paused. "Em, I didn't mean physically."

"At first it was tough. They was all pushing me around; Ben get this, Ben get that. One day I did a good turn for one of the prisoners. He was an ex-pimp and got into an argument with some of the inmates. Three of the prisoners started to beat him up. They was about to beat him to death. Everyone was standing around cheering. I stepped in front of him and asked them to stop. The three of them started to laugh and could not stop laughing for a couple of minutes. They then stopped laughing and one of them grabbed me by the throat and started to choke me. Just then Big Al and his men arrived. It turns out that the pimp was Big Al's cousin. The three prisoners ended up in hospital and Big Al made it known that if anyone messed with me, they were messing with him. That was three years ago. Nobody dares to say boo to me now. I keep my nose clean and keep out of the way of trouble."

Jake pointed to Ben's top pocket. "Show me the picture of Ben Junior again."

Ben had the widest of grins as he reached for the picture in his top pocket, almost in haste.

He showed it to Jake. "My pride and joy."

"When did you last see him?"

"Oh, I haven't seen him for over four years. He saw me in here a couple of times but the last time he seemed quite distressed, so I thought we had better not expose him to these surroundings. Letitia was not so sure, but I was insisting that I didn't want him here."

"And how is he now? Does he talk about you or want to see you?"

"Well, Letitia says that over past couple of years he is reluctant to talk about me and seems to be embarrassed in front of his friends when they talk about their daddies. But I am sure once I get out that I will be able to sort things out slowly."

"Ben, I think maybe you should have trusted Letitia."

"What do you mean?"

"Well, the longer he doesn't see you the more difficult it will be for him to bond with you."

Ben scratched his head. "But I am worried about him seeing me in prison and not liking me."

"He is eight, isn't he?"

"Yes. I mean he will be eight in a couple of months."

"I can assure you that he is old enough to understand. He knows between right and wrong. Meet him here. Explain to him that you made a mistake in your life, that you deserve to be in jail, that you regret what you have done and have learned your lesson. Tell him that you are sorry for what you have done, but that you have paid your dues to society and that now you hoped that Ben would have it in his heart to understand and forgive you. Then promise him that from now on you will always be there for him."

"Do you think it will work, Jake?"

"Ben, trust me, Junior needs you and he will be able to understand what you tell him."

"Well, I'll talk to Letitia later and see what she says."

Just then one of the prison guards came to the table. The other four inmates got up and walked off. Jake looked at him and picked up his plate to walk off too. The prison guard put his hand on Jake's shoulder. "You stay."

Ben put his head close to Jake's and whispered, "I don't like this, Jake."

Jake whispered back, "Don't worry, I have been waiting for this."

"What do you mean?"

"Well, I dreamt last night that Big Al stabbed me."

"Holy shit!"

Jake put his hand on Ben's shoulder, "Don't worry, Ben. That's not the way dreams work. It means he is going to get at me in some way, but it doesn't mean he is literally going to stab me. It's an analogy."

Ben shrugged his shoulders. "Whatever, but I have no idea what you are talking about!"

Ben sat there waiting for the guard to speak. "Ben, you can go."

Ben got up quickly and picked up his plate. He had taken a couple of steps when he stopped and looked at Jake's plate, he then looked the guard and back at the plate. The guard tipped his head towards the plat., "Go ahead, he won't be eating anymore."

Jake joked, "Ben you must have worms, 'cause you eat like a horse and are as thin as a rake."

Ben showed a very nervous smile and looked at Jake sheepishly. Jake nodded, "Go ahead, take it." Ben grabbed Jake's plate and ran off towards another table.

The guard looked at Jake and pointed at the kitchen. "You are wanted for washing up duties."

Jake looked over the guard's shoulder towards the kitchen. "This is a bit irregular, isn't it?"

"Hey, I am just following orders."

Jake shrugged his shoulders. "I guess washing dishes can't be that difficult."

Jake followed the guard to the kitchen door. He bumped into the guard who suddenly stopped at the kitchen door. Jake looked at him with surprise. "What, no escort?"

The guard pointed towards the back of the kitchen. "The sink is in the back room."

With that he walked away. Jake looked at the guard walking away. He looked at some of the inmates seated and a number seemed to be looking towards him. A couple of them suddenly looked away to avoid eye contact. There was something that was incongruent, but he could not put his finger on it. He whispered to himself, "I must be dreaming." He then pinched the tip of his left thumb with his right thumb and index finger. "Ouch, okay maybe not!"

As he walked into the kitchen, he noticed the small number of staff working there dropped what they were doing and left the kitchen hurriedly. He walked towards the back room, turning around on the way and looking at the last person to leave the kitchen in haste. He shook his head but was still trying to figure out what was bothering him about the dining room as he walked into the back room. He suddenly realised what had caught his attention. There standing in front of him was Big Al. As he turned around, he could not see any of the door or even its frame as Atlas and Nigel were standing in between the door and him.

Jake spoke with remarkable calmness. "Oh good, Big Al, I see you are going to help me with the washing up. Do you want to wash up or dry up?"

Atlas smirked. Big Al looked at him and Atlas immediately shut up.

Big Al walked back and forth for a few moments with his hands folded across his chest. He suddenly stopped. "I'll get straight to the point. I hear you killed Sarah Miller."

"You may hear a lot of things; I am sure most of them are not true."

Big Al grabbed Jake's right forearm. His grip tightened for a few seconds. Jake tried to free his arm but realised that he had no chance of pulling his arm away. He began to shake the fingers of his right hand. He then tried to use his left hand to release Big Al's grip. This time Nigel seemed amused and smirked. All of Jake's attempts were in vain. Eventually Big Al let go. Jake closed his right hand into a fist and released the grip again a few times, as if to bring the circulation back into his fingers.

Big Al pushed Jake. Nigel had held a chair behind Jake and Jake fell into the chair. Big Al leaned towards Jake until his nose was almost touching Jake's. "My cousin tells me you raped her and then killed her."

"I did no such thing!" Jake sounded indignant.

"You know we tolerate a lot of things in here, but rape and murder of young girls is not acceptable. Especially when it is a friend of my cousin."

Jake was trying to pull his head back and away from Big Al's, but there was no room for his head to go backwards. "Look I am not afraid of you, and I haven't killed anybody."

"Some say you buried her alive."

"They say a lot of things, but I am telling you I have not killed anyone."

Big Al suddenly put his right hand across Jake's throat and gripped tight. "My sources tell me otherwise. Now you can have your fancy lawyers who will get you off with technicalities, but in here we look after our own."

Jake tried to say something but the grip around his throat was so tight that he could not speak. He began to make some grunting noises.

Just then Ben walked in. He put his head in between the two shoulders of Nigel and Atlas. "Big Al, Jake is really a nice guy, I am sure he didn't kill his wife."

"What the fuck are you doing in here?" Big Al shouted. "Are you tired of living?" In turning his attention to Ben, Big Al let go of Jake's throat.

Jake slouched over and coughed a few times.

"Get the fuck out of here before I turn on you," Big Al shouted again. By this time Atlas was pulling on the back of Ben's collar, so much so that Ben's feet were nearly off the ground.

Jake put his hand on Atlas's forearm. "Put him down, let him go, he has nothing to do with this." Jake turned to Big Al, "Look he has nothing to do with this, please let him go."

Big Al nodded to Atlas. Atlas let Ben down.

"Ben remember you have Junior to think of, don't worry about me, I can look after myself," Jake said in a hoarse voice.

Ben reluctantly turned around and walked away.

Big Al walked to the dirty dishes and picked up a large kitchen knife. He walked towards Jake. "You are lucky you were interrupted. If I kill you now Ben will end up in trouble. That's him and me all square now."

He took the knife and suddenly stabbed Jake on his left upper arm. Jake let out a yelp. Big Al then turned the knife whilst it was in Jake's arm. "You see guys, this guy is so careless, I was washing up the knife and he fell onto my hand."

Atlas and Nigel laughed.

He then brought his face very close to Jake's. "If the bleeding or poisoning doesn't kill you, I will see you again and finish the job."

With that he threw the knife into the washing and walked out with Atlas and Nigel following him.

Jake stood there as the blood poured down his arm. He noticed that there was also blood squirting out at short intervals. Jake looked around and saw some tea towels. He took one and put it around his arm above the cut that was bleeding heavily. He tied a knot in it and tightened it as a tourniquet. He held one end in his teeth and pulled the other end hard with his right hand. He took a second tea towel and pressed it hard on the bleeding site. He walked out towards the dining area. By this time the blood was pouring down his arm onto his shirt which was virtually covered in blood. His trousers were also covered with blood.

As he walked into the dining area, Ben was standing by the door looking very anxious. There were also plenty of the inmates looking expectantly at the kitchen door.

Ben shouted as he saw Jake, "O my God! Someone call the guards, we need to take him to the medical quarters."

Most of the inmates got up and walked away. A couple of them walked towards Jake. At that point Jake lost consciousness.

CHAPTER 31

The Shark

Jake opened his eyes and at first all he could see was a blurry vision of a nurse in a uniform.

"Mister Chapman, can you hear me? Mister Chapman?"

Jake grunted. His eyes began to focus and he saw the nurse more clearly. She was a young pretty nurse with her short blond hair held back by her hat that was pinned to her hair. "Have I died and gone to heaven?"

The nurse laughed. "You are obviously not too bad if you can joke at a time like this!"

Jake tried to get up and as he leaned on his left hand, he let out a yell. "Shit! I mean ouch. I am sorry, nurse."

"Don't worry, Mister Chapman, I've heard a lot worse. I am sure it is sore. You are due your morphine injection again."

"No thanks, no morphine for me."

"Fine, I can give you some tablets instead. I will get the doctor. I will be back soon."

Jake grabbed her hand. "Sorry nurse how long have I been sleeping for?"

"You were in theatre for eight and a half hours, and that was yesterday. Your artery was severed, and the surgeon was worried about losing the arm, but the shark was eventually able to repair the artery."

Jake interrupted. "That's the shark the inmates mention, the prison surgeon."

"Yep that's him."

"Is he a vascular surgeon?"

"No," the nurse shook her head, "but there isn't much he hasn't done surgically. He got fed up with inmates losing limbs and dying while they were waiting to transfer to a district medical hospital."

Jake looked at his left hand and moved his fingers and winced with the pain.

"And you had severed tendons. You needed twelve units of blood! The blood banks were able to transport ten units to us urgently or you would not have made it." She looked at his arm. "How is the arm, sore I'm sure."

Jake let go of her hand. "Thanks, that's not too bad."

She touched his fingers. "Can you feel this?"

"Yes. It feels slightly numb though."

"We'll let the doctor know."

"Will I be able to play the piano?" Jake asked.

"Were you able to play the piano before?"

"Very badly."

"In that case no," she laughed.

The nurse left the room. Jake looked at this left arm. He had pyjama bottoms on, no top, and his left arm was heavily bandaged at the top. He had a drip in his right arm. He moved the fingers of his left hand again and winced with pain.

The doctor entered the room along with the nurse. The nurse had a glass of water and a couple of tablets which she offered him.

"No that's okay, nurse, I am fine." As he waved his left hand, he let out another yell.

"Go ahead, Mister Chapman, you don't need to be a martyr, it's only tylenol."

"Thanks." Jake took the tablets and swallowed them with the help of the water.

The doctor reached out his hand and shook Jake's hand lightly. "Good afternoon Mister Chapman. My name is Doctor Sharkey."

Jake interrupted, "Ah, so you are the shark."

"That's right."

"No offense meant," Jake added quickly.

The doctor smiled. "None taken. The fact that my first name is Finn doesn't help. Imagine going through school being called Finn Shark. I guess my parents have a good sense of humour."

"You must be good to repair arteries."

"In here sometimes you have to do the best you can. You get some horrendous injuries in here. For example, I am sure anywhere else you would have had a plastic and a vascular surgeon working on your arm."

"I am not sure if that is very comforting."

"Well let me check, Mister Chapman." He stepped closer to Jake. "Can you move your fingers?"

Jake moved the fingers of his right hand. "There doctor, perfect."

The nurse burst out laughing, joined in by the doctor.

"Very funny, Mister Chapman," said the doctor after he had finished laughing. "Now let us see if you can move the fingers of your left hand which was operated on."

Jake grimaced as he moved the fingers of his left hand.

"That is very good," said the doctor. "The pain is to be expected. Now can you feel me touch your hand?"

Jake nodded every time the doctor touched a part of his left hand. "Yes but feels slightly numb."

"Very good. I'm confident you will have full sensation in the next three to four weeks or so."

"I thought I saw an arterial bleed, and my personal nurse tells me you repaired the artery."

The doctor looked at Jake "Are you medical?"

"Clinical psychologist."

"Yes, there was an artery bleeding." Doctor Sharky looked over his shoulder at the door and lowered his voice. "The official line is that I repaired your artery, unfortunately I did not have the facilities to repair it. I had to tie it off. But there should be enough collateral circulation to compensate." He got closer to Jake and lowered his voice even more. "If they find out I tied off your artery and repaired your tendons they would stop me practicing here and the insurance company would probably stop me practicing ever again. So, your notes will carry the official line. But I can assure you that if I had transferred you to a tertiary hospital you would at best have lost your arm, if not your life!"

"Don't worry, doc, your secret is safe with me. And I am very thankful."

"Mister Chapman, I am sure you are tired, but I have to ask you this." The doctor looked towards the door. "There are some prison authorities who would like to question you. Nurse Collins here told them you need your rest, but they were very insistent to speak to you ASAP. I told them that at least I will ask you."

"That's fine, doc, no problem."

The nurse looked concerned. "Are you sure Mister Chapman?"

Jake smiled. "That is very sweet of you, Nurse Collins."

"Debbie."

"Debbie, thanks, but I am fine. I will have to see them, if not now later, so I will get it over and done with."

"Okay," said the nurse, "but just press the buzzer if you need me, or if you want rid of them."

Jake smiled. "Thanks Debbie. If I was fifteen years younger, I would be looking your phone number."

The nurse laughed. "I am sure my husband would have something to say about that."

Jake and the doctor laughed. Jake said, "Oh doctor, many thanks for your efforts."

"You are welcome," said the doctor as he walked out.

A very short time later Debbie walked back in with two men. She stood by the door. The older of the two looked to be in his early sixties. He had a brown suit on, which looked to be quite a few years old. The creases on the jacket sleeve and back suggested it was being used as a daily uniform.

He approached Jake and offered his hand. "Hello Mister Chapman, I'm Edward Bell, the prison warden. This is Mister Ian McDonald, my deputy."

Ian looked to be in his mid-fifties and wore an equally drab suit which was beige in colour. The trousers and jacket were full of creases. His crew-cut dark hair give him a semblance of order.

Ian reached across the bed to shake Jake's hand. "Ouch!" Jake exclaimed as Ian leant on his left arm.

"I am sorry, Mister Chapman."

"That's okay, don't worry about it. I'll ask the nurse to rub it better," Jake smiled.

Ian looked at Jake with a blank face. "Will that not make it worse?" he asked earnestly.

"Never mind," said Jake as he shook his head.

Mister Bell turned toward the nurse. "Nurse would you mind leaving us alone for a while?!"

Debbie left the room.

"Mister Chapman—" said Mister Bell.

"You can call me Jake."

"Yes Jake," continued Mister Bell, looking rather serious. "we would like to speak to you about the prisoner Albert Miller, generally known as Big Al. We understand that he stabbed you; is that right?"

Jake eyes flicked from one visitor to the next. "Carry on."

The warden continued, "Well yes anyway. We have had our eyes on Big Al for a long time and have been looking for an opportunity to nail him. If you could testify to what happened to you, we will be able to place him in solitary confinement for a very long time. It will also help to break up the mob structure. More importantly we think that there is obviously some collusion from the guards and we hope to remove this pernicious internal influence from our establishment once and for all."

Jake had a wry smile on his face. "And what do I get in return? My other arm stabbed or a knife in my heart?"

The deputy leaned forward to speak.

"Ouch, you are leaning on my arm!" Jake said rather loudly.

"Oh sorry, Mister Chapman. We can't promise anything, but what we can do is speak to the prosecution team and ask for leniency with your sentences."

Jake sat up with some difficulty. "Are you guys for real?"

The warden looked indignant. "Whatever do you mean?"

"Firstly, the prosecution will have no interest in anything you say, secondly, if I go back to this prison there is no way I will survive more than a few days."

"We can arrange for your transfer to another prison," the deputy interjected.

"No thanks. Thirdly, you have your own problems and I have mine, you will have to fight your own battles and I will fight mine. Fourthly, I am innocent and have nothing to worry about. And finally, this was an accident. Big Al was washing the knife and I turned around and the knife went into my left arm."

"Mister Chapman," the warden said, "we understand that you may be scared of the repercussions of speaking to us, but we can assure your safety. We can certainly place you in secure quarters or transfer you."

"No that will not be necessary, gentlemen. I have nothing more to add."

Debbie suddenly walked into the room. She stepped forward. "Gentlemen, Mister Chapman has not been well and needs his rest now, so if you would be kind enough to leave."

The men got up. The deputy leaned on the bed to get up. "Ouch," Jake yelped.

"Sorry."

The warden took out a card from the top pocket of his jacket. "If you change your mind, Mister Chapman, please contact me."

"Sure."

"Thank you for your time."

"Goodbye Mister Bell."

The deputy was about to reach over to shake Jake's hand. Jake held up his right hand. "That's okay, you don't need to shake hands."

"Goodbye Mister Chapman," he said.

"Goodbye gentlemen."

The two of them walked out.

Debbie approached Jake's bed. She pulled up the bed sheet and neatly placed it over Jake's bare chest, folding the top part back and adjusting the top so it was in almost a horizontal line.

She thought for a moment. "Do you mind me asking you something, Mister Chapman."

"The name is Jake; go ahead."

She continued. "Seriously Jake, are you not scared, do you not think you would be better co-operating with them?"

"Well nurse–"

"Debbie, I like to be called just Debbie," she quipped.

"Well, just Debbie …"

She laughed.

"Well, Debbie, I hope you were not eavesdropping!"

"Jake what do you take me for?! Of course I was! But my motives were pure, I was worried about why they had come to visit you and wanted to be able to interrupt if needed."

"Their guarantee means, pardon the French, Jack shit! The laws in the prison are made by the hierarchy on the inside, not the outside. I am sure if someone wanted to kill me, he would find a number of ways of doing it. If I go away to some other prison, I may have to face the same thing again. In fact, Debbie I would say that it is the opposite of what you say."

"What do you mean?"

"The problem is that I have no fear. If I were to die tomorrow, I would not care. I have in fact nothing to live for."

"Oh that is so sad."

"Don't worry about it. I am not worried. You can take the drip down now. I am ready to go back my cell."

"Are you sure you are ready?"

"Absolutely."

"Okay, but I will have to check with the Shark."

Debbie returned with the doctor.

The doctor came to see Jake. "Sir, are you sure you don't want to stay here a while longer?"

"No doc, you are busy enough anyway."

"It's no bother to me, I'm usually here till nine p.m. or later most nights."

"What about your wife?" Jake pointed to the ring on his ring finger.

"Oh, she doesn't mind. She keeps herself pretty busy. She is either at one of her sisters' houses, with one of her girlfriends or at a jewellery-making club or something like that."

"It sounds like you have a very comfortable arrangement."

"Yes we do." The doctor paused. "Wait a minute were you being sarcastic?"

Jake sat up on the bed, pushing himself up gingerly by leaning on both his hands. "Well I worked for years as a psychologist. I often found workaholics to be in two groups; broadly speaking. Those who were very dedicated to their work or were needed; and those who used their work to hide from life."

"Hide from life?" asked the doctor, raising his eyebrows. He looked at Debbie. "Debbie would you mind giving us a few minutes?"

Debbie nodded and walked out quickly.

Jake looked at Debbie as she walked out. "She has such a wonderful nature."

The Shark nodded. "And she is brilliant at her work. I would be lost here without her. One nurse and one auxiliary nurse is all I have here … So you were saying about life."

"Yes! Life! Problems that they had to face in the real world. Perhaps their families … Perhaps their spouse … their wife!"

The doctor sat on the edge of the bed. He thought for a while. "You know, I don't understand women. No, what I mean is that I don't understand Helen." He looked at Jake. "That's my wife, Helen."

"Yes, I gathered that. Carry on."

"Well, I just sit there at the dinner table and don't seem to have anything to tell her. Any subject that is brought up seems to have a yes or no answer and the conversation is over before it has started. She doesn't seem to want to touch me anymore and seems to push me away anytime I go near her."

"How long are you married?"

"We just had our fifth anniversary. She didn't even want to go out, said she was tired and had a headache."

"Do you love her?"

"Oh, I adore her, but have a feeling she no longer loves me. In fact, I have a feeling that she might be having an affair."

"What makes you think that doc?"

Finn hesitated, "Well." He walked to the door and closed it. He came to the right side of Jake's bed. He pointed to the right-hand side of Jake's bed. Jake nodded and moved slightly to the left of the bed. Finn sat down. He hesitated, "Well, the other day I asked her if she was all right or was she feeling ill. She replied that she was fine and had been out shopping all day. I asked her what she had bought for herself. She said nothing as nothing grabbed her."

"Well doc, that's not unusual for a woman, is it?"

"Here's the thing, Jake. I had noticed when I went upstairs to change that the bed had been slept in."

"Are you sure it wasn't from the morning?"

"No, she always makes the bed in the morning. She has her routine."

"Well doc, what are you going to do about it?"

"Oh, I don't know."

"Did you not say you adore her?"

"I truly do but can't seem to connect with her."

"Well doc, you need to go and tell her how you feel, you may be surprised!"

"I guess you are right." The doctor stood up. "I'll chat to her when I get home tonight."

Jake shook his head, "Doc, doc, doc. Not tonight, not an hour from now. You need to go to her now!"

"But I have a lot of things to do before I finish."

"Is anyone dying or going to die before sunrise?"

"I guess not."

"Well doc, go to her."

"You are right, I will go straight away before the mood leaves me. I'll surprise her."

"Atta boy."

Finn was walking off at pace when Jake called him. "Doc, just one thing!"

"What is it?"

"She didn't make the bed up."

"What?"

"She didn't make the bed up."

"I have no idea what you are talking about Jake but I have to go now." He walked away briskly.

CHAPTER 32

Doc Arrives at Home

Finn arrived at home carrying a small bunch of flowers. He opened the door and closed it very quietly. He took his shoes off and tiptoed in his socks through the kitchen. He put his keys on the kitchen table very quietly. He peeped into the living room and didn't see her. He went into all the downstairs rooms and did not see her. He walked to the stairs and noticed her blouse on the bannister. He lifted it and smiled. He tiptoed up the stairs. He walked into the bedroom showing off the flowers. He saw her in bed and shouted, "Surprise honey. Wasn't expecting you in bed at this hour. Are you all right?"

Suddenly there was some movement in the sheets in her crotch area and a man jumped up from under the sheet and said, "Oh fuck!"

She sat up and said, "Oh shit!"

Finn dropped the flowers. He looked from her to him back to her and then walked out of the room.

Finn was seated at the kitchen table when the man walked past him, tucking his shirt in as he was walking out.

The doctor shouted as he was about to open the door. "Do COME again!"

The man was about to walk out but stopped and turned around. "What sort of man are you? If I found a man in bed with my wife, I would kill them both!"

"I see," said the doctor rather calmly, "so being a man means you can screw another man's wife, but if someone screws your wife you can kill them both?"

The man opened his mouth, paused and closed his mouth again, he opened the door to leave.

The doctor shouted, "Oh, before you leave, man to man, I feel I have to tell you this."

The man walked back in, somewhat reluctantly, holding on to the door frame and was situated so he was half in and half out the door. "My wife has syphilis and chlamydia. That's why I don't sleep with her. My bum is so sore from all the penicillin injections. I was told if I hadn't got it in time, I may have become sterile. So, every so often she has to get her needs satisfied by an unfortunate bloke. I hope you were wearing a condom on your tongue."

The man went red in his face, he was about to say something but stopped again. He had a worried look on his face. He went out and slammed the door.

A few minutes later his wife came down. She was only wearing a beige silk dressing gown. She shouted at Finn, "Did you tell Stanley that I had syphilis?"

"You forgot the chlamydia!"

"What!" she shouted.

Finn spoke with a slightly raised voice, with a sarcastic tone, "Let me get this right, I have come home and found you in bed with a man, and now I have to apologise to you? And who the fuck is Stanley?"

"He's a nobody."

"It didn't look like a nobody when his face was buried in your crotch."

Helen put her head in her hands and started to sob.

"Was it Stanley who was here two weeks ago?"

Helen looked surprised, "How did you …"

"So, I was right."

Helen wiped some tears and walked over to the kitchen table and took a couple of tissues from a tissue box.

"Well, was it Stanley?"

"Finn, what do you want me to say?"

"I don't know, honey. You tell me. I would never have taken you as having sex with anyone but me, and certainly not in our bed!"

Helen started to sob again.

Finn walked toward the kitchen window and looked outside. "How long have you known him? Where did you meet him? I suppose what I am asking is do you love him?"

"Do we have to talk about his now?" she said between sobs.

"I need to know."

"Is it enough to say that no I don't love him, or in fact care much for him."

"Well, Helen, it didn't look like it when he was going down on you."

Helen put her head in her hands again and continued to cry.

Finn wiped a few tears from his eyes and kept looking outside the window. He then came down and sat opposite Helen. "Do you want a divorce?"

"I don't know! I just know that you feel like a stranger to me and in fact I think that you can't bear to be in my presence. You can't talk to me about anything, you hardly look at me or touch me. You hardly notice anything I wear, have not given me a compliment in I don't know how long. In fact, all you care about and have passion for is your work and saving lives. I am a nobody to you!"

"That is not true!"

"Well, it's no good you saying that, I am telling you how I feel and how you make me feel."

There was silence for a while.

In between sobs Helen asked, "And why did you come home so early anyway?"

Finn walked upstairs and came down with the bunch of flowers. "I came home to tell you how much I love … how much I adore you."

Helen dried her eyes and took a big breath. "Why did you stay?"

"What do you mean?"

"You didn't leave. You stayed here!"

"I stayed …" He looked at the ceiling for a few seconds. "Gosh, that is a very good question. Why did I not just walk out?" He reached out and held her hand. "Helen, I don't want to lose you, I adore you."

She got up and clenched her fists and jumped up and down, "That is not fair! That just is not fair!"

"Whatever do you mean?"

"Well, it would really make me feel a lot better if you screamed or shouted at me or broke a plate against the wall. It's not fair that you are being so nice to me, it makes me feel so much worse. Can you at least just for once slap me or shake me vigorously or something that will make me feel better?"

Finn squeezed her hand. "Aha! I get it now. I see what Jake was saying. You didn't make up the bed."

"Finn you are beginning to scare me now, what exactly are you talking about?"

"When I was leaving, Jake shouted out 'she didn't make the bed'."

"Who the hell is Jake?"

"He's a psychologist that I treated."

"Oh."

Finn continued, "You always make the bed, you have OCD about it. So, if you went to bed with someone during the day, why wouldn't you tidy up after?" He nodded. "Unless … Unless, you wanted me to notice. Why would you bring someone to our house and take a chance of sleeping with them at this time? Unless you subconsciously wanted to be found out."

"And what sort of a silly person would do that, may I ask you …"

"Someone who cared for her husband and was not looking for a new relationship or sex for that matter, but wanted him to notice her, to be jealous."

"Wow, that's incredible, did you just work it out?"

"No Helen, Jake must have worked it out earlier today, but just left me a clue." He looked her in the eye. "Well is it true? Are you done with me, or do you still love me?"

"Did you come here to tell me you love me?"

"Yes!"

"And you brought me flowers?"

"Yes."

"I feel so terrible, I just wanted someone to look at me the way you used to a few years ago, to touch me the way you used to. You can't even bear to look at me now." She got up and walked towards the window. "But every time Stanley touched me, I shuddered, and felt empty inside me. It had no feeling, hollow. When you used to touch me, my heart felt like it wanted to jump out of my chest … Oh dear. How can I find the words to say how sorry I am?"

"Honey, you won't believe this, but I sincerely feel that I should be the one apologizing. Instead of showing you the affection I have for you, I was staying at work to avoid you and was cross with you when all I too wanted was your affection."

"If you are trying to make me feel guiltier it is working. Please can you at least punch me once to make me feel better."

Finn reached across the table and raised his hand and after a pause stroked her hair and placed Helen's hair behind her ear on one side. "Honey I could never hurt you; you are the most precious thing to me."

"Even more important than your work and saving lives?"

"The most important thing to me in my life."

Helen smiled. "So, what now?"

"Would you like to dance?"

"But there is no music."

"This can be arranged, just let me get some slow music on Spotify."

Finn started the music and they danced slowly, she rested her head against his chest and for a while they just swayed slowly. Finn suddenly stopped and squeezed her real tight.

She smiled. "Are you trying to break my ribs?"

"No darling, just letting you know that I will never let go of you, just thought I'd let you know."

"That is a wonderful thing to say. Perhaps we should spend some time just talking and getting to know each other again."

Finn nodded. "It's easy to drift apart. I am all for that."

CHAPTER 33

Young Love

It was seven a.m. Gabby got off the bus at Fifth Avenue. She looked around anxiously and suddenly stopped. A broad smile lit up her face. She walked up in a circuitous way and stood behind Geno. She put her hands over his eyes. "Guess who?"

"Oh, it's Martha of course."

"What?"

Geno lifted her hands and held on to them. "You fell for that one, didn't you?"

Gabby slapped him on his arm. "Haha. I should have known better." She laughed.

"Coffee?"

"Sure thing, Geno, but I'm buying."

Geno stepped to one side and with a wave of his arm invited her to go forward. "In that case after you, signorina."

They both got coffees and sat on a bench in a small area with a few benches and some trees. Some of the trees still had a few red leaves, what was left from the autumn transition.

Gabby put both her hands around the coffee cup. "The best thing about a cup of coffee on a winter's morning is that it warms your hand."

"I know what you mean," said Geno, doing the same thing.

There was silence for a while. Geno was the first to speak, "You are right, it is strangely nice to watch people walk by."

"Yea. I sometimes wonder if it is a type of voyeurism."

"I don't think so. I assumed everybody does it at airports."

Gabby took a sip of her coffee. "I like watching interactions between couples."

Geno laughed. "I know what you mean. Are the couple fighting? Are they young lovers? How much affection does one give to the other?"

"Yes, and body language of couples. Perfect, for example look at that girl with the guy." She pointed across the road, "Her body language is so flirtatious. It is as if she is saying 'I am available, I like you'."

"Yes, and he is trying to look calm and cool and aloof, but you know inside his heart is thumping."

Gabby turned to Geno. "That's the way I was when I saw you earlier."

"What, you mean flirtatious?"

Gabby slapped his arm. "No you dummy. I mean my heart was racing." She paused. "And what about you?"

Geno blew on the fingers of his right hand and brushed it against his coat. "No, I was cool and calm with a pulse of fifty."

Gabby hit him again.

Geno kissed her on the lips. "Does that give you the answer?"

Gabby wiped a tear off her face. "Oh my!"

After a few seconds she looked across the road. "Look at that mother, look at the way she is tenderly stroking the hair of her daughter. Is there anything more beautiful in life?"

"Now Gabby, don't be getting broody on me."

Gabby laughed. "Yes, let's not go there for now. My next challenge is to pass my driving test."

"How is that coming along?"

Gabby shrugged her shoulders. "Well I've had a couple of lessons, but time seems to be a problem."

"Well I was going to drive you to work, so why don't you drive there?"

"No Geno, not in morning traffic. Speaking of work, I need to go, and I'm sure you have places to go, people to see."

Geno lifted his coffee cup. "Maybe a few more minutes till we finish our coffee?"

Gabby slid her bottom so she was right next to him and hooked her arm round his. "Yeah, a few more minutes."

CHAPTER 34

Ready for Court?

Jake walked into the visiting room and sat behind the dividing glass and picked up the phone. Lucy picked up the phone on the other side of the glass.

"Are you okay, Jake?" She looked concerned.

"Thanks for asking, I'm fine, minor injuries." Jake pointed to the bandaging on his left forearm. "Should make a full recovery in a few weeks."

"I had asked to see you in the private room, but they said you had declined that."

"Yes," Jake nodded, "I have things to do."

"I made a request to move you to a more secure place but the warden, Mister Bell, told me that you don't want to be moved."

Jake nodded. "Yes I am happy to stay here, Lucy."

"Mister Bell assured me he would help in any way he can."

"If he had had any power, he would sort out the corruption inside here," Jake added.

"Do you not think it is dangerous to stay here?" Lucy looked very concerned.

"Perhaps, but I will take my chances."

"Jake do you have a death wish or something?"

"No, I just don't care that much one way or the other."

Lucy paused for a few moments. "What is the deal with this guy, Al is it?"

"Yeah, Big Al is his full title. He is the chief in here."

"I mean what is it with him and you? Why is he picking on you?"

"Sex offenses are a no-no in here. And it is his belief that I … that I … Well that I raped Sarah Miller and then killed her."

"That is a bit high and mighty of them, isn't it?" said Lucy, raising her eyebrows.

"They have a different set of rules in here. I also gather there may be some connection between Big Al and Sarah Miller."

"What is that?"

"I am not certain; she may be related to or a friend of his cousin or something."

"Are you sure you don't want me to intervene?"

Jake nodded again. "There are times in life you have to fight your own corner and take the bull by the horns, so to speak, and I feel I need to sort this out by myself."

"Can you explain to me why?"

"I don't know if I have a logical explanation. Just a gut feeling that I will come to no harm, and that I feel I need to see this through."

"Well I hope you know what you are doing 'cause I fear the worse."

Jake looked at Lucy and smiled and was silent for a while.

Lucy broke the silence. "What exactly is going through your mind right now, because I am finding it difficult to understand you. I mean I am worried about you being killed, and you are sitting there smiling."

Jake chuckled. "That's exactly it, Lucy. I was just thinking that you should get a life."

"What?"

"You heard me right, Lucy. I am a total stranger who is in prison with murderers and gangsters and what-not. You should be opening the tender aspects of your heart to those who are closer to you, to those who are deserving of such a privilege. You shouldn't be sprinkling your emotional energy on unworthy characters like me."

Lucy seemed quite taken aback. "Jake I have never met anyone like you. I am used to giving advice to my clients. But it seems like every time I am with you I learn something new about others."

"Or perhaps about yourself."

"Yes, about myself too. Anyway, Jake, I would hardly describe any human being as unworthy, especially not you. I mean look at you; you are walking into a scenario where you might get seriously injured or eve … well, I worry even killed. And you are concerned about me. I don't think I have ever met a client who is more worried about me than themselves."

"Well Lucy, maybe it's because your clients weren't able to see what a pure heart you have."

Lucy blushed. "Gosh, Jake, I don't know what to say."

Jake smiled again. "Why don't you tell me the main reason why you are here. I believe it is to ask me if I want the case to be put back because of my state of health."

Lucy became a bit fidgety. "Jake, I wish you would stop reading my mind, you make me nervous."

"I can't read your mind, Lucy. It was just a logical deduction."

"Well whatever it is, it is still disconcerting."

"I am sorry to make you feel uncomfortable."

"Oh no Jake, I wouldn't say I am uncomfortable, it's just that I like to be in control of the discussion with a client, and I seem to follow you rather than the other way round."

"Well as you said it, I am no ordinary client. I will take it as a compliment."

"It was meant as a compliment, Jake. When this case if over, I would be fascinated to sit and chat with you over coffee about things."

"Like what sort of things?"

"Oh many, many things!"

"Miss Walker, are you asking your *client* out on a date?"

Lucy blushed very prominently this time. "Oh God. No. I mean. It was …"

"I'm just pulling your leg, Lucy."

"You can see, Jake, I sometimes say things as I think them and it gets me into trouble sometimes. Not a very good quality for a lawyer."

"Yet, some would describe it as a refreshing honesty."

"Anyway, all I meant is that I enjoy talking to you."

"The answer is no!"

"Oh well, I understand …"

"No Lucy, I would be honoured to have coffee and a chat with you. But no, I don't want the case delayed, I would like to go ahead."

"Are you sure?"

"Yes, I am one hundred percent certain."

"And are you sure you don't want to transfer to a safer prison? I think you are in danger."

"I am willing to take that chance, Lucy," Jake said very assuredly. "Now if you don't mind, I am very hungry."

"Sure, give me a call if you need me to do anything."

"Thanks for your concern," Jake said as he put the phone down and got up. He turned around and walked away with purpose.

Lucy sat there with the phone in her hand. She shook her head as she put the phone down. Her expression demonstrated a lot of anxiety.

CHAPTER 35

Court Reconvenes

"All rise for Judge Temple!"

Everyone stood up. Jake got up rather gingerly.

The judge sat down.

"All be seated."

Everyone sat down. Again, Jake was the slowest to react and the last to sit down.

The judge looked at Jake for a few seconds and then at Amanda. "Miss Jackson, I gather your client had an unfortunate accident in prison. He has the prerogative to request a delay in proceedings and I am happy to give this serious consideration! Are you … perhaps I should say, is he happy to proceed?"

Amanda looked at Jake and he nodded.

"Yes, your honour, even though he is not fully recovered he is happy to go on."

The judge sounded rather stern. "Miss Jackson, he is either ready or not!"

"Sorry your honour, yes he is ready."

"Very well then the court will continue." He turned to the jury. "May I remind you to ignore anything you may have seen or heard in the media. You are morally bound to ignore any comments or opinions you have heard from anyone about Mister Chapman, positive or negative, or any comments about this case. Please do not read the newspapers or listen to any news about this case, and indeed you are forbidden to engage in any social media interactions about any matter pertaining to this case. Have I made myself clear?"

He looked at the jurors and they all nodded. "Very well, we can then proceed."

The judge then opened the file in front of him. "Mister Gomez, please state, or should I say re-state, your initial presentation!"

Andy jumped to his feet like a greyhound that had been released from the trap. Peter put his hand on Andy's forearm. Andy stopped and leaned forward so his ear was near Peter's mouth.

"Slow and steady wins the race."

Andy smiled. He walked towards the jurors and slowly walked across their benches, making eye contact with each of them. "Ladies and gentlemen of the jury. I would ask you to look at Mister Chapman for a few seconds." He then became silent and stepped to the side so they could see him.

"Well, ladies and gentlemen look at him; do you think he is guilty or innocent?" He became silent again.

The jurors' eyes were looking at Andy and suddenly they all looked at Jake. Amanda looked somewhat puzzled. Lucy was looking at the jurors slightly apprehensively. The judge was staring at the jurors. Some of the jurors were intently looking at Jake and a couple of them looked at each other.

Andy broke the silence. "Ladies and gentlemen. Stop whatever you are thinking. This is my point. You will be looking at this gentleman and trying to decide if he is capable of killing someone. You may hear that he was stabbed by an inmate and feel sorry for him. He may have been very good at his profession as a psychologist and helped a lot of people. I am now asking you to get rid of any prejudice you may have right now. You don't need to deduce anything in your mind. Just empty your mind of all preconceptions and listen to the evidence. Then you can make up your mind."

Some of the jurors faces literally seemed to indicate that they had relaxed, a few were nodding, and a couple were smiling. None of them had a smile as wide as Peter North. He sat back on his chair and nodded his head, a nod that was barely visible, but his smile was indication of his satisfaction.

"Ladies and gentlemen, members of the jury. Over the next few days the prosecution will show that this man you see sitting there …" He pointed to Jake and stepped aside so they could all see him. "This man has killed not one, but two young girls. Two unfortunate girls who met the wrong, EVIL person at the wrong time. He snuffed out their lives. We will show beyond any shadow of doubt that he was their killer. In one instance, he told someone, no less than a detective, that Charlene Mills was dead, before her death had hit the news. A sample of his pubic hair, yes I repeat of his pubic hair, was found on the body of Sarah Miller, a person he claims he has never seen."

One of the ladies in the jury gasped on hearing this and held her hand to her mouth.

Andy nodded. "Yes ladies and gentlemen, I have little more to say, the evidence will speak for itself!"

He walked slowly and sat down.

As he sat down Peter gave him a thumb's up under the table and did not show a smile this time.

The judge looked at Amanda. "Would the defense like to present its case?"

Amanda took a sip of her water and got up slowly. "Yes your honour." She seemed very calm, as if she had not heard anything from the prosecution.

She walked to the jurors and smiled and looked at them individually. She smiled again. "Members of the jury. I would make the same request as Mister Gomez. Please do not make up your minds until you have heard ALL the evidence. Have you ever had a premonition yourself that something was going to happen, perhaps deja-vu, a dream relating to an event? None of these are a crime. We will be able to show that our client, Mister Chapman, a servant to the community and so many people, indeed had no direct contact with any of the two innocent girls that were murdered. Mister Chapman … Jake, knew neither Charlene Mills, nor Sarah Miller. He never met them, so he obviously had nothing to do with their deaths."

She seemed to end abruptly and slowly walked back to her seat. She caught everyone by surprise. A murmur filled the room and people spoke to each other quietly. Lucy whispered to her, "I thought you were not going to talk about dreams and premonitions."

Amanda whispered back, "We are up shit creek, it's damage limitation!"

The Judge spoke. "Mister Gomez, are you ready to question your witnesses?"

"Yes, your honour. The prosecution would like to invite Doctor Morrow, one of the state pathologists, to the stand."

"Go ahead." The judge nodded.

Doctor Morrow walked to the stand and stood there.

The bailiff asked him, "Doctor Morrow, do you promise to speak the whole truth?"

"I do."

"Please be seated."

Andy Gomez approached the bench. "Doctor Morrow, for the benefit of the jury and everyone else, would you inform us how many pathologists are there in the state of New York?"

Doctor Morrow was taken aback a bit.

Andy quickly added, "Sorry Doctor Morrow this is not a quiz, just a rough estimate."

The doctor seemed to relax. "I can't give you an exact number, but it's over three hundred or so."

"Is it fair to say that you are, Doctor Morrow, one of the top pathologists in the state of New York and that you often lecture at pathologist conferences and that you have written a book which has been referred to as the 'Gold Standard' in pathologist circles?"

"Mister Gomez, that is not for me to say."

"You are being modest, Doctor Morrow. Let me quote the NYSSPath, the New York State Society of Pathologists, summary by the president of the association, and I quote, 'If you have not read Doctor Morrow's book, 'The Hidden Clues', then stop whatever you are doing next week and read this book. This is the gold standard for all pathologists.' End of quote."

Doctor Morrow seemed unmoved. "Well that is someone's point of view."

Andy turned to the judge and raised a number of A4 papers he had in his hand. "Your honour I present this report as exhibit one, it is the autopsy report. In this report it states that Charlene Mills was killed by a blow to the back of the head, she had facial injuries and chest wall injuries. Doctor Morrow, from the nature and pattern of the injuries, can it be deduced that the killer was left-handed?"

"Yes, the direction and pattern of injuries strongly indicates that the killer preferred to use his left hand ... or fist."

"Your honour, it has been established and agreed by all parties that the defendant, Mister Chapman, is left-handed."

The judge looked at Amanda who nodded. "Carry on, Mister Gomez."

"Doctor, did the autopsy reveal any signs of forced vaginal penetration?"

"No, there was some semen in her vagina, but it did not match Mister Chapman's DNA."

"How long could the sperm have been there for?"

Doctor Morrow thought for a couple of seconds. "It may have been there for two days or longer."

"So Charlene Mills could have had intercourse up to three days prior to being killed and would have some semen inside her."

"Yes, that is correct."

"And you are one hundred per cent sure that was not the defendant's sperm?"

"Yes, there is no question about that. In fact, with the cooperation of her boyfriend we have matched the semen with his DNA."

"Your honour, unless the defense objects, we will not disclose his name, for the sake of anonymity."

The judge looked at Amanda. Amanda nodded. The judge turned to the scribe. "Let it be known that the defense is agreeable to this request."

Andy turned towards the judge. "Your honour, I would like to focus on Sarah Miller's autopsy and reserve the right to call Doctor Morrow back to the stand at a later date if needed to question in reference to Charlene Mills."

The judge was very brief, "Granted."

"Doctor Morrow, I would like to focus on the findings of Sarah Miller."

Doctor Morrow nodded.

"Is it your finding that the pattern of injuries indicates that the killer, let's say, also preferred to use his left hand?"

"Or hers," Doctor Morrow answered.

Andy smiled. "Indeed, or hers."

"That is correct. The assailant inflicted the damage to Sarah Miller's face and chest wall with the left hand or fist."

"Doctor Morrow, I am going to refer to one point about Sarah Miller's autopsy report. Hair samples were found under the nails of the body of Sarah Miller?"

"That is correct. Two to be precise."

"And you have analysed the hair samples?"

"Not me specifically, but yes the samples of hair have been analysed by our forensic team. It was suspected to be pubic hair, and this was confirmed by further analysis."

Amanda stood up. "Objection, your honour, the site of the hair is speculative."

The judge turned to Doctor Morrow. "Can you verify that this is from the pubic area as this may have a bearing on the intent of the assailant."

"There was a sweat gland attached to the hair, which was an apocrine gland that you get in the pubic and armpit region. The skin gland from normal skin is slightly different. The shape of the hair suggests it is almost certainly from the pubic region."

The judge turned to Amanda, "Over-ruled."

Amanda sat down.

Andy continued, "I suppose, Doctor Morrow, ignoring for now the exact site of the hair, is there any doubt that it matches the suspect?"

"No, there is no doubt."

"I understand that you have obtained samples of pubic hair for forensic testing from the accused?"

"Yes, that was obtained by our forensic doctor, that is fairly routine."

"And does that hair match the accused, Mister Chapman?"

"Yes, it does."

"So, you are saying that the hair was definitely that of the accused?"

"Well, polymorphic testing …"

Andy interrupted Doctor Morrow, "Doctor Morrow, please give your information in such a way that even a lay person like me would understand."

There was a trickle of laughter across the court room.

"Apologies Mister Gomez. Simply put, a hair sample does not always contain DNA material, however if the hair follicle is attached to the hair, that is so to say if the root of the hair is still attached, that root or follicle is rich in DNA."

"And this DNA material was contained in the hair sample found on Sarah Miller's body?"

"Yes, and it was an exact match with Mister Chapman's DNA."

"So we can surmise that Sarah Miller got Mister Chapman's pubic hair under her nail by trying to protect herself from his sexual advances?"

Amanda and Lucy both jumped up at the same time. "Objection!" they both shouted.

Amanda looked disapprovingly at Lucy who sat down quickly.

The judge looked at Andy, "Mister Gomez, you should know better. Sustained!" He turned towards the stand. "Carry on."

Andy walked towards his desk and rubbed his chin. "Doctor, I'll re-phrase the question: so, from a forensic perspective she would have had to get pubic hair under her nail or nails, therefore he would have exposed his privates to her prior to this?"

This time Amanda stood up. "Objection! Calls for speculation on behalf of the witness."

The judge was quick to answer, "Sustained."

Andy seemed determined to press the issue. "Doctor Morrow, in your opinion, how did the pubic hair get under her nails?"

Amanda was up again. "Objection, calls for speculation."

"Sustained. Mister Gomez, please stop repeating the same question in a different way!"

Andy was not going to let go. "Doctor Morrow, is it possible to get a sample of someone's pubic hair through their clothes?"

"I wouldn't have thought so."

"So, the answer is no?"

"Yes. I mean the answer is no. It is not possible."

"Doctor Morrow, you mentioned earlier that it is routine practice to obtain samples of the suspect's pubic hair in forensic sampling?"

"Yes, it is."

"What other samples do you routinely obtain?"

"Buccal swabs for DNA testing – that's from inside the mouth, that is the cheeks; plus swabs from the penis, pubic hair samples, nail scrapings … those would be the most common."

"Doctor Morrow, what are these samples used for?"

"Well, they can either be used to see whether any genetic material from the alleged victim is on the accused or vice versa."

"So Doctor Morrow, if you found semen from the accused on the victim, that would be proof of a sexual encounter between the two?"

"Yes, although on its own it does not imply rape, it does confirm a sexual encounter between the two."

"And so, Doctor Morrow, if a suspect has stated that he has not met the victim and you were to find pubic hair from the victim on the accused, what would you then conclude?"

"It would be a proof that the accused was lying, that he had met the victim. Also, in a normal course of self-defense one would expect hair from the forearm or chest under the nails. Pubic hair under nails, in my experience, have only been present in cases of sexual violence."

Andy said, "Thank you." He looked rather pleased with himself. Peter smiled at him and gave him a subtle wink. Amanda, on the other hand, looked very disgruntled.

Andy walked towards his own bench and in a soft voice said, "Doctor Morrow, just for the record, and I do realise that the body was discovered a year after death, but would there be any way of knowing if there was forced vaginal penetration?"

"No, any injuries like that would cause soft-tissue damage. Any evidence would be destroyed with changes to tissues after death."

"You did, however, have an unexpected finding in the … let's say, pelvic area."

"Yes indeed, there was a cell phone SIM card in the pelvic area."

Andy went to a desk and lifted a transparent plastic bag. "Your honour, this is exhibit number three." He held it up and raised it so everyone could see it. "Your honour, I will refer to this at a later time."

Judge Temple nodded.

Andy then turned towards the jury. "Again, just to be clear, Doctor Morrow, is there any doubt whatsoever, in your expert opinion, that the hair found under this murdered girl's nail was that of the accused sitting over there?" He turned around and extended his right arm to its maximal length and pointed to Jake.

"No, Mister Gomez, no doubt whatsoever."

"Thank you, Doctor Morrow, I would like to thank you for taking the time in your busy…" He suddenly became aware of the judge glaring at him. "Yes, thank you doctor, that will be all."

The judge turned to Amanda. "Your witness, Miss Jackson."

As usual Amanda took her time and took a sip of water. She looked at the notes in front of her and, put the glass down and walked towards the stand.

"Doctor Morrow, would you say that you are one of the top pathologists in the state of New York?"

Doctor Morrow answered without any hesitation. "These are not words I have ever used."

"But other people have said this about you?"

Doctor Morrow shrugged his shoulder. "That is not of importance to me."

"I understand, doctor, and I appreciate your modesty. Certainly, I will not question your authority in forensic pathology. However, would you say that anybody can make a mistake?"

"Yes Miss Jackson, we are all fallible."

Amanda quickly turned away from Judge Temple so his frown would not distract her.

"Doctor, I would like to ask you about a case that you appeared in as a professional witness. In the case of state versus Lance Smyth, that's Smyth with a Y, I wonder if you remember the case or would you like me to jolt your memory?"

The doctor smiled a broad smile. "Yes I remember it well."

"For the benefit of the court, I will mention this part. There were allegations of rape against Mister Smyth and there were intimate samples taken. To be specific you had to obtain swabs from his penis, three types of swabs is that correct?"

"Yes, that is correct Miss Jackson."

"And you took those samples from Mister Smyth?"

"Yes."

"And is it correct that when the evidence was presented the penile swab samples showed that they were taken from a Mister Philip Morrow … that was you?"

There was a gasp from a lady in the court room.

Doctor Morrow seemed totally unperturbed and continued to smile. "Yes that is right."

"And how was that, doctor?"

"When I was signing the sample bags, I put my name instead of the person I was taking the sample from."

There was laughter around the court room.

The judge hit his gavel hard against the wooden block. "Silence!" There was sudden silence. He stared at Amanda. "And your point, Miss Jackson."

"Yes, your honour, I am getting to it right now."

"Doctor Morrow, I am simply agreeing with you that we are all fallible. We can all make mistakes."

Doctor Morrow simply smiled and was very calm. "I will not argue with that."

The judge was not smiling, rather he was frowning.

"So, Doctor Morrow, would you agree that some experts would say that genetic sampling is not one hundred per cent accurate and that a genetic sample may be compatible with more than one person?"

"Yes, there is not universal agreement on the degree of accuracy of samples and some fringe pathologists state that it is only accurate to one in perhaps a few thousand people. But over ninety nine percent of us accept that it is accurate to more than one in over a billion."

Amanda looked at the jurors. "But it may be wrong?"

"No, not in my opinion."

The judge was getting more restless. "Miss Jackson please approach the bench."

Andy put up his hand as if in a classroom. "May I too, your honour?"

The judge showed his agreement with a very slight nod of his head.

Andy approached the judge's seat. The judge whispered but his whisper did not hide his annoyance. "Miss Jackson, if you wanted other people's opinion then you should have invited them to be here. You are getting close to badgering a man of great respect, and I must say he has stayed very calm. Now, if you want to cross-examine him, continue. But don't use him or any other witnesses to pronounce your own opinions!"

It was Amanda's turn to raise her hand. "Your honour I was just …"

Judge Temple raised his eyebrows.

"Yes, your honour, understood."

Andy walked back. Amanda went to her notes and looked at them.

The judge said sternly. "Miss Jackson, any further questions?"

"Just one your honour." Amanda approached Doctor Morrow. "So you are agreed that not all pathologists agree that DNA samples can be used to indicate an exact match of a person?"

"That would be correct."

"That will be all, your honour, thank you Doctor Morrow."

The judge looked at the witness box. "You may leave." He smiled at the doctor.

Doctor Morrow smiled and looked very calm. "Thank you, your honour."

As Amanda sat down Lucy nodded. "Good job of a hopeless situation."

The judge directed Andy Gomez, "Your next witness please."

Andy stood up. "Your honour we would like to call Detective Derek Johnston to the stand."

The judge sounded very authoritative. "Detective Johnston, please come forward."

Derek walked to the stand and the bailiff swore him in.

The judge said, "Please be seated."

Andy looked at his notes for a few seconds. He put his notes down and approached the witness box. "Detective Johnston, I understand you have been assigned to investigate the deaths of Charlene Mills and Sarah Miller, is that right?"

"Yes sir … That is along with Detective Jim Sterne."

"Sure," said Andy, slightly caught off guard. "Can you please tell the court when you first came in contact with the accused, Mister John Chapman?"

"Yes, it was the night of November the sixteenth, the night that Charlene Mills' body was discovered."

"Detective, can you describe for the benefit of the jury the circumstances of your meeting with Mister Chapman," he raised his voice and looked towards Jake, "the accused."

Derek continued, "Quite fortuitously we stopped at a bar called Mexicano, a few blocks away from the murder scene–"

"Can I interrupt you before you go on, Mister Johnston, I do apologise, but do detectives usually frequent bars when working or after a crime scene?"

Derek gave a chuckle. "No Mister Gomez! It's just because on the crime scene we got a lot of mud on our shoes and Jim … Well, we wanted to clean our shoes!"

Some of the jury laughed quietly.

"Thank you, detective, carry on!"

"Well whilst in the bar Mister Chapman happened to be sitting beside us. During the conversation that ensued he mentioned, out of the blue and unprompted, that we should feel sorry for the girl who had been killed that night. He mentioned the one with the red shoes."

"Detective, what exactly were the words he used?"

"He said something to the effect that the girl who had been killed that night in Manhattan, beside the disused cement factory, the girl with the red shoes."

"Detective, are you certain about his statement?"

"Absolutely, Detective Sterne and I both recalled almost exactly the same words."

"And Detective Johnston, how did …" he looked towards Jake and pointed, "How did the *accused* say he heard about this murder?"

"He mentioned that he had heard it on CNN News. He mentioned that a black newsreader had read the news."

"And, Detective, you looked into this claim?"

"Yes, we did indeed. In fact, no broadcast studio had any info about this murder. We contacted CNN and they had not read this item of news. The press were all alerted by our captain the next morning. None had knowledge of the murder."

"And Detective, did you find out any other info from CNN?"

"Yes, they informed us that they had no black newsreaders on their staff."

Andy suddenly said, "That will be all, Detective Johnston, thank you very much." He walked quickly to his seat.

The judge turned to Amanda. "Any questions, Miss Jackson?"

Amanda was taken by surprise and had been taking notes. She put her pen down and had to flick through the papers in front of her.

She picked up an A4 page. "Detective Johnston, how long have you been working in the homicide team?"

"About three months, Miss Jackson."

"So the Charlene Mills case would be the first murder case you are investigating?"

"Yes, but Detective Sterne—"

Amanda interrupted, "Detective Johnston, please answer the question."

The judge turned to Derek. "Detective please answer the question asked."

"Yes, your honour." He turned towards Amanda. "Yes, this is the first case I am investigating."

"Detective, how many murders are there in New York annually?"

Derek was silent and seemed to be thinking.

Amanda interrupted, "Perhaps I should make this easier for you, how may murders were there in Manhattan last year?"

"Last year there were five hundred and fifteen murders in New York."

"That is very precise, Detective!"

"Yes, it's because I had to look up some facts before applying for a homicide detective position."

"My math isn't the best, Detective, but if we work out the average over fifty-two weeks, that would be about ten a week, is that right?"

Derek thought for a couple of seconds, "Yes, about ten and a half a week."

Amanda smiled and turned toward the jury. "Obviously, your math is better than mine." Most of the jury laughed aloud but quickly went quiet.

"So, Detective. There is more than one murder a night on average, and please you don't need to work out the exact stats."

The jury laughed louder and slightly longer. Derek smiled. "Yes, that would be correct."

"Now Detective Johnston it looks like you have some knowledge in the matter. Would you agree that certain nights there are no murders?"

"That is correct."

"Then, Detective, by a simple calculation we can deduce that on certain nights there may be three of four murders?"

"That is the case, Miss Jackson."

"So Detective, is it not possible that a person may get mixed up with different murders?"

Derek sat forward. "But there were no other murders in Manhattan that night."

Amanda was abrupt, "Detective, please answer the question."

The judge leaned forward and in a calm voice explained, "Detective Johnston, you are not being asked to make any conclusions, simply answer the question."

Derek sat back. "I am sorry, your honour." He turned to Amanda, "Please repeat the question."

"The question, Detective, was – and please pay attention – is it not likely that a person hearing about a murder on the news may get confused between one murder and the next, if there are several murders in one night?"

Derek looked apprehensive. He hesitated. "I … guess so."

Amanda turned to the judge. "That will be all, your honour."

The judge was about to speak to Derek when Andy stood up. "Your honour, as we have the right to recall any witness, rather than wait can I pose a couple of questions to Detective Johnston?"

Amanda had just sat down and stood up. The judge raised his hand and showing her the palm of his hand looked at Andy. "Yes, Mister Gomez, this is within your rights and I will allow it."

Andy approached the witness box. "Detective Johnston. Can you explain again how many murders there were on Manhattan the night of Saturday November the sixteenth?"

"Just the one."

"That of Charlene Mills?"

Derek nodded. "That is correct."

"Had there been any murders in the previous couple of days?"

"In fact, no."

Andy continued, "Had any girls been murdered in the previous week?"

Derek shook his head. "No, as I had not been tasked to investigate a murder case, I was keeping a close eye on all murders in New York over the previous month."

"Had anyone been murdered beside that or in fact any other cement factory, disused or otherwise?"

"No Mister Gomez." Derek shook his head again.

"Finally, Detective Johnston, had any girls, and in fact anyone, been murdered who was wearing red shoes?"

Derek shook his head even more emphatically. "Definitely not."

"Thank you, Detective, that will be all."

He sat down.

The judge looked at Amanda. "Because of the circumstances would you like to cross-question Detective Johnston again?"

Amanda shook her head. "No your honour, but we would like to reserve the right to recall Detective Johnston."

The judge nodded. "You may leave Detective Johnston, thank you."

The judge looked at Andy. "We still have some time today; would you like to call your next witness?"

Jim pushed his arms against the arms of his chair and half lifted himself up, ready to be called to the stand.

Andy looked at the judge. "No, your honour, that will be all for today. We were not able to get any more witnesses for today."

Jim was halfway up from his chair, before he slumped down and looked very surprised.

Lucy was surprised and looked at Amanda.

The judge banged his gavel. "That will bring proceedings to an end for the day. Court will reconvene tomorrow morning at nine a.m."

The judge got up. The bailiff pronounced, "All rise for the judge!"

Everyone stood up.

Andy looked towards Amanda and smiled.

Peter North whispered to Andy, "What about Detective Sterne?"

Andy whispered back, "I am taking a slight risk; I think we have done enough with the one detective; I am also anxious about what might be unearthed if Detective Sterne is cross-examined. I am worried the jury may get distracted about his slightly shady past and question the authenticity of the evidence and impartiality of NYPD."

Peter smiled. "Andy, you are a genius!"

Lucy looked at Amanda. She whispered, "Why did they not call Jim?"

Amanda looked at Andy and smiled. "Very shrewd move." She looked at Lucy.

Lucy looked at Jim, "Ah. I see!"

"Lucy, I think this is even going to be tougher than we thought. I had underestimated Andy."

"What are our chances of acquittal do you think?"

"Well kid, they were hovering in the one to two precent before today, now they are much smaller."

"So, what is the next move?"

Amanda sat back. The court was fairly empty, Jake had been taken away quickly and there were a handful of reporters in the back of the room on their cell phones reporting back.

Before Amanda could answer Andy approached her and Lucy. "Well Amanda, this is your client's last chance to plead guilty. If he does so we can drop the charges to a lesser charge of manslaughter due to diminished responsibility due to mental illness. You pick what you prefer, alcoholism, depression …"

Amanda interrupted. "Andy do you not have anywhere else you need to be? My defendant is innocent of these crimes and has no intention of pleading guilty. If I were you, I would go and look at all the facts because you have a fight on your hands!"

Andy smiled. "Very well then, see you tomorrow."

Amanda nodded.

Andy nodded his head. "Lucy."

"Have a good night, Mister Gomez."

Andy turned around, picked up his papers, and left.

Amanda looked at Lucy whose face was as red as a beetroot. "Have a good night Mister Gomez? You forgot to say sweet dreams Mister Gomez!"

"I am sorry Mandy, I said it before I knew what I was saying." Lucy paused, "Well at least you put on a brave face."

"You always have to. But no doubt he knows he has a strong case."

"Why did you not consider the option of guilty plea?"

"Oh, I have, and I will ask Jake, but we both know what he is going to say."

Lucy nodded. "What is our next move?" She looked concerned. "Are there any moves left?"

Amanda smiled and looked at Lucy. "Kid, there is always a next move, there is always a chance." She slowly stacked the papers in front of her into a neat pile. However, it seemed to be absentmindedly, as her thoughts seemed to be far away. She put the papers down. She looked around the room. There were only the two of them left. She sat back and seemed to relax.

Lucy waited patiently, knowing something was brewing in Amanda's mind.

Amanda finally spoke. "I remember when I was about fifteen, I was in my bedroom crying. My father was going past the room. He must have heard me. He knocked gently and I didn't answer. He slowly opened the door and walked in. He sat on my bed and asked me what was wrong. In between sobs I told him that I fancied Tim. In fact, I think I told him I was in love with him and just found out he had asked another girl to go out with him. Tim was six foot two at sixteen and the star of our basketball team. We had been smiling at each other for a while and I hadn't been brave enough to approach him and he seemed quite shy. I had just heard that he had asked Sandra, one of the cheerleaders, to go out with him. My dad put his arms around me and tried to console me. I said things like Sandra was butt-ugly – actually she was gorgeous – and that Tim was no-good and not my type anyway. My dad just nodded, gave me a hug, and left the room. I could have strangled him. I remember thinking at that moment that I hated my dad too. I was very quiet at dinner and my mother kept asking me if I was all right and I kept saying I had a bad headache. After dinner, I excused myself to go to lie down in my bedroom and take some painkillers. My mother said sure, but my dad held my hand and said he wanted to show me something. I tried to pull away, but his grip was so tight that I couldn't free myself. He looked at me and smiled. I felt he wasn't going to let go and felt compelled to follow him. He took me to the sitting room and walked me to the shelves in one corner. I had no idea what he was up to but was hoping to get whatever it was over and done with so I could go to my room and cry and feel sorry for myself and remind myself how much I hated Tim, Sandra, and my dad.

"My dad pointed to the trophy on the shelf. It was in the shape of a knight, as in the chess game. I had never noticed it! 'Did you know I was the school champ in chess?' Actually, what I wanted to say was 'You insensitive jerk, how can you talk about chess when my whole life is about to finish.' Instead I instinctively said, 'No dad, I never knew that.' He must have known I was miles away, so he held my face in his two hands and turned my face towards him. 'Darling, please pay attention to me.' He smiled. Strangely his smile just melted my heart. I nodded. He continued, 'You know, I was playing in the final of the school chess competition. I always reckoned I was better than Jessie, but I made one silly mistake in the final and I was ironically a knight behind. As I had a losing hand, I realized that I had nothing to lose so I started to play in a chaotic and irrational manner. I pushed all my pawns forward, exposing my king to all-out attack and danger. Jessie got really flustered and began to play defensive. The short of the story is that I marched two of my pawns forward and ended up with two additional queens, won the match and the rest is history. Now darling, do you know what you need to do?' He winked at me. I nodded.

"Well the next day I approached Tim first thing. He was standing with two of his mates. I told him that I had heard that he was going to go out with Sandra. I wished him good luck and turned around. After a couple of steps, I suddenly turned around and looked at him over my shoulder and whispered but loud enough for his mates to hear. I said, 'For your sake I hope she can kiss as well as I do.'"

Lucy was on the edge of her seat, "Well, what happened?"

"Oh nothing much, except Tim and I were kissing and cuddling at the back of the gym after school."

Lucy laughed.

Amanda continued, "I came home that evening in a chirpy mood. My mother told me my headache must be away. I looked at my dad and winked and said, 'Yes, the pain is away completely, thanks to the medicine dad gave me.' My mother looked quizzically at me dad who was smiling at me."

"I guess you went out with Tim for a while then?"

"Are you kidding me? He was crap at kissing. I dumped him the next day!"

Lucy laughed. When she stopped, she asked, "So what is our next move then?"

"We have a couple of options but let me think about them overnight."

CHAPTER 36

Jim Meets Mary-Beth

Jim was seated in the open area in the mall. He was sipping a latte from a big mug when a lady approached his table. She had shoulder-length black hair that was brushed immaculately. She was wearing a knee-length mustard coloured skirt with a black blouse. She had a black quilted coat with a hood hanging on her arm.

She approached Jim rather tentatively, stopped a yard away from the table and then took a short step forward.

"Are you Jim?" she asked rather timidly.

Jim looked at her with a rather surprised look. He looked over her shoulder and looked at her again. As he put his mug down, he realized he had a froth of milk on his upper lip. He quickly wiped it off.

"Yes," Jim said, instinctively looking around the mall very quickly again.

The lady reached out her right hand. "Hello, I'm Mary-Beth. Derek's wife."

Jim sprang to his feet. "O my goodness, this is a pleasant surprise. What brings you here? How did you know …?"

Mary Beth laughed. "Yes, I thought you'd be wondering how I knew it was you. Derek mentioned to me last night that he was meeting you here for coffee before you went to question one of his contacts. I was shopping in the neighbourhood so I thought I would drop in to meet you."

"That's very kind of you to come over. Although I would have thought you would have done most of your shopping in Queens rather than coming to Manhattan."

Mary-Beth smiled. "Spoken like a true detective. If the truth be told Derek has spoken so much about you, I couldn't resist the opportunity of meeting you face to face." She looked at the empty seat. "Do you mind if I sit down?"

"Oh I am sorry Mary-Beth, you caught me by surprise and I forgot my manners. Do sit down. Please."

Mary-Beth sat down and took off her black leather gloves.

"Would you like a cup of coffee?"

"I would," Jim looked around to catch the eye of the waiter. "But I won't have the time."

Jim turned around. "Derek won't be here for fifteen to twenty minutes."

"Yes, but he likes to keep his work and private life separate and I am best leaving before he arrives. I just couldn't resist this chance. You see, even though he is a wonderful husband and we do a lot of work for the church together, I still feel there is a part of him I don't know at all." She paused.

Jim resisted the temptation of saying anything. He just picked up his mug of coffee and took a sip of it.

Mary-Beth eventually continued. "Well it is as if he has two lives, two marriages. Once he leaves the house and goes to work, I feel I don't know the man who goes away. He rarely talks about his work or his feelings about work." She smiled. "With the exception of you. He constantly talks about how good you are and how much he is learning from you."

"Well, Mary-Beth, you know what they say, you can fool some of the people some of the time!"

"Oh no Jim, you are being modest. I have no doubt it is all true."

"Okay so what do you want to know about our work?"

"Well actually nothing in specific. I mean outside of our life I know he likes fast cars and loves to watch boxing. But I just want to get a feel of what you are like so I can picture Derek at work and feel that I am closer to him in some way."

Jim put down his mug. "I'm sure you know that he has come here with a glowing reference and seems to be lined up for higher things."

"Yes, I know that not many get to work in homicide at such a young age. Still that is a side of him that is totally in a dark room for me and I feel I cannot be in touch with. Sometimes I think I am not worthy enough to be married to him."

"What do you mean?"

"Well Jim, you know that he saved a child's life by giving him CPR for about an hour?"

"Yes actually I heard that the other day. The child was left for dead."

"That's right. You know he became very unwell after that and was hospitalized because he got carbon monoxide poisoning from performing CPR. He inhaled the carbon monoxide because he gave the child mouth-to-mouth resuscitation."

"Gosh, I didn't know that. Derek is too modest to self-glorify."

"Well, Jim, you don't know the half of it. Everyone says that Derek and I raise a lot of funds for the church, but in fact it is Derek who is the brains behind the operation and organizes all the coffee mornings, car boot sales etc."

"He is an impressive guy."

"That he is! But also, he seems to worship the ground I walk on, sometimes I feel embarrassed and so unworthy of such adoration."

"Well Mary-Beth, I am sure you are worthy of his attention."

"But still I feel that at times he is a different person once he leaves home and would love to know what he is like at work."

Jim paused for a few seconds. "You know that a lot of wives of detectives feel that their husbands have two marriages, to them and to their work. No doubt it is the same for husbands of the female officers."

"I know, but I thought this would change and I would be more in touch with his work as time went on, but I think if anything I have got further away from him."

"Now you know why there is such a high divorce rate in cops."

Mary-Beth was silent.

"I am sorry Mary-Beth, that was a bit insensitive, I didn't mean it that way."

"Don't worry, Jim, you haven't said anything I haven't thought about."

"I'm sure he has told you about my ... our late miscarriage."

"No, he hasn't actually. I'm sure he was waiting for the right moment to mention it."

"I think I lost him a bit then. It was a difficult time for me. I became really depressed and he was ever so sweet and caring. But I think since then he doesn't want to ..."

"Go ahead Mary-Beth."

"Well I was so low that I think he doesn't want me to get pregnant again."

"These things can take a long time to get over." Jim sat up and said in a cheerier voice. "Well I am sure when you have two or three little ones running around it will be different and you will see a different side of him and much more of him."

"That may be a long time," exclaimed Mary-Beth.

"How do you mean?"

"I suppose it will take us both a while to get over the miscarriage. It's silly but sometimes I think he is closer to you than he is to me."

Jim thought for a second. "Mary-Beth let me explain to you what it is like out there. You put on your jacket, pick up your badge and gun and leave the office. The moment you leave the office you are totally dependent on your partner and vice versa. One mistake by you, a momentary lapse and your partner could be ... well in a lot of trouble. So, the bond you develop is unique in a way that even someone you are married to might envy."

"Well," Mary Beth said, looking rather disappointed.

"I am sorry if I have made you feel worse! That wasn't my intention. You should see him when he talks about you. His eyes light up. He looks like a different person. In fact, he makes me jealous."

"Wow, Jim. You have just made me so happy."

Jim leant forward. "Don't ever compare the cop partnership to love at home. Be proud of what you have. Every cop gets a number of partners during their career. Hopefully he or she will only have one spouse for life."

"Thank you so much, Jim. I can see why he is so full of praise for you."

"And likewise, Mary-Beth."

Mary Beth let out a big sigh. "I think on that wonderful note I will take my leave. Maybe this can be a private moment between us."

"My lips are sealed."

Mary-Beth got up and Jim got up in politeness. She hugged him and turned away and walked quickly with a smile on her face.

CHAPTER 37

Friends in Low Places

Jim braked suddenly, so much so that Derek was flung forward in the passenger seat and his seat belt locked, lurching him backwards even more violently.

Jim turned his head around and peered over his left shoulder. He reversed the car fairly fast, cutting back across an intersection. A car crossing the intersection had to swerve suddenly and tooted the horn. The car then came to an abrupt stop and the driver got out of his seat and started to wave his fist. "What the hell sort of driving is that, you moron!" his voice seemingly rising with each word.

Derek anxiously looked at the driver and then looked at Jim. "You nearly killed us both!"

Jim did not seem to take any notice of the driver who was still shaking his fist and shouting obscenities. He looked at Derek. "You are still alive, aren't you?"

"Only by the grace of God!" Derek quipped.

Jim looked over his left shoulder again, moving his head from side to side.

"Is that the guy?" asked Derek, looking at a person on the sidewalk.

"No, it's the Red Sox cap made me think it was Joe. Not many guys wear a Boston Red Sox cap in the Big Apple. But that guy is too tall to be Joe."

Just then the driver of the car had walked up to Jim's window and started to slam the window with his fist. "You moron, what the fuck sort of crazy driving is that? You backed on to a main road!" Jim shook his head in annoyance but still did not look at the driver.

"Do you hear me, you fucking asshole! I am going to call the police right now."

Jim was very calm. He shook his head and told Derek, "No it's definitely not Joe."

The man again rapped on the window. "Did you hear me? Come out and I will show you a piece of my mind," he clenched his hand into a fist. "and my right hook."

Jim lifted his right hand off the steering wheel and held it up. "All right, I'm sorry man."

Derek's face was getting red and he suddenly burst out shouting, "Who the hell do you think you are?"

The man was about six foot six and had a physique of a body builder. He continued to shake his fist. "Come out here and say that."

Derek shouted back, "Do you have a clue who you are fucking with?" as he reached across Jim to roll down Jim's window.

Jim put his hand on Derek's wrist. "Stay cool, kid, it's not worth it."

A taxi driver got out of his yellow cab and started to shout, "What sort of an idiot parks his car in the middle of the road?"

The first driver rapped Jim's window even harder.

Derek pushed Jim's hand away. "I'll show him not to mess with us."

Derek suddenly opened his own door and got out. The man walked towards Derek, his fists clenched. He had a white T-shirt on, which was very tight-fitting. His upper arm muscles were all tensed and looked like they were going to tear the T-shirt. As he got close to Derek, Derek suddenly reached towards his back and pulled out his gun.

"Go on! Who is the moron now, punk?"

The man had a look of horror on his face and took one step back. He put up his hand. "Hey look man I am sorry, but your friend nearly killed me."

Derek's hand was shaking slightly. "Yes and another word from you and I might just finish the job!"

The man slowly took a step back with his hands in the air and looked at Jim pleadingly, as Jim was getting out of the car.

Jim walked very slowly and calmly towards Derek. The driver looked pale.

"Look mister," he said his voice slightly quivering, "maybe I got a bit carried away."

Jim reached his right hand towards his waist. The man looked even more anxious. Jim pulled out his NYPD police badge. He then put his hand on Derek's gun and using one finger pointed the barrel away from the man. He then realized it was pointing towards the crowd that had been gathering. He then slowly pushed the barrel of the gun towards the ground. He lifted his badge very high. "All right, NYPD, homicide. I'm afraid there has been a terrible mistake, you can all disperse."

He then looked at Derek, pointed to the man in the Boston Red Sox cap and said in a serious voice, "Sorry Detective, my mistake, this is not the man we are looking for. He just looks like him."

"You scared the shit out of me, man!" the driver said with a quivering voice.

Jim then stood in front of the man so he was between Derek and him. "Sorry man, this is a case of mistaken identity. We thought we saw a suspect. We are looking for a dangerous man." Jim then pulled out a card from his pocket. "I'm Detective Jim Sterne, if you have any queries do not hesitate to call me, or you can come down to the precinct for a chat. You have a right to make a complaint."

The man was visibly shaking. "No man, I don't want no trouble." He looked hesitantly over his shoulder. "Can I go now?"

"Sure, sure, I am sorry," said Jim.

The man walked backwards and with his two hands half raised. "That's all right, man, just minding my own business, I don't want no trouble!" With that he walked quickly but still backwards towards his car and got in and drove away, spinning his wheels as he drove off.

Jim put his badge away and shouted to the crowd. "All right the fun is over, you can all carry on."

He looked at Derek. "Are we good to go?"

"Sh..sure, sure."

They both got into the car and Jim calmly drove off. The two of them did not speak a word for a few minutes.

Derek finally spoke. "Does it not piss you off the way people carry on in public?"

Jim nodded. "It sure does, but not as much as cops pulling out their guns on members of the public."

"The man was about to break your window!"

"Yes Derek, and I nearly caused an accident. You could be suspended if he were to report you."

"Well he won't, because he is chicken shit." Derek paused and looked at Jim. "Unless you are going to report me? Are you?"

Jim looked at Derek. "Report what? Did you see anything?"

Derek smiled, "I saw nothing."

Jim nodded. "Make sure you keep your gun packed away unless you intend to use it."

"Okay. Point taken. Won't happen again." He paused for a second. "But he deserved to be taught a lesson."

Jim shook his head, "My! Aren't we stubborn?"

Derek looked at Jim. "Look at Mister Whiter-Than-White, I have heard about your reputation!"

Jim glanced at Derek briefly. "And what reputation is that?"

"Well you don't need me to tell you."

"Oh, but please do tell me," Jim said, smiling and with a hint of humour. "What is it exactly that you have heard about me?" Jim looked at Derek. He was very calm.

"Well." Derek eyes wondered in different directions. "I suppose I am best being direct."

Jim jumped in. "You haven't held back today, so why start now?"

"Well, the word on the street is that you would do anything to get your man. Including planting evidence."

Jim was quiet for a few moments. "Do you believe everything you hear?"

"You tell me, Jim."

"Well first of all I don't always get my man. Just nearly always! Secondly, planting evidence is a criminal offence. Let's just say I have never put anyone behind bars who was not guilty."

Derek nodded. "So how would you describe it?"

"I would describe it as making the prosecution aware of certain facts that are not obvious." Jim nodded. "That would be a good description. But my conscience is clear, I … I need say no more."

Jim was scanning the pavement as he was talking.

"So who is this guy?"

"Which guy?"

"You know who I am talking about, this Joe character. How do you know him and what do you think he knows?"

"It is a long story."

"Come on, Jim, I wasn't born yesterday. What are you hiding from me?"

"I just don't want to teach you bad habits, Derek."

"It's too late for that. That idea went out the door the day I met you."

Jim laughed. "Okay, I suppose I owe it to you." Jim had come to an intersection and stopped talking. He looked left and then straight ahead. "Eeny meeny miney moe, where-should-I-go, let's see now."

After a couple of seconds there was a loud blow of the horn from a yellow cab behind, followed by two short blasts of the horn.

"Okay, three blasts of the horn means left."

"Well?" said Derek.

"Have you heard of the D'Agostino case?"

"Was that the drug dealer guy, that got off scott free on a technicality?"

"Yes, although I am sure you heard that he was topped shortly after by a rival gang."

"Yeah I heard of that too."

"Well it was pretty much known to us that D'Agostino and his mob were responsible for a series of gang crimes, in particular a number of murders. To be honest most of us in homicide were quite happy if they all knocked each other off one by one, but the NYPD hierarchy felt under pressure to do something, as the public were getting very nervous and also a number of innocent bystanders had been hurt in some of the shootings. Once a grenade was thrown into a restaurant, that was the final straw. Few of the rival Conti family mob were killed. Unfortunately, a judge's daughter and her newlywed husband were also killed in the restaurant. That's when it was decided to take some sort of action. We moved in on D'Agostino."

"Was that not a narcotics team bust? I heard they made a mess of the evidence."

"Yes they had been tailing him for about three years, but the homicide squad were collaborating with them, and our captain, Will, who had just got his present job, was keen to make a good name for himself and asked me to do all I could to nail the son of a bitch."

Jim stopped at another junction. "Now let me remember where I found Joe last year. Hmmm, Let's try right this time." He turned right and drove very slowly on the inside lane. So slow in fact that a bicycle overtook him, the rider giving him a quizzical look as he went by.

"D'Agostino was as slippery as an eel, and it was proving very difficult to get anything on him. I was tailing him once and saw Joe in the area. I recognised Joe from a photo in the D'Agostino file. I stopped him. He looked really nervous, like shifty. I searched him and he was carrying a kilo of the white stuff. He told me that he was out on bail and that in fact he had gone clean a couple of years ago. He said he worked in a local pizza place doing deliveries at night. It was late December, and he needed some extra cash to buy presents for his two kids. Said he was doing a one-off delivery of cocaine. I didn't believe him for a second, but I had no interest in arresting him but was also worried about drawing attention to us. So, I let him go. As he was leaving, he told me that he owes me one. The guys actually trailed him for a few weeks, and it turned out that he had gone clean. But for someone who is allegedly clean he seems to know a lot and I would call on him occasionally for info on the ground. He says he spends the daytime going around different bookies, but I have my suspicions. Anyway, I have more use for him on the ground and he has been of value in nailing two murder cases."

"So, what was it they got D'Agostino on?"

"His right-hand man, Jimmy One-Ear, so called because he had one of his ears cut off when he was fifteen years old, was handling and delivering drugs from he was twelve. Jimmy had some sort of dispute with D'Agostino. The squad thought D'Agostino suspected Jimmy had been putting his hand in the cookie jar and had threatened that if Jimmy didn't put the money back he would kill his son. Just to show him he meant business he cut off his other ear. It took the hospital twenty-four hours to stop the bleeding. Jimmy One-Ear, or should it be Jimmy No-Ears, immediately sent his wife and son to Europe somewhere and went to the Feds. He asked for immunity for spilling the beans on D'Agostino. The short of the story is that the narcotic squad contaminated the evidence they had picked up. Jimmy found out a week before the trial that his wife and son had drowned in what was described as a boating accident in Switzerland. Jimmy was found dead – allegedly a suicide – and D'Agostino walked free, only to be shot dead by forty-six bullets a week later. I guess the godfathers felt he had too much heat on him and was becoming a liability."

"Well," said Derek, "at least there is some justice in the world."

"Except that the baton of drug dealing has just been passed to someone else."

"So I guess Joe now owes you a favour?"

"Yep, I get a lot of my info from guys who owe me."

"So, this is what they mean when they say you like to run with the fox and hunt with the hounds?"

"Well I think sometimes you have to sacrifice something less important for what is of more value, after all."

Jim pulled the car near the kerb and stopped suddenly. "You see the guy with the Red Sox cap, that's Joe."

"The guy sitting on the short garden wall?"

"Yep, that's him. He looks like he is waiting for someone, doesn't he?"

Derek nodded. "What is he doing, selling drugs?"

"No, I don't think Joe would work at that level now. I suspect he carries money for guys, big sums of cash. In any case, I don't wanna know!" Jim looked through the back and side windows of the car. "Tell you what, I want you to go and ask him to come and see me in the car. He wouldn't want to be seen with me, the last time I approached him he got very scared. I think he is worried about being watched."

"No problem," said Derek as he reached to open the car door, "I can do that."

Jim held Derek's forearm. "Derek, you look like a cop, and he'll probably disappear before you reach him. Take off your jacket."

"But it's very cold out here!" Derek saw the look on Jim's face and took his jacket off.

Jim looked at him. "Okay take your tie off too."

Derek took off his tie. "Is this okay?"

"No, you are still too clean cut, pull your shirt out of your trouser."

Derek did as commanded.

Jim opened his glove compartment and took out a cap with the New York Yankees NY on it. "Put this on."

Derek put on the cap. "That's more like it. Now you can go!"

Derek got out of the car. He was about to tuck his shirt back in his trousers, but he looked down and pushed it out again. He walked on the opposite side of the road that Joe was on. He looked across the road and noticed Joe looking at him. He quickly looked away to his left and started walking down the road away from Joe. Joe followed Derek's movement with his eyes for a while and then seemed to lose interest. Derek walked about a hundred yards up the road and then crossed the road and walked back towards Joe. He kept well away from the wall that Joe was sitting on. The last twenty yards Joe was looking at him directly. Derek suddenly turned around and walked straight toward Joe. Joe looked past Derek and also to his left and right. Derek went over and sat down on the wall a yard or so from Joe.

Joe looked at Derek and then looked towards Jim's car.

"Nice morning," Derek said, looking at Joe.

"That's a matter of perspective, isn't it?" said Joe.

"Suppose so. Better morning for a Yankee fan than a Red Sox fan, after last season."

Joe turned around and looked at Derek. "I'm sure a cop didn't come all the way here to talk about baseball with me."

"What makes you think I am a cop?"

Joe looked towards Jim's car. "Is this your partner in there?"

Derek paused for a second. "Okay you got me, it's Jim, he wants to talk to you."

"Jim who?"

"Jim Sterne."

"Shit! Should have known!"

"Well are you coming?" Derek said, not sounding convinced.

Joe looked around a little nervously. "Tell you what, why don't you get up and get into the car, if you go down the street take the next right three times running. Don't look to your right, but you will end up beside that Launderette to our right. I will get in the car there."

"How can I be sure that you won't run?" Derek asked.

"Because if Jim wants to see me, he will see me one way or the other."

"Okay we'll see you soon." Derek got up and walked to the car and was about to get in the back seat.

Jim put his hand on Derek's chest. "Make sure your shoes are clean."

Derek checked both shoes, top and bottom, "All clear, boss."

Jim nodded towards the back of the car. "In that case you can get in."

After a few seconds the car drove off.

Joe waited a minute and walked in the opposite direction.

Jim stopped the car just before the intersection near the launderette. Joe had walked around to the intersection and looked around before quickly opening the front passenger door to Jim's car and jumping into the front seat.

Joe looked anxious and looked around in all directions and still without looking at Jim pointed to the left. "Start off quick and take a left just here and drive for a few blocks!"

Jim drove off. Joe slouched down in the seat, so his head was barely above the bottom of the window.

Jim looked at Joe. "Anyone in particular watching you, Joe?"

Joe shook his head. "No, I just don't want anyone to think that I am a rat. Anyway, you should be looking where you are going or you'll cause an accident."

Jim looked forward. After he had driven a few blocks Joe sat up. "Right Jim, you can stop here."

Jim looked in his rear-view mirror and stopped after indicating. "Well how are you keeping, Joe?"

"Let's cut through the crap, Jim, you are not here to ask about my health, nor is your friend interested in the fate of the Boston Red Sox." Joe turned around and looked at Derek, "Even though I am glad to say that the curse of the Bambino is gone once and for all."

"I'll keep it brief," Jim said as he switched off the car. "I want information on the girl that was murdered last year. She had disappeared and her body was recently dug up. You know her name was Sarah Miller. She was a high-class escort. What do you know?"

Joe looked out Jim's window at some guy who was sitting on the steps of a doorway, with earphones in his ears, for a few seconds and then turned to Jim again. "What makes you think I know anything about a call girl, Jim? In fact, I can categorically say that I don't know anything about this law girl you talked about."

Jim smiled. "Come on Joe, if anything happens in this neighbourhood and you don't know anything about it, it is not worth knowing. Anyway, you said the law girl, how did you know she was a law student?"

"I said call girl, and I know nothing about her."

"No Joe! You definitely said law girl!"

Joe looked at the guy sitting on the steps. He had an i-Pod in his hand and seemed to be choosing his music on it. He then put the i-Pod in his pocket and walked away. Joe then looked through the back window of the car and turned around, fidgeting nervously. "Okay Jim, I will help you out this one time, but it will be at a cost to you."

"All right Joe, you never asked for money before, but how much are we talking about?"

"It's not money we are talking about. Look Jim, you did me a big favour before, and I in turn have helped you whenever I could. But now I am a family man and have got away from all the stuff from the past. I don't want nobody thinking I am involved in any of the shit that I used to be in; and frankly you meeting me like this is going to give the wrong people the wrong ideas." Joe stopped to looked out his own window and then looked back at Jim. "So I will do you this one favour, but after this we have to say goodbye for good!"

Jim looked at Joe "Joe, I …" He paused. "Okay fair enough, it's a deal."

"Thanks Jim, my whole family is indebted to you, but this is the final meeting."

Jim nodded. "Okay, so what do you know about the law girl?"

Joe turned around and looked at Derek. "I'll tell you all I know, which is not a lot, but first of all this amateur friend of yours must leave us alone."

Jim shook his head. "Sorry Joe. I did not introduce you. This is Derek, my new partner. Derek, this is Joe."

Derek reached his hand to shake hands with Joe. Joe ignored Derek and turned to Jim again. "Trust me, you don't want this guy here when I tell you what I know."

"Sorry Joe, this is my partner, and we have no secrets, this would not be a good time to start."

"But Jim—"

Jim interrupted, "Come on Joe, we are just wasting time, let's just get on with it."

Joe looked back at Derek and shrugged his shoulders. "Okay but don't tell me I didn't warn you! Well the story on the street is that the girl was killed by someone who frequents this area regularly, if you catch my drift." Jim looked at Joe.

"Are we playing a game of charades here, Joe?"

Joe fidgeted uncomfortably and seemed reluctant to speak.

"God damn it, Joe, you are wasting both our time, will you just tell me what it is you don't know and we can all get the hell out of here!"

"All right Jim, the story is that the guy is a cop!"

Jim looked back at Derek and they looked at Joe and laughed out loud. "Come on Joe, you have got to be kidding me. A cop, who frequents this area a lot!"

Joe seemed more anxious than ever.

"All right Joe, what is it that you are not telling me?"

"For God sake Jim, I did warn you. You asked for this. The word is that it is YOU, Jim! You have been seen regularly around the area and people became suspicious and found out you were a cop."

Jim laughed. "Come on Joe I didn't come all this way to …" Jim looked at Derek. "Derek, would you mind leaving for a few minutes?"

Derek nodded. "Sure Jim."

Derek got out of the car and waited for a few minutes outside the car. Joe eventually got out and adjusted his baseball cap and looking around started back towards the direction they had driven there.

Derek got into the front seat of the car. "What was all that about?"

Jim started the car. "Don't worry, Derek, just a case of a misunderstanding." And with that Jim drove off.

*

Next morning Jim and Derek were in Jim's office when the phone phone rang. Jim answered the phone. "Jim here … Yes Captain … Right away, Captain!"

Jim put the phone down. "Let's go, the captain wants to see us."

Derek got up. As they got to the door Derek stopped. "Jim, I need to tell you something."

Jim opened the door. "I'm sure whatever it is it can wait because the captain can't!"

Derek seemed a bit hesitant. "I would like to just have a couple of minutes."

"Later Derek, trust me when I know by the tone of the captain's voice it is something urgent."

"All right Jim."

They arrived at the captain's office. Will was speaking to another man who was in his office.

"Good morning Jim, Derek, can I introduce you to Captain Ken Patterson from the Narcotic squad. Ken, Detective Jim Sterne and Detective Derek Johnston."

"Good morning gentlemen."

"Good morning Captain," said Jim.

"Good morning Captain," said Derek, and they shook hands in turn.

Without wasting any time Ken passed a photograph to Jim. "I believe you know this man."

Jim took a look at the photo and immediately sat down.

"What is it, Jim?" Derek asked at he looked at Jim. "You look a bit pale."

Jim passed the photograph to Derek. Derek looked at the photograph. It was of a man with a bullet wound to his head. "Isn't that Joe what's-his-name that we spoke to …" Derek stopped speaking and looked up with a guilty look on his face.

Jim spoke quietly, "Yes Captain, I saw him yesterday and we questioned him. When did this happen?"

Ken sounded irritated. "Last night. Do you realise the narcotics squad has been working with Joe for the past year? He has been giving us inside information. You just blew his cover and messed up the whole operation."

Jim took the lead. "I am sorry Captain, I thought Joe had left all that behind him."

"Well he has for sure now." Ken said in a very stern voice. "Now can I show you some more photographs?" He picked up a couple of photographs.

Will stood up. "Ken I will take it from here. After all, it is my department."

Ken looked at Will for a couple of seconds and then nodded. "All right Will, but I would like an explanation."

"I promise you that, Ken."

Ken nodded, and with a quick nod of the head he said, "Gentlemen." He walked out of Will's office.

Will looked at Derek. "Son, would you mind giving us a few moments alone?"

"Sure Captain," Derek said as he looked at Jim and quickly left the room.

"I'm sorry Captain, I had no idea. I know that Joe always was in the know and could have given me some sort of a lead." Jim then noticed that Will was not paying any attention to him. "Sorry Captain, what is it?"

Will gave him a couple of photographs. Jim looked at one photograph and then the next one. He handed them back to Will. "Well they are not my best side, but I do look well in both of them."

"Jim this is not a time for jokes."

"Sorry Captain, so narcotics got pictures of me? I am judging by the blue shirt I am wearing that was yesterday with Joe. I suppose you are going to give me an explanation about the other photos?"

"Yes Jim, the other two photos show you coming out of a house in the red-light district, near to where Charlene Mills used to frequent."

"Will, it's a long story. I would rather not get into it now, but you don't think I had anything to do with Charlene's death, do you?"

"No that's absurd, Jim. But as Ken explained, Joe has been passing on information about the Chiesi gang. It was actually mainly about money laundering, which is what Joe was very good at, in his heyday. Anyway, when you met up with Joe, they had to question Joe, he seemed very loyal to you, but eventually he had to tell them why you had seen him. They then went back and looked at these pictures in a very seedy area of town, with some other pictures of you entering a prostitute's apartment. They asked around and Ken tells me that you are reported to be there on multiple occasions."

"Where is this all going, Will?"

"Well Jim, Ken saw me personally, partly because Joe had told them that rumour had it that you may have killed Sarah."

"Will, you have got to be kidding me!"

"Just hear me out, Jim. They had pictures of Derek meeting with Joe, so I had to speak to Derek, and he also verified what Joe had told you."

"Will, don't tell me you believe any of that shit about me being involved with Sarah Miller's murder?"

"No Jim, not for a minute, but the rumour has spread like wildfire and Captain Patterson is under pressure to show the police are seen to have some leads."

Jim got up and walked to the glass door of Will's office. He noticed Derek sitting at his desk, looking anxiously at him. Jim walked back to Will's desk. "Well Will, is this the part that you ask me to hand in my badge and gun and tell me not to have any more involvement in the case?"

Will smiled. "Jim you have been watching too many movies. This is the part where I tell you to step it up and nail the son of a bitch that is guilty and get the heat off my back. Look Jim, I know you don't always play it by the book, and in fact I don't want to know all the ins and outs of whatever the hell you do. All I know is that this is bullshit, and I won't give it a second thought. But I am still under pressure and I need something more than what we have. Remember it's not just your ass on the line, it is also mine."

"Thank you, Captain. I'll try my best." Jim walked to the door.

"Jim come back and sit down."

Jim walked slowly back and sat on a chair. "What is it, Captain?" he said, looking a bit anxious.

"I have known you for a long time. Can I trust you to be very discrete?"

"Are you going to tell me that you killed her, Captain?"

"Very funny, Jim. But you need to promise me what I tell you will never be disclosed to anyone."

"You can trust me, Will."

"Not a soul!"

Jim saluted, "Aye aye, Captain."

"How well did you know Joe?"

"I had seen him on a few occasions. That day he did look very nervous and shifty, I assumed he was involved with some sort of dirty dealing somewhere, although in a strange way I was very fond of the guy and I genuinely thought he was going to get out of the business all together a couple of years ago. He always gave me the impression that at heart he was a family man, but perhaps had been caught up in the drug scene from an early age and couldn't extricate himself out of the mess."

"Yes, I never understand how drug dealers can wreck so many lives but can have so much love and loyalty for their own family."

Jim scratched his head. "I suppose underneath it all, all of us are looking for the same things in life."

"Did Joe tell you about his family?"

"He never stopped talking about his family, at every opportunity. In fact, that day he told me that he had moved his family to Detroit for a better education for his children."

Will pulled his seat forward and leaned over and spoke more quietly. Instinctively Jim leant forward. "Jim, Joe's family were moved to an unknown location a few months ago. Joe had given the narcotics squad enough information to crucify the Chiesi gang multiple times, but he had always said he would not testify, as he would never be sure of his family's safety. They had been working on catching the gang red handed. When they saw you with Joe, they had to step it up, and now they have the guy who was cooking the books of the gang. The mob got suspicious that there was something cooking, they threatened the book-keeper, and he wants out. Anyway, Joe isn't dead. This is a mock killing. Joe is on his way to join his family, a place which even he did not know the location of when he left!"

"Joe's parents are still alive, aren't they?"

"They are the only other people who know. His brother and sister don't even know that he is not dead. But apparently, they were not very close. They knew he was involved in criminal activities and have both disowned him and not spoken to each other in years."

"How come Ken gave you so much info, Will?"

"It's an unsaid rule amongst captains. Sometimes you give out information, but in return get some useful information. It is accepted that this additional info may be of help at some stage, but also that it is never shared."

"Have you ever shared privileged information like this before with anyone?"

"Never. That's sacrilegious!"

"And what info are you going to give Ken?"

"I'm working on that. Ken wants your scalp; I suppose to divert attention from his own squad. But that's my problem for now. Now get out there and get me something of use."

"Yes Captain." With that Jim got up and left.

CHAPTER 38

Bennie Meets Dad

Ben sat in the visitor's area looking anxiously at the door. Every time the visitor's door opened and some relatives walked in, his head dropped. He looked at the guard. "How much time left for visiting, sir?"

The guard answered mockingly, "Don't worry, you are not the first one to be stood up. Who in their right mind would want to visit this piss-hole?" He laughed.

Ben asked again, "I am sorry, sir, but would you mind telling me what time it is?"

The guard stopped smirking, he looked at his watch. "Twenty minutes left. You should have stayed in your cell and read a book."

Outside the visiting room Letitia was holding Bennie's hand. She had a dark brown dress on with a floral pattern and frills at the neckline. She started to pull his arm towards the visiting room. "Come on, we are running out of time to see your daddy!"

Bennie had maroon cords on with a white long-sleeved shirt buttoned to the top. "I don't want to go in there, mamma, I am not coming in."

"Please darling, your daddy wants to see you."

Bennie stamped his foot. "Well I don't want to see him."

"He will be very sad if we don't go in, Bennie." Her voice sounded slightly angry and was slightly raised.

"Well I don't care. He never cared about my feelings, so why should I care about his?"

Her voice got louder, "BEN, we have to go in."

Bennie stamped his foot again. "I DON'T WANT TO!"

Letitia suddenly twisted her ankle. She stopped pulling and let go of his hand. She walked over to a chair and sat down and rubbed her ankle. There were a few tears rolling down her eyes. Bennie walked over with a tear in his face and sat on her lap. "Mamma, I am sorry to upset you." He wiped a tear from her face.

Letitia seemed to be strangely calm all of a sudden. She took out a handkerchief from a pocket in her dress and wiped her tears away. Her face lit up suddenly with a smile. She gave Bennie a big hug. "You are right, Bennie, you don't have to go in if you don't want to. I shouldn't be forcing you to go in."

She pulled a chair facing her and patted the chair. "Now Bennie, I want you to sit here and listen to me."

Bennie sat down and faced his mother.

"You are right, Bennie, you are now nearly eight, and you will soon be a man. I sometimes forget how much you have grown. So, I need to talk to you like a man."

Bennie suddenly smiled and stopped arching his back and sat up, fully erect.

"Do I have your attention, Bennie?"

"Yes mamma."

"Firstly, if you don't want to go in there, I promise I won't drag you in. The only way is if you want to come in with me. Okay?"

"Okay mamma."

"Now tell me, Bennie, who loves you more than anyone in the world?"

Bennie thought for a second. "God does, mamma!"

Letitia laughed. She stroked his cheek. "Yes my darling, you are absolutely right. You have been taught well. God loves us more than we love ourselves. I am so proud of you, my son."

He smiled and seemed so pleased with himself.

"Now tell me, Mister Ben, what person loves you more than anyone in this world?"

"That will be you, mamma."

"That is right. And Mister Ben, have I ever asked you to do something, or do you think I will ever ask you to do something, that will hurt or harm you?"

"No, but mamma …"

"Now shoosh Bennie, please answer me."

"No, never mamma."

"Now Bennie, do you remember last Saturday morning when I had been working my night shift in E R and needed to sleep?"

"Yes mamma."

"And what did you want?"

"I wanted to go to the park and play with my new skate board, and grandpa couldn't take me because he was sick."

"Yes Bennie, and what did you do?"

"I was jumping up and down on your bed and you wouldn't get up."

"Yes Bennie, and what did you say?"

"I said … mamma if you love me you will come to the park with me."

"Yes Bennie. And what did I do?"

"Even though you were very, very tired, you took me to the park."

"Yes Bennie. And now behind those doors is your father. Also, he is my husband, and I love him very much. I am going to see him with or without you. But Bennie, if you love me you will come in to see him for my sake. Just remember, I may never again in my life ask for something like this."

Letitia suddenly got up and walked towards the door. She stopped at the door and Bennie did not move. She walked in the door and closed it behind her. Ben Senior got up and smiled as he saw Letitia. He tried to look around her and realized that Bennie was not there. He slumped to his chair.

Suddenly the door opened behind Letitia and the guard held the door open. Bennie walked in. Ben Senior jumped to his feet and was about to run forward when Letitia raised her hand and he stopped after one step. He continued to smile and sat down. Letitia smiled and mimed, "Thank you."

Bennie walked behind his mother and was content to peep around her to look at Ben. Letitia came over and hugged Ben. Bennie was glued to the back of her.

They all sat down. Ben held Letitia's hand. "How are you, my love?"

"Good Ben, looking forward to you coming home."

Ben looked at Bennie. "Hello Bennie, it's nice to see you."

"Yes sir. Thank you, sir."

There was silence for a few moments. "Bennie I would like to have a man to man chat with you. Your mother and I thought that it's … well, overdue."

"Yes sir."

"You see, Bennie, a lot of guys come to prison and blame this and that and others for their bad fortune, but I deserve to be in here."

"How is that, sir?"

"Well, you see, I loved – I mean love your mother so much, and then you came along and I wanted to look after the two of you and thought that a life of working as a helper to my uncle making furniture was not good enough. So, I wanted to make some extra money to give you two the things that other families have, like a better house, more clothes, house utensils for your mother."

Letitia looked at Ben Senior and interrupted, "Surely you know now, Ben, that none of those things are important to me."

Ben nodded. "I know now, but at the time I felt you deserved better. Anyhow Bennie, some of the guys I know told me that if I drive a car for them, I would get a thousand dolla. Even though I didn't know they had guns, I should have known they was up to no good. I thought it was easy money. So, I did wrong and I have paid my dues. I have no complaints, just annoyed with myself. I have learnt my lesson. Do you understand?"

"I think so, sir. You mean you are punished for being bad?"

"That's right, son. In a way, maybe it is better that if you do something wrong, you pays your punishment in this life, so that when you go to the next life God will not be as hard on you as you have paid your dues. Do you understand?"

"I think so, sir. You mean God won't throw you in the fire?"

"What makes you think God will throw people in the fire, son?"

"Well sir, the minister said on Sunday that if you are bad there will be fire and beanstones in the next life."

"Beanstones? Ah, you mean brimstone?"

Ben looked at Letitia. "What's that he said mamma."

Letitia smiled. "Brimstone."

Bennie looked at Ben. "Yes beanstone."

Ben laughed. "Well son, let me see if I can explain. Do you think your mother would ever throw you in the fire?"

"No sir, she loves me, she always looks after me." He looked at her and smiled. "She will never do anything to hurt me."

Letitia smiled at Bennie.

Ben continued. "What happens, Bennie, when you do something that mamma doesn't like?"

Bennie looked at Letitia. "She stops talking to me and stops smiling at me, and I feel terrible."

"Has your mother or I ever hit you?"

"No sir."

"So you see, son, when you love people and they love you, you don't need to use violence or fire to let them know they have done wrong, they just know themselves. So, you see if you have done something wrong, God doesn't have to throw you into the fire or hit you with stones. You just know you have done wrong and feel terrible. That is worse than any fire. Do you understand?"

"Yes sir. That makes perfect sense. What the minister said didn't make sense to me anyways. I didn't think God would throw people in the fire if he loves everyone."

Letitia wiped a tear from her eye. She looked at Ben. "That's amazing, you have taught him more in a few minutes than he has learnt in years of going to church!"

Ben held Letitia's hand. "Well Letitia, I may be a bit simple in my thinking at times but is it not true that truth is also usually very simple."

Letitia smiled. "Ain't that the truth! And I love you the way you are."

Bennie reached and tugged the bottom of Ben's shirt. Ben stopped looking at Letitia and turned to Bennie. Bennie asked, "Sir, how will you look after my mamma; are you going to go out with men with guns again?"

Ben smiled. "No son! I have been learning how to be a proper carpenter in here, and I plan to work with my uncle Jimmy and be honest for the rest of my life."

"That is very good." Letitia looked pleased. "By the way, Ben, I meant to say. You uncle says he is getting on in years and, 'cause of his heart, he would like to reduce his hours of work and wants you to take over the furniture business."

"That is great, Letitia. Only problem is that although I have learnt a lot about carpentry, I know notting about running a business …"

"Don't worry, Jimmy said he would be there for the next couple of years to look after the business side of things."

"That is great—"

One of the guards shouted, "VISITING TIME OVER! EVERYONE OUT PLEASE!"

Ben approached Bennie who pulled back a bit. Ben looked at Letitia. He then reached out a hand toward Bennie, who shook hands with him.

"It was lovely to see you, Bennie, I am sorry I did not do this earlier."

Bennie withdrew his hand. "It was nice to see you, sir."

Ben got up. Letitia kissed him on the side of his cheek, very close to the corner of his mouth. "I'll try and come down again in the next couple of days."

Ben held her hand for a couple of seconds and then let go. "That would be nice." He then waved to Bennie. "Bye son."

Bennie had his head slightly tilted downwards. "Goodbye sir."

Ben stood there as the two of them went outside the door without looking back. He had a tear in his eye and big smile on his face.

Letitia and Bennie were walking away when Bennie stopped suddenly. Letitia had gone a step ahead and stopped. She noticed he had a few tears on his face. "What is wrong, son?"

Bennie's crying got a bit more noticeable. "What is wrong, Ben?"

Bennie sobbed, "I want to hug my daddy."

Letitia wiped his tears. "I'm sure that will be okay." She walked him back to the door.

The guard put his hands across the door. "I'm sorry ma'am, visiting hours are over."

Letitia looked at the guard and looked at Bennie. The guard nodded with his head and opened the door, "Go on, son, but be quick."

As Bennie entered the room Ben was walking away. Bennie shouted, "DADDY."

Ben turned around. Bennie ran and jumped up into his father's arms. "I love you daddy!"

Ben hugged him firmly. "I love you so much, son."

"Will you come home soon, daddy?"

"You can be sure of that. I will be on my best behavior and come home to look after you and your mamma."

"Thank you, daddy."

Ben put Bennie down, "Now son, you had better rush back."

Bennie looked at the guard. He reached up and Ben lowered his head for Bennie to whisper to him, "He looks like he is going to put us in fire and beanstones, daddy."

Ben laughed out loud. "You are right, Bennie! We had best both disappear!"

Bennie ran back and held Letitia's hand and waved to Ben as they went out the door.

Letitia held his hand as they walked away. "Well Bennie, are you happy now?"

Bennie was hopping along. "Yes mamma, I will tell all my friends and my teacher that my dad is a carpenter and is coming home soon."

"That's great."

Bennie thought for a second. "Mamma?"

"Yes son?"

"Is that what blackmail is?"

"What, son?"

"Well mamma, when you said if you love me you will come in to see daddy?"

"What do you think?"

"I think so, mamma. I think you blackmailed me, didn't you?"

"Where do you think I learnt it from?"

"Was that from me, mamma?"

"What do you think?"

Ben nodded.

"Mamma?"

"Yes honey?"

"Why do you always answer a question with a question?"

Letitia thought for a second. "Well son, is it not a lot better when you answer your own question?"

Bennie nodded.

Letitia stopped suddenly. "You do know you are adorable, don't you, darling?"

Bennie thought for a second. "Where do you think I learnt that from, mamma?"

Letitia thought for a second. She smiled and patted the tip of his nose. "Very good!"

"One more question, mamma?"

"Shoot."

"I like being treated like a grown up. But does that mean you will stop calling me Bennie?"

Letitia stroked his hair. "No honey, you will always be my Bennie."

CHAPTER 39

Jake Asks to See Big Al

Jake walked straight to the dining hall. The majority of the inmates were seated in the dining room. Heads turned around as Jake joined the queue. There was a lot of inmates nudging each other or pointing towards him with their heads. If he was not conspicuous enough before, the bandaging on his left arm certainly made him stand out. Jake picked up a plate and held it up to be served. As he raised his tray he winced and clenched his left wrist and relaxed it again and shook his hands a few times. He walked towards James, the same person who had served him the spaghetti. His white outfit was once again in pristine condition.

James looked rather nervously at Jake. Jake smiled at him. "You look too classy to be working here. You should be serving at the Ritz in London. You must love your job."

"Yes, sir, I do." There was a respect in his manner which was a far cry from his attitude on Jake's first day. He then looked behind him and stepped forward so he could whisper to Jake. "By the way, I feel terrible about what happened to you. I wish I could do something, but it is hard to swim against the tide. I am looking to get married next year and cannot afford any hassle at work."

James placed a ladle full of pasta onto Jake's plate. To Jake's surprise he filled the ladle again and put some more pasta on Jake's plate.

Jake smiled. "Thank you very much, I am starving." He then leaned forward. "Listen about the other day, I know you have no choice in the matter. Don't worry about it. You are right, you can't swim against the tide. Anyway, I always say you have to pick your fights."

"Thank you, sir."

"Don't mention it."

Jake stood for a moment looking around the tables. He saw Ben at a table. He walked over and sat beside him.

"Hi Jake, are you okay, I was worried about you, how is your arm? You bled a lot, I thought you was sure to die. You must have bled a whole heap? Are you sore?"

"Which question do you want me to answer first?"

Ben laughed. "How are you?"

"A little bit sore and a bit numb," he clenched his left fist a few times, "but fine otherwise. Are you okay, Ben?"

"Sure, I am fine."

"I mean with Big Al. Were there any repercussions of your intervention in the kitchen the other day?"

"Big Al just saw me later that day and said that we was now even and that I am on my own from now on." Ben sat upright and looked very excited. "But listen Jake, I really want to thank you. I have some exciting news!"

"What is it? Is it about Junior?"

"Bingo! I spoke to Letitia that night. She told me that all along she had wanted Bennie – she likes to call him Bennie – that all along she had wanted him to keep seeing me. Well she brought him over the next day. Junior seemed very, well kinda shy or anxious, or …"

"Apprehensive?"

"That's it, Jake, he was very apprehensive. I wish I could talk like you …"

Jake interrupted, "You express yourself just fine, Ben. You wear your heart on your sleeve and that's what I love about you."

"Hah, that's funny, that's exactly what Letitia says. Anyhows; Bennie came over and was very shy and couldn't speak a word to me, so I sat him down and told him just as you told me. Well I was in tears, Letitia was in tears, and Junior was so happy to see me. He then hugged me and said, 'I love you daddy'. Well Jake, my heart just melted. Letitia has told me that he now has put up a picture of me in his bedroom and has bought a calendar and is marking off the days till

I go home. He is also telling everyone that his daddy is coming home soon. So, I just don't know how to thank you."

"Ben, you just did. It's just part of my job as a psychologist to help people, so don't mention it again."

Jake then pointed to Big Al's table. "Ben, what is the story with Big Al and the guards, why is it he gets so much freedom? I mean I know that there is mob rule in prisons, but I never imagined that the prison guards would be so accommodating with the bad guys."

"Well just a few years ago it used to be hell in this prison. Many of the guards was attacked from time to time and on a couple of occasions stabbed. In turn they got their own back on the prisoners whenever they could. There were plenty of inmates placed in the isolation chamber on a regular basis. They often came back with multiple injuries. The guards was smart, there was often no bruising or anything to show the injuries. Even when there was a lot of bruises or bad injuries, it was hard to take up a case against the guards as you were fighting the system. The prisoners, as you can imagine, then wanted revenge, and so on and so forth. Then Big Al arrived on the scene. The story goes that he was a godfather in one of the Bronx gangs. You have to admire what he did. He met with a few of the top guards – I have no idea how he managed that. The word is that the guards and their families all went on expensive holidays later that year. As a result of the meeting with the guards a meeting was set up right here in the dining room when all the different leaders of the various gangs in different sections of the prison were invited to this very hall. Not all of them attended, but most did. He made a pact with them, that if he could be the boss in here he could guarantee them certain freedoms, no solitary confinement, more regular visits from families, even … what's the word?" Ben looked up toward the ceiling.

Jake quickly added, "Conjugal rights?"

"That's it, Jake, even conjugal visits. He would get them virtually anything they wanted smuggled into prison, from magazines, cigarettes, food, and even drugs. Initially most of them laughed at him. The next week he invited them to a meeting where they were served rib-eye steak and champagne. That did it for most of them. A few still were not buying in, that included Nigel and Atlas, who were top dogs at that stage. Big Al took them on directly. In that very meeting

Big Al challenged Nigel to a fight. Nigel laughed at first. He then accepted and with arrogance walked towards Big Al. He threw a punch at Big Al. To everyone's surprise Big Al held Nigel's punch with his left hand. He looked Nigel in the eye and said, 'Kid that was your second mistake!', in a flash he pulled out a knife with his right hand and made three cuts on Nigel's forehead, two vertical ones on either side of his forehead and one diagonal one joining the two. That is how Nigel has a giant N on his forehead. Nigel stood there with blood gushing out of his forehead and looked stunned. Big Al pushed him, and Nigel fell to the floor. Big Al wiped the knife on his shirt and looked Atlas straight in the eye. 'Well, anyone else want to challenge me?' he said. Atlas had his fists clenched. He relaxed them and smiled. Atlas reached out his hand towards Big Al and said, 'Anyone who has the balls to stand up to Nigel like that is okay in my books.' Big Al paused for a second and then shook Atlas' hand. As time went on everyone heard about the incident and all rallied behind Big Al. Nigel and Atlas both became very friendly with Big Al, especially Nigel, who has totally committed himself to looking after Big Al. I have heard that their families outside are well looked after."

Ben leaned forward and whispered, "Rumour is that Big Al may have anywhere up to five hundred million dolla in various accounts. Anyhow, since that day Big Al sets the rules; however, he consults with the other leaders and gives them certain privileges; in fact he has even brought in call girls for them, amongst other things. In turn the guards have not had any bother from the inmates. Any trouble with the guards and it is dealt with by the leaders themselves, or worse still by Big Al. Word has is that the guards are very well looked after outside, but that is very hush-hush."

Jake spoke after a pause, "Wow, that is extraordinary. I suppose I can see how it suits mutually. But how does Al manage to get all the money to keep everyone happy?"

Ben smiled. "Don't you worry about that. It is well known in here that when Big Al was arrested, his life was under threat and he was offered police custody. They had caught him red-handed with laundered money. It's hard to know how someone so high up in the mafia would get careless, I have heard from an inmate in here that he had got over-confident and got careless. Anyways, his solicitors could not get him out of that one. Big Al may have had some sort of contract on him but in typical Big Al fashion he invited the various members of

303

the gang to a meeting and assured them of his loyalty. He said that he was not going to move his family anywhere, and in fact said that he wanted them to stay in the house of the Bambino, now the new godfather. The family stayed at the Bambino's house, almost as hostages. Big Al would not spill the beans to the feds and got twenty-five years for money laundering. But I understand he is like a god to the mafia. Turns out that Big Al was a big family man, and he was quite happy being an inmate so long as his family were safe and comfortable. Unfortunately, a rival gang broke into the Bambino's house one day and shot his family. Big Al's wife was also shot. His daughter was not at home, but in a funny twist she was killed by someone else a year or so later. They don't think it was gang related. Big Al apparently has his millions in bank accounts around the world. However, he has made this place his home and seems to be happy to live in here with his kingdom. I guess he has nothing left in life and no reason to leave here. He is probably safer in here anyways."

"I can see how it is win-win for the guards and everyone in here," said Jake.

"Well it is. But probably one day it will all blow over and hell will break loose. But for now, the guards generally ignore the punishments and beatings of the inmates amongst themselves, and on occasions even cover up for the inmates."

"Well Ben, I'm sorry I got you into trouble. Just make sure you don't get involved any more if things get ugly."

"What do you mean, Jake?"

"Just keep your nose clean, I need to sort out something with Big Al."

"But I am worried about you, Jake."

Jake looked at Ben straight in the eyes. "Look Ben, just think of Letitia and Junior. Don't get involved. There is nothing you can or should do that would make a difference. In fact, come to think of it, I am going to sort out this matter once and for all right now."

Jake pushed his plate towards Ben. "Here Ben, make sure you eat all of it."

Ben looked at Jake anxiously. "Where are you going?"

"Straight into the lion's den."

"Jake!" Ben said in vain as Jake walked towards Big Al's table.

Big Al had a spoonful of food on his spoon and put it down as he was laughing so loudly that the food was falling off his spoon. Atlas and Nigel were also laughing uncontrollably, so they were all caught off guard when Jake got to the table.

Jake sat on the bench on Big Al's side and slid his bottom so he was sitting shoulder to shoulder with Big Al. He put his right arm around Big Al's shoulder. "Care to share the joke?"

Nigel and Atlas seemed frozen for a short period, the look on their faces suggesting they couldn't believe what they had seen.

Big Al quickly composed himself. "If you want to keep your arm attached to your body, remove it immediately."

Jake seemed jovial. "Sure, what are we eating?"

He lifted his right arm and reached towards Big Al's plate. He picked up a longish slice of cucumber and looked at it, turned it round to see the other side. He raised his eyebrows. "Looks very fresh."

He put the slice of cucumber in his mouth and began to chew it. He then reached over to pick up another piece. Atlas seemed to have recovered from his frozen state. He reached over and grabbed Jake's arm. Jake looked rather surprised. "Gosh you are very agile for someone so big!"

Big Al tilted his head upwards just once. "It's okay, Atlas, he knows not to do that again."

Atlas let go of Jake's hand. Jake withdrew his hand and shook it as if to get life back into it.

Big Al looked at Jake. "I presume you are not here to share my meal."

"No," said Jake, sounding rather cheerful. "I believe you and I have some unfinished business."

Nigel stood up. "How dare you walk here and threaten Big Al." He walked around the table towards Jake. He grabbed Jake's collar. "I could crush your skull right here."

By this stage no one was eating, and they were all staring at Big Al's table. Some were leaning over to see around other prisoners that were in the way.

Big Al looked very composed. "That's all right, Nigel, let's hear what he has to say, this should be amusing."

Nigel let go of Jake's collar.

Big Al spoke again, "You have two minutes, unless I get bored before the two minutes is up."

Jake had a quick look around the room. All eyes were staring at him. Two of the guards had taken a few steps so they were closer to Big Al. One of the guards reached for his gun. Big Al looked at him, raised his hand and shook his head. The guards walked away.

Jake fixed his collar and shirt so that it was sitting tidy. "Well you see, Al."

Nigel interrupted "It's Big Al to you!"

"You see, Big Al, I think …"

Big Al stood up. "Sorry I'm bored. Let's go into the kitchen, we need to wash up again. You can either walk in yourself or you can be dragged in."

Jake sounded very calm. "That's okay, I know the way." He started to whistle as he led the way.

Jake was already a few paces ahead walking towards the kitchen. Atlas whispered in Big Al's ear, "Big Al, do you think this could be a trap?"

Al shook his head. "No chance of that. I already know that he has turned down the offer to take action against me. I had assumed he was scared, but now I am not so sure. Big Al has no fear, let's go." He then pointed towards Jake. "You had better go ahead of him; it doesn't look good if he is in front of us. I'll see you in there shortly."

"Sure Big Al." And with that Atlas walked quickly ahead with Nigel following closely behind. They got ahead of Jake and walked towards the kitchen.

As Jake was going past James, the young man serving the food, the man looked anxiously at Jake. Jake smiled and winked at him.

The prison guard at the kitchen door stood aside to let them in. Atlas and Nigel walked into the kitchen. Atlas stood at the door and pointed to the dining hall by slightly tilting his head. The few staff who were working in the kitchen began to walk out at a brisk pace. Jake walked into the kitchen area. Atlas pointed to the same room where Jake had been stabbed.

"Big Al will be with you shortly," said Atlas. "Just sit here." He pulled up a wooden chair and picked up a cloth and hit the chair with the cloth, causing some flour to rise from it.

Jake sat down. He looked at Nigel. "You need to shave your head soon; the white hairs are coming through."

Nigel just grunted.

Jake turned to Atlas. "You, on the other hand, are looking sharp, my man."

He held out his hand for a high five. Atlas turned his back to Jake and looked towards the door. Jake looked at his hand and rubbed his hand on his shirt. He looked around the room and whistled the tune of 'There May Be Trouble Ahead'.

Big Al walked into the room. Atlas and Nigel walked over to the door and stood shoulder-to-shoulder, blocking any view into or out of the room.

"This is déjà vu," said Jake.

Big Al walked towards Jake. He grabbed Jake's collar with his left hand and put his right hand into his back pocket. He pulled out an old-fashioned shaving blade that he flicked open. "It is time for a shave, a very close one."

He held the blade on the left side of Jake's neck and pressed it near his jugular. He increased the pressure, causing an indentation under the knife.

"Give me one reason why I should not cut your jugular right now?"

"Do I not get a last wish?" asked Jake, sounding a little nervous.

Big Al paused for a second and then pulled back the knife. He then let go of the collar. "I can't figure you out. Okay I will give you your one wish, what is it? And don't tell me you wish to be left alone or some such shit."

"No," said Jake, sounding a lot calmer, "I would like to drink a cup of cappuccino with you."

Big Al rubbed his chin and looked rather bemused. "What the fuck are you about anyway? I tell you what, I am intrigued enough to see what your game is."

He snapped his fingers. "Nigel, will you get us two cups of coffee right away."

Nigel looked at Big Al quizzically.

Big Al snapped his fingers. Nigel said, "Sure Big Al," and rushed out.

Nigel left the room. Big Al looked at Atlas and nodded towards Jake. Atlas walked towards Jake and lifted him off the chair. Jake was momentarily in the air the with legs still folded as if he was seated. He straightened himself and pointed his toes to the floor, but he could not reach the floor.

"Could you please put me down, Mister Atlas, remember I have a last wish?"

Atlas carried him towards the sink and turned him round and pushed him against the sink. Jake put his two hands against the sink. Atlas frisked Jake very thoroughly and made sure Jake was not hiding anything in his underwear by grabbing his genitals and squeezing them hard.

Jake looked around to Atlas. "You are impressed, are you?"

Atlas grunted. He frisked Jake down to his shoes and then took Jake's shoes off to check inside them. "All clear, Big Al." Jake put the shoes back on.

With that Atlas pushed Jake onto the wooden chair again.

Nigel arrived with two cups with rising steam from them. He handed one to Big Al and one to Jake. "Sugar?" he asked Jake.

"Yes please."

Nigel showed Jake his middle finger.

"I suppose I can manage without."

Big Al pulled a chair in front of him, with the back of the chair facing Jake. He sat on the chair with his legs astride. He leaned his two arms on the back of the chair, his coffee in his right hand.

Big Al was losing patience. "I hope you enjoy that coffee because it is the last thing that will probably pass your lips in your lifetime. By the time I have finished this cup of disgusting prison coffee, if you have not given me a reason not to kill you, your next bed will be the pathologist table."

"Can I ask you first what your connection is with Sarah Miller?"

"You can, but it is only losing you time."

"Well what is your ..." Jake stopped mid-sentence. He turned his head sideways to read a tattoo on Big Al's right wrist, which became apparent as he raised his hand to take a sip of his coffee.

Jake read the inscription in italics 'Sarah'. He looked up at Al. "Mister North called you Albert Miller! Is Sarah YOUR daughter?"

Big Al looked at Atlas. "Our friend is a bit slow, isn't he?"

Jake looked stunned. "Are you ..." He paused as if not wanting to ask the question. "Are you Sarah's father?"

"Yes, you little shit; and I have no intention of any smart-ass lawyer getting you off the hook for killing my daughter."

"Holy shit," Jake was open-mouthed, "you couldn't make that up."

"You are losing precious time and I am losing patience."

"Big Al you have to believe me when I tell you that I did not kill your daughter. In fact, I never met her."

"It's not what I have heard. You were having a line with her and knocked her off when your wife realised you were having an affair."

"No Big Al, I never met her. It sure as hell wasn't me who got her pregnant."

Big Al got up from his chair suddenly and threw his chair to the ground. He put his coffee near the sink. "What the fuck are you talking about her being pregnant?" He picked Jake off the chair and put the shaving knife and held it against Jake's throat. Some of Jake's coffee spilt on the floor.

"Big Al, listen to me." Jake touched his neck and on lifting his hand noticed some blood on his fingers. "At least give me the chance to explain."

Big Al pushed Jake down, causing him to fall back onto his chair. The chair tilted backwards and was only prevented from falling by Nigel holding it. Some of the coffee spilt on Jake.

He pointed to the door with his head. "Boys, can you give me a few minutes alone? I can handle this."

"Are you sure, boss?" said Nigel rather nervously.

Big Al kept looking at Jake. "I've got this, Nigel."

Atlas grabbed Nigel's arm. "Come on buddy, Big Al has nothing to worry about."

Atlas and Nigel left the kitchen, Nigel looking somewhat reluctantly backwards as he left.

"You didn't know she was pregnant? I thought your connections would have told you that." There was quite an echo in the big empty kitchen.

"Let me worry about my sources later, now explain yourself before I lose my patience."

"My wife, Tracey, was a social worker. She was helping Sarah. Some married guy was seeing Sarah regularly. Somehow, she got pregnant, she must have missed a pill, or Tracey thought it was because of a tummy bug. Anyhow she got pregnant. In fact, the reason Tracey helped Sarah is because I had a dream about Sarah. Well in fact it was about her baby."

Big Al's face was very flushed, and his hands were held tightly in fists. "How could you have had a dream about Sarah if you hadn't even met her?"

"The same way I had a dream that you were going to stab me with the exact same knife that you stabbed Nigel with."

"So what if you had a dream?" Big Al asked.

"Well the short story is that Sarah was under pressure from this jerk to have an abortion. Tracey helped her to give the child up for adoption."

"That is bullshit! The police never mentioned her being pregnant! I don't believe a word of what you are saying!"

"Think about it, Big Al. How would I make up a story like that? Tracey, my wife, was a very trustworthy person and she told no-one about the pregnancy. Except me. And that was because her client, Sarah, was anonymous to me at the time."

Big Al started to pace back and forth. He grabbed Jake by the collar again. "You mean I have a grandson?"

"It's a little girl, Big Al. And please, you are choking me."

Big Al let go of the collar and Jake rubbed his neck.

"A little girl. Where is she?"

"The identity of the parents is secret."

Big Al could not hide his excitement. "Carry on with your story."

"Well it seems as soon as the baby was gone, Sarah disappeared. My wife was killed at the same time. Since then I have spent my life pickled in Jack Daniels."

"So you think the same guy has killed your wife and my daughter?"

"That would be my bet. And your best chance to get to the killer is for me to stay alive and go through the court case. If you kill me the case will be buried alongside the memory of Tracey and Sarah."

Big Al picked up his chair which was lying on its back on the floor. He placed it, this time, the right way around in front of Jake.

"What did Sarah tell your wife about me?"

"I have to explain that Tracey didn't tell me much about her cases."

Big Al interrupted, "Listen Jake, this is not a court of law. I just need to know a bit more about my little daughter. Tell me all you know." There was a warmth and softness in Big Al's voice.

"Okay Big Al, I will tell you what little I know. I had a dream that Tracey was holding a baby, so when Tracey met Sarah who secretly told her that she was pregnant, she saw that as a sign that she should help Sarah. Sarah had mentioned to Tracey on one occasion that her father was some big shot, I think those are the words she used, but she wanted to be independent and manage her own life and go through law school by herself." Jake paused and looked at Big Al. "You know she worked for an escort agency?"

Big Al nodded. "You know, she was all I cared about. My wife knew about Sarah. Cathy, that's my wife, was very understanding. She knew I had a daughter from an extra-marital affair. She never asked me anything about Sarah's mother or what had happened. She was just happy that I supported Sarah and her mother. She just wanted an assurance that I did not love Sarah's mother and a second condition was that I never talked about her mother. God bless her soul, Cathy that is; she was killed by a rival gang a few years ago. Our daughter, Katie, was killed a year later. As Sarah grew up, I saw her regularly. As she grew older, she began to figure out that not all I did was on the right side of the law – putting it mildly. Anyway, she began to resent me more and more. In fact, I think that is the reason why she went to law school. To put guys like me behind bars. I offered to pay her fees, buy an apartment for her, buy her own house. She would have none of it. At the young age of sixteen she cut all ties with me and worked as a waitress to support herself. I always thought she would see sense and come running to me for money. I then found out that she was an expensive hooker. I wanted to kill any guy that touched her. I even sent her a cheque for a million dollars. I thought that would sway her. She never cashed it."

Big Al walked to the sink and stretched both his elbows and placed both hands on the sink with his back to Jake. "My father used to beat me; my mother disappeared from our house when I was six. I left home when I was twelve and was a carrier for a drug dealer. I worked my up, anyway I suppose in a way I feel responsible for Sarah's death. I also feel responsible for the death of the only two other people I cared for, my wife and other daughter, Katie." Big Al seemed to suddenly break out of a trance. "I am not sure why I am telling you all this."

He then grabbed Jake by the collar again. "You are either telling the truth or are a very good liar. I have not decided which one yet. You certainly have a lot of balls to confront me in this way. I will tell you this, if I find out that you have had to anything to do with Sarah's death, I will not rest until I cut you up in pieces."

"That's fine Al. Can I call you Al?"

"Don't push your luck!" Big Al walked towards the door and after opening, stopped, and looked back. "Pray to God I don't have to come after you, here or anywhere. If I find out you had anything to do with my daughter's death, the police will not be able to find any parts of your body to identify." With that Big walked away.

Atlas and Nigel followed Big Al. The prisoners kept their heads down and continued to eat their meals. Atlas, Nigel, and Big Al left the dining room. Ben looked very anxious and kept looking at the kitchen door expectantly.

Jake walked out a few seconds later into the dining room. He came out whistling the tune of 'I'm Still Standing' by Elton John. Heads turned around, some looking bewildered. Jake walked to James and picked up a plate. "My appetite has come back. Any chance of seconds?"

"Sure thing."

CHAPTER 40

Gabby meets Paolo

Gabriella walked outside the golf club restaurant and was standing in the same place as she always did when waiting for her taxi. She looked at her watch; it was five minutes to five.

She suddenly felt two hands cover her eyes. "Guess who?"

Gabriella shouted with excitement, "It must be Andrew, my fiancé, who else?"

Geno removed his hands from her face and looked at her in surprise. "What the hell?"

Gabriella pointed to Geno's face. "Gocha!"

Geno pointed a finger at Gabriella and shook it at her. "You … you …"

Gabriella grabbed his finger and kissed it. "You are not going to swear at a lady, are you?"

"I never fucking swear!"

They both laughed.

"Are you all set to meet Paolo?" asked Geno, he sounded enthusiastic.

"Are you sure it's not too early?" asked Gabriella, slightly hesitantly.

"Gosh you look so nervous, don't be, I'm sure you will get along like a house on fire!"

"Well … Okay, I suppose."

Geno grabbed her by her elbow. "Come on, it will be great."

On the way to the bar, the two of them continued where they left off previously, talking all the way in the car.

They arrived at the bar and walked in. Geno had his arm around Gabriella and was looking frantically around the room. "Let's go to the counter, he should be here somewhere."

They arrived at the counter and Geno tapped on Paolo's shoulder.

Paolo turned around and saw Gabriella. "Oh!"

Gabriella looked at Paolo. "Oh!"

There was a few seconds of silence and Gabriella's face was visibly red.

Paolo hesitated for a few seconds and then reached out his hand. "So you are Gabby, Geno told me you are gorgeous, but he didn't tell me how much." He then reached over and kissed her on the cheek.

Gabriella blushed. "Geno exaggerates a lot. Long time, no see … I mean I couldn't wait to see you. Geno wanted this to be a surprise!"

"Well it sure was. What would you like to drink? The pleasure of buying is mine, Gabby."

"I'll have a G and T, on the rocks."

"And you, Geno, usual beer?"

"Yes, a Budd will do me fine."

There was a stool free next to Paolo'. Paolo got up, "You two guys sit down, I can stand for a while."

Gabby put her handbag over her shoulder. "Will you gentlemen excuse me for a couple of minutes, I need to powder my nose."

"Sure," said Paolo.

Geno also nodded.

Paolo pointed to the bartender. "Could I have two Buds and a G and T on the rocks."

"Sure partner," said the barman cheerfully.

Geno and Paolo sat down.

The barman took the top off two bottles of Budweiser. "Glass, gentlemen?"

They both said, "No," almost simultaneously.

Paolo took a sip of his beer. He slapped Geno on the back of his shoulder.

"Come on, you're very quiet, why don't you tell me how the two of you exactly met?"

Geno took a sip of his beer. "Well Paolo, maybe you should tell me how you and Gabby met!"

"Oh shit. Didn't think you would have spotted that."

"I would have spotted it from across the room."

Paolo looked towards where the ladies room would be. He took a small sip of his beer again. "Shit, you couldn't write the script!"

Geno remained silent.

"Geno, I don't know where to start."

"Well Paolo we have a very short time, so why don't you just spit it out, so to speak."

"Right Geno. You know the way I am very fussy with my girlfriends?"

"Carry on, Paolo, the pause is not helping me at all, I feel rather flat as it is."

"Sorry Geno, this is so difficult." He hesitated. "Where do I start?"

"Paolo, just get to the point!"

"Okay Geno, but this is hard!" He hesitated and took a sip of his beer. "Geno, do you remember we were chatting once, and I told you that I once had a one-night stand?"

"Yes, it was at a Christmas party and it was the daughter of a policem …" He stopped mid-word. Geno's shoulders slumped suddenly, "You mean you had a one-night stand with the girl of my dreams?"

Paolo shook his head. "God Geno, I don't know what to say."

"New York has a population of over eight million, over fifty percent of these are female, and you had to have a one-night stand with the girl I would probably marry."

The guy on the stool besides him turned around. "Hey buddy if it's any consolation, I–"

Geno put up his hand. "Look buddy, not one more word, turn around and look that way. NOT A WORD!"

The man turned around quickly.

Geno leaned with his arms on the counter and put his head between his upper arms. He lifted his head. "So, what happened next?"

"What?" Paolo looked surprised.

"Well I want to know what happened after the one-night stand."

"Well Geno, we woke up in her place, both had sobered up. The first thing I did was promise myself that I would never get drunk again, and never have. She seemed like such a nice girl and she wanted to meet me again, but I just couldn't get myself to go out with a girl who would go to bed with a guy on the first night."

"Is that not a bit hypocritical?"

"I know it sounds incongruous, but I had never done anything like that before and never since, but as nice as she was, I just couldn't. No doubt she didn't think highly of me because of it, and I just didn't think it would work."

Geno shook his head. "Who said truth is stranger than fiction? Was it Oscar Wilde or Mark Twain?"

The man on the next seat turned around again, "I believe it was Mark Twain."

Geno stared at him intently. The man put his hands. "Sorry, I'll mind my own business."

Geno kept staring at him. "You had better or this bottle may go where the sun don't shine."

The man pointed to a seat across the bar. "Oh look a free seat … I'm outa here!"

With that he got up and walked away quickly.

"So, where does that leave you?" asked Paolo as he put his hand on Geno's shoulder.

"Well Paolo, every time I kiss her, I will probably think I am kissing you, and that is not a pleasant thought! I think I should I go."

"No I'll go," said Paolo, standing up. "See you tomorrow partner."

Paolo got up and they hugged.

Paolo put his hand on the back of Geno's neck. "I am so sorry, Geno."

"You know, Paolo, it is so strange that maybe it was meant to be."

"Well I'll leave you to it then," Paolo said.

Geno nodded.

A short while later Gabriella walked to the counter and sat at the stool.

She picked up her glass of gin and tonic and took a sip. She pointed to the beer bottle that was on the counter. "Is Paolo in the gents?"

Geno was rather quiet. "No he had to leave."

"Right." Gabriella looked straight ahead towards the bottles of spirit held up by brackets behind the counter wall.

There was silence for about a minute.

Gabriella shook her head. "Shit, I knew this was too good to be true."

Geno looked at his beer bottle and took a sip of it.

Gabriella turned around and held Geno's chin with her hand and turned his face round so he was looking at her. "Geno, if we don't at least talk this over for a few minutes we might regret it for the rest of our lives."

"Okay, I'm listening. What should we talk about?"

"Well, does that really change anything?" She paused. "Forget I said that." She took another sip of her drink. "I had better go."

"I can take you home."

"No Geno, it's best I take a cab. I have your number, you have mine, let's see how we feel after a few days."

"Sure," said Geno.

Gabriella got up and kissed him on the cheek. She seemed to be about to say something, but then didn't and left.

Geno sipped on his drink slowly over the next ten minutes or so. He sat there deep in thought, shaking his head occasionally. He then took out his cell phone and tapped on his contact icon. He went to the G section and selected Gabriella. He slowly reached towards the phone with his finger. He then pressed the 'Delete' button. A prompt came up, 'Confirm delete; yes-no?' He paused for a few seconds and then pressed 'yes'.

CHAPTER 41

Friend or Foe?

The judge turned to Amanda. "Would you please call your next witness to the stand."

Amanda looked at Andy. "Your honour, the defense calls Detective James Sterne to the stand."

Andy stood up. "Your honour, the defense has not asked Mister Sterne to be here for questioning."

Amanda answered quickly. "Your honour, Detective Sterne has provided a witness statement and Detective Johnston has also referred to the fact that his story of meeting the defendant in the bar was corroborated by Detective Sterne. The defense is happy to recall James Sterne at a different time if needs be."

The judge looked at Andy. "Mister Gomez, you do realise that the defense has the right to question this key witness. If your client is not ready this questioning can be postponed to a different time."

Andy was not as composed as usual. "Your honour, if I could have a couple of minutes to speak to Detective Sterne?"

Jim stood up. "I am quite happy to get on the stand."

Andy seemed reluctant. "I guess that is okay, your honour."

The judge looked at Jim. "Very well then Detective Sterne, you may take the stand."

Jim walked up to the stand.

The bailiff approached Jim. "Would you please raise your right hand?"

Jim did so.

"Do you promise to tell the truth, the whole truth and nothing but the truth?"

"Yes," Jim said quietly.

The judge interrupted. "Could you please speak up, Mister Sterne."

"Sorry, your honour. Yes, I do," Jim said much louder.

The judge pointed to the chair. "Please take the seat."

Jim sat in the witness box.

Amanda looked at a sheet of paper for a while, it seemed to increase the tension in the court room. She took the customary sip of water.

Amanda approached Jim. "Detective Sterne," she said very formally, "you are a homicide detective?"

"Yes."

"For how many years?"

"About twelve."

"I believe you have quite a reputation."

Jim looked puzzled. "I'm afraid I don't understand?"

"I mean, Detective, that you are known for getting your man much more often than not."

"If you mean the murderer, yes, I stop at nothing until I get the guilty party, but I'm not sure about the reputation bit."

"Detective, stop at nothing?"

"Yes, I don't rest until the case is put away."

Amanda walked toward the jury. She rested her hand on the jury box wooden wall. She looked back at Jim.

"You don't stop at anything? Hmm. Detective Sterne, does that include planting evidence?"

Andy jumped up. "OBJECTION! You honour, the witness is not on trial."

The judge was very calm. "Over-ruled, based on the statements and the need to establish his credibility it is a fair question."

Andy slumped down.

Jim thought for a second. "Your honour, can I take the fifth amendment?"

The judge nodded. "That is within your rights."

Jim didn't look at Amanda. "I will take the fifth amendment. I refuse to answer on the grounds that it might incriminate me."

Amanda continued. "Very well, Detective Sterne. Have you ever planted evidence?"

Jim looked towards the floor. "I refuse to answer on the grounds that it might incriminate me."

"Detective, do you know of anyone that you have put behind bars that are there that perhaps would not be there if evidence had not been tampered with?"

"I will take the fifth amendment."

"Detective Sterne, are you guilty of imprisoning suspects by misrepresenting evidence?"

Andy jumped up. "Objection, your honour."

"Sustained, Miss Jackson, you are repeating the same question."

"Detective Sterne, do you not feel guilty about putting innocent members of the public behind bars?"

Andy jumped up again. "Objection, your honour!"

Judge Temple raised his voice slightly. "Sustained!"

Amanda put up her hand. "Withdraw the question."

The judge looked at Amanda. "Miss Jackson, you should know better. The jury will disregard the last statement of the defense. Continue, Miss Jackson."

Amanda nodded. "Detective Sterne. You have been investigating the Sarah Miller case for the past few weeks, is that right?"

"Yes," Jim said rather quietly.

"I am sorry I am not sure everyone heard you," Amanda said quite curtly.

Jim sat up in his chair and said loudly, "Yes Miss Jackson."

"And you believe that the defendant Mister Jake Chapman is guilty of this murder."

"Yes, I am fairly certain."

"Fairly certain, Detective Sterne, does that mean that you are harbouring some doubts?"

Jim looked a bit taken aback and hesitated for a couple of seconds before he replied. "It is not my job to be a hundred percent certain, but all the evidence we have gathered has shown to be, beyond reasonable doubt, that he is the culprit." Jim sat back a bit and seemed to be pleased with his answer.

"However, you demonstrated some doubt initially?"

The judge interrupted, "Miss Jackson, I believe Mister Sterne has responded to your question appropriately."

"But your honour, I would like to indicate that the police have some doubt–"

The judge interrupted, "Miss Jackson, I am going to have to ask you to desist in this line of questioning."

"Very well, your honour." Amanda turned away from the judge and was smiling.

She walked up across the front of the court room, in front of the judge's bench and without looking at Jim she asked, "Detective Sterne, are you familiar with the rumour that a policeman has been visiting the so-called red-light district of Manhattan regularly?"

The DPP, Peter North, stood up quickly. "Objection, your honour, the court should be dealing with the facts, not rumours."

The judge spoke quickly, "Sustained. Miss Jackson, you should know better than that."

"Sorry your honour," Amanda looked at Lucy and seemed to have a hint of a smile.

She continued, still not looking at Jim, "Detective Sterne, have you been frequenting the red-light district?"

Peter North jumped up again. "Objection, your honour, the detective is not on trial."

"Miss Jackson where is this going?" The judge frowned at Amanda.

Amanda turned towards the judge. "Your honour I am trying to establish whether the witness may have known either the victim, a friend of the victim, or have any connection with the perpetrator."

Peter North stood up again. "Your honour, if Miss Jackson is pointing to a police officer being involved this is totally speculative and unsubstantiated."

The judge thought for a second. "I am going to allow the line of questioning for now, but I am warning you, Miss Jackson, if this deteriorates into a fanciful farcical distraction, I will personally hold you responsible."

"Yes, your honour."

Amanda walked over to her desk and looked at her papers. She whispered to Lucy, "This is where I get my own back and also get one up for women. You could say a kick in the balls for all the cheating no-good men."

Lucy seemed very apprehensive. "Are you sure this is a good idea?"

"Never been more certain." With that Amanda took a sip of her water.

Amanda walked up slowly and calmly towards Jim and crossed her arms. "Mister Sterne, do you regularly visit the red-light district of Manhattan?"

Jim looked at Peter North, who just shrugged his shoulders. "Yes."

Amanda looked at Jim. "Sorry I didn't hear you properly."

"Yes, I do."

The was a loud murmur around the room.

The judge banged his gavel. "Please maintain order!"

"How often do you visit this area, Detective Sterne?"

"Roughly once a week."

"I'm sorry, I didn't hear you."

The judge turned to Jim. "Mister Sterne, can you talk as if you are talking to the last row of seats, to ensure everyone hears you."

"Yes, sorry your honour."

"Now please answer the question again."

"Yes, I go there once a week."

The whispering around the court room was a lot louder this time.

The judge banged his gavel a lot louder. He shouted, "Quiet, please, in my court!"

"And do you spend the nights with a prostitute?"

Jim seemed to be searching for the right words. "Well I know what this sounds like–"

Amanda interrupted him. "Would you please answer the question!"

"Yes, I do."

"And would you like to tell the jury what you do there all night."

"Well not all night, just most of it." Few of the public burst out laughing. Jim looked up in surprise. He continued, "We talk."

Amanda raised her voice "Do you mean to say that you spent the night with a prostitute, and you spend most of the night talking? That is a little hard to believe!"

The prosecution attorney stood up. "Your honour, I object, where is this leading to?"

The judge looked at Amanda. "Yes where is this leading to?"

The prosecution attorney stood up again. "Your honour, this is totally unnecessary!"

Amanda replied quickly, "Your honour, I would like to establish the witness's credibility and possible lack of impartiality in the case."

Peter North stood up and sounded annoyed. "Your honour, the witness has an impeccable record in the police force, his credibility and impartiality are not in question, nor is he on trial here for his social activities." He suddenly stopped, having realised that he had chosen the wrong words. "What I mean to say is that this is hostile questioning of the witness."

Amanda walked back to her seat. "I guess I don't need the answer to that question. I withdraw the question, your honour." She looked at the jury with a wry smile. It was noticeable that some of the jurors were smiling too.

Amanda sat beside Lucy and whispered, "Take that you son of a bitch!"

The judge nodded. "Objection sustained." He turned to Jim "You don't have to answer."

Jim looked pensive. "I would like to respond, your honour. If the esteemed attorney, Mister North, is questioning my conduct, no doubt everyone will have a question mark on my ethics and all my colleagues will have doubts about my conduct."

Peter North shuffled uncomfortably in his chair and stood up to speak. "Your honour, I would like to ask for a short recess."

The judge nodded his head and banged his gavel. "Very well, under the circumstances I will allow this. The court will have a fifteen-minute recess."

*

Andy Gomez, Peter North, and Jim were seated in an interview room. Andy sat forward. "Jim, I don't think this is a good idea at all, it will not help the case and it will certainly not help your reputation, whatever the outcome of your story."

"Andy, I hear what you are saying, but if Peter here has doubts over my 'social activities', what do you think my colleagues and everyone else is going to think? I already have my ethics questioned and now I am being questioned not only about my morality and honour, but also some may think I am guilty in some way."

Peter looked a bit subdued. "I am sorry Jim, it is so unlike me to say anything like that, but I have to say Amanda worked it very well." He paused. "I had heard that the two of you are an item. Is that right?"

"Were," said Jim, "were an item, until recently!"

Peter nodded. "It all makes sense now, I was a bit baffled where this was all going! It does seem a bit unprofessional."

Jim smiled. "Well, Peter, as they say all is fair in love and war."

Andy nodded. "She is very shrewd, it certainly does not make the police look very professional, and gets the sympathy of the jury."

Jim nodded. "Andy you have hit the nail on the head, I need to say my piece to maintain the reputation of the NYPD and also it is my only chance to redeem myself."

"Okay," said Peter, leaning forward, "run the story by us so we can have a heads-up."

"I am sorry, it is too difficult for me to go over it twice, you are going to have to trust me on this."

Peter looked at Andy. "Okay Jim, but if it gets difficult let me know and we can get a recess or ask to speak to the judge privately."

"Okay," said Jim.

They walked back to the court room.

*

"Would everyone stand up for the honourable judge, Mister John Temple." Everyone stood up and sat down after the judge sat down.

The judge looked at Jim, who was seated in the chair. "Mister Sterne, are you sure you want to go ahead, because you are not accused of anything and are under no obligation to speak."

"I would like to, your honour."

The judge nodded. "Very well, go ahead. Miss Jackson, would you ask your last question again?"

Lucy looked at Amanda. Amanda picked up her glass of water and took a sip again. It was as if she was savouring every moment. The courtroom became totally silent.

"Mister Sterne, how many different prostitutes did you see?"

"Just the one."

"Oh, that is very touching!"

Peter North jumped up. "Objection your honour, she is badgering the witness."

"Sustained, Miss Jackson, my patience is running thin!"

"Yes, your honour." She turned to Jim, "What was her name?"

"Cindy."

She paused. "Mister Sterne, I asked you during your regular visits to this prostitute–"

The judge interrupted, "Will the counsellors please approach the bench."

Andy Gomez and Amanda approached the judge's bench.

The judge switched off his microphone. "I am getting a bit irritated with this, I do not want my court room to be turned into a charade. Now, Miss Jackson, please be quick and get to the point, I am losing patience."

Amanda nodded. Andy returned to his seat.

"Mister Sterne, the question is during your visits what were you doing all night?"

Jim looked straight at Amanda. "We spent a few hours talking. I asked her about her job, about her family—"

Amanda interrupted, "That's very touching."

The judge snapped, "Miss Jackson, this is the last such comment I will tolerate."

"Yes, your honour."

The prosecution attorney looked very nervous and fidgety. He looked at the judge who had his eye firmly fixed on Jim.

Jim suddenly became aware of all eyes staring at him. He looked at the jury and then looked around the room. He felt very uncomfortable and thought for a second he couldn't go through with what he was going to say. He then took a deep breath and sat more upright as if he had just mustered the courage to say what was on his mind.

"I have been seeing Cindy on a weekly basis since she got pregnant five years ago. I suppose I need to give some background information." He looked at Amanda who looked very pale. He put his index finger under his collar as if to loosen it. He quickly looked away as he found it difficult to concentrate on his thoughts.

"I first met Cindy – that is not her real name, but if it is okay with the court I will refer to her as Cindy."

The judge nodded and was leaning forward in anticipation. "Carry on for now."

The whole court room was absolutely silent, the anticipation was palpable.

"I met Cindy over five years ago. I was working on a homicide case which involved a drug ring. We collaborated with the drug squad. In the process we were tailing a pimp. In one of our raids, I apprehended a couple of call girls."

The judge interrupted, "You are referring to prostitutes."

"Yes, your honour. Cindy was one of them. I was about to lock her up in a cell for the night when she pleaded with me to release her. I was totally unmoved by her appeals and her tears and as she persisted, I grabbed her arm and pushed her into the cell. She fell on the floor and was in tears. I suddenly became remorseful of my harshness and picked her up. She embraced me and was sobbing and for a few seconds I didn't know what to do. She suddenly said that she was pregnant."

The judge interrupted, "I am sorry to interrupt, Mister Sterne, but can you confirm that you were not the father of the unborn?"

Jim replied quickly, "Oh, good God, no, your honour, that was the first time I met her."

"Carry on then. Making sure everyone is clear on the topic," said the judge, leaning forward.

"Well I felt there was something very touching about her embrace. I felt terrible that up to that point I had not treated her as a human being. Coupled with the fact that I had pushed a pregnant woman to the ground. As there was another girl in the same cell, I asked Cindy to get up and follow me for further questioning. I released her and told my colleagues that I was going to use her to acquire inside information and that I would be visiting her the following week. I did visit her the next week and she was straining in early pregnancy and did not want to go to hospital because she could not afford it. I took her to hospital and paid her hospital bills. Anyway, to give you a condensed version of the story I visited her nearly on a weekly basis."

Jim plucked up the courage to look at Amanda again. She looked totally dazed. Jim suddenly realised that he had to clarify matters. He continued, "I should add that it was not a romantic relationship. I helped her through the pregnancy, financially mainly, but also for moral support. After her baby was born, a beautiful girl, I made a pact with her. I would support her daughter financially if Cindy promised to take a course to pursue an alternative career before her daughter reached school age. I had – have no family and it made me feel good I suppose. Cindy enrolled part time in a secretarial course, which she has just finished. Her daughter knows me as uncle Jim and I occasionally take her out by herself. And that it is why I visit Cindy on a weekly basis."

Jim looked at the judge. The judge turned to Amanda. "Does that answer your question, Miss Jackson, or do you have any further questions?"

Amanda shook her head and then raised her hand. "I do have one more question to ask."

"Go ahead."

"Do you mean to tell me that you spent a few hours a week with a girl and you are not romantically involved with her?"

"Objection, your honour!" Peter North looked red in the face.

"Sustained."

Jim put up his hand, like a child in a classroom. "Your honour, there is something else I would like to say."

The judge shrugged his shoulders "Go ahead, if you feel compelled, but you are not under any obligation to do so."

"I would like to, your honour."

Jim looked Amanda straight in the eyes. "Well you see I couldn't be romantically involved with her, or with anyone else, because I have known for a while that my heart belongs totally and indivisibly to someone else." He paused and took a deep breath. "You see, I am madly in love with you, Miss Jackson, I mean Amanda."

Amanda's mouth was half open. "I beg your pardon!" she said without realising what she had said.

"You heard me right, I love you! And the other night I had planned to ask you to marry me. In fact, I am asking you in front of all these people. Mandy, will you marry me?"

There was a hush in the court room. Lucy's mouth was open as she stared at Amanda expectantly.

Amanda turned to the judge. "Your honour, this is totally irrelevant to the case."

The judge looked bemused and had a mischievous-looking smile on his face. He turned to Jim. "Why, I have never said this before, but I don't know what to say!"

Murmurs broke out throughout the court. Amanda, whilst looking at Jim, could feel every eye boring into the back of her head.

Amanda turned to the judge. "Your …" She had to clear her throat. "Your honour, could I ask for a recess."

The judge raised his small gavel. "I need a coffee break. There will be a 30-minute break." He slammed down the gavel three times.

Everyone got up. Amanda ran out of the room before the judge had barely left his seat. Lucy followed her, struggling to keep up.

Jim sat there for a minute staring at his shoes. He suddenly felt completely idiotic. He got up, and hardly looking up he started to walk out of the courtroom. As he walked down the courtroom towards the exit all eyes followed him step by step. It seemed to take forever. As soon as he got outside the room, he took a few deep breaths. He waited for a few minutes to try and compose himself. He then began to walk briskly towards the defendant's room. He knocked at the door fairly furiously. Lucy opened the door. She turned towards Amanda. Amanda turned towards the window, away from Jim. "Tell him he can come in."

Lucy whispered softly to Jim, "She says–"

Jim interrupted, "Yes I heard."

Jim walked into the room and closed the door. "Mandy … Amanda …"

This time Amanda jumped in. "What were you thinking?! You are making a mockery of my case. How could you?!" She paced up and down. "I mean, what were you thinking? Do you realise …" She suddenly stopped and turned to Lucy. "Could you leave us alone for a few minutes?"

Lucy nodded and went towards the door. She opened the door and looked at Amanda and looked at her watch. Amanda said, "I'll see you in a few minutes."

Lucy looked at Jim. Somehow Jim felt as if she was looking at someone who is about to walk to his executioner. Lucy shut the door behind her.

Jim walked towards Amanda. "Honey, I'm sorry to …"

Amanda grabbed Jim and pushed him towards the chair beside him. She then gave him a light shove, causing him to slump onto the chair.

Jim put up both his hands, "Amanda, I'm–"

Amanda cut him short, "Won't you ever shut up." She then pulled up her knee-length skirt halfway up her thighs and placed her left knee beside his right thigh. Jim looked at her left leg and looked at her. He climbed up the chair a little bit, straightening himself as though trying to dig himself into the chair. Amanda lifted her right knee and placed it beside his left thigh so that she was now sitting on his lap astride. Jim's mouth was wide open. She grabbed his face with both hands and kissed his lips for what seemed to Jim to be a few minutes. After a while he had to push her back.

"Hold on, I need to breathe!"

"Well …" Amanda looked at Jim.

"Well what?" asked Jim, looking surprised.

"Well, have you taken your breath?"

Jim nodded silently. Amanda kissed him passionately again, rising up so much that Jim was looking up towards the ceiling. He gripped her hair, running his hands up and down her head.

Amanda leaned back and with her left hand stroked Jim's hair. All Jim could say was, "Wow!" He held both her arms with his hands and pushed her back a little bit. "I thought I had offended you!"

Amanda shook her head, looking into his eyes with a tear coming out of her eye. "That is the most romantic thing I have seen in my life. And I was very touched by what you did for Cindy."

Jim said, "Well …"

"Well what?"

"Was that dramatic enough of a proposal for you?"

"O Jim, much more dramatic than I ever dared to imagine."

"Well?"

"Well what?"

Jim grabbed her left hand and rubbed her ring finger where a ring would be worn. "Well, yes or no?"

Amanda put her finger on his lips. "Of course, darling. YES, YES!"

Just then there was a knock at door and Lucy walked in. Amanda jumped from Jim's lap and looked sheepishly at Lucy whilst fixing first her skirt, then her hair. She then pointed at Jim, wagging her finger. "And no more shenanigans in court please!"

Lucy said, "Aha!" She looked at Jim and winked. Jim got up and left the room. As Amanda was walking out Lucy put her hand in front of Amanda's chest, stopping her. Amanda looked at her and said, "What?"

Lucy reached into her bag and handed her a brush. "It must be very windy in there!"

As Amanda walked into the courtroom, she looked very serious and sat down in her seat. The judge looked at her, "Are we ready to go?"

Amanda said, "Yes your honour."

The judge looked at Jim who had retaken the witness stand. "I trust all matters are resolved?"

Jim looked at the judge and raised both thumbs ever so slightly and winked. "Yes your honour."

Amanda stood up. "Your honour, I will ask that the last remarks of Mister Sterne be eliminated from the records. They are irrelevant to the case and I would ask the witness to stay on the subject at hand."

The judge replied, "Duly noted." He turned to Jim, "Please answer the relevant questions only." He looked at the scribe. "Please delete the last two sentences of Detective Sterne."

"Yes, your honour."

The judge turned to Amanda again. "Any further questions?"

"No, your honour."

"Mister Gomez, do you have any questions?"

"Yes, your honour."

"Detective Sterne, can you confirm the following. Detective Johnston has testified that the defendant, Mister Chapman, talked about the murder of Charlene Mills, prior to general information being given to the press."

Jim nodded, "That is correct."

"And Detective Sterne, you do not have to answer this question." He paused for a few seconds. "Have you planted or misrepresented any evidence in this case?"

Jim shook his head. "Absolutely not!"

"That will be all, your honour!"

The judge turned Jim. "You are dismissed."

The judge looked at Amanda. "The court will recess for lunch, you can call your next witness at two p.m. after we reconvene."

He stood up.

The bailiff announced, "All rise for the judge."

Leaving the court, Jim approached Amanda. "Can I come to your place for a cup of coffee later tonight?"

Amanda leaned over until her lips were very close to his ear and whispered, "Only if you promise your intentions are totally dishonourable."

Jim smiled. "That will be one promise that is easy to keep!"

Lucy finished putting her papers in her briefcase. She looked at Jim and said, "Is that grin on your face permanent?"

Amanda kept looking at Jim. "Jealousy will get you nowhere. Now let's meet up with Jake, we'll need to have a chat with him."

CHAPTER 42

Damned if You Do, Damned if You Don't

Lucy looked at Jake. "Would you like some coffee?"

Jake nodded. "Yes please, milk and sugar."

Lucy poured three coffees from the pot on the side table in the interview room and placed the sandwiches on the table and then gave each one a side plate. "Please get something to eat."

"Thank you, Lucy." Jake put a couple of sandwiches on the plate. "I don't feel like eating, but I guess I'd better eat before going on the stand."

Amanda took a sip of her coffee. "Jake, are you sure you are happy to go on the stand?"

"I guess so." Jake didn't sound sure.

Lucy turned to Amanda, "Do you still think this is a good idea?"

Amanda chuckled. "I think it is a terrible idea. I would be very concerned about the cross-examination. But I have to be honest. The prosecution are so confident, they have hardly called any other witnesses. The jury will have paid a lot of attention to the fact of the detectives' account of Jake's knowledge of Charlene Mills' murder. There was a lot of specific info and the question marks I have created in their minds about Jim's credibility will not be enough to erase that. The genetic evidence is very compelling and I'm afraid." She looked at Jake. "And it pains me to say this, we have little or no chance of winning the case. When you are losing a chess game badly, you have to take risks." She took a big breath. "So we are damned if we do and damned if we don't, but I think our only hope is for you Jake to get on the stand and appeal to enough members of the jury that you are some sort of psychic and hope it leaves a hung jury."

Jake nodded. "Hey I know that my story is far-fetched. I am sorry I have dragged the two of you into this apparent mess. All I can say is that I could not kill anyone. I have lost sleep as to the genetic evidence. In fact–"

Amanda interrupted, "Jake, you don't need to say anything."

"I understand, Amanda. Perhaps there is nothing more to be said."

*

Everyone took their seat in court.

The judge asked Amanda, "Miss Jackson, who is your next witness please?"

"Your honour, the defense calls Mister Jake Chapman to the stand."

There was quite a loud murmur in the court room. Jake got up and was sworn in. He seemed to shift his bottom a few times from side to side, trying to get comfortable.

Amanda, as usual, took her time and took a sip of her water. She walked towards Jake.

"Mister Chapman, how do you feel, having been accused of killing your own wife last year?"

Jake was silent for quite a few seconds,. "Well, at first I thought was a joke. It took a while to sink in. I sort of wish it had gone to court so I could clear my name of any suspicion. Even though the case was dropped, I think in a lot of people's mind I would have been deemed to be guilty."

"However, the case was dropped as they did not have evidence to prove you to be guilty?"

"It was a matter–"

Amanda interrupted, "Mister Chapman, you are not on trial for your wife's death. It will suffice if you answer the question."

"Sorry Miss Jackson; yes, they had no proof of any such thing as I had not done it."

"Mister Chapman, I am sorry to pursue this line of questioning. But was your wife, Tracey, insured for her life?"

"Yes, we had dual life insurance."

"Dual, Mister Chapman?"

"Yes, we were both insured, if either died the other collected the insurance money."

"And would you mind telling the court how much money you received from the insurance company when she died."

"Nothing."

"Nothing?" asked Amanda, sounding genuinely surprised. "Why not, did the insurance company refuse to pay you?"

"No, I did not make a claim."

"And why would that be?"

"Well Tracey was my world. Without her I had no need for money. I had nothing I wanted to do, nowhere to go without her. Even food has had no taste."

"So you took solace in alcohol?"

"Yes, it's a sad and recurring story I have come across in my profession as a psychologist. I guess I just wanted to die as I had nothing to live for."

"Thank you, Mister Chapman." She hesitated for a few seconds. "Mister Chapman, did you kill Miss Charlene Mill?"

"No, I've never met her. Sorry, *had* never met her."

"And what about Sarah Miller, did you kill her?"

"No, I never met her either."

"But you were aware of her case?"

"Well, actually not by means of direct contact. My wife, Tracey …" he paused and looked down. "Could I have a glass of water please?"

The judge nodded and the bailiff brought over a glass of water. Jake drank half a glassful and put the glass down. Andy shook his head.

Amanda sounded sympathetic. "Mister Chapman, are you okay to continue?"

Jake nodded.

"Continue Mister Chapman. What was your association with Sarah Miller?"

"Yes, my wife Tracey was a social worker and a champion for the needy and ones who were wronged or underprivileged. She knew Sarah Miller was in trouble and helped her."

"Would you care to say what sort of trouble?"

"I would rather not. Even though my wife gave me some details about Sarah, it was in the assumption that I did not know the person. So, I would rather not give details of the case."

"Mister Chapman, I understand you have dreams from time to time."

"I guess we all have dreams."

"Perhaps rather than the philosophy, Mister Chapman, we can just deal with your story, if that is okay?"

"Oh, I am sorry, yes I do have dreams."

"That's all right, Mister Chapman. And thank you. So, what sort of dreams do you have?"

"Well, different sort of dreams–"

Amanda interrupted, "Let me be more specific. Do you ever dream of future events?"

"Don't we all?"

"Mister Chapman …"

"Sorry, yes I do."

"Do you mean you actually dream of things that are going to happen in the future?" Amanda raised her eyebrows, looking sceptical. No doubt asking questions that the jury were thinking.

"Sort of."

"Explain how that works."

"Well," Jake thought for a while. "You don't, or I should say I don't always see directly what is going to happen. For example, I may dream that a dog is going to bite me, and inevitably I know that someone is going to be attacking me in some way or another, but not physically, some sort of assault which is often not a physical event."

Amanda nodded. "I think I see; can you give me another example?"

"Well …" Jake was thinking again. "For example, one night I dreamt that my cousin was in hospital getting intensive investigation and was told that he had a heart complaint. When I phoned him the next day, he told me that he was actually taken to ER the previous night, had tests done and had pneumonia."

Amanda rubbed her chin. "So your dream was wrong?"

"Oh, not at all. The nature of my dreams is to give me a glimpse in the right direction, in a theme or general scenario, but it is not prophetic in that it is not accurate in every detail."

Amanda nodded. "I think I see. But you can see how this might seem far-fetched to a lot of people?"

"Yes, absolutely. However, I have been taught to speak the truth, so I have to say it as it is."

"Taught by whom, Mister Chapman?"

"Oh, my mother. In all the years I knew her she never told a lie, nor spoke ill of anyone. I couldn't lie if I tried."

"Mister Chapman. Going back to your theme of dreams. Have you ever dreamt, let's say, of sports matches, NFL, NBA, baseball results? Perhaps horse racing?"

"I'm not comfortable talking about this."

Amanda approached the stand and leaned on the seat. "Mister Chapman, we are trying to establish the pattern of your dreams."

Jake nodded. "Yes I do have some random dreams of that nature."

"Would you sometimes dream of horse races, for example you may dream that a horse is a faller in a race, or that a certain horse is a winner?"

"Yes, I used to, but these have stopped for some reason."

"So, Mister Chapman, you are saying that you would dream of a race and see who the winner is?"

"Rarely, but yes."

"So you must have made bucketsful of money betting."

"I never bet."

"Why is that?"

"Dreams are there for a higher purpose. I would be defiling them by using it to bet."

"What does that mean? What would be the higher purpose?"

"Well, according to my limited understanding, dreams of random events, like horse racing, would give me the confidence to trust my dreams and to be alert for one which I have to take heed of."

"So, you didn't bet on horse races, but you gave the details to others?"

"Yes, a few acquaintances made a few bets, but when I realized the level of betting I stopped passing info. Anyway, that phase of dreams stopped at that time."

"So, you have at times told some people that a certain horse is going to win a race or have a fall at a certain obstacle?"

"Yes."

"And at another time, for example, you dreamt that your sister was going to have a car accident and warned her to wear her seat belt?"

"Yes, that did happen."

"For example, Mister Chapman, when you dreamt your wife was in danger and could be killed?"

"Yes, I should have paid more attention to that dream."

"Finally, Mister Chapman. You are clear in your mind that you never met Sarah?"

"Yes. I had definitely never met her!"

"So Mister Chapman, when you told the detectives, on the night of the sixteenth of November, that a young girl was killed, you may have indeed had a dream about this murder?"

"It's the only explanation I have. But some of my dreams are very vivid and I have difficulty knowing whether the memory is from a dream or from a real-life event. It is probably made more difficult to distinguish between dreams and real event because I was intoxicated most of the time."

"Mister Chapman, how can you explain the fact there was forensic evidence incriminating you? I mean your hair sample was on Sarah Miller's body!"

"Well, I am not a scientific expert. Perhaps meeting my wife would have somehow cross-contaminated Sarah's body."

"Thank you, Mister Chapman, that will be all."

The judge turned to Andy. "You may question the witness."

Andy got up.

"Forgive me Mister Chapman for not applauding your generosity—"

The judge sounded very stern and interrupted Andy, "Mister Gomez, this is not a theatre, please do not use the questioning for making cheap comments. Members of the jury please disregard that last comment."

Andy nodded. "I apologise. I will re-phrase my comment." He put his hand on his chin. "Mister Chapman, is it not true that the only reason you did not collect the life insurance payment of your wife is that there was heat and attention on you from the police and you had to put on a brave face?"

"No, that is not correct. I had no interest in it."

"Mister Chapman, I have a recorded conversation from you to Assurance Insurance Company a week after your wife's demise. You asked them how quickly you could cash the claim. Is that right?"

"Well, that was because—"

Andy put up his hand. "Please Mister Chapman, I wasn't asking for reasons. Can you confirm that you did phone them and wanted to get the money as soon as possible?"

"Well, yes I did, but—"

Andy stopped Jake short, "Thank you, Mister Chapman."

He walked to his desk and Anita handed him a paper; Andy gave her a quick wink and whispered, "Good job, just in time!"

He turned towards Jake. "Mister Chapman, you were a regular customer at the Mexicano Bar, were you not?"

"Yes, you could say that." Jake smiled.

"You would tend to have a few drinks most nights you were there, is that right?"

"Yes, as I have said before I, sadly I may add, took solace in alcohol."

"How did you pay for your drinks?"

"Well, I didn't have a lot money, so I owed them, or was helped out."

"Mister Chapman, is it not true that you never paid for drinks in the last few months? In fact, your horse tips – whatever fanciful way you have of describing them – these tips were rewarded by free booze, lifts back to your house, occasional meals and so on and so forth, is that right?"

"That's not the way I would look at it."

"Whichever way you look at it, Mister Chapman, do you deny the favours you got?"

"No, I don't."

"Thank you."

Andy walked over to the table, he put the papers he had in his hand and picked up another set of A4 pages and flicked through them. He studied one of them.

"Mister Chapman, is it not true that you murdered Sarah Miller in cold blood, for whatever twisted reason? She tried to resist your attention and affection, you exposed your privates to her, she pushed you away, in the process she got your pubic hair under her nails. You got angry and killed the poor young girl as she had refused to accede to your advances?"

"No Mister Gomez, I had never met Sarah!"

"So your hypothesis is that your wife somehow carried some of your pubic hair, it accidentally got under the nail of Sarah Miller, and then she was killed by someone else?"

"I know it sounds farfetched, but as I never saw her, it must be the only reason."

"Well, you are absolutely right there, it is very farfetched. That's because it is a lie."

"As I had never met her there can be no other explanation!"

"Mister Chapman, where were you on the night of Saturday November sixteenth, the night of Charlene Mills' murder?"

"I was at the Mexicano bar drinking."

"Mister Chapman, I believe you have said that you have been taught never to tell a lie."

"Yes, that is correct."

"In that case I would also like to remind you that you are under oath. So now I am going to go back to witness statements from Detectives Sterne and Johnston. Let me see …" He walked back to his desk and flicked through the papers he had on his desk. "Ah, this is it. On the first interview one of the detectives asked you if you remembered seeing them previously, and do you remember what your answer was?"

"I believe I told them that I did not remember seeing them the night previously."

"That is correct. Now if you do not remember seeing them the night before, do you remember seeing anyone else?"

Jake looked very uncomfortable. "Yes."

"Yes, you remember?"

"No, I mean, yes I agree with you, I don't remember meeting anyone on that night."

"Is it not true that you had a slight altercation with Detective Johnston, of which you recalled nothing?"

"Yes, that is right."

"In fact, Mister Chapman, do you remember anyone you have met over the past month, after nine p.m."

"My life is a blur after about four p.m., I usually start drinking in the morning – or I should say I used to – then I generally drank all day."

"So, Mister Chapman, I put it to you that you have probably met a lot of people that you do not remember, would that be accurate?"

Jake nodded. "Yes, that would be accurate."

"Mister Chapman, would it be safe to say that you may have met Charlene Mills and not remember the event?"

Jake was slow to respond "I gue … guess so."

"So, Mister Chapman, you agree that you may have met Charlene Mills?"

"Ye … Yes."

"Is it then possible that you would have had an altercation with her and not remember this, as happened with Detective Johnston?"

"I don't think that would be very likely."

Andy raised his voice, "But Mister Chapman it is possible."

"I guess so."

Andy turned to the jury. "I will take that as a yes!" He turned to the judge. "Thank you, your honour, that will be all."

The judge faced Amanda. "Any further questions from the defense?"

Amanda jumped up. "Yes, your honour."

She approached Jake. "Mister Chapman, why did you call Assurance Insurance?"

Jake seemed relieved. "It's because I thought I would have to go to court and didn't have enough money to pay a solicitor. Once I found out that the charges were dropped, I lost interest in the money."

"Thank you. And one final question. To the best of your knowledge, have you ever met or seen Charlene Mills or Sarah Miller?"

"No, I have not!"

"Thank you, Mister Chapman." She turned to the judge. "That will be all, your honour."

The judge looked at Jake. "You may step down, Mister Chapman."

Jake looked jaded. "Thank you, your honour." Jake walked to his seat beside Amanda.

The judge looked at Amanda. "Does the defense have any other witnesses?"

"No, your honour."

The judge stated, "Very well then, the court will recess until the morning."

Jake was about to sit down when he suddenly called out, "Your honour, I wonder if I could ask how your daughter is doing?"

The judge looked quite taken aback. "I beg your pardon?"

Jake did not seem to notice Amanda elbowing him in the ribs. "I wonder if her abdominal pain has settled."

The judge's voice was visibly louder, "I am going to ask you to stop speaking."

"Sure judge, I only ask because, even with my limited knowledge, I know that an ectopic pregnancy can be very dangerous."

The judge stood up and was visibly red. "Mister Chapman, you have overstepped the boundaries of moderation. I find you in contempt of court. I will delay the suitable punishment for this until my rage has subsided."

He hit his gavel very hard. "Everyone dismissed."

Jake turned towards Amanda and Lucy. Lucy looked at Jake. "What in the name of heaven was that all about?"

Jake looked surprised. "But Lucy, you gave me that information."

Amanda looked at Lucy indignantly. Lucy shrugged her shoulders. "Amanda, I have no idea what he is talking about."

The guard had come to take Jake away. Amanda nodded. "Go on Jake, we'll chat in the morning, but for God's sake, don't say another word! To anybody!"

Jake nodded and left quietly with his head bowed.

Amanda and Lucy sat down. Jim walked towards Amanda. "Honey, if you would like to cancel tonight, I will understand."

Amanda held Jim's hand. "No Jim, I would like some company tonight. Believe it or not, I have gone over my summing up presentation a few times already."

Jim kissed her on the cheek. "Pick you up at eight?"

"Make it seven."

"Sure, see you at seven."

When the court room was empty Lucy sat forward. "I thought you did well to put some doubt in the face of such damning evidence."

"I did my best but I'm afraid it's nowhere near enough."

Lucy nodded. "Do you want to go over the summing up?"

"No, I have been summing up in my mind for a long time. I have never been involved in such a hopeless case!"

"Yes, I agree," Lucy nodded. "Not helped by the nonsense at the end about the judge's daughter. Does he even have a daughter?"

"You know, Lucy, I have no idea, but no it does not help anything."

Lucy nodded. "What would say about our chances now, Amanda?"

"I only have two words that will sum it up: we're fucked!"

Lucy smiled sadly. "Couldn't have put it better myself. So, what now?"

"It's been a strange day. I am certain that I am losing the biggest case I have been involved in. But the only thing on my mind is that I have been proposed to. I plan to forget about the case for the rest of the day and savour every moment."

"Gosh, I nearly forgot about that!"

"Yes, let's have a cup of coffee together and then I can go and soak in a hot bath and get ready for the night."

"Aha!"

"Shoosh you, no more said. Let's go. There is a bar across the road. Many a drink and coffee has been had there by lawyers, both happy and sad."

"I bet," said Lucy, laughing.

*

They arrived at the bar and sat down on two stools. Amanda beckoned to the lady behind the bar. She came towards them. "What can I get you, ladies?"

Amanda was about to speak when Lucy held up her hand. "Shhh." She pointed to the TV up at the back of the bar. "Could you turn that up please?"

The caption under the picture of the news reader said, 'CNN breaking news – Jake Chapman, verdict due tomorrow.'

The bar lady turned up the volume. The female TV presenter said, "We now bring you a report about the murder of the young girl behind the disused cement factory in Manhattan. The case which has become known as The Lady with the Red Shoes."

Amanda slowly turned her face and looked at Lucy, who had likewise turned her head to look at Amanda. The lady reading the news was black.

The lady behind the bar broke the silence. "Would you ladies like me to come back?"

Amanda replied, "No I'll have a whiskey!"

Lucy was next, "I never drink before eight p.m., but I'll have a whiskey too."

CHAPTER 43

To Bed at Last?

Jim listened on his phone, "Hello Ahmad, can you talk?"

"Sure, Mister Jim."

"Are working now? You know I only get my car valeted by you, if you are not working, I will wait."

"Yes, Mister Jim, I am working, please come down. Even if I wasn't working, I would have come in for you."

"Okay Ahmad, see you soon."

*

Ahmad was busy cleaning Jim's car. Jim kept looking at his watch. "Ahmad, is this going to take much longer?" he said, pointing to his watch.

"Mister Jim, you know if I don't have it in perfect condition, you will be the first to complain."

"I know, I know, but this time it seems to be taking a long time, even though it was valeted recently."

"I know, Mister Jim, but you have bloody muck in the front and the back of your car, and I only have one way of cleaning. That is perfect or nothing! Anyway, Mister Jim, do you have a date or something tonight?"

"Got it in one, Ahmad. I'm sorry, just very nervous about tonight."

"Is she hot, Mister Jim?"

"Pardon me?"

"Your date, I think with a sexy car like this you will date some sexy broads."

"Ahmad, my days of me chasing broads is long gone. But she is gorgeous, yes!"

"In that case you had better be going. Let me just give you your invoice."

"No need for that, I will just pay in cash."

"No Mister Jim, my boss here insists on giving invoices. He was investigated by the IRS once and his accountant has told him to give out an invoice for every bit of work and all monies go through the till." He took out an invoice book from his overalls and wrote on it, tore off the top page and handed it to Jim.

Jim had a look at it. He reached for his wallet and stopped. "Hold on a second, Ahmad. No wonder the IRS are investigating your boss. This invoice is numbered fourteen thousand two hundred and twenty-four. That's an awful number of valets per year!"

"No Mister Jim, it has a dummy number."

"Come again?"

"It is a business trick. You have an extra number at the beginning, so it looks like we are very busy. Mister boss doesn't want the customers to think he has a small number of clientele and therefore not good at what he does. If you take away the first one, it makes it four-thousand-something invoices this year."

"I see. Well look, you got me in a good mood. Here is fifty dollars, thanks a lot."

"Are you sure, Mister Jim, this is far too much?"

"That's okay, Ahmad. Anyway, I like you, so it's a pleasure."

Ahmad put the fifty dollars in the till and put thirty dollars in his pocket. "Well Mister Jim, now that's three reasons why I like you!"

Jim was about to get into his car and suddenly stopped. "Oh, I'm dying to know what the other two reasons are, Ahmad."

"Well Mister Jim, the first one is this; you call me by my proper name. AH MAD. Some people call me AAH MAD, or AMAD, or AKMAD, or AKHMAD, or AMED. The list goes on, you call me like me mother and father call me AH MAD. The second reason is …" He looked back from the workshop towards the office and his boss in the office looked up at the same time. He looked down at his paperwork again. Ahmad lowered his voice. "Do you remember me from before, Mister Jim?"

"Sure Ahmad, I see you here regularly."

"No, I mean from about nine years ago, when I was fourteen years old."

Jim shook his head. "Maybe you should keep this to yourself."

"No, Mister Jim, I would like to tell the story. Because that is the day that my life changed."

"Oh? You have me intrigued."

"I was parading the streets with my cousins who were older than me. We were in a gang and I thought I was a big shot because I was given a knife to carry. I thought I was so cool. My cousins told me I had to prove myself worthy to be in their gang. I nearly wet myself. I gave them the knife back and said I was not going to kill nobody. They all laughed. My older cousin who was eighteen said, 'No, you silly ass. That is the car of the father of our rival gang. You have to slash the tyres.' I was so relieved that I took the knife off him and ran to the car and slashed one of the tyres. As I turned around to slash one of the other tyres, I bumped into you. My cousins all disappeared in a flash. You stood there with your hands on your hips. I pointed the knife at you and you just laughed at me. Then before I knew what had hit me you had my arm behind my back and I dropped the knife. You then held me by my ear and showed me your badge. I wet myself on the spot."

"Ah yes, I remember something like that, I think I was just amused. So how did that change your life?"

"You probably don't remember, Mister Jim. I begged you not to arrest me, I said that my parents were God-fearing Muslims and that my father would kill me and my mother would die of shame. You looked at my wet trousers. Then you said, Okay son I will let you off, but only if you repair the damage.' I asked how, and you walked me into this very shop and told the owner that I had to work here until I had paid for a new tyre. I have been working here since."

"Well Ahmad, I am glad to hear that."

"That's not all of it, Mister Jim." He paused and then looked at Jim. "My cousin Saleem was killed the next week, his throat was cut from ear to ear and a few of my other cousins were injured. I could have been dead! Now you know why I have given you my personal number to call me whenever you need anything done to your car!"

"Well what can I say, Ahmad, your fabulous work had repaid me several times over."

"No, Mister Jim, I will always be at your service."

Jim put his hand on Ahmad's shoulder. "Well I have to go now. I like you a lot, but my hot date takes priority."

"Thank you very much, Mister Jim. Any time. And that's very kind of you. And you probably don't need this advice, but make sure you take condoms with you so you don't have to speed out late at night!"

"What? Oh goodness, I never … Better rush. Thanks, Ahmad."

"See you again, Mister Jim."

*

It was about six thirty p.m. Amanda got out of the shower and wrapped a large turquoise towel around her body and a matching smaller towel around her hair after she had dried it a little. She went over to her antique mahogany chest of drawers and opened the top drawer.

She took out two pairs of knickers, one black and one red. She held the black one in front of her on top of the towel and swayed her hips from side to side. She put the black pair down and did the same with the red pair.

"Hmm," she said out loud to herself, "black or red, Jim, which one to knock you out?" She went through the process again and still seemed unsure. Her cell phone rang. She put the two pairs of knickers side by side and went to her phone by her bedside table with her eyes fixed on the knickers.

She picked up the phone. The light on her cell phone was flashing and the cell phone screen read 'Jim Sterne'.

She flicked open her phone and remained silent.

"Hello?" Jim's voice seemed almost apologetic.

Amanda remained silent.

"Hello, can you hear me?" Jim was shouting a little bit.

"Jim please don't tell me you have to cancel."

"I am so sorry honey but …"

"O Jim, you can't be serious. Do you know what I am doing at this precise minute? I am choosing my sexy lingerie for you. Don't tell me you are going to stand me up, tonight of all night."

"Amanda let me tell you something. Hold on a second, why exactly are you putting on sexy lingerie?"

"Never mind that, Jim, and tell me what's up, or perhaps you just shouldn't bother. I mean tonight of all nights!"

"There is nothing I would like better than spending the whole night with you. In fact, let me tell you a secret. There is not a night has gone by over the past few weeks that I have not gone to bed thinking about you."

Amanda interrupted. "There is a but coming though, isn't there?"

"Well my pops needs my attention."

"Oh dear honey, I am sorry, is he okay?"

"Yes and no. He is not sick sick, but has a catheter to drain his bladder and it has blocked and I need to take him to ER to get it changed. He is in slight discomfort at present but I'm sure he'll be pretty distressed soon. I promise to come over to you as soon as I bring him back home."

"No, you won't!" Amanda quipped.

Jim's voice was slightly tremulous. "What do you mean, you don't want me to come over to your place?"

"No. Because I want to come over with you and your dad. I would like to meet him. That is if he doesn't mind me accompanying him on such a delicate matter."

"Hold on and I will check with him."

Amanda could hear Jim talking to his dad. "Pops do you mind if Amanda comes along with us to the hospital? She wants to meet you."

She faintly heard his dad, "Are you missing a night in bed with a gorgeous girl on account of me?"

Jim covered the phone and laughed. "Don't worry about that, Pops, I intend to spend lots of nights with her."

Jim spoke to her again, "Yes he would love to meet you, Amanda. Do you want to meet up at ER?"

"No silly. I want to come to his house. Give me the address and I will meet you there. We can go to ER in my car."

Jim gave Amanda the address and put the phone down and suddenly looked anxious. "Pops, we need to tidy the place up."

"My, oh my. I've never seen you so nervous before."

"Well you know what they say about first impressions. No offence meant about your place, although it's not too bad."

"Yes, but when you live on your own, you do get a bit sloppy. Right son, why don't you tidy the papers over there, and I will take the dishes to the kitchen … and just drop the papers along with the clothes in the bedroom … and … well let's do that first."

"Okay Pops, I'll do the papers first and take them to your bedroom on top of your bed and you can sort them later."

"That's fine, Jim."

Jim picked some copies of newsletters and a pile of envelopes and papers. Just then an A4size paper fell from the pile. Jim looked at it with his two hands full.

"Holy shit," he muttered. He shouted, "Pops, what is going on here?"

His dad shouted from the kitchen, "What's that, son? I can't hear you."

Jim walked into the kitchen. He paused for a second and looked around the kitchen. "Pops you need to look after your place a bit better."

"I know, son, but since your mom died, I have little to get excited for at home."

"What about your lady friend, the blind date, I thought she was, let me quote you, 'hot and sexy'!"

"No, that's all over now."

"What happened?"

"It's a long story, son, and with a very distended bladder, I don't feel like long stories, and with a catheter in my willie I certainly don't need to be reminded of anything hot or sexy."

Jim laughed.

"Anyway Jim, what was it you wanted to tell me?"

"Oh yes," Jim said as he lifted the A4 paper. "I wasn't prying or anything, but I dropped this piece of paper and when I picked it up, I noticed that it was your bank statement."

"That's all right, Jim, I have nothing to hide from you."

"Well I have to ask you. You have deposits of ten thousand dollars, thirteen thousand dollars, and twenty-one thousand dollars all in the past year. Are you dealing drugs?"

"Oh yes, those. You won't believe me if I tell you."

"Try me, Pops."

"I put three bets of one thousand dollars each with odds of nine, twelve, and the last one at twenty to one."

"You have got to be kidding me! Since when do you bet on horses? You know nothing about horses. And anyway, as you know the bookies have three windows for collecting money and one for paying out, so they get you in the end!"

"Yes, but I had a hot tip. Or I should say tips!"

"And who exactly is this tipster?"

"Can't tell you, I'm sworn to secrecy. He doesn't give tips often, once every few months, but they are solid tips. Never failed. There are only about a dozen of us in the loop, and we are sworn to secrecy."

"Are you sure it is legitimate and legal?"

"I can assure you of that. All I can tell you is that his nickname is the Oracle."

"Well I will say is that if I find out you are involved in an illegal ring, I will personally hand the money back. You know I hate any sort of corruption."

"Well son, you'll just have to trust me on this one."

"Okay Pops, you know I trust you."

"Now make yourself a cup of coffee while you wait for Amanda, I would have one, but my bladder will complain."

*

Amanda walked to the door of the apartment; she checked the address on the piece of paper in her hands which had the number 17 written on it. She made a fist with her right hand and was going to knock the door but held back. She couldn't believe how nervous she was. She fixed her hair and brushed her skirt. "This is silly!" she whispered to herself and rapped the door quite loud, perhaps to give herself the illusion that she was confident.

Jim opened the door within a second. He came out and pulled the door behind him so it was almost shut. He grabbed her face in his two hands and kissed her very passionately. "Whoof," Amanda exclaimed, "I could get used to this."

"I am so sorry, honey."

Amanda held a finger against his lips, "No I was a bit thoughtless; I should have known better."

"Thanks for understanding and thanks for coming over."

"Don't mention it," Amanda said. It was her turn to kiss him.

There was a loud voice from inside the apartment, "Are you two lovebirds going to be long, because my bladder is about to burst."

"Sorry Pops." Jim went in and Amanda followed him in. "Pops, this is Amanda Jackson, Amanda this is Pops. Sorry, Jim Senior."

Jim Senior reached to shake Amanda's hand. "You are as gorgeous as Jim had said."

"Well thank you. Nice to meet you. Two Jims, what am I going to call the two of you around the dinner table?"

Jim Senior answered, "Call me James."

Jim held Amanda's hand. "You can call me anything, so long as you keep calling."

Jim Senior held up the urine-collection bag which had a tube running into it from the catheter. "You see this bag should be full and only has a small amount of urine in it, so now let's go."

"Right. Right," said Jim as he rushed to pick up his overcoat and car keys. "It's quite cold out there, Pops, and it's raining a little bit, you'll need a coat."

"Is it okay to go in my car, Jim?"

"Sure Amanda."

At the car Jim was about to help James into the back seat. "I'm not an invalid you know; I just have a catheter in."

Amanda walked up and opened the front door. "James would you like to sit in the front with me, we have a lot to talk about."

"I would certainly like that, ma'am."

"Jim you can sit in the back."

"Oh well thank you very much," Jim said with a tone of humour as he got into the back seat.

Amanda started the engine and with that started to talk to James. "Well James you can be the co-pilot. It is the Western General Hospital we are going to?"

James answered, "Yes that is correct. The ER entrance is at the back of the hospital."

"Now tell me about your job. You were in the Navy, weren't you?"

"For forty years, I travelled to …"

The conversation went on all the way to the hospital, interrupted only by occasional directions from James. On a couple of occasions Jim tried to butt in but was soon stopped by Amanda. "Do you mind, we are having an intelligent conversation."

"Sorry to disturb you," was all Jim would add sarcastically.

When they arrived at the hospital the two of them stopped talking for the first time. James then broke the silence, "You know, there is one thing I hate about going out since I had the catheter inserted six months ago."

"What is it?" Amanda asked.

"It's carrying this damned urine bag everywhere. That's why I rarely go out now."

Amanda asked, "Have you not had an outpatient follow up?"

"No, every time I phone they say that there is a large waiting time, or the doctor is on vacation. I think it's because I don't have premium insurance they could not be bothered dealing with me."

"We'll see about that," said Amanda with an irritation in her voice.

They got out of the car. Amanda went to the side of James where he was holding the urine bag. "Give that to me."

"What?!" asked James.

"What?!" asked Jim in a louder voice.

James shrugged his shoulders. "Okay if you say so."

Amanda took the urine bag and put it behind her handbag so it was very much concealed. "Now put your hand through my arm." She bent her elbow to allow James to put his hand around her elbow. "Now are you ready to go out, James?"

"Yes darling." He waved a hand towards Jim. "Garçon, would you please park the car and maybe you could give it a wash as well."

"Very funny." Jim was smiling but he could not hide this thrill at what he was seeing.

Amanda and Jim were seated outside in the general waiting room whilst James' catheter was being changed. Jim whispered to Amanda, "I can't believe I am in ER instead of being in your apartment holding you in my arms."

"Maybe you have lost your chance to find out."

"Maybe not?" Jim asked inquisitively.

"We'll see." She paused, smiled and whispered in his ear. "It's been a long time."

Jim said rather loudly, "A long time since wha …" He cleared his throat as realisation dawned on him. "We'll try and get matters here sorted quickly!"

A nurse came up to the two of them. "Mister Sterne, the doctor will see you now."

As they got up, she put her hand in front of Amanda's chest. "Sorry miss, this is a delicate matter and the doctor will see him privately."

Jim's father shouted through the door which was slightly ajar. "That's okay, I wouldn't mind … in fact I would like Miss Jackson to be in here as well."

The nurse nodded. "You can both now see Mister Sterne."

"Thank you," Amanda and Jim said simultaneously.

When they went into the clinical room James was sitting on an examination couch with a big smile on his face. He gave the thumbs up to Amanda and Jim as they walked in. He pointed to the drainage bag that was at the side of the bed and was bulging with urine. A male doctor in his fifties was measuring the urine in the bag and then wrote down the volume on the chart. He was seated on the edge of the couch. As Amanda and Jim walked in, he looked over the top of the chart momentarily and then continued to write.

Amanda walked over to him and shook his hand. "Good evening Doctor …?" She looked towards his badge.

"Doctor Hagan." He made a gesture to get up although his buttocks barely left the couch. He shook her hand and then began to flip over the pages of the chart.

The doctor got up and spoke to James. "Mister Sterne you should be okay for now. I will see you at the clinic in three months."

He put the chart under his arm and turned around to walk out.

Amanda very casually asked him, "Doctor Hagan, may I ask what Mister Stern's PSA is?"

Doctor Hagan seemed to stop in his tracks. "I presume you are talking about his Prostatic Specific Antigen level?"

"Yes doctor, his PSA."

The doctor looked a little flustered. He quickly turned the pages of the chart back and forth. "Emm, let me see."

He suddenly stopped and asked, "May I know who you are please?"

Jim walked towards him. "I thought you would never ask. I am Detective Jim Sterne of NYPD." He reached over and shook the doctor's hand.

"And I am Amanda Jackson, law attorney."

Doctor Hagan seemed to swallow very hard. "Just out of interest, what is your specialty?"

"Medical negligence." Amanda raised her eyebrows.

The doctor tried to swallow his saliva but seemed unable to.

Amanda said casually again, "His PSA?"

"Oh right." He flicked back and forth over the pages of the chart again. "Oh yes, his last PSA was fourteen point two, previous to that it was eight point six."

"What date was his PSA last taken?"

The doctor looked a bit flustered; he flicked the pages of the chart back and forth. He then stopped on one page. "It seems like it was six months ago."

"That is a long time ago. Is that not a little high, Doctor Hagan, and rising as well?"

The doctor closed the chart and turned to James. "Mister Sterne, I have to apologise, I have not seen you on the last couple of attendances at the clinic. May I suggest that we keep you in overnight for some tests, and perhaps a prostatic biopsy as well."

James replied, "That's okay by me. I will only get in the way of these two lovebirds anyway."

"I will go and organise the tests." And with that Doctor Hagan left a room and seemed to breathe a sigh of relief as he walked out.

James looked at Amanda and winked at her. "You sure scared the crap out of him. I didn't know you specialised in medical negligence."

"Nor did I," Jim said, looking surprised.

"I don't now, but I did for a while as an understudy."

Jim pinched his dad's cheek with his fingers. "Pops I love you dearly, but do you mind if I go on my date now?"

Amanda laughed.

"Go already." James motioned with his two hands toward the exit door. Jim laughed out loud.

*

As they were getting into Amanda's car Jim asked, "Do you want to stop on the way to get something to eat?"

"No!" said Amanda. "Eating is not on my mind at the minute."

Jim nodded. "I am happy to skip food."

Amanda looked towards Jim as she was driving. Jim looked back. Amanda didn't say anything.

"What?" asked Jim.

Amanda shook her head.

"What is it?" Jim asked again.

"Nothing Jim, it's just that …"

"Yes?" asked Jim.

"Well you haven't said a word since we left the hospital!"

"Gosh, I'm sorry sweetheart, it's just that there is something bothering me."

"Have I upset you, Jim?"

"O God no! In fact, if I hadn't been madly in love with you by tonight, I would be so by the end of the night."

"Okay Jim, now that you have redeemed yourself tell me what is so important that it can preoccupy you on a night like this?"

Jim was reluctant.

Amanda seemed impatient. "Go on spit it out!"

"Well Mandy … Do you like me calling you Mandy?"

"I like that but get on with it!"

"Well Mandy, I was thinking about Jake."

"Oh, come on, Jim, you know I can't talk about the case with you."

"I understand, but just hear me out, you don't have to say anything, just listen to me, is that okay?"

"All right. If I must."

"Well I am wondering what Jake's motives would be. I mean, why would he want to kill his wife? What if he was not having an affair, nor was she that we are aware of. I don't think he has any interest in money. His life is devastated since she died. In fact, I understand he did not cash in the cheque for her life policy. And why would he kill Sarah?"

"Carry on," said Amanda, taking short looks at Jim whilst driving. Jim on the other hand was staring straight ahead.

"Well I saw Jake in the pub that night, and you interviewed him soon after. Now that I know him a bit better, I find it hard to think he would walk the streets looking for sex!" He looked at Amanda. "Well are you going to say anything at all?"

Amanda shook her head. "I'm sorry I don't want to say anything until the case is over. I'm sure you understand."

"That's all right, Mandy, I have it off my chest, let's drop it for now."

They arrived at Amanda's house. They walked into the hall and Amanda put her handbag and keys on top of a tall table with an oriental design on it. She switched on a large lamp and switched off the main lights. She took off her shoes and stretched her arms skywards, went on her tiptoes, and stretched her whole body. "I am pooped."

"If you are too tired, I can leave."

"Jim you are not going anywhere tonight that is outside the four walls of my bedroom, get it?"

"Yes ma'am."

"Anyway, a quick drink will sort me out. Would you like one, is it whiskey you like?"

"That would be nice."

"Don't go far," Amanda warned. "I'll be right back."

Jim started to walk around and before he realised he had opened a drawer to look at what was inside. He quickly shut it and talked to himself, "Shit, once a cop always a cop!"

Amanda returned with a crystal glass in each hand. She handed him a glass that was filled a third of the way up with whiskey.

He took the glass from her. "Thanks honey, just what I need."

Amanda waved one of her fingers in a very seductive way. "Follow me."

Jim put up his hand as if to ask permission to speak. "I will be in right after I watch the New York Knicks on the box."

"Very funny." Amanda laughed. She hooked one of her fingers on the belt of his trousers and pulled him along.

"I suppose the ball game can wait," he said, smiling.

She led him into the bedroom. She took off her blouse and unzipped her skirt and let it drop to the floor. She was wearing her black see-through lingerie. She turned around and Jim could see part of her behind, as her knickers only covered half of her buttocks.

Jim could only say, "Wow, worth waiting for."

"Well what are you waiting for, are you going to get undressed too or not?"

Jim was fidgeting trying to take off his shirt and he eventually gave up and took it off over his head without undoing the buttons. He threw it across the room. He took his shoes and socks off before he dropped his trousers to the ground and was standing there in his boxer shorts.

"Well now we can hardly make love with your boxers on, can we?"

"Let me take a leak first." Jim got up to go to the bathroom. As he walked towards the bathroom, he pulled down his boxer shorts slightly to reveal the top of his buttocks. Amanda whistled, "Nice butt!"

Jim pulled up his boxers as he walked to the bathroom. He walked back and jumped into the bed. Amanda said, "It's my turn now."

Jim sat up and folded his arms across his chest. Amanda said, "Cover your eyes."

Jim put his hands on his eyes while obviously spreading his fingers apart so he could see through them. As Amanda walked to the bathroom she stopped and wiggled her bum. She then turned her head and looked over her shoulder. "Is that cute enough for you?"

Jim shook his head. "No, it's not cute, it's dead sexy! Get back in here quick."

Amanda shouted from the bathroom, "Tie a knot in it till I get there."

Jim shouted back, "I never knew you were so funny."

Jim was seated high up on the bed with his arms folded. Suddenly Amanda shouted from the bathroom, "James!"

Jim shouted back, "Oh shit, my mother used to call me James when she was angry with me."

"Come here please, Jim."

Jim walked into the bathroom. Amanda had her hands on her hips. "What do you see?"

Jim replied quickly, "A nearly naked girl."

"Look harder!"

Jim scratched his head. "A nearly naked girl and a nearly naked guy who is standing around looking at her."

"Be serious!"

"Come on, give me a clue."

Amanda pointed at the toilet. Jim walked towards it, "I'm sure I flushed."

Amanda took the toilet seat and swivelled it up and down. "See this, you are meant to keep it down."

Jim put up his arms high. "Guilty as charged! I am sorry, I have lived on my own for a long time!"

Amanda then pointed to the lip of the toilet bowl. "And no pubic hair please."

Jim took a piece of toilet tissue and lifted the hair and took it close to Amanda's face. Amanda pulled away. "Oh that is disgusting." She then waved the back of her hand, beckoning him to go away. He threw the tissue in the toilet bowl.

Jim left the bathroom and went to bed. Amanda joined him. She got into bed beside him. She lifted his right arm and put it around her shoulder. She began to stroke his chest. "I like playing with your hairy chest."

Jim looked at her hand. "I'll give you half an hour to stop."

Amanda laughed, "I didn't know *you* were so funny."

There was a silence for about a minute. Amanda tapped Jim's temple, "Hello, are you there?"

"Sorry I was just thinking about Jake."

Amanda quickly replied, "I thought we had agreed not to talk about the case."

Jim thought for a few seconds. "Do you think he is guilty?"

"Why do you ask?"

Jim was ponderous. "I don't know, there is something bothering me."

Amanda was obviously not going to be dragged into the discussion. "Sorry I cannot discuss the case with you, especially not in bed!"

"Ok sorry. By the way, you don't have to stop stroking my chest."

Amanda smiled. "If you play your cards right you can stroke mine."

Jim seemed to be in deep thought again. Amanda looked at him. "Can I ask you something?" she asked a little nervously. The tone of her voice made Jim give her his full attention.

"What is it?"

"Do you think I am too old to have a child?"

"How old are you again?

"Thirty-six."

"Well, I'm not a doctor, but I would say you couldn't have any more than six children."

Amanda slapped his chest again. "I'm serious."

"Do you really want children?"

Amanda looked Jim straight in his eyes. "Yes, I would love to be a mummy. How do you feel about that?"

Jim stroked her hair. "I would love to be a dad. Why don't we start the practice now?"

He kissed her. She suddenly stopped and started to laugh. Jim looked puzzled, but Amanda just seemed to laugh louder.

"What is so funny?" Jim asked indignantly.

Amanda stopped laughing. "A thought just came to me, that you will not allow any children in the back of your car in case they make a mess."

Jim nodded his head. "You are damn right, no one will make a mess of the back of my car!"

Amanda laughed again. "That is right, no one gets in the back of your car."

Jim suddenly sat up, pushing Amanda back. Amanda rubbed her neck and shouted, "Ouch that hurt."

Jim looked at her, "What was it you just said?"

"I said, ouch that hurt!"

"No before that."

Amanda looked surprised. "I just said no one will be allowed in the back of your car."

Jim said, "No, you said no one gets in the back of your car."

Amanda was rubbing her head and still looked baffled. "What is the difference?" Jim was staring at the ceiling. "Jim, you are miles away again."

Jim grabbed her face and kissed her on her lips. "You are absolutely right."

Amanda was losing patience. "What the hell are talking about?"

Jim smirked. "The missing link! God I am so stupid!"

Amanda looked puzzled. "What is it?"

"I can't discuss the case with you. What time is it? Oh, good it's only eleven thirty. I have to make a phone call."

He got his trousers from the floor and took out his cell phone. He walked towards the bathroom whilst waiting for a response from the number he had called. He looked at the toilet and walked back into the bedroom. He was pacing up and down and muttering to himself. "Come on, answer, come on, answer."

"Okay good, Paolo. What are you up to?" He listened for a few seconds before he said, "Dishes will have to wait. We have to meet at the precinct." He listened again for a few seconds. "Good see you in 45 minutes or so. I have to talk to someone on the way."

He came across and hastily put on his trousers and was buttoning his shirt when he noticed Amanda looking at him. He came and sat at the edge of the bed, "I'm sorry honey …"

Amanda put her hand across his chest. "You don't have to explain; I've entered this relationship with my eyes wide open. My turn will come too."

Jim kissed her forehead. "Thanks for being understanding." He leaned over and kissed her again. "And thanks for helping to solve the case!"

Amanda looked more puzzled. "Huh?"

"Never mind for now."

He put on his socks and shoes with the tail of his shirt still hanging out. He was about to leave when he came back and asked her, "Would you be able to delay the verdict tomorrow?"

Amanda said, "Why what is it?"

"I'm not sure and I can't say now."

Amanda replied, "Well darling, you know I can't ask for a delay without new evidence."

Jim tucked his shirt in. "Gotta go."

Amanda held his hand as he was getting up. "Will I see you later on?"

"I don't think sleep is on the menu tonight. In any case if I do get to bed it will be late and I will only disturb you. Goodnight." He kissed her lightly on the lips. "But please whatever thought you had a few minutes ago, please hold on to it."

Amanda shrugged her shoulders. "Goodnight."

Jim dialled a number on his cell phone. As he was buttoning his shirt, he got a reply. "Geno, Jim here. Can you talk?"

Jim pulled up his trousers. "Can you meet me in my office? ... Paolo is on his way ... hope to be there in about forty-five minutes ... And listen don't tell anyone else, just trust me on this one ... Great, see you there."

CHAPTER 44

The Missing Link

Jim stopped outside the Mexicano bar. As he got out of the car, he went to the passenger side and pulled forward the front seat and reached as if to get into the back of the car and got out of the car again. He did it a second time. He paused, shook his head, and closed the passenger door.

He walked into the bar. He walked into the men's room and stood and looked at the urinals for a short time.

A man was urinating and looked over his shoulder. "Hey buddy, you are not one of those perverts, are you?"

"No. Sorry. I have lost a piece of paper and can't find it. That's me off. Toilets are very clean, aren't they?"

The man responded. "You don't mind if I don't talk to you while I'm taking a piss!"

"Sure, sorry, just thinking aloud."

Jim then walked to the bar counter. "Oh good, Alfonso, I was hoping you would be here."

Alfonso nodded with a smile. "Good evening, I don't get too many nights off, Detective Sterne."

"You remembered my name?"

"It took a while for the penny to drop. There was something bugging me and then I figured out what it is. A Jim Sterne comes here regularly, and you look a little bit like him, so I figured you were his son."

"Yes, my dad doesn't get out much these days."

"I would still be in touch with him though."

"How is that then?"

Alfonso was tidying away small containers of peanuts from the bar counter. "It's a long story."

"Everyone seems to have long stories tonight. Could you get me a coke please?"

Alfonso poured the contents of a small coke bottle into a glass. "Ice?"

"Sure."

Jim drank a bit of the coke. He looked at a couple sitting at the other end of the counter. He lowered his tone slightly. "I came here to ask you about John Chapman. When I came here the first night, what did you call him?"

"Jake."

"No before that."

Alfonso looked at the couple sitting at the bar and saw they were busy talking to each other. "The Oracle."

"I thought I remembered you saying that. My dad used the same name. So, Jake has been giving you tips for horse racing?"

Alfonso nodded. "There are only a dozen of us in the ring, so to speak. Although Jake stopped giving us tips a while back when he realized there was a ring of us."

"So if that's the case, why are you still working, you should have retired by now?"

"Well it's not that straightforward. It started by Jake watching races at the bar. He would occasionally say things like that horse falls at the fifth hurdle or that horse won by three lengths. Then occasionally before a race we would ask him if he knew the winner and he would say yes. A few of us started to bet on these tips. After a few weeks, he became very uncomfortable with this. So, he made me promise that we would not bet more than a certain amount and that we would not tell another soul. I asked him if I could just tell one more person and he said yes. So, I thought your dad could do with a break, so I included him along with a couple of others. It seems like everyone just told one more person and before you knew it, there was at least a dozen betting every few weeks and the size of the bets became larger. The big bets happened on a race every three months or so, but then Jake suddenly stopped giving tips."

"What about Jake?"

"He never bets. I don't think he has any interest in money at all."

"Figures." Jim got up. "Thanks for the information." He got up and took out a single note of money on the counter. "And thanks for helping my dad."

"My pleasure." His eyes seemed to widen when he noticed it was a hundred dollars. "Any time, Jim."

Jim got into his car and started it. He took out his phone and looked at his contacts. "Ahmad, Ahmad, please answer."

He listened for a few seconds. A sleepy voice answered, "Hello?"

"Ahmad?"

"Yes Mister Jim."

"Ahmad I am so sorry to phone you so late, but can you clarify something for me?"

"Don't tell me, Mister Jim, it's been so long that you have forgotten how to put on a condom!"

"What?" Jim then laughed out loud. "Haha Ahmad, very funny! No, this is business."

"What about your hot date?"

"Had to leave it, Ahmad."

"Mister Jim, has anyone told you, you are a very sad case?"

"Yes Ahmad, all the time!"

"So what can I help you with, Mister Jim?"

*

Jim walked into his office to find Geno and Paolo waiting for him.

Paolo was sitting on one of the two chairs facing the desk and Geno was seated on the edge of Jim's desk. "Must be important," Geno said, pointing to his watch. "I had my feet up sipping on a glass of red wine when you called."

"Don't sweat, Geno, this is just a cop's life."

"I suppose so. What time is Derek coming at?"

Jim pointed to the empty chair, beckoning Geno to sit there and he sat on his leather chair. "Derek was busy, he couldn't make it."

Geno looked surprised. "What is he doing that is so important?"

"I'll explain later."

"Okay!" said Geno. "So why are we here?"

"There is something bothering me. I am not sure how to put it exactly …"

Paolo smiled. "It's not like you to be lost for words, Jim."

"Well …" Jim was hesitant again. "Let me say it straight. I think this Jake character, as odd as he is, and as weird as his dreams thing is … Well I think he might not be our man."

Paolo nodded. "Hmm," he muttered.

Geno turned toward Paolo and had a look of astonishment. "Don't tell me now that you agree with Jim!"

Paolo shook his head. "No the thought would have never crossed my mind, except that's exactly what my mama said. She said that is not a man that would kill anyone."

Geno leant forward. "But Jim, you were sure all along. It's not like you to get it wrong! What about the fact that he knew about Charlene Mill's death before it hit the press? And if that's not enough, what about the forensic evidence?"

"Be patient, Geno. First of all, I want us to have another look at something else."

Jim started to pace back and forth in the room. Paolo and Geno followed his movements as if they were watching a tennis match, transfixed on his every move. There seemed to be a pregnant pause, as if they were waiting for an inspired revelation from Jim.

Jim suddenly stopped. "There has to be something in the SIM card. There must be some information there that she wanted us to get. I think we have missed something!"

Geno shook his head. "Jim; Paolo and I have been over the numbers ten times. We have contacted everyone in the address book. They are all accounted for."

Paolo suddenly sat upright. "Shit, I am so dumb."

Geno turned around to him. "Whatever are you talking about?"

"Shit, shit, shit! They are all accounted for except the invalid number."

"Yes, but there were insufficient numbers, only nine instead of ten. What was the name … David, wasn't it?"

"Yes Geno, but remember the name David was in inverted commas. This means that it probably wasn't his real name."

Geno hit himself on the side of his head. "Damn it, I'm stupid! I think we are on to something!"

Jim frantically went over the pages on his desk, turning them over in such haste that a number of them fell onto the floor. Geno and Paolo went over to the table, peering over both of his shoulders. He finally lifted one of the A4 papers in the air. "This is it!"

He put his index finger on the paper and went down the list of names. He then lifted it and tapped the paper a few times. "Could this be a clue to the son of a bitch?"

Geno and Paolo were leaning forward trying to get a closer look at the number.

Jim sat on his chair and Geno and Paolo went right back behind him to look at the number.

Jim read it aloud, "212-456182. 212-456182. I'm damned if can make anything out of this. Who do we know in the cell phone industry? Could there be any 9-digit numbers?"

Geno shook his head. "No we have checked that, there are none. We also added the numbers zero to 9 at the end of the number. All ten numbers were a blank. One of them was called David. We thought we were onto something, but then he turned out to be a World War II veteran who was in a wheelchair. Two were housewives, three dead numbers. So, nothing really"

Jim stood up and said very excitedly, "Thank you, Ahmad."

"Beg your pardon?" Geno looked slightly bewildered.

"A dummy number, Ahmad mentioned a dummy number."

Paolo spoke this time, "Would you care to elaborate?"

Jim sounded excited. "She didn't want anybody else or possibly the killer to get a whiff of the clue, so she has put in the two-one-two to disguise it. Maybe it's a hidden zip code or birthday or something."

Paolo came over to Jim's desk. "This leaves four-five-six-one-eight-two." He repeated that a few times. "It certainly is not a local zip code. I hardly think she would leave a zip code for another state, as the killer has to be local."

Geno looked at Jim. "Do you mind if I use your note pad here?"

"Go ahead, be my guest."

Geno wrote on the piece of paper and read aloud, "Four-five, maybe he was born on April fifth."

Jim nodded, "Of course, in the year six thousand one hundred and eighty-two of our Lord!"

Geno shrugged his shoulders. "Do you have any other ideas?"

Jim answered quickly, "Sorry Geno, not a good time for sarcasm."

Paolo seemed to be absorbed in his own thoughts. "I think we have to separate them in some way. For example, four five six and one eighty-two."

Jim suddenly bolted up from his chair. "It's a registration number."

Geno looked puzzled. "What registration?"

Paolo nodded, "That's it, a car number plate! It must be personalised."

Jim nodded back. "Let's leave in the last three or four digits and see what we can do with the first two or three." He picked up his phone and flicked through his phone book of his desk. He dialled a number and held on for a few seconds.

"Herbie is that you?" he asked as he was busily writing on the note pad. "Listen I'm sorry to phone you this late."

Paolo and Geno heard the voice on the phone, "This is early for you, Jim!"

Jim chuckled, "You are too kind!"

"What can I do you for?"

Jim continued, "Do you have access to your computer? I want a match for a number plate." He paused for a few seconds. Jim then looked up at Geno and Paolo and said, "He says he is going to access his computer."

Jim continued to write on the note pad.

"Okay Herbie, and thanks again. Could you run a match for the following numbers; we have a six-digit number: four-five-six-one-eight-two. I was thinking of maybe changing the first two or three digits to letters and the leave last three or four as numbers. What do you think?"

He listened again, "Yes we think it is some sort of a coded message … Yes I agree, let's hold on to the last four digits and forget the first two numbers. So, this would give us some letters and 6182." Jim suddenly stopped. "Herbie do me a favour, would you just check all vehicles ending in four five six one or six one eight two. I'll put you on hold."

"I should have twigged much earlier myself!' Jim said, shaking his head as if in annoyance.

"Why do you say that?"

"You know what Amanda told me tonight at her house?"

Paolo looked surprised. "You mean you were at Amanda's house tonight?"

"Yes we were in bed, but that's another story. She said that I wouldn't allow kids in the back of my car because they would make a mess."

Paolo raised his eyebrows. "Jim, do you mean you were in bed with Amanda and got up to come here?"

Jim nodded.

"Mama Mia!" said Geno shaking his head. "You are a lost cause. She will never forgive you."

"No Geno, this time you got it wrong. If I am right, she will be forever thankful to me."

Geno looked at Paolo and remarked, "So what are we missing here?"

"I believe I have found the missing link. As I was saying, I was with Amanda and she said, 'you will never allow kids in the back of your car.' As you know I am very fussy about my car. The slightest dirt and I have to get it valeted. I had valeted my car a few days before Charlene's murder. The night we found

Charlene Mill's body, Derek and I had to walk through the mud to the crime scene. We got back to the car and my car was a complete mess, so I had to get another valet done today."

Geno was losing patience. "So, your car was a mess."

"This is the bit that I missed. When I left the car for a valet today, Ahmad, the guy who always cleans my car, was cross with me. He told me that I had only got it cleaned just recently and he had to scrape mud off the front and back mats. You see, when we left the crime scene Derek got into the car with dirty shoes. When we stopped at a bar, he was going to reach in the back of the car, and I stopped him. The only way he could have got mud on the mat in the back was when we arrived at the scene and he leaned into the back to get my coat!"

Geno nodded. "So, he must have had the mud on his shoes before you got to the scene. Which means that he was already on the crime scene before he got there with you."

Jim nodded. "Which means he was the one who murdered Charlene!"

Geno shook his head and looked bewildered. "I just can't believe that would be possible. Let me guess, you never did ask Derek to come here, did you?"

Jim nodded ever so subtly and replied quietly. "No I didn't."

Paolo said without thinking, "We should know that anything is possible."

Jim looked up. "Geno, would you break into the personnel office and check Derek's file, especially his date of birth."

Geno looked surprised. "But that's illegal Jim!"

Jim replied, "Don't worry, I won't tell if you don't."

Geno looked at him with an open mouth. "You can't be thinking …" He stopped as if there was no need to finish the sentence. "I'll get into his personnel file."

Jim suddenly put the phone mouthpiece back against his mouth. "Sorry, go ahead Herbie. Let me write this down. An Alfa Romeo Sports reg number DJ 6182 It's registered to a …" He put his pen down. "Thanks Herbie, yes the four five must be the fourth and fifth letters of the alphabet, D E. Must be for Derek. Much obliged Herbie, owe you big time."

He put the phone down and looked at Paolo.

Paolo asked, "Is it registered to a Derek Johnston?"

Jim nodded.

Paolo said, "I wonder if his date of birth is going to be June first, 1982?"

After a few minutes Geno returned. "Not much on his file, except for various commendations. But guess what his date of birth is?"

Paolo nodded. "We know, first of June 1982."

Geno asked, "I suppose the car was registered in his name?"

Jim and Paolo nodded.

Geno seemed puzzled, "What about the pubic hair, I mean that seems pretty damning?"

"You are right," Jim replied, "that was the part that really closed my mind to anybody else. I have to say that was an ingenious move by Derek. You see, the night of the discovery of Charlene's body we stopped at a bar. We met Jake at that bar. It was fortuitous on Derek's part. In any case when we were at the bar Derek went to the toilet to clean his shoes. When he came back, he mentioned how clean the toilets were. I then asked him to escort Jake to the gents. He brought Jake back and had to go back to wash his hands, I presume he spotted some pubic hair on the urinals and they were very clean beforehand he must have known they belonged to Jake. I can't be sure, but I think he went back to the body and planted the hairs on Sarah's fingernails and then arranged the anonymous phone call."

Paolo got up and grabbed his black leather jacket. "I guess I'll see you guys in the morning."

"Off to sleep?" Jim asked.

"Oh no!" was the response. "I am off to contact the twenty-four-seven security agency. I am hoping they still have the tapes from the time of Sarah's disappearance. I don't think there will be copies made anywhere else. I'll let you know if I find anything. I hope they live up to their name and are available twenty-four-seven."

"Good luck," said Geno. "I am off to my bed. I am no use to anyone."

Paolo chuckled, "I will need luck, it's a long shot, but you don't ask you don't get. I'll either get some coffee on the way or failing that some match sticks."

Jim leaned back in his chair. "I'll stick around for a couple of hours, getting my thoughts together. I'll have to see how I can put other bits and pieces together so it all makes sense."

CHAPTER 45

Initial Morning of Sentencing

Jim looked at his watch. "Shit!" He thought for a second and took out his cell phone and dialled a number. "Come on Amanda, answer it, answer it!"

"Hi Jim," he heard, he breathed out a sigh of relief. "I hope you are phoning to apologise about last night."

"Thanks for answering. Listen we don't have a lot of time, but I need your total attention."

"Okay Jim, I am in the middle of getting dressed, but fire away, because I don't have a lot of time either and I have to get in early."

"Well Amanda, I would suggest you sit down, because … Well I have little doubt that Jake is innocent. We have some evidence that someone else is the guilty party."

There was no response from Amanda.

"Hello Amanda, are you there?"

"Yes, I'm here. But what … What the hell is going on, Jim?"

"I have evidence that strongly implicates someone else."

"Would you care to tell me who this is?"

"I would, Amanda, but you have to give me a few hours on this one. It may be late morning."

"Jim we are about to meet the judge this morning and I don't have time to go over a plea to him to allow more time. I can't be left hanging like this."

"I know, but you just have to trust me on this. I will be speaking to someone shortly and should be able to get back to you soon after."

"Jim, I know we are friends—"

Jim interrupted, "I thought we are more than that?"

"We are, Jim, what I mean is that you are asking a lot of me at this critical time."

"Well it's your call."

There was a pause. "Okay Jim I will speak to the judge as soon as possible. But get back to me as soon as you can."

"Thanks Mandy. And I love you."

Amanda was quiet again for a few seconds "That is the first time you have said that."

"Well actually the second. Remember my proposal in court?"

"Of course, how could I forget?"

"And it won't be the last, you can count on that. I will get back to you ASAP."

Jim was about to hang up when he heard Amanda, "Oh Jim?"

"Yes?"

"I love you too."

"You are right, Mandy, it is nice to hear it. See you soon honey."

"Okay darling."

*

It was Friday morning, and the final summing up was due to be done that day, along with the jury's decision. Amanda and Lucy had arrived in court early and walked to the judge's room.

Amanda knocked at the judge's door. "Come in."

Amanda walked in, Lucy following her in.

Amanda stood timidly with her hands clasped in front of her whilst the judge was writing something and appeared to be concentrating quite intensely. He looked up after a few seconds, still with his reading glasses on. "Oh good morning Miss Jackson," he nodded, "Miss walker."

Amanda looked like a schoolgirl who had just been ordered to the Principal's room. "Good morning, you honour."

"Good morning," said Lucy, positioning herself so Amanda was between her and the judge as if she needed a shield.

The judge looked amused and looked back and forth between the two of them. There was silence. He then said, "I don't know what you are going to ask, but I get the distinct feeling that the answer is going to be no!"

Lucy looked at Amanda who unusually seemed to be lost for words.

The judge broke the silence again, "Well come on, spit it out, I promise to listen to you carefully."

Amanda got to the point, "Your honour, I have just spoken to the prosecution team and they have declined but I would like to request an extension of the case."

"Please sit down," said the judge.

Amanda sat on one of the chairs and Lucy slid into a chair next to her, trying to be as inconspicuous as possible.

The judge put his pen down, took off his slim reading glasses, folded them, and put them down on the table. He sat back and again looked back and forth between the two of them. He folded his arms together in front of his chest. "Well now that it highly irregular and exceptional. I presume you have acquired new evidence for the case? If you present it to me, I will show it to the prosecution team and will get back to you. But I am warning you, it must be very strong evidence to sway either me or the prosecution."

Amanda paused for a few seconds. Lucy had her hands clasped together and seemed to be nervously squeezing them.

Amanda then acquired enough courage to say, "Well your honour, there is new evidence, but I am not sure how concrete."

The judge sat forward and placed his arms on the table. "Pardon?"

"Well, you honour," Amanda continued, "it's sort of a hunch."

The judge raised his eyebrows. "Miss Jackson, tell me this is the first of April and this is an April fool's joke." He looked at her and Amanda said nothing. He puffed out his cheeks. "Right tell me what you mean by a hunch."

"Well Detective Sterne thinks that are some irregularities and he has been up all night looking into the matter. He phoned me less than a couple of hours ago to say he has some leads but has not able to finalise anything as yet. He feels pretty sure if he has the weekend he will be able to come up with something."

"Well what are the leads?"

Amanda went quite again for a few seconds. "Well your honour, he couldn't tell me, so I don't know."

"Surely, Miss Jackson, Detective Sterne was a witness for the prosecution. Why exactly are you having off-the-table conversations with him?"

Amanda shifted her bottom to one side of the chair and then the other, leaning on her arms. "Your honour, it's not what it seems, it's just that …"

The judge put up his hand. "You know what, I would rather not hear any more. No evidence, no extension. Please close the door behind you, I have to work on my summing up."

He put on his glasses, picked up his pen, and began to write again.

Lucy put up her hand as if asking permission to speak, "But, your honour…"

The judge peered over his glasses. "Yes, what is it?"

In fact, Lucy was very relieved that the judge's phone rang. She visibly breathed out a sigh of relief, perhaps she could think of something over the next few seconds.

As soon as he picked up the phone the irritation in his voice was very clear. "What is it, Liz? I specifically asked not to be disturbed!"

Amanda and Lucy could hear the voice at the other end which sounded slightly anxious. "Your honour, it's your wife, she says it's urgent."

"Well then put her through please … Hi honey what's up?"

The anxious voice could be heard faintly by Amanda and Lucy.

"Hello John, it's about Jill. She was not well this morning. I didn't want to disturb you. I took her to ER. She had tummy pain and the doctor examined her. He said it was a urinary tract infection. He gave Jill some antibiotics. I have just put her to bed and am on my way to buy some painkillers for her. Phone me when you get a break."

"Okay honey, thanks for phoning."

He put the phone down and looked up at Amanda. "Where were we, oh yes." He turned to Lucy. "You were just going to present indisputable evidence, weren't you?"

Lucy was struggling to speak. She stuttered her words, "Your honour I was just going to say that …" She paused and looked at Amanda, as if for inspiration.

"Damn it, girl, will you spit it out!"

Lucy suddenly said, "Your honour, was that about your daughter?"

The judge responded before he could think, "Yes it was my wife, Jill is going to be fi …" He did not finish the word 'fine'. He looked at Lucy. "This is extraordinarily odd, but it couldn't …" Again, he stopped and stared at the phone.

Amanda looked at Lucy and Lucy looked back. Lucy then looked at the judge. "Your honour, what if Jake was right?"

The judge shook his head. "In the name of God, there is no way …" He paused and looked at the phone again. He then picked up the phone and frantically dialled a number. He was rapping his fingers on the table and his impatience was obvious. "Come on answer, come on answer. Oh Good. Honey it's me, where are you?"

"In the car, just driving out of the driveway. I'm going to the drug store to buy some Tylenol."

"Please stay on the phone and go back inside. You need to ask Jill something."

"Why honey, what is it?"

"Ann, please do as I ask."

"Okay John."

The judge picked up the phone and started to walk up and down with the phone pressed against his ear.

Amanda asked, "Would you like us to leave, your honour?"

Just then Ann's voice could be heard again. The judge seemed oblivious to the presence of anyone else in the room. "Ann please trust me in what I am going to ask you to do."

"Ok John, but what is the matter?"

"Ann, time might be of the essence. Please ask Jill if there is any chance at all, even a slim one, that she might be … well, could she be pregnant?"

"But …" It seemed like Ann had to acquiesce.

There was a few seconds' hesitation. Then her voice could be heard, "She says no."

John thought for a few seconds. "Honey did she hesitate when you asked her the question?"

Ann responded, "John, you are not in a courtroom now!"

"Honey trust me! This is very important!"

There was silence for a couple of minutes during which John kept rapping his desk with his knuckles. Then Ann's voice could be heard, "John, let's just say she has been worried because after she spoke to the doctor, she is not sure, and thinks she may be a bit late."

"Late for what …" John suddenly stopped. "Ann, listen to me very carefully! Pay very close attention to what I am saying. This is an absolute emergency. I want you to dial 911. Tell them that Jill is very ill and has a suspected ectopic pregnancy. I'll turn my cell phone on. Phone me as soon as you know which ER she is going to and I will meet you there."

"John you don't really think that …"

John interrupted, "Please trust me, just go ahead and do it."

"Okay John."

The judge put the phone down. He looked at Lucy and then Amanda. "I can't believe I am doing this, but I will personally wring Mister Chapman's neck if this is a false alarm.'

He put on his jacket. "I will inform the court that the hearing is postponed until Monday." He turned to Lucy again. "What you were going to say, is it urgent or can it wait?"

Lucy waved her hand, "Oh, it can wait, your honour!"

With that the judge was out like a shot.

Lucy and Amanda just looked at each other, both with their mouths slightly open. Amanda said, "You don't think she could have an ectopic pregnancy?"

Lucy said, "You know, it won't surprise me."

Amanda asked Lucy, "By the way, what were you going to tell him?"

Lucy raised her eyebrows. "I don't have a clue. Let's say I was saved by the bell!"

Amanda took out her cell phone from her bag. "Whatever is the matter with his daughter, let's make good use of the time."

She dialled a number and after a couple of rings it was answered. "Jim you won't believe this, but the case is postponed until Monday."

Amanda listened briefly. "Don't even ask now. I will explain later."

She got up and Lucy followed suit. "Come on, Lucy, I would like to see the expression on the face of the prosecution when I give them the news."

CHAPTER 46

Jill in Hospital

Shortly before ten a.m. the ambulance arrived at the hospital with the blue lights flashing. Jill said to the paramedics, "Please, I can walk in myself."

One of paramedics put his hand on her shoulder as she lay on the trolley. "I know that, sweetheart, but I will get into trouble if you do. So, for my sake will you please allow us to wheel you in?"

Jill accepted, "Okay but this is ridiculous! I only have a little bit of pain; I wish my mom would stop making such a fuss."

The paramedics wheeled Jill into the waiting area with her mother following close behind. A black nurse approached the paramedics. She had a navy-blue uniform that was immaculately clean and pressed. Her badge read 'Isabel Jones, senior nurse'. She was in her forties and had a kind smile. She looked at the paramedics. "What is the story here, gentlemen?" she asked as she instinctively put her hand to feel Jill's pulse.

The paramedic who had spoken to Jill seemed to be the senior of the two. "Abdominal pain, Sister. This is Jill Temple, twenty-two-year-old; she was here earlier on and was diagnosed with a UTI, but her pain is slightly worse, and someone has mentioned ectopic pregnancy but not sure where that diagnosis emanated from. She has no fever, her pulse is raised at one-twenty, and her BP is quite low at eighty-over-fifty."

She looked at Jill. "Were you not here earlier on? I recognise that beautiful turquoise blouse."

Jill smiled back at the nurse. "Yes, my mother is making such a big fuss, I only have cystitis."

The nurse waved and a porter came to her. She looked at the paramedics. "Thank you, gentlemen, we will take it from here."

She beckoned the porter, "Would you please take this young lady into cubicle five please?"

"Certainly Isabel."

The porter wheeled the trolley from the waiting area into the treatment area and pulled the curtains around Jill. He stood outside the cubicle. "I'll be here if you need me."

Nurse Jones walked into the ER cubicle. "Do you have much pain?" she asked Jill.

Jill tried to sit up and winced as she did so. "Well not much different from bad period cramps if you know what I mean?"

The nurse smiled. "I am very lucky that way. How is the pain compared to before? The doctor gave you some analgesia, has it improved?"

Jill put her right hand on her lower abdomen on the left side. "It had eased slightly but now it seems to be slightly worse and more focused on the left side."

Isabel took Jill's blood pressure and temperature and recorded it on a sheet. Ann looked on anxiously.

Just then the doctor walked in. He was in his early twenties. He was unshaven and looked rather tired. Isabel pointed to him and looked at Jill and Ann, "I think you met Doctor Tomaszewski, he's our intern. He saw you earlier. I am dealing with another emergency and will be back soon." She left the cubicle.

He had a look of surprise on his face and spoke with a sight accent, "Wasn't expecting you to see you so soon! Has the pain not eased? Did you take the antibiotics?"

The doctor approached to examine Jill's abdomen. He looked at Ann. "Would you like to wait outside?"

Jill held her mother's hand, suddenly feeling very anxious. "No I would rather she stayed with me." Ann held Jill's hand with both her hands.

The doctor shrugged his shoulders. He pushed her blouse up, exposing her abdomen up to her bra line. He then tried unsuccessfully to push her skirt down, tugging down her skirt without any success and was looking at the sides of the skirt. Jill winced with pain as he tugged slightly harder.

Ann spoke to the doctor, "Allow me, Doctor."

Ann unzipped Jill's skirt on the side and pushed the skirt down a few inches.

"That's fine," said the doctor.

He looked at Jill and with a very stern face said, "Let me know if it hurts."

He pressed down on her lower abdomen on the left side and Jill jumped up and shouted, "Ouch, that hurts!"

Ann looked very cross as she looked at the doctor. She pushed the hair off Jill's face and stroked her forehead.

The doctor sounded somewhat cross, "Well your condition is as before. As I explained, a urinary tract infection can cause a lot of abdominal pain and your urine dipstick test, so to speak, had blood and protein in it, suggesting the same. Let me look at your bloods again and ask the lab to look at the urine sample under the microscope."

As the doctor left, the porter popped his head from behind the curtain and noticed Ann's anxious look. He pointed towards the clinical area and mimed the words, "I'll get the nurse."

Ann smiled and mimed back, "Thank you!"

The porter winked.

The doctor had walked to the nursing station and flipped the pages on the flip board back and forth.

The porter approached Isabel. "Isabel, I think that young girl needs you. Doctor Tomaszewski wouldn't know an ectopic from a pituitary tumour and needs some help!"

Isabel looked somewhat startled. "You certainly have picked up the lingo, haven't you?"

The porter nodded. "Years of pushing patients around, you pick up a thing or two, especially when a doctor is lost."

Isabel nodded. "You are right, he is a very good intern, but his gynae knowledge is crap."

Isabel quickly walked into the cubicle. The doctor followed her in.

She smiled at the doctor. "Well Doctor Tomaszewski, what is your diagnosis?"

"Well, nurse, emm …" he leaned over and looked at her badge, "Nurse Jones, it's the wrong side for her appendix, as suspected it is a UTI and should resolve over the next twenty-four to forty-eight hours."

"Good doc. I was just wondering with the significant abdominal pain that perhaps we should ensure there are no surgical or gynae problems. Perhaps we should consult the specialists just to be sure, after all it will do no harm."

The doctor stopped reading the chart and looked up. He approached Jill again. "Allow me to examine your abdomen again." Again, as he pressed on her tummy, Jill shouted.

He cleared his throat. "Well, nurse, emm …" he leaned over again to look at her badge, "Nurse Jones, will you speak to the surgeons and let them know there is possible case of appendicitis. I believe they are operating on a GSW and might be a while." He stopped to study Jill's chart. "Please take some bloods, FBC and electrolytes, erect IV fluids and keep her fasting."

Isabel was very calm. "Very well, Doctor Tomaszewski, just thought I should mention that there is a possibility of ectopic pregnancy."

Doctor Tomaszewski seemed to be irritated and was a little snappy in his response, "Her last period was less than four weeks ago, so this is not a possibility!"

Isabel said very quietly, "Then you don't mind if I perform a pregnancy test, do you?"

The doctor shrugged his shoulders. "It is going to be negative but if you insist go ahead." He threw the chart on the trolley and walked out saying, "Let me know if her condition deteriorates."

As he walked away Isabel whispered, "Oh no I won't!" She turned to Jill. "He is very good, but can be stubborn. By the time he's finished he will learn. So, darling, when was your last period?"

Jill said, "I thought it was four weeks ago, but now I am not sure; also, it was very light, not my usual, just for a day or so."

"Do you use contraception?"

Jill looked at her mother and looked back at Isabel. "We use the rhythm method, he doesn't like condoms."

Isabel smiled at her. "We can have a chat about that later! Let me phone the labs. Your urine sample will still be there. I will request a pregnancy test. It will only take a minute."

The nurse walked to the nurse's station and was on the phone for a couple of minutes. Ann was staring at her whilst holding Jill's hand very tightly.

Jill had a tear in her eye. "Mom, you are not upset with me, are you?"

"Shoosh my love," Ann replied with a couple of tears rolling down her eye. "Don't be thinking about anything like that. All I want is for you to be okay."

Nurse Jones walked back into the cubicle a couple of minutes later. She sat on the edge of the bed and held Jill's other hand. "Listen Jill, the news is that you ARE actually pregnant. You are going to need an ultrasound scan. You may well need an operation."

A few tears ran down Ann's face and Jill tightened her grip on Ann's hand.

Isabel smiled and seemed very calm. "Don't worry, you two, everything will be all right, you are in the right place at the right time, now don't worry!"

Just then another nurse walked in behind the curtains. "What do you need, Isabel?"

Isabel seemed very business-like all of a sudden, "Take bloods for FBC, electrolytes. Crossmatch her for four units of blood. Call the gynaecologist on call and tell them that we have a probable ectopic pregnancy. No, in fact tell him that we have an ectopic pregnancy. Ask the clerk to phone theatre and tell them to prepare for an emergency operation. In fact, I will speak to the gynae intern myself."

She then lowered her head until she was very close to Jill who looked very anxious. She stroked her hair. "Don't worry, darling, you are in safe hands here. You probably know that an ectopic pregnancy is a pregnancy which has lodged in one of your fallopian tubes. It is easy to treat, but if left for too long, it can rupture and be a bit dangerous."

She looked at Ann, "Don't worry. Now I must go and get the gynaecologist."

John arrived at the ER. He rushed to the reception desk. "Hello, my name is John Temple; my daughter Jill Temple was brought here by ambulance a little while ago."

The young girl behind the desk looked at the board behind her. "I'm sorry I don't see her name on the board, let me check the computer."

One of the paramedics was standing at the reception desk. "Excuse me, ma'am, I brought her in, she was taken straight to the treatment area. I can take this gentleman there."

The reception clerk said, "Sure, that's good of you to do that."

John asked the paramedic, "Is she okay?"

"Jill was fine when we brought her in, I'm sure she will be fine. Here you are."

John could see Jill through the parted curtains. "Thank you, sir."

"It's a pleasure," said the paramedic.

John rushed in and stood at the opposite side from Ann. "What did the doctor say?"

Ann tried her best not to look too worried. "Well actually the doctor wasn't so sure, but a pregnancy test is positive, and I think she almost certainly has an ectopic pregnancy."

"So is our Jill going to be okay?"

Jill talked with a little smile on her face, "Dad, I am right here, don't talk about me in the third person!"

John hugged her. "Oh honey, I am sorry, I have been so worried. So, what exactly is happening now?"

"I am going to need an operation, dad, nothing to it!"

"Yes John," Ann added, "the nurse assures us that everything is going to be okay."

Just then Isabel returned with a wheelchair. "Darling we are going to take some blood samples …" She looked at John. "Sorry who are you?"

John instinctively put out his hand. "Hello I'm John Temple, her father."

Isabel shook his hand and looked at Jill, almost questioning her with her eyes. Jill said, "You can be frank."

Isabel continued, "We need to get some more blood tests and an urgent scan, as she is going to need an operation."

Jill was beginning to perspire a little bit. "That's fine, nurse, but the pain is getting worse, I'm feeling a bit lightheaded."

Isabel checked Jill's pulse, and said, "Never mind, darling, just stay as you are." She popped her head around the curtains. "Nurse Smiley would you come here quick, bring the IV set with you." She grabbed a nurse who was walking past. "Would you go and tell Pat behind the reception desk to fast bleep the gynae intern. Ask our intern to come here pronto!"

She came back beside Jill. "Is your tummy very sore?"

Jill looked very uncomfortable. "It's getting very sore."

"Don't worry, darling, we'll get you sorted out soon."

She took out a tourniquet from her pocket and put it around Jill's left forearm and then turned to Ann. "There may be a bit of internal bleeding, we'll have to speed things along." She then turned to John. "Could I ask you to wait in the relatives' room, Pat behind the desk will show you there, I'll speak to you as soon as I have any further information."

Doctor Tomaszewski ran into the cubicle.

John held Ann's hand and they walked to the reception area. When they got to the reception desk John leant on the desk. He looked at the name badge of the girl behind the counter, which confirmed she was Pat. Pat was on the phone. John tried to speak to her whilst she was speaking. She held up her left hand whilst she was still talking on the phone. "Yes, it's cubicle five in ER. Nurse Jones is requesting a fast bleep. Thank you." She turned to John and noticed that Ann was crying.

John said softly, "Relatives' room please."

Pat turned to her colleague besides her. "Kate, could you take over for a couple of minutes?"

"Sure, no problem Pat," was the answer.

Pat came around the reception desk. "Please follow me."

She held Ann's elbow very lightly and walked to a side room which was marked 'Relatives' Room'. "Come on in, I don't think there is anyone in here." She peeped round the door and then walked in, "Yes it's empty. There is coffee here and water. If the phone rings pick it up, occasionally we would communicate with you on the phone, for example if an operation is ongoing. We will let you know as soon as we have any information. Mrs …"

John answered, "Temple, Ann Temple and I'm John Temple."

"Yes, there are also some tissues there. I will get back to work, it's very busy. You can pick up the phone and dial zero for an outside line and one-zero-zero one if you want to speak to me. Bye now."

Ann was finally able to speak, "Thanks for your kindness, Pat."

"You're welcome." With that Pat left the room.

Ann started to cry quite uncontrollably. John put his arms around her. "Don't worry, honey, she is in good hands."

Ann spoke in between the sobs, "What the hell is going on, it's like a bad dream!"

John pulled her tight into his chest. "I know honey, I know." He felt a bit helpless and for a brief moment seemed more worried about Ann than Jill. "Would you like some coffee?"

Ann shook her head, drying her eyes with a tissue.

John asked again, "Some water?"

Ann nodded. "Yes please."

John walked to the water cooler and filled a plastic cup with water. "Here you are."

"Thanks John." She took a very small sip and put the cup down. "How did you know she was sick and didn't just have a urine infection?"

"Do you mind if I leave the explanation to later? I am too upset right now to elucidate the point."

"Sure. Would you like a sip of water?" She picked up the plastic cup.

John took the cup from her and took a small sip. He placed the plastic cup on a coffee table in the room.

Ann remained seated while John paced up and down in the room. Ann finally spoke to him, "Do you have to pace? You are making me worse."

"I am sorry, honey; you know I always pace when I'm nervous. This reminds me of when you were delivering Jill, twenty-two years ago. I was pacing up and down the maternity room so much the nurse told me they would have to replace the carpet."

Ann looked up. "I don't know if I want to remember that early morning."

John walked to her and held her face in his two hands. "I know, I realised there was something wrong when the doctors started to run into the delivery room. You bled so much they said you were lucky to make it. I never told you this, but at the time I resented Jill being born and wished you had never got pregnant."

Ann looked very sad. "Oh John, please don't say that!"

John smiled. "Don't worry, Ann, once you were okay, I began to appreciate the beauty that had been born. You know I adore her as much as I worship you." A tear ran down his cheek. "I wouldn't give Jill up for the world."

Ann grabbed one of John's hands and kissed it.

Just then Isabel walked into the room. She seemed somewhat cheerful. "Hi guys, the gynaecologist has performed an ultrasound scan. She is definitely pregnant and has an ectopic pregnancy. They are preparing theatre and she will be going up shortly. She has had nothing to eat over the past four hours, apart from the antibiotics and analgesics she has taken. But she will be all right for theatre. I would like to let you know about the risks of the operation—"

Ann interrupted, "Nurse you have been very kind. Look, you don't need to tell us anything. Just make our daughter better. Just one question, will she lose her ability to have children?"

"I should hope not," said Isabel very calmly, "she has two fallopian tubes and can manage with only one, but they will try and preserve the one that has the foetus in it."

Isabel held her hand and smiled. "I'll be on my way. I am sure she will be fine." She got up and walked out in a hurry.

Ann whispered quietly, "God bless you."

John took a big sigh. "I feel a lot happier now."

Ann replied, "So do I now. Somehow I know she is going to be okay. Maybe I will have that cup of coffee now."

John poured two cups of coffee and sat down in the room for the first time. He looked at Ann and seemed to be in two minds as to whether to speak. He asked somewhat reluctantly, "Did you know Jill was sexually active, I didn't even know she had a boyfriend ..." He seemed to pause in mid conversation, "assuming of course she had a steady boyfriend and it was not casual."

"John!" Ann said indignantly, "what sort of a daughter do you think we have?"

"I don't know, on the way over I was thinking of how little I know of her life. When she phones us, she talks to you for an hour and I say a quick hello and goodbye and very brief chat. Now that I think of it, she usually asks me about my cases and I just generally ask her how she is!"

"John, Jill is a lovely girl. She has been going out with Tom, Tommy, for a few months. She thought about it long and hard and a couple of months ago asked to meet me for lunch. She said that she had thought about this carefully and felt that she really loved him and she wanted to let me know that she was thinking of going on the pill and had thought about going to have sex with Tommy–"

John interrupted, "Oh Ann, please don't use those words about my, about our daughter."

"What words, having sex? It didn't bother you when you asked me when we were dating!"

"Yes, but that was after two years!"

Ann nodded. "Yes John, but times have changed."

John pushed his hair back on both temples with his hands. "I wish they hadn't. Anyway, honey why did you not tell me about your chat with her? You didn't even tell me she had a boyfriend."

"Do you want me to answer that, you are a very intelligent man."

"Let me guess; I am so busy with my work and so engrossed in my profession that I was not aware what was happening in my own life. I suppose Jill's behaviour is a consequence of me!"

"Oh darling." Ann reached across and held his hand. She was within a couple of inches of his face. "You are a most wonderful father. Jill adores you. You know when we had lunch together she said that one of the reasons she had not gone out with anyone for a long time was that anyone she met could not compare with you. In fact, Tommy was so different that she liked him because she said it was like comparing apples with oranges."

John puckered his lips together. "Is that meant to make me feel better? I still feel as if I have been totally out of touch with my daughter's life and with you."

Ann stroked the side of his hair. "Do you want me to be honest?"

John shrugged his shoulders. "Go ahead, be honest!"

"Well it's not that bad, it's just that ..." she hesitated.

John seemed to be a bit calmer. "Go ahead, I want to know."

"Well, you are a wonderful father. But over the past few years you are always giving her advice and well, I hate to say it, but it's as if you are at work and making decisions for her." She paused again. "When did you last hug her, when did you last spend time with her like you used to?"

John walked away and was pensive for some time. "I suppose you are right, since I have become a judge, I have been totally preoccupied with my work. Some of my best moments in life are when it was just the three of us on holidays."

Ann smiled. "She used to love going in the swimming pool with you, or swimming in the sea."

"I'm afraid my pre-occupation with my work has adversely affected the cohesion and conviviality of our family structure."

"And John, perhaps when you communicate with her, you could use plain language!"

"What do you mean?"

"Perhaps you could tell Jill that you have been so busy with work that you have not paid attention to your family. Like in simple English."

"Oh, sorry Ann. Yes, you are right, maybe I should be different at home than at work. I can't believe that now my little girl is pregnant. I somehow feel responsible."

Ann sat down. "Please don't blame yourself. By the way, John, are you going to tell me how you knew she was pregnant, let alone had an ectopic pregnancy?"

"Well, believe it or not, John Chapman asked me in the court room, no less, if my daughter was okay!"

"Are you talking about Jake, the accused in the trial?"

"Yes, most people now know him as Jake."

"How did he know you have a daughter?"

John scratched his head. "Well I don't know. At first, I thought he had read it somewhere. He then asked me if her tummy pain had settled. I was very upset but somewhat taken aback. He then went on to say that there are serious complications of pregnancy and that ectopic pregnancy is life threatening. He asked if she was okay. I rebuked him severely and reserved his punishment."

Ann looked amazed. "Wow this is a little spooky, how is that possible?"

John shrugged his shoulders. "Search me. I am starting to feel a bit uncomfortable with the case, and I must say that the guy has grown on me, although his stories have seemed a bit far-fetched."

Ann thought for a second. "Maybe not so far-fetched now, I would say!"

It was about an hour and a half later when Isabel walked in with an older doctor. Ann and John stood up. "Please sit down." He pointed to the chairs.

John and Ann sat down. Ann looked slightly anxious. "Is she all right, Doctor?"

The doctor smiled, "Hello Mister and Mrs Temple. I am Doctor Stevens, the resident gynaecologist. She is fine, Mrs Temple. She was about seven weeks pregnant. The pregnancy was in the left fallopian tube. We were able to conserve the tube, but needless to say she has lost the foetus. Her condition is stable. She had begun to bleed internally and had in fact bled a lot. We had to transfuse her with six units of blood. I would say had she not been in hospital I dread to think what would have happened. If I were honest, I would say she probably would not have been alive."

Ann gasped and held John's hand very firmly. The doctor held her other hand. "Don't worry, she is out of danger. She is in recovery now but will be transferred down to ward eight E in about two hours. Is there anything you would like to ask me, because I have another emergency to attend to?"

John spoke this time, "Can you assure me that she is safe?"

"Absolutely," was the doctor's response.

"How soon can we see her, Doctor?" asked Ann.

"The recovery nurse will be in soon to take you to her, she is just being monitored in theatre recovery."

Ann shook his hands with both her hands. "We will forever be grateful to you, Doctor."

The doctor got up. "You should thank her family doctor, or whoever it was that diagnosed the ectopic pregnancy at home. Were it not for that I have little doubt that you would have lost her!" With that he left.

Isabel got up. "Is there anything you want to ask me?"

Ann shook her hands again with both her hands. "You've been a real darling, many thanks for all your help."

"It's all part of the service. In all the confusion, we have not had any insurance details. Pat will attend to you shortly to get these details if that is okay?"

"Sure, Sure!" said John, "Naturally."

Isabel also shook John's hand and walked out.

As soon as she left the room John said, "Well I'll be damned. My daughter's life saved by the chap we are trying to put away for life!"

*

About two hours later a nurse entered the room. "Mister and Mrs Temple?"

Ann jumped up and said slightly hesitantly, "Yes?"

"Jill is awake now. She is very well and would like to see the two of you."

They followed the nurse to Jill's room. She was lying down and tried to sit up. Ann went forward and hugged her very tightly. "Stay as you are, darling. I am so glad you are well!"

After about a minute John said, "Eh-mm, eh-mm, can I cuddle my only daughter!"

Ann stepped back, wiping away some tears. Jill stretched her arms out and John hugged her so tight Jill shouted, "Ouch dad, watch my tummy!"

"Sorry honey, got carried away."

Jill smiled and said rather weakly, "Reminds me of the bear hugs you used to give me."

John smiled and kissed her on her forehead.

John held Jill's hand, "I'm afraid that my …" he paused and looked at Ann, "Jill I think that I have been so busy at work that I have forgotten to pay attention to my family and its wellbeing."

Jill looked surprised. "Are you feeling all right, dad?"

"What do you mean, honey?"

"I would have expected you to say that you have been so preoccupied with your occupation or career that it has adversely affected the dynamics and conviviality of our family life."

John smiled and looked at Ann. Ann looked up towards the heavens and rolled her eyes.

"What?" asked Jill.

"Never mind," said Ann, pretending to be upset. "Like father, like daughter. They do say an apple doesn't fall far from the tree!"

John kept on laughing. Jill smiled, "Mom, did you tell dad to use plain English with me?"

Ann nodded.

Jill held John's hand. "But mom, you know I think dad is perfect, you don't need to change him for me."

Jill stopped smiling. "Dad, are you disappointed with me?"

John smiled and stroked her forehead with his thumb. "No honey, I am disappointed with myself for allowing myself to get distant from you." He kissed her on the forehead again.

He turned around and looked at Ann. "I was just thinking, why don't the three of us go on holiday together after this case. We have always talked about going to Europe, maybe Paris or a visit to Rome."

Ann paused for a second. "What about the big case you have been preparing for?"

"Well Ann, I think they can manage without me, but I can't manage without my girls."

Ann looked at Jill. Jill smiled. "I would love that, just the three of us."

Ann hugged both of them. "It's a date!"

John paused. "Jill, maybe we should ask if you would like to invite Tom along?"

Jill thought for a few seconds. "Mom and dad, I don't know yet if I want to marry Tommy, I may well do, but whoever I marry I will spend the rest of my life with. I would like just the three of us to go away together. Like the old days!"

CHAPTER 47

Big Al's Request to See Jake

Jake was eating his dinner and chatting to Ben when Nigel came over to the table. He was short and to the point. "Big Al wants to see you in his office."

Ben looked at Jake anxiously. "Don't worry, Ben, everything is cool … I think!"

Jake followed Nigel. Most of the prisoners turned around to look at Jake as he went past.

As Jake walked into the kitchen, he noticed that the kitchen staff were not scampering out as they had before.

Jake went into the same back room. Atlas and Big Al were already there.

"Cappuccino Jake?" Big Al had a mug in his hand with steam coming out of it.

"Why thank you, Big Al."

Nigel held out two small sachets. "Sugar?"

"This is very touching, Nigel, you remembered."

Nigel grunted.

Big Al looked very relaxed. He sat down on a chair. "Sit down, Jake, I have some news to tell you."

"Are they letting you out?" asked Jake. His tone suggested it was said more in jest than belief.

"No, although I am working on that too." Big Al got up and started to pace up and down and seemed very excited. He finally stopped walking and faced Jake. "This is one of the most difficult challenges I have faced. I had to bribe a lot of people; you are talking mega bucks. I also used up a couple of my favours with two of my top connections, but Big Al stops at nothing."

Jake sounded a little impatient. "Well put me out of my misery and tell me what the news is!"

"I have found Anna."

Jake looked puzzled. "Big Al, maybe I am missing something, but who the hell is Anna?"

Big Al put his right hand across his chest. "My little granddaughter!"

"You have got to be kidding me?" exclaimed Jake. "I thought all that stuff is highly confidential. I didn't think social services could be bribed!"

"Especially when it's the Social Services in another State. Yes, but everybody and everything has a price. It so happens this one was very costly."

"Well Big Al, I am delighted for you." Jake paused for a second. "But why are you telling me this?"

"Well I just wanted to thank you for helping me to find my little Anna. This means that I owe you one favour. And when Big Al owes a favour, he owes big time. If there is anything you ever need you come to me and I will sort it out for you. But I will stress to you, Jake, this favour counts for nothing if I find out you had anything to do with my Sarah's death."

"Well Big Al, I am flattered. What are you going to do now? Surely you will not be able to speak to her."

"Jake, for a psychologist you sometimes don't listen very well, do you? As I said; everyone and everything has its price. I will give the parents an offer they can't refuse."

"You are not going to threaten to kill them, are you?"

Big Al looked indignant. "What do you take me for?"

Jake smiled. "A criminal with no conscience."

Big Al laughed and seemed in jovial mood. "Touché! No, I don't need to harm them. That would only complicate matters anyway. Social services will be more difficult to deal with than a young couple. A house in the Bahamas and a cheque with enough zeros on it usually does the trick."

Big Al looked at Jake who remained silent. "Well Jake, come on, say something, you must be happy for me, not to mention the favour that I owe you."

Jake looked at Atlas and Nigel and then looked at Big Al. "Big Al could I speak to you in private?"

Big Al looked at Atlas and Nigel, and then looked at Jake. "You know they are always with me and sometimes I don't even realise they are there."

Big Al clicked his fingers. "Boys I will see you outside. In fact, you can go back to the dining hall, Jake and I have a lot to talk about."

Atlas left the room. Nigel looked at Big Al and seemed reluctant to leave. "That's okay, Nigel, I am safe with Jake."

Nigel left the room. Big Al smiled. "He is very protective of me. His son was in trouble and looked like he might end up in prison. Nigel came to me in desperation, so I spoke to a friend of a friend. The judge saw sense, I owe the friend a favour and Nigel owes me big time. And that is how the system works."

Big Al looked at Jake. "Somehow I thought you may be glad for me for finding my granddaughter. I suppose I have no one else to share the news with. I can't afford to have any emotional interaction with Nigel and Atlas. So, you were the only other person who I could think of, and I was dying to share the news with someone."

Jake looked at Big Al. "Big Al, can I be honest with you?"

"Sure, why not."

"You are a selfish prick!"

"What the fuck do you mean?" Big Al walked towards Jake and grabbed him by the throat. "I could break your neck in one instant. What the fuck do you mean? No one talks to Big Al like this."

Jake stood up and grabbed Big Al's hand and somehow managed to prize it away from his neck momentarily.

"Well whether you like it or not you are going to sit down and listen to me. So, shut the fuck up and for once in your life, listen."

Big Al looked shocked. He pulled his hand away from the vicinity of Jake's neck and slumped heavily onto a chair.

"Now listen to me, Big Al, you are not going to see Anna, contact her in any way, contact her parents, or in any way get into her life."

Big Al looked dumbfounded. Jake continued. "You only know one way to live. You live by the sword and you will die by the sword. You have a lot of connections and a lot of influence. You are young and strong. But you won't be the alpha male forever. Soon a young buck will challenge you, you will have to vacate your throne. You will run out of favours and will be watching over your shoulders all the time. What then, Big Al? What will happen to Anna?"

Big Al was silent.

Jake pulled a seat forward and sat facing Big Al. His tone softened, "You know, I was watching a nature programme some time ago. It was about these birds; I think they were called sea birds. The eggs were hatched, and the mommy and daddy birds fed them day after day after day. Then one day it was time for the bird to leave the nest. The only problem was that the nest was a few hundred feet above ground on a cliff. The baby bird looked down the cliff and made some tentative flapping of his wings but seemed reluctant to jump. The daddy bird stood behind him and just gave him a gentle nudge towards the edge. The baby bird had to jump. Within a few seconds the bird was flapping its wings and soon was flying and was able to soar the heavens. You see, Big Al, you are that daddy bird. In order for your little Anna to fly you have to push her away. You have to let her go so she can fly. If you keep her in your nest you will be happy, but she will die, if not physically, her spirit will die."

Nigel ran in. "Are you okay, Big Al, I heard some shouting?"

"Of course I'm okay. You don't think a little fuck like him could harm me, do you? I am Big Al after all, no one hurts me.' He looked at Jake. "Now stop your bullshit talk about birds and leave me alone."

Jake sat there looking at Big Al.

Big Al shouted, "ARE YOU FUCKING DEAF? GET THE FUCK OUT OF HERE!"

Jake got up and walked towards the door, he stopped at the door and looked back. He opened his mouth to say something and stopped and walked out.

Nigel quickly walked in. "Sorry Big Al, I just got worried when you didn't come out."

"That's okay, Nigel, don't worry about it. Now leave me be!"

*

Several hours later Jake's cell door was opened. The guard stepped aside, and Big Al stepped in by himself.

He came in and sat down.

Jake spoke first, "Sorry I can't offer you a cappuccino."

Big Al smiled. "That's okay, maybe if we ever meet on the outside."

"Look, Big Al, I am sorry, I was a little bit over the top back then, I don't know what came over me, I think I said a little bit too much."

"Jake no one has spoken to me like that for years."

"I am sorry if I offended you."

"No kid, I like it. You certainly have some balls."

"That's the second time you have told me that."

Big Al laughed. "I admire your courage; you are the only person who has stood up to me in here."

Big Al got up and walked to the prison door and held on to the bars. "I have arranged for my solicitor to hand over a cheque of one million dollars to Anna's parents."

"I suppose I understand that Anna is your only family and you want to get in touch with her. I suppose in some way it might make up for losing Sarah."

"No Jake, nothing will make up for losing Sarah. Well, maybe you are right, maybe that was partly in my mind. But in any case, I have thought about what you said and sadly I agree with you. I realised that even though I have never met Anna, I love her so much. In fact, I love her so much that I would rather she soared the heavens than stay in the nest with me. My solicitors will put the money in a trust fund for Anna which she can have when she is twenty-five years old. It will of course be given anonymously."

Jake stood up and walked towards Big Al. He put his arms around him and hugged him. Big Al wiped a tear from his eye.

Just then the guard came to Jake's cell. "Is everything all right, Big Al?"

Big Al pushed Jake away. "Sorry kid, you are not my type, try your luck with someone else."

Jake smiled and so did the guard.

Big Al looked at the guard. "That will be all."

The guard unlocked the door. Big Al walked out and pulled the door shut behind him. He then opened the door again and whispered, "By the way I would like it if you call me Al!"

Jake smiled. "Sure thing, Big Al. I mean Al."

Big Al was about to walk away when Jake spoke to him, "Emm Al. About this favour …"

"Yes, anything for you, Jake."

"I would like you to continue to look after Ben in here. He doesn't have long to go and I would worry that they would take advantage of him in here and his release would be delayed. You see, at heart he is just like you, a family man."

Big Al smiled and nodded. "Consider it done." He started to walk away and turned around. "I suppose I shouldn't be surprised you didn't ask for a favour for yourself." He turned around again and walked away.

CHAPTER 48

Jim Senior Meets An Accountant

Jim looked at his father as they were walking along. "Pops, I couldn't begin to tell you what sort of a week I have had."

"Tell me, son, I have all the time in the world, I am not even sure if we will find this banker guy here."

"Maybe I'll tell you some day, but for now let us focus on the task at hand."

They walked along the promenade where Geno and Gabby had had their night-time picnic.

"Are you sure this is the right place, son? This is a large area."

"Yes Pops, Geno was very precise. He said the tramp was sleeping here."

They heard a voice from behind, "There's no tramps here! Just homeless people."

Jim Senior was startled. They saw a man sitting on a bench, dishevelled, with a long scruffy beard and a dirty overcoat with a blanket over his legs, the blanket that Geno had given to him.

Jim Junior turned around. "Are you Rick Balance?"

"It's BAA LAAnce." Rick sounded disgruntled.

Jim Junior responded, "Yes sir, Geno did mention that you are particular about your name."

"And who would Geno be?" The man burped. "Excuse me."

"That's a cop that was here a week or so ago."

"Oh yes, the one on the romantic date."

"That's right," said Jim Junior. "I wasn't sure if you would remember."

"Oh I don't remember much about him, except that he was a bit slow on the uptake. But his girlfriend now, she was different. She spoke my sort of language. I really enjoyed the bottle of Irish Jamison's I bought after that night. Better than the usual cider."

Jim Senior looked at Rick. "That's a bit sad, do you not think?"

Rick snapped, "I am sure you are not here to shower pity on me, so whatever it is be quick because I am very busy."

Jim Junior looked around the place with a smirk on his face. "You have somewhere to go, someone to see?"

"Yes, I need to be off in a few minutes to the homeless shelter to get some soup for my lunch. I don't get food every day and have not eaten for two days." He burped again, "Excuse me, I get a lot of acid when I don't eat for more than one day."

Jim Junior continued, "Well, Mister BAA LAAnce. We would like some financial advice."

"Why would you get advice from a tramp – as you called me?"

Jim put up his hand. "I am sorry, Mister Balance, I meant no offence. We heard you were an ex banker and we would like some financial advice."

"Do you have an appointment?"

Both father and son laughed. "Are you serious?" asked the father.

"I need to refer to my appointment book first," Rick said as he smiled. "I am sorry but old habits die hard, couldn't resist it. And how much are you prepared to pay for this advice?"

Jim Junior put his hand in his pocket and took out a fifty-dollar bill. "I heard this was your going rate."

Rick laughed and reached out and grabbed the note folded it in four and put in his sock. He shook Jim's hand. "It's a deal. Now you are a smart cop, not like the other fella. He was very slow."

Jim Senior put a file on the bench and opened it up.

"What are you doing, sir?" Rick snapped.

"I am showing you my accounts. Is this not what we agreed on?"

"Yes, but not in my bedroom, please, let's step into my office which is over there." He walked over to a bench which had a wooden table fixed to the ground and another bench on the opposite side. "This is my office!" He sat on one side and pointed to the other. "Please be seated."

Father and son sat down beside each other on the bench opposite Rick. Jim opened the file and gave his accounts statements to Rick.

Rick put his hand top of the pile. "Before I look at this, how can you be sure you can you trust me?"

Jim Senior shrugged his shoulders. "Beats me, none of this makes sense to me!"

Jim Junior looked at his father. "No, it doesn't make sense to me either, but Geno had a hunch and I don't think there is any harm listening to you."

Rick kept his hands on the files as he spoke, "Well if you ask me, anyone who goes to a park and asks a total stranger, and a tramp no less, for financial advice must be either totally bonkers or have very good instincts."

Jim Junior smiled. "For our sake I hope it is not the former but the latter."

Rick pulled the papers towards him and studied them for a couple of minutes, going back and forth over some of the pages. He then folded the papers into a neat pile and handed them back to Jim Senior. "Oh, oh. No thank you. Look guys I don't know what sort of shit you are into, but I am not touching this."

Jim Senior looked surprised. "What do you mean?"

"Look guys, I was in the banking business for twenty years, I started when I was twenty-two and became bankrupt when I was forty-two, that was two years ago. I lost my job, my home, my family … well everything in life that I care about. I know a dodgy account when I see one. I see at several intervals deposits of cash into the account, starting as small sums going out and large sums being deposited, with the sums getting larger and larger and some five-figure sums being deposited."

Jim Senior laughed, "That is horse racing winnings."

Now Rick laughed. "Listen guys, for all I care the money is from your piggy banks. I have heard it all. I was dishonest and I paid for it. I am not one of those guys who blames others or society or my upbringing for what I did. I was a selfish arrogant greedy human being and I got what I deserved. I don't know whether I'll ever get on my two feet again, or see my wife and two children again, but I have promised to myself that I will never ever do anything immoral, let alone illegal."

"Honestly Rick, I won this in horse racing, it's a long story, but they are genuine, and I have the chits from the bookies from each winning."

"Are you being totally honest with me, Jim?"

Jim Senior nodded. "I guess you saw my name on the accounts." He reached out his hand.

"Jim Sterne, Senior." Rick shook his hand. Jim pointed to his son, "Jim Sterne Junior." The son shook Rick's hand.

Rick was still holding the papers in his hand near Jim. He pulled them back and began to study them again. He nodded. He then reached into his sock and took out the fifty-dollar note, unfolded it and handed it back to Jim Junior, "Deal is off!"

Jim Junior asked, "What is it now?"

"Well," said Rick, "the stakes are higher. You didn't tell me the sums involved."

Jim Junior didn't take the money from Rick. "Did you or did you not swear yourself to honesty in the future, sir?"

Rick looked a bit surprised. "That I did, sir!"

"Well then we shook on the deal and as part of being an honest banker for the rest of your life, you have to honour your promise."

"God you drive a hard bargain, okay I will do it, but I still think I was hoodwinked."

"A deal is a deal, Mister Banker!" Jim senior said, smiling.

Rick nodded and started to fold the fifty-dollar bill. Jim Senior reached and took the money from Rick. "What now?" asked Rick

"Wait a minute," said Jim Senior. "Can I ask you a question?"

"Ask away," said Rick.

"Where do your wife and children live?"

"I don't know. After I went bankrupt, we had to sell the house, in fact it ended up being re-possessed. It was ironic. I had ruthlessly re-possessed so many houses and now I was on the receiving end. My wife was keen to move to her parents' house in New Jersey so the children could have stability and go to a nearby school. I didn't want to go there and stayed in my folk's house in Brooklyn but slowly drifted and the rest is history. I have not seen or heard from them in about eighteen months."

Jim Senior looked very empathetic, "Would you like to see them again?"

Rick shrugged his shoulders.

Jim Senior continued, "Let me ask you another question. How long will it take you to give me advice about my finances?"

Rick shook his head. "It will take me quite a while to work things out, I shouldn't be even taking your money. I really would need to make some preliminary enquiries about bonds and shares and interest rates and so on before I can give any advice. I wouldn't be confident that I can give you good advice without some research. I think I would have to decline."

Jim Senior continued, "But given time you would be able to give me advice?"

Rick nodded. "I can assure you that given time I would give you the best advice. I may have been dishonest for a while, but I *was* very good at what I did."

"Well, here is the deal …"

Jim Junior put his hand on his father's. "Pops do you not want to discuss whatever it is you are going to offer him with me first?"

"Well, son, it is now your turn to trust me."

His son moved his hand away and shrugged his shoulders. "Okay Pops, it's your money."

His father nodded. He then turned to Rick. "Here is the deal. No fifty dollars. You can come and stay with me for a few days, a week or so, or the few weeks that it takes to sort out my finances. In return you get food, bed, and shelter, and I also get someone to keep me company for a short while. What do you say?"

"Pops, are you sure, I mean—"

Rick interrupted, "Really? I am a total stranger and for all you know might be a mass murderer!"

Jim Junior thought for a short while. "On second thought, Rick, are *you* sure? My father doesn't stop talking once he starts, and he will have your head turned. This is your chance to save yourself."

Rick looked towards the other bench where he had a duffle bag with all his possessions in, and two blankets. "I am not sure about leaving my home here, I am sort of very used to it, and the cops rarely bother me now."

Jim Senior put his head close to Rick and said rather quietly, "I have two words that will most definitely change your mind."

"What? Are you going to say Irish whiskey?"

"No actually the two words are *hot bath*."

Rick looked towards the bench again. He reached out his hand and Jim Senior shook it. "We have a deal?" asked Jim.

"We have a deal!" replied Rick.

CHAPTER 49

Lucy Visits Jake

Lucy walked into the all familiar interview room of the prison and sat behind the desk. She fidgeted nervously and tapped the table with her fingers. After a few seconds she stood up and started to pace around the room. A few moments later she sat down and started to tap the table with her fingers again. She looked at her watch, stood up again, and started to walk around the room. The door opened. The prison officer walked in and Jake walked in after him.

"Would you like me to stay in?" asked the prison officer.

"Whatever for?" replied Lucy looking very surprised.

"Just routine question, ma'am." The prison officer replied as he nodded his head. He walked out and closed the door behind him.

"Good morning Jake, please take a seat."

"Thank you." He sat down. "This is an unexpected visit!"

"Well yes." Lucy paused and walked towards the wall with her back to Jake. She was quiet for a few seconds. She then turned around and faced Jake. "I …" she stopped and cleared her throat, "I guess I owe you an apology."

Jake looked surprised, "In your words, whatever for?!"

"I guess you would not have heard."

"Heard what?"

"Sorry, yes, I will get to the point." She went over and lifted her chair and brought it from behind the table where it was across from Jake's chair and put it to the side of the table. "The judge's daughter became very sick yesterday. I phoned his office this morning and he personally phoned me back. I guess it was to say that she had had an ectopic pregnancy. He said that the reason he was giving me this delicate information was that if you had not said what you had said in the court room, his daughter would almost certainly have died!"

She pushed her chair forward and looked Jake in the eye. "He said that you saved his daughter's life. Now he is not sure if he will be able to proceed with the case but is wary of having to nullify all that has been done."

"Well I am delighted that she is well. But I don't really feel that I have done anything. But it is good of you to come all the way here to give me that information." He looked at her and smiled. "I suppose though that is not the only reason why you are here."

Lucy sat back and hesitated again. "I am not sure how to say this … but I wanted to come here to ask you this. You see, I want to believe in this fantasy world of yours, but I find it difficult to see how someone can see into the future. And why is it that you should be able to have these dreams and nobody else I know? It seems a bit farfetched, but then this dream of yours about the judge's daughter has spooked a lot of people. Does this mean you are some sort of a prophet, and, if so, how could you kill someone?"

Jake laughed out loud. "Please, a prophet, I certainly am not!" He continued to laugh.

"But how could you be so precise?"

"Well actually, all I remember is that you had told me that the judge's daughter had had an ectopic pregnancy and it was so vivid that for an instance in the court room I had a flashback of your words. Perhaps I dreamt about this situation here and now and didn't realise that I had heard it in a dream!"

"But how is it possible, I don't understand?"

"Have you never had dreams about events that in some shape have come true in the future?"

"Not really …" she paused and stood up. She walked away from the table and stood facing the wall. "Well actually I remember another dream that I had; when I was twelve years old my mother got sick one day. She went to the doctor and was admitted to the hospital because she was jaundiced. She was told she had cancer of her pancreas. She died within weeks and I was devastated. I adored her …" she paused as she wiped a tear from her eye. "Anyway, I couldn't accept the fact that she wasn't there, at home with me. My father tried his best to console me, but I cried myself to sleep every night. Then one night I had a dream about her. I dreamt that I was lying in bed and she was singing me a lullaby. It was 'Somewhere Over The Rainbow'. When she finished, she kissed my forehead and stroked my cheeks with the back of her index finger. The next morning, I recounted my dream to my dad. I was in tears. My dad was not very emotional, but I saw a few tears roll down his face. 'Lucy,' he told me, 'that is the song your mommy used to sing to you every night until you were nine months old. After the age of nine months you slept like a log as soon as you were placed in your cot and did not need a lullaby. After singing that song she would kiss your forehead and stroke each of your cheeks with the back of her index finger.' As my dad told me this he stroked my cheeks as I had seen in my dream. 'You see Lucy,' he told me, 'your mommy is letting you know that she will always be with you.'"

Lucy frantically looked in her handbag. Jake reached into his pocket and pulled out a tissue and handed it to Lucy. "One of the very few privileges I am allowed."

"Thank you," Lucy said as she wiped the corner of her eyes. "I am sorry, I didn't mean to get that emotional."

"You don't have to apologise for a natural human emotion."

"Spoken like a true psychologist."

"I am sorry I didn't mean to be analytical."

Lucy interrupted him, "No actually that was a bit unfair, I guess I was trying to cover my slight embarrassment. After all, this is hardly a natural lawyer-client discussion."

"Ain't that the truth? But then maybe what is natural for one person isn't natural for another."

"I guess so." Lucy looked at Jake intently. She paused, "So you still haven't answered my question."

"Which one?"

Lucy was silent for a few seconds, lost in thought. "Tell me Jake, how does this dream thing work? I mean, how do you know what the dreams mean?"

Jake thought for some moments. "It's hard to explain." He scratched his head. "I'll be damned if I can understand most of mine, let alone anyone else's dreams. But some dreams have a certain meaning, an inner reality. Perhaps if I explain what my mother explained to me, it might be the simplest way. Where do I start?" He stared at the ceiling for a while. "My mother used to talk to me about my dreams all the time, and most of the time she confused the hell out of me. My first memory is when I had the mumps. I remember when I was about four years old, being sick with a very high temperature. I dreamt that there were wild animals running after me and there were about to catch me when I suddenly woke up from my sleep, screaming. My mother ran into my bedroom. I told her about my dream. She laughed. She told me not to worry and that when people were sick or have taken certain medication or had poisons in their system the brain can be affected, and they would have bad dreams. She explained that was why my dad would occasionally see rats climbing up the walls and that alcohol did that to the brain. And my temperature had caused me to hallucinate. Then a couple of years later when I was six, I had to appear in my school's nativity play. Again, I woke up crying and told my mother that I was on stage and was about to say my lines when all my teeth fell out. She laughed again and stroked my hair and told me not to worry and that I was just worried about messing things up and assured me I would be all right. I didn't fully understand her explanation at the time. It took me years to realise that what she was explaining to me was a phenomenon that I saw in a lot of my clients. For example, they would dream that they had turned up for their exam and had forgotten to study–"

Lucy interrupted, "Or for example I would dream of turning up in court and start speaking to the judge and realise I was fully naked!"

Jake chuckled. "Yes indeed, that is the same sort of dream. What I realised that my mother was explaining to me was that our anxieties can crystallise in our dreams into a reality. So, I often told them that those dreams told them what was bothering them in their subconscious, and by dreaming about it, the concern came to the fore and they should tackle what was bothering them, i.e. in your case it would be prepare your case better."

Lucy nodded.

"So, my mother explained to me that the first dream had a physical cause, the second one was the concern of the mind. That takes us to the other type of dreams. Dreams that are often confusing, mysterious, obscure, and enlightening all at the same time … And often a pain in the ass."

Lucy laughed, "And why is that?"

"Because they still baffle me too and can make me very apprehensive when I see things which are not pleasant."

"So, when did you first have a dream like this one?"

"Yes, I was coming to that. When I was about eight, I had the first dream that I recall being of the mysterious type, or perhaps a spiritual nature. I should explain that my father was an alcoholic and would have been very abusive to my mother. Don't get me wrong, he was a very charming man and loved by all, but most didn't see the other side of him. My sister and I hated him being drunk because he shouted at us and was abusive to us; like saying that we were a waste of space, stupid, draining all his money and so on and so forth. More importantly my mother was terrified of him when he was drunk but she tolerated him, until one day he slapped her hard when in a drunken stupor. She fell to the ground and her scalp bled a little. Next day he did not remember hitting her and was very apologetic and even brought her flowers. What he didn't know was that my sister, Freda, and I could hear her crying all day. That night she ran into my room because she heard me crying. She told me not to worry and that my father would not harm her again. I told her that I was crying because of a dream I had had. I explained to her that I had dreamt that it was the heart of winter and my sister and I were sleeping in our separate bedrooms. My father was outside the house and he was hammering at my bedroom wall with a sledgehammer until a few bricks fell, allowing the snow and the cold to come in. My mother was outside the house meticulously putting each brick back in place. My dad would then proceed to my sister's room and knock out a few bricks with the sledgehammer. My mother would then run to her side of the house and replace the bricks. This went on and on and my mother was getting exhausted, she was getting really cold and her fingers were bleeding. She finally got so exhausted that she fell to the ground. She was crying, freezing, and the blood from her fingers made the virgin snow red. My father did not stop. He continued with the sledgehammer and knocked out more and more bricks. Then suddenly there was a rumble and the whole house shook and all the bricks and mortar and roofing fell down as the whole house collapsed. Amazingly every bit of debris managed to miss my sister and me. We stood there without having to duck or take shelter as everything collapsed around us. Then I woke up and cried. To my surprise my mother did not laugh this time. She wept, but they were tears of joy. She kissed my head several times and kept saying, 'bless you my son, bless you my son'. Many years later she told me that she had wanted to divorce my father but was worried as to how it would affect me and Freda. My dream had reassured that with the house, that is the marriage breaking down, Freda and I would be protected and would come to no harm. She then divorced my father and I had never seen her so happy prior to the divorce."

"Wow!" Lucy exclaimed. "That is some dream for a young child. How is it that you have these dreams? In fact, how is it even possible if the events haven't even happened? I mean how can you have heard me saying that the judge's daughter had an ectopic pregnancy when I didn't even know he had a daughter?"

Jake paused for quite a while and then his face seemed to light up. He suddenly sat up and looked at Lucy. "Can you wait for a short while and I can show you something?"

Lucy looked surprised. "What is it that you are going to show me and why do I have to wait?"

"Well Lucy you just have to trust me on this, there is no point describing it to you. I will have to go and get something."

Lucy reached into her bag and took out her diary. "Let me see," she turned over the pages of that week. "Nothing on Saturday evening, nothing on Sunday evening, nothing on Monday evening, in fact clear all week, I suppose I can wait here a while longer!"

"My God I was right; you need to get out a bit more. Do you not have a boyfriend?"

"I hate to admit it; I have finally decided to give up on men. Maybe the romantic thing is okay for some, but it is not for me."

"You have no idea how many times I have heard those exact words, more often followed by people finding romance."

"Well maybe for others, but looking around me, no thanks. Anyway, what was it you were going to show me?"

"Oh yes," Jake stood up. "I'll be back in a few minutes, don't go anywhere."

Jake opened the door and was greeted by the guard. "I need to get something to show Miss Walker."

The guard looked at his watch. "I think you are stretching things; I will have to speak to the supervisor."

Jake nodded, "That's okay, tell him I need to see Big Al."

The guard looked at his watch again. "I guess you still have some time left. I will take you there."

It took several minutes before they got to Big Al's cell. He was lying on his bed with his knees bent and legs crossed, moving his feet to the sound of the music playing.

"Is that Pink Floyd?" Jake asked.

Big Al jumped up. "Hey Jake what's up?"

"I need to ask you a big favour, Al."

"Well it all depends how big the favour is! I guess I can extend another favour to you. Do you want to speak to me in private?" He pointed at the guard.

"No Al, it is actually not private at all. I just need to borrow two radios for a few minutes."

"Hey don't worry about radios, you can have a loan of my expensive Hi Fi, amplifiers, speakers, the lot, for as long you want."

The guard raised his eyebrows, looking very surprised. Big Al tilted his head to the right and with that the guard walked away and waited a few cells away.

Big Al looked towards the guard looking at Jake. "This is the beginning of the end."

Jake looked at the guard and looked surprised. "What do you mean?"

"They are not used to seeing anything but hardness from me, and as you aptly described, just like the alpha male in a pack that loses his authority over the group, with any perceived weakness he will be challenged for the top spot. My heart has been touched with something, and now I can't go back."

"Well I am sorry if I have brought this on you."

Big Al smiled at Jake. He reached into the top pocket of his prison shirt and brought out a picture of baby Anna. "What you have given me cannot be replaced by anything this prison, or indeed the whole world, has to offer." He stared at Anna's picture. "Forty-nine years of living, umpteen years or so in this prison, all the ups and downs, doesn't compare to what I feel for Anna." He looked at Jake. "It probably seems strange to you, with all the misdeeds I have done that I should be so sentimental."

Jake smiled. "I know exactly what you mean. In fact, when I practiced I had a poem framed on my wall, it went something like this:

I spent day and night toiling for a better life

I amassed gold and silver for my delight

But alas at the dusk of my life I pondered

I had not collected that which fulfilled my heart."

"That is exactly what I mean. I can see why you were a good psychologist."

"Nobody said I was good!"

Big Al laughed. "Who wrote the poem by the way?"

"In one of my inspired moments I reflected on why so many of my patients were unhappy and it just came to me."

Big Al looked at the guard who was staring at him and his features changed to a stern one suddenly. "What is it you need again?"

"I need two radios, but they need to be exactly the same."

"Consider it done, Jake, come back day after tomorrow and I will have the state-of-the-art ones for you."

"You don't understand, Al; I need them right now! And they need to have batteries in them."

"Oh, that complicates matters." He beckoned the guard with his index finger. "Charlie, I need to go and see Shifty the spark. You can lock Jake in my cell, I will vouch for him."

Charlie looked around, "Sh … Sure." He sounded unsure.

"Don' t worry, Charlie, it will only take a few minutes."

A few minutes later Big Al returned holding two radios and showed them off as if he had a trophy. "This is the best I could get, they are not identical, in fact one of them is ancient, the other one is pretty good though, but it's all I could do at short notice, the batteries being the stumbling block."

Jake looked at him. "No actually this is perfect, better than I had planned. Let me test them."

He switched both on and tuned them to stations.

"I am curious as to why you are desperate for one radio, and am dying to know why you need two, and why so urgently?"

"Will explain later, Al, need to go now."

Big Al held Jake's upper arm and Jake stopped. "You may have a bit of bother with Billy at the primary exit of the cells, tell him …" Big Al came close to Jake and whispered something in his ear. Jake smiled and nodded.

Jake was escorted by the guard and at the primary exit of the cells Billy put up his hand. "Hello, hello … What do we have here? Do you think you live at the White House? Nothing is allowed out of the cells." He stood erect with his chest puffed out and had a huge grin on his face. "I need a specific letter from the warden to allow these bad boys through!"

Jake looked disappointed. He handed the two radios to Billy. "I am sorry, here you are, Billy. Would you mind giving them back to Big Al?" He paused and had an inquisitive look on his face. "By the way, Billy," he went close to Billy's ear, "Big Al wants to know how your daughter Lauren is doing."

Billy's grin suddenly disappeared. He looked at the guard who looked a bit flustered. He then quickly composed himself. "Of course sir, you are quite right, the paperwork was delivered earlier, it slipped my mind. Please go on ahead."

Jake arrived back at the meeting room. He found that Lucy had her head resting on her arms on the table and was asleep. She was startled when the door was closed.

"Oh gosh I must have dozed off."

Jake stood there with a radio in each hand. "If you are tired, I can go away."

"Oh no, I am even more mystified at what you are going to show me!"

"Well probably not worth the anticipation." He put the radios on the table.

"I have already set the stations, so I want you to listen to the music."

Lucy looked at Jake. "I think the time inside has got you a bit muddled!"

"Bear with me, Lucy." He then turned on the old radio. There was a man talking. "Em, this was not part of the plan, you need to wait a bit longer. This is my favourite radio station; it plays beautiful classical music."

Lucy shrugged her shoulders. "I am not going far."

"Right this is it. Wow this is amazing, it's playing one of my all-time favourites, 'Sheep May Safely Graze'."

He stopped talking and closed his eyes and listened. His head moved slightly from side to side as he listened to the music.

Lucy looked quizzically at Jake. After about half a minute she coughed slightly. "Jake, this is beautiful, but am I missing something?"

"Oh sorry Lucy, I got carried away with the music." He turned off the radio. Now I want to play the music on this other much more modern radio." He turned on the new radio and closed his eyes, listening to the music.

Lucy looked even more astonished. The music was barely audible, and the sounds were predominated by crackles. This went on for about half a minute. Lucy coughed again. Jake opened his eyes. "I am sorry, Jake." She passed her hand over her head. "I think your point has just gone over my head. I don't get it."

"Well Lucy, it is simple. You see you have two radios that have exactly the same potential. In fact, it could be argued that this new radio is superior and should have a better quality of sound. But unless they are tuned in to the right wavelength, they cannot play the right music."

"Thanks for that enlightenment, but you went to a lot of trouble to show something that you could have told me in a few seconds."

"Well my point is this. As human beings we have a lot of potential. Some say that we use less than ten percent of our brain capacity. The point is that there are a lot of people who tap into the metaphysical world that is around us. People who have dreams, premonitions, instincts – these people are in fact not special, or necessarily gifted. In fact, as the two radios showed, the more modern radio that had the poorer sound quality had much more potential, but this potential is not realized if it that does not tune in to the right frequency. The fact is that a lot of people are not aware of their higher self, a part of them that transcends the physical barriers that are imposed on us. So, it is as if some people are tuned in to the right frequencies and therefore tap into the world that is as close to us – as close as the airwaves that surround us. Does that make sense?"

All Lucy could say was, "Wow."

"Well does it make sense?"

"Yes actually it makes perfect sense. But do you mean we are all able to have dreams?"

"Well I think that different people will probably develop different qualities. I have no doubt that in the future we will have better awareness of our higher self. So, I don't see myself as being special or gifted. But for whatever reason I can tune into the right frequencies at certain times but know that there are millions of folks out there with more potential than me but have not tuned in to the right frequency."

"I guess that makes sense. So, are you psychic too?"

"No, I am not psychic in the sense that we normally see psychics. I have just learnt over the years that certain vibes I get from people, and I have learnt to trust some of the positive ones and the negative ones. My first reaction is usually right."

Lucy looked Jake in the eyes, "So what did you think of me when you first saw me?"

Jake looked at his watch. "If you don't mind, it has been a long day, and I am sure you are more tired than I am, can we call it a day?"

Lucy blushed a bit, "Oh I am sorry. Yes, I will go now."

Jake smiled. "It is very good of you to come and see me. But I would rather not go down certain avenues right now."

Lucy looked embarrassed. "Sure thing, no problem. I will see you soon." She picked up her handbag, got up, and quickly left the room.

As she left the room Jake hit his head on the table three times. "Shit, shit, shit!" He muttered to himself. "You idiot!" He got up and walked out.

CHAPTER 50

Do Tell Me

It was Sunday morning. Paolo walked into Jim's office. Jim was asleep on his chair with his hands on top of his desk and his head rested on his hands.

Paolo walked up to him and shook his shoulder gently. "Jim." He got no response. He shook Jim a bit more forcefully and called him louder "JIM, JIM."

Jim suddenly bolted up. "What, what?" He looked at Paolo and looked around the room "Where am I? Oh shit, what time is it?"

"It's seven thirty."

Jim looked round the room. "What day is it?"

"It's Sunday."

"Oh right. Oh yes, I remember now." Jim put his nose towards his armpit and inhaled deeply. "O God I stink! Did you get any sleep?"

"Yes, I got home at four a.m., slept for an hour, but more importantly was able to shave and have a shower."

Jim noticed that Paolo had a file in his hand. "What do you have?"

"You'll find this interesting. I was able to track down the head of twenty-four-seven security. It took me a whole day to track the right guy. I convinced him to get out of his bed at 1 a.m. He was astute enough to have backed up all the tapes of the street surveillance that the police had reviewed pertaining to the days surrounding the murders of Tracey Chapman and Sarah Miller. In fact, he said that he had kept a copy under his mattress at home, in case the other copy went missing. Anyway, at first, we didn't see anything, but we thought about going backwards in time day by day. We were about to give up when I suddenly noticed this. I have printed some pictures from the video."

Paolo opened the file and put a few pictures on top of the desk.

Jim had a look at them and nodded. "Good job, Paolo, leave them with me, I'll have to phone the captain."

"All right Jim, Ciao."

Jim dialled a number on the phone. "Will, I need your attention!"

After a few minutes of talking to Will, Jim put the phone down. He then dialled another number. He listened to the ringing tone and tapped his desk. The ringing tone then stopped, and he heard an answering machine, "The number is not available, please leave …"

*

Jim picked up his desk phone and dialled a number. "Derek, I know you are busy at church, but please phone me as soon as you get a chance."

After a couple of minutes Derek phoned Jim. "Derek, we have had some new evidence that has come to light, we need to look at it urgently."

After a few seconds he spoke again. "Yes Derek it is urgent. Could you come in as soon as possible? … Great, see you here soon."

*

Derek stood at the door of Jim's office. "Would you like coffee?"

Jim replied, "No thanks."

Derek walked into Jim's office smiling. "It's not like you not to want coffee. Gosh you look dreadful."

Jim looked very stern. "Sit down, Derek. And yes, I've been up all night assessing some of the facts of the case."

Derek sat down. "You look very serious, Jim. Is it because the sentencing has been delayed?"

"Actually Derek. No! That is not the reason."

"Oh, what is it, Jim?"

Jim didn't answer and walked to the door and closed it. He walked slowly back to his chair without saying a word. He sat down and leaned back. He rested his chin on his two thumbs with his hands covering his mouth. He stayed silent for quite a few seconds. Derek began to fidget slightly, looking slightly uncomfortable.

"What is it, Jim?"

Jim took a deep breath. "Why did you do it, Derek?"

"Whatever are you talking about?" Derek said, looking even more uncomfortable.

"Where had you been the night before we went to inspect Charlene's body?"

"Jim, are you questioning me?"

"Derek, please answer the questions."

"Okay, if you must know. I was at home, most of the day and went to the mall to buy some items of clothing and then came over here."

"Did you buy anything nice?"

"No, as I recall I didn't see anything I liked. What is all this about?"

"Derek there was mud on the mats in the back of my car, after we left the scene."

"Yes of course, Jim, if you remember I grabbed your coat from the back of the car."

"Yes, you did, Derek, but that was before we went to the site. You didn't set a foot in the back of the car after we went to the murder scene!"

Derek hesitated for a few seconds and sweat precipitated on his brow. "What does that mean, Jim? I must have got mud on my shoe before we got there."

Jim smiled. "Sure. Must be a lot of mud in these malls these days." Jim held up an A4 paper and looked at it briefly. "Do you recognize this car?"

He handed Derek the A4 paper that had a printed photograph on it. Derek had a look at it. "The picture is very blurry; I can't see much." And handed it back to Jim.

Jim handed another A4 picture to Derek. "This is the number plate blown up. Do you recognize it? Mary-Beth told me you like fast cars."

"When did you see Mary-Beth?"

"I bumped into her at a mall."

"Were you questioning Mary-Beth, Jim?"

"No, actually, Derek, she came to see me to find out more about you, but let's not talk about that now."

Derek looked at the second photo. "It's a bit blurry, but it seems to be the number plate to my car."

"Yes," said Jim, "and it's a black spitfire convertible." He handed him another photo. "Do you recognize this person with a cap on? Looks a lot like you."

Derek had a look at the photo. "Have you been following me?"

"No Derek, that is a photo taken from the surveillance camera outside Sarah's flat a week before she disappeared."

Derek put the photos down and sank into his seat. "Crime never pays."

Jim remained silent for a while. "Mary-Beth mentioned you like to watch boxing, did you used to box?"

Derek was silent for a short while. "I used to have terrible trouble with anger when I was growing up. At the age of thirteen my father thought I should take up boxing. He thought it would help me to control my anger. He was right, the only problem is when I got angry, I vented it more forcefully."

"And you learnt to use your left hand?"

Derek nodded. "Yes, I made sure I didn't use my right hand."

"So why did you do it, Derek?"

They talked for about twenty minutes.

Derek finally said, "I guess I should speak to my solicitor."

"Okay Derek, I will organize that. For the record I am deeply shocked and was very fond of you."

"And likewise Jim, I really liked you."

CHAPTER 51

Final Court Scene

It was Monday morning ten a.m. Judge Temple asked for silence in the court. There was no letting up in the murmur that pervaded the court room. He hit his gavel very loudly twice and shouted, "SILENCE IN THE COURT!" There was a sudden quiet.

He was silent for a few seconds. "The prosecution team have withdrawn all charges against the defendant Mister John Chapman." He then hit his gavel on the sound block and said, "Case dismissed!"

Jake clenched his fists and punched the air and whispered, "Yes!"

Amanda had a hint of a smile as she leaned forward, enough to be able to see Peter North. Peter tipped his head ever so slightly, just enough for Amanda that he had acknowledged her victory. Amanda's smile broadened as she nodded back in acknowledgement.

Lucy leaned back on her chair and sighed loudly, which seemed more like relief than anything.

A murmur had broken out in the courtroom after the announcement. The noise escalated by the second.

The judge then hit his gavel loudly and the courtroom slowly went into silence. All eyes were turned towards the judge and there was some expression of surprise from the lawyers.

John Temple was quite for what seemed a long time. He then spoke, "I …" There was a slight quiver in his voice and he swallowed his saliva. He then took a sip of water from a glass and cleared his throat. "I feel it is important that I also mention this." He paused again. "This is most unprecedented. I had mentioned that Mister Chapman was in contempt of court. I would like to say that firstly I am withdrawing that statement. Secondly I am lost for words as to how to thank …" He paused and again his voice as quivering. His eyes seemed somewhat watery. He looked straight at Jake. "Sir, I don't know how to thank you. I don't know how you were able to tell me my daughter was going to be ill, but you saved her life. I want to thank you from the bottom of my heart and my wife and I are forever in your debt." He then got up and walked out quickly.

The bailiff hastily announced, "Please be upstanding for the honourable Judge Temple leaving the court room."

Everyone stood up, except for Lucy who seemed to be in a trance. Amanda nudged her. Lucy jumped to her feet and muttered "Oops!" By the time she got up the judge had left the court room.

When the judge left the room there was a momentary silence again. The noise level suddenly escalated to a crescendo. Andy Gomez turned towards Peter North. He shook Peter's hand and appeared to be about to say something and then just shrugged his shoulders. Peter patted him on the shoulder a few times. "You did well, Andy. This is the sort of case you don't mind losing. After all, we are in this business to ensure justice is done, and in this case, justice was done. Also, one thing I have learnt in this job is that a dose of humility now and then is character-building. I'll see you Monday morning in the office." He was about to walk away and stopped. "By the way, Andy, gather your things from your office and clear it by Monday."

"Oh!" said Andy, looking apprehensive.

"I have seen enough to know that you are the man to take over the DPP post. You are moving into my office next week. I will be going on a vacation and won't come back. You have the use of all my facilities from next Monday."

"Okay Peter, so long as I get to keep my own PA!"

"That you can do."

"Maybe you should let me break the news to her in case she does not want to move."

"Sure thing, Andy. See you in two weeks."

They busily put their papers into their briefcases and walked out unceremoniously.

Amanda looked at Lucy who was staring into space. "Well, what are you thinking about?"

Lucy looked at Amanda and had a look of disbelief on her face. "Did we really win the case?"

Amanda sounded very chirpy, "You better believe it, kid! And I'll tell you what, enjoy it while you can, because you will also have a lot of lows over the years."

Lucy shook her head. "You know all along I never thought we had a hope in hell of acquitting Jake."

Amanda seemed a bit more serious, "Well Lucy, remember, you *always* have a chance!"

Lucy nodded. "And yes you are right, the truth is a mirage!"

Jake was waiting for his moment to interrupt. He reached across and Amanda shook his hand. Jake then grasped her hand with both of his and said, "If you two think it feels good, imagine what it feels like for me, to have my life back, in more ways than one. I always thought I would come out of this okay and that the truth would somehow manifest itself, but for a while I began to doubt it! It's hard to put into words. I think getting justice for Tracey is more important to me than my own freedom!"

Amanda shook his hand firmly. "Jake it's very rarely I would say this, but I really got you all wrong and I apologise for that."

"Look Amanda, I am, and forever will be, thankful to you and Lucy. Looking back on the whole situation I can see how my story was not plausible, and my indifference was totally unhelpful. But were it not for the perseverance of you two I don't think I would have had a chance."

Amanda smiled. "You are welcome." She paused. "Emm, could I have my hand back please?!"

"Oh certainly." Jake smiled and let go of her hand. "You owe a lot to Lucy. She kept me going at certain points when I felt like giving up completely."

"Yes, I know and I am going to thank her shortly."

Amanda looked at Jake and then at Lucy. After a couple of seconds, she said, "Oh right! Okay then, I'm out of here!" She hurriedly finished putting her papers away and turned to Lucy and said, "I'll handle the press outside and then I have to meet the senior partners later on and report back on the case. Company policy on homicide cases. Do you want to meet up for a drink later this evening?"

A voice over Amanda's shoulder said, "No she can't meet you tonight, because you are otherwise engaged!" It was Jim.

Amanda turned around and said in a surprised tone, "I am?"

"Yes, you are," Jim replied. "You have a date tonight!"

Amanda shrugged her shoulders. "Since you put it that way, I suppose I have no option. I'll see tomorrow, Lucy." She hugged Lucy and whispered, "Well done, kiddo, it was a pleasure working with you."

Lucy whispered back, "I learned from the best."

Amanda started to walk away, Jim was standing there awkwardly. She nudged him with her elbow, "Come on, Jim."

Jim replied, "Okay, but I just wanted a word with Jake."

Amanda tugged his elbow. "You can tell him later. Anyway, we have heard the script. You are sorry you got it wrong, you thought he was guilty, and didn't believe him, and now you feel like shit, etcetera etcetera."

"Well not exactly in those words, but I suppose you have made a good synopsis."

"Okay then let's go."

The two of them were walking towards the court exit.

Amanda said, "I am looking forward to a night of wining and dining, relaxation, and …"

"And …?" asked Jim with a mischievous look on his face.

"And relaxation, what else?" said Amanda with a twinkle in her eye. As if to change the subject she quickly asked, "How is your pops?"

"Oh he's doing well. He hasn't shut up talking about you and praising you."

"I suppose you two have each other at Christmas every year?"

"Yes," replied Jim. He shook his head, "But he is going to miss me this Christmas!"

"Why is that, Jim?"

"Well I am rather proud of myself."

"How is that?"

"I was able to go," he bent the index and middle finger of both hands as if quoting, "*online* … and book a ticket to Maui from the coming Friday for two weeks, so I guess Pops will miss me."

"Ah Jim, I am surprised at you. Going to Hawai'i on your own while your poor ill father is left here on his own at Christmas."

"I was going to chat to you about all this tonight, but now that we have started, I feel compelled to carry on. Firstly, he is not ill, thanks to you he is on treatment and doing well and due to have an operation in a few weeks to sort out his prostate problem. He also has a friend to keep him company. Secondly, I am not going on my own."

"Oh …" Amanda was silent for a few seconds. "Who are you travelling with, male or female company?"

"Now Mandy, do you think I would go on vacation to Maui with a man?"

"I see …" Amanda looked a bit apprehensive. "I think I know who it is. It's Candy or Cindy, whatever her name is; isn't it?"

Jim scratched his chin. "Now, there's a thought, I didn't think of that. Let me get my bookings and see if I can change and take her instead."

He took out two printed airline tickets. "Let me see. This one is for Jim Sterne, and this one is for …" He showed her the ticket. It read 'Amanda Jackson'.

"You have booked me a ticket? Gosh you haven't even consulted with me. I have the debriefing to do with the firm most of next week and a couple of cases to review …"

Jim put his hand over her mouth. "Shush. Now just listen to me. I have a number of things on my desk, in fact my desk is covered with paperwork. But Pops made me realise that sometimes in life you can't keep waiting for things to happen, you have to seize the moment. Now I have given you most of the week to sort out anything you need to at the office. The two of us are then going to Hawai'i together on Friday. We will have a lot to talk about there."

"And what exactly is there that we need to talk about?"

"Now Mandy I would have given you more credit. We have to discuss the wedding arrangements, and also …"

Amanda held his hand lightly and tenderly, "Also what, Jim?"

"I want to get the back of my car messy!"

"I beg your pardon, is this your idea of being romantic?"

"Oh, sorry Mandy, it didn't come out the way I meant it. What I mean is that I would like to talk to you about having children. I don't want to wait any more."

Amanda seemed very emotional all of a sudden. "I will be ready for Friday morning."

Jim held out his right arm with the elbow slightly bent. "Shall we dine, darling?"

Amanda smiled and put her arm around his elbow and they walked away.

*

Lucy and Jake had still not looked at each other. Lucy fidgeted with her papers aimlessly.

Jake looked around the room. "It's very busy and noisy here."

"It's likely to be busy for a while."

"Do you mind if I come around to your office on Wednesday morning to thank you when it's a bit quieter? I'm sure you will be busy tomorrow."

"Sure Jake, what time were you thinking of?"

"Oh, whatever suits you, is ten a.m. okay?"

"That's perfect, meet you for coffee then."

Jake held her right hand with both of his. "Thank you so much." He paused. "Actually this feels more right." He hugged her.

Lucy smiled. "My pleasure."

CHAPTER 52

Mary-Beth Visits Derek

Mary Beth asked the guard. "I am sorry, but will I not be able to see him in a private room?"

The guard smirked, "Miss this a maximum-security prison. You'll be asking for conjugal rights next!"

Mary-Beth couldn't hold back a tear that fell from her cheek onto her coat. She fumbled in her coat pocket for a tissue. The guard seemed unmoved. "Miss I can get you a tissue if you want."

Mary-Beth turned her side to him so he couldn't see her tears. "No, that's okay I have one here somewhere."

The guard pointed to the corner of the room. There were a number of wooden tables with four plastic chairs around each, all of which were attached to the floor by means of chains and screws. "Look Miss, if you go into the corner table you will at least have a bit of privacy."

Mary-Beth got up, having got a disposable tissue from her pocket, and with her back to him said thank you and walked to the table in the corner. She looked around the room. A Hispanic lady had just come in with two children under the age of five. Three other women had come in and again after standing and looking around all had gone to tables that had no one sitting on the table next to it. There were a few guards standing strategically around the room so everyone could be observed. The prisoners started to walk in one at a time. They all had dark grey tracksuit bottoms on with a light grey T-shirt.

Eventually she saw Derek. She gasped. He was slightly bent over and unshaven and his T-shirt was quite creased. He came over and sat beside her. There was silence for quite a long time as he looked at her and she gazed at the floor.

He then reached over and held both her hands. She pulled back her hands as if startled and suddenly slapped him very hard, so much so that he nearly fell back. Two of the guards suddenly came toward them.

Derek held up his hands. "That's okay guards, please let us be."

Mary-Beth was now crying loudly.

Derek held up his two hands towards the guards. "Please let us be, we are okay." Mary-Beth had again turned her back on them. Everyone else in the big room was looking at them.

One of the small children was crying loudly, "Mommy, I don't want to be here, can we go home?"

Her mother embraced her and kissed her on the cheek and stroked her hair. "It's okay baby, people are just upset when they are here, don't worry it's nothing bad."

One of the guards tapped Mary-Beth on the shoulder, "Ma'am, if what you did is repeated, we will have to ask you to leave." Mary-Beth just nodded as her shoulders bobbed up and down as she shed tears.

The guards walked away.

Mary-Beth sniffled before she could talk. "I am sorry for creating a scene."

Derek replied, "Mary-Beth, you have nothing to be sorry for, I deserve this and more."

She now looked angry. "YES YOU DO! If all these people were not here, I would slap you again. How could you?" She then raised her voice in a mixture of what was both a whisper and a shout at the same time, "How could you?!"

He reached to hold her hands again. She pulled her hands back. "Are these the same hands that you have killed three people with? And to think you stroked my hair with the same hands. I was sick about four times this morning. I didn't even want to come here."

"And why did you, is it because you love me?"

"You cannot love someone with all your heart and suddenly turn the tap off, but I think – no, I am sure – that in time I will have put any feelings for you locked firmly away in a safe in my heart. I will throw the key out and never access it again."

"And did you come here just to tell me that or did you want to ask me why?"

Mary-Beth hesitated, "Of course I want to ask you why, but I am scared of what you will say. And I am scared …"

Derek spoke, "You are scared that I will have killed others."

"Yes, that you would have … Oh my god, I can't even say it. Derek, you have taken human life. All those Church meetings, all the charity work, saving the life of a child, all your kindness. How could you, why would you ever …?"

"Mary-Beth, please at least hear me out. I know nothing I say will make you feel better, but I know that if I don't tell you anything, you will look back on this day and think why did I not ask him to explain himself."

"Okay, but I am not sure I will be able to endure it."

"Please at least let me explain without interruptions, I know you may be upset at certain things, but I need to tell you the whole thing. Is that okay?"

Mary-Beth nodded.

Derek looked at the guard who seemed to be leaning towards him to hear. "Do you mind, can I at least have a bit of privacy?"

The guard took a few paces to his left and turned his attention to another table.

Derek instinctively reached for Mary-Beth's hands and pulled back quickly. "After the miscarriage you were not …"

"Don't you dare!" Mary-Beth said very loudly. The guards turned towards them again. Mary-Beth whispered, "Don't you dare blame me for this, Derek."

"Mary-Beth I would never do that, now you promised that you will allow me to tell you my part without interruption. Please allow me this."

Mary-Beth nodded.

"After the miscarriage you were upset. So was I. But you were always such a cheerful and jolly person. You were so low …"

Mary-Beth inhaled deeply.

Derek raised his arm. "Please allow me to continue."

Mary-Beth nodded.

"Well I couldn't bear to see you like that. I felt like I didn't want to continue living. I realised that without you my life was hollow. I promised myself that I would never allow you to get like that again, and that I would never get you pregnant again."

"Is that why you haven't made love to me since the miscarriage?"

"Of course, why else do you think?"

"I thought you didn't find me attractive anymore, or that you were upset because I was not fertile enough, or perhaps your job is all you really cared about."

"Good God, no! Anyway, I need to get this off my chest. One day I stopped a girl for drink-driving. Her name was Sarah Miller."

"Please don't refer to her by her name."

"Well, she said she was an escort for high-class people and was at a party and had to drink some champagne to keep up appearances, as she called it. She said she was a law student and that if she got charged it would close a lot of doors for her career. She was tearful, but I was my normal intransigent self when it came to charging people. She suddenly crossed her legs – and I am ashamed to say this – she crossed her legs and there was a long slit in her dress which exposed her legs up to her upper thigh. She asked me if there was anything she could say or do that would make me lenient. I was so startled by the whole thing. I don't know what got into me. I told her that she was in no fit state to drive, that I would take her home and decide on the fate of her charges after that. When I got to her home, she invited me upstairs. It was as if I was not in control of myself, as if I was looking down on myself telling myself 'what the hell are you doing, don't do this, this is not like you.' But I seemed to go on until the inevitable happened that night. After that I dropped in on her once a month or so. This went on for a few months, until one day she told me she was pregnant. She was sure it was my child."

"Oh my God, Derek. Are you telling me that you had a child?"

"Please honey, let me finish."

"Don't call me honey."

"Okay Mary-Beth, just hear me out. I didn't want her to have the child, but she wouldn't hear of it. I pleaded with her. Then one day I got angry at Sarah … sorry I got angry at her and hit her across the face. She stopped communication with me and approached social services. This is when Tracey Chapman got involved. She eventually gave the child for adoption …"

"Oh my God, you have a child. I can't believe this."

"Yes."

"And you kept this from me?"

"I don't even know whether it is a girl or a boy. She gave up the child for adoption in another state and I don't know where the child is."

Mary-Beth shook her head. "I don't know you at all. So, then you bumped them both off."

"Well I saw her once again and I got really angry at not knowing who or where my child was, and I hit her again … There is an angry side of me that I hate that you haven't seen. Anyway, I lost my temper and before I knew it, she was on the floor and not breathing. I tried CPR, to no avail. Just then she got a text from Tracey Chapman saying that the name of the person that she is involved with needs to be disclosed as he may be dangerous. So, there I was, I had accidentally killed a girl, but now I wasn't sure if the social worker knew my name or not. So, I was thinking of telling you that night that I was going to hand myself in. Then when I saw you that night, you looked so perfect. We were doing so much good for humanity, I guess I felt that the life of a call girl was not as important as what we were going to do to help others. If I was honest, I would say that you are my world. Yes, I really love my work, but really outside of you, everything else in the world seemed imperfect or unimportant to me. I guess I justified killing Tracey in order to keep our perfect world intact. To ensure your happiness, after all, that is all that I have wanted in life."

"And the other poor girl, Charlene? I guess you wanted to gratify yourself and lost your temper with her too?"

"Yes, her death was such a freak accident. She ran out of the car and I grabbed her. She struggled. I didn't mean to but punched her before I knew it. I sometimes forget the strength from my boxing days. She fell backwards and died instantly."

Mary-Beth had a look of disgust. "I guess she was an inconvenience to my perfect life too."

"Well, I don't in any way feel right about what I have done, but you know you are my world, and that is all I care about."

"Derek … I feel sick even using that name. How could you live knowing you have killed a human being?"

Derek paused. "You may find it a strange answer. The answer is that I can't. Each day became more bitter than the last. You may have noticed me becoming more withdrawn over the past year."

Mary-Beth got up. "Maybe in years to come I may be happy to have heard your story, but at the moment I just feel numb. This 'perfect world' that you describe is living hell for me. You are not the man I loved. I can't stand the sight of you, and I never want to see you again."

She walked away without looking back. "Guards please escort me out."

He called out to her, "Mary-Beth!" She turned around. He looked at her for a few seconds, "You should know, Mary-Beth … It is important that I say that the pre-pondering emotion is one of relief. These hands have taken human life and I feel relief that I am able to confess. But before you go, I would like to see you once more." He stared at her and smiled. "You know I worship the ground you walk on. If you were to search the whole Earth, you won't get someone who loves you as I do!"

"Maybe so, Derek, but even the best medicine in the world can be poisonous." She walked out and he stared at her, she never looked back.

CHAPTER 53

Andy Gomez Gets Ready For A New Office

Andy walked past the secretaries. Sandra looked up and, as if unsure, said, "Good morning Andy."

Andy nodded without looking at her and went on to his room.

Andy walked around his office looking at various objects around the room. He then went to the window and looks at the Manhattan skyline.

There was a knock at his door. The knock was repeated and was louder. He suddenly looked back towards the door. "Oh, sorry Sandra, I was miles away."

"Are you okay?"

"Oh yes. Come on in, Sandra. Do come in and sit down." He pointed to a sofa chair that was at the other side of the room away from his desk. "Sit on the comfortable chair."

"I thought these chairs were for VIPs."

"Today, Sandra, you are the VIP."

Sandra sat down and put her notebook on her lap.

"Before I say anything, I am not sure how to say this, but I think you should address me more formally in front of other staff. That is Mister Gomez and not Andy."

"Oh, I do apologise Mister Gomez."

"Andy."

"Pardon?"

"Please call me Andy."

Sandra smiled, "Yes Andy I understand. I am sorry."

"Don't apologise again, especially as something funny happens inside me when you say Andy!"

"What do you mean?"

"Em … I would like to talk to you about something else."

"Yes, I noticed when I came into your office that you were miles away. Are you okay? I mean with losing the case and so on."

"Absolutely. Winning a case is always important to me, but I studied law because my parents fostered a great sense of justice in me. Put away your notebook, you are not going to need it."

Sandra put the notebook on a small table beside her, putting the pen on top of it. She looked very anxious. She crossed her legs and sat back.

"I'm going to tell you a story that I do not recount often," he kept looking out the window and continued to talk. "When I was young my father lost his job in a newspaper firm. He was wrongly accused of stealing money from the petty cash and was fired. It was the talk of the town and my mother became very upset. She was the daughter of a judge and she felt that they had brought shame onto the family. Her father was a most wonderful man and he tried to reassure her that he trusted Frank, my father. But my mom became very ill and died mysteriously a few months later. The forensic investigators initially thought she had committed suicide, but they did not find any evidence of it. My father always maintained that the newspaper firm had caused her death through stress. He said that she was so ashamed that she simply lost the will to live. My father blamed himself at first, but then became even more determined to clear his name. He fought his cause for two years. Eventually he took the newspaper firm to tribunal and won his case. Even though he gained little financially, he said he was so happy because justice was more important than money to him, and he was happy that his name and the family name had been cleared. So, you see, I would never want anyone charged as being guilty if they are innocent. So, I am very content with the outcome of the case."

He walked over and sat on the edge of his desk, facing her.

"Well Mister Gom … I mean Andy," she smiled, "Where does that leave you with reference to taking over as the DPP?"

"I start next week, Sandra. I thought you girls knew everything?" he teased.

"Well Andy, obviously not everything!" She hesitated. "So, who will be the new deputy that I will be the PA for?"

"Yes Sandra, I meant to talk to you about that. I have been thinking about this a lot." Andy got up and walked towards the window and stared out, he was silent for a while. Sandra looked quite anxious. Andy kept looking out the window while he talked, "You know I still find it strange looking at the Manhattan skyline and not seeing the Twin Towers."

"Andy, you are making me very nervous!"

He turned around. "Gosh I am sorry, Sandra, I feel a bit philosophical today. Where was I? Yes. Sandra, you have worked in this office for a long time and have acquired a lot of experience that perhaps is different to what the DPP needs."

Sandra interrupted, "I understand, Andy, I can't be your PA as the DPP as I am needed here, or perhaps someone with better skills in needed in the DPP office."

"Sandra, you are not on the ball at all today, are you? No, what I am trying to say, and failing miserably, is that you and I will have to interview for the PA post for the Deputy DPP and you will be moving up to work as the PA to the DPP, that is my PA."

"And Andy, you are assuming that I will accept the job?"

Andy walked over and sat on the seat beside her. "Gosh, I am sorry, Sandra, that was very presumptuous of me. Would you like the job?"

Sandra slapped him on the upper arm. "Don't be silly, Andy! Of course, I would like the job. I would love the job. Are you kidding me? I can't imagine myself working for anybody else."

"Of course there will be some changes to your working conditions."

Sandra raised her eyebrows. "There's always a catch. What exactly are the changes?"

"Well I hasten to add that your new pay scale will reflect the change in your working conditions."

"Counsellor please answer the question!"

"Haha, very good, Sandra. But this may take a few minutes."

"That's okay, Andy, I have all day!"

"Yes, but I was hoping to discuss this over dinner … tonight."

Sandra looked at him and smiled. "Man, this is the worse invitation I have had for a date in my life!"

Andy laughed, "And I bet you have had a lot of invitations."

"Are you kidding me? Not the way you work me in here. I have no time for a social life!"

"Well, you haven't answered my question yet."

"Well Andy, I will go out on a date on one condition."

"And what condition is that?"

"That we don't talk shop."

"Well Sandra, I am a bit out of practice, can I at least start talking about work to break the ice?"

"Okay I will give you that much, but I am sure there is a lot more we can talk about."

"Like what?"

"For example, Andy, you can tell me whether you look at every girl's behind when they leave your room or just mine."

"How did you know … Oops I just incriminated myself, didn't I?" He waved his hand. "Now get that aforementioned pretty little derriere of yours out of my office. I will pick you up at seven."

"Do you know where I live?"

"Yes, I had to look it up to see what restaurants would be easier to get to."

"Oh, you have done your homework. I am flattered. Where are we going?"

"I can't tell you that, but if you don't wear a long dress you will feel out of place."

"Well now, Andy, I can certainly tell you that I have not been on a date ever when I wore a long dress."

Andy waved his hand. "Out, out."

Sandra got up and in a flirtatious way said, "See you later, Andy."

She walked towards the door and when she was at the door Andy said, "Sandra?"

"Yes Andy?"

"Just yours!"

Sandra looked over her shoulder at her behind. "It's not a bad toosh if I may say so myself!"

She walked out.

Andy whispered, "Hmm, it's edible!"

Sandra walked back in. "Sorry what did you say?"

Andy answered quickly, "I said 'It's admirable'."

"Oh, I thought you said something else!"

"Out! Out!" He mockingly shouted and waved the back of his hand.

Sandra laughed as she walked out.

CHAPTER 54

Big Al's Surprise Visitor

The guard talked to Big Al through the metal bars of the cell door.

"Big Al, you have a visitor."

"Who is it, Steve?" Big Al sat up and turned down his music.

"I don't know, Big Al, I was told that it is confidential."

"Hmm …" Big Al rubbed his chin. "I guess if I don't go to see I will be up all night wondering who it was."

Steve unlocked the cell door. "Follow me, Big Al."

After going through a couple of gates Big Al stopped, "Hey wait a minute, Steve, this is not the way to the common visiting area!"

"No Big Al, did I not mention? It is in one of the private interview rooms."

"Fuck me. He must be a big wig. It is not the warden, is it?"

"Don't think so, Big Al. The warden meets everyone in his palace, his office. He wouldn't be seen anywhere near the interview rooms."

"Quite right, Steve. He likes to show everyone he is boss. Know why he is not the boss?"

"Why?"

"To be the big boss you have to have big cahoonas. What does he have in his boxers? Two peas."

Steve laughed out loud, "Big Al, I didn't know his balls were that big."

Big Al laughed and slapped Steve on the back.

Steve opened the last door and pointed to an interview room which said,

'Solicitor Interview Room 1'.

"I'll be outside waiting for you. I am in no rush."

"Sure thing, Steve, thanks."

Big Al walked in and could only see the back of a person sitting on a chair facing the back wall.

Big Al seemed a bit apprehensive. "Do I know you?"

The chair swivelled around. "Hello Mister Miller."

Big Al smiled. "Well, fuck me! If it isn't Detective Sterne!"

Big Al stepped towards Jim. Jim stood up but said quickly, "Cameras are on."

"Oh right!" said Big Al and reached out his hand. Jim shook it.

Jim pointed to the seat facing him. "Please sit down, Mister Miller."

Big Al walked around and sat on the chair facing Jim.

Jim sat down and pointed to the camera on the ceiling. "Camera is on but there is no sound."

Big Al looked at the camera and turned his chair slightly, "Well we had better make sure they don't read our lips."

Jim smiled. "Ever the cautious."

Big Al reached out his hand and shook Jim's hand again. "Well to what do I owe this pleasure? I wasn't expecting to see you in here!"

"Well Mister Miller …"

"Please call me Big Al. Everyone in here does."

"Sure Big Al. And you can call me Jim. I thought I would come and see how you are doing in this shit hole."

"I'm doing fine, Jim. I heard you got some stick in court. The chick lawyer gave you a hard time about planting evidence. Your reputation took a bit of a battering."

"Yes and no, Big Al. You know the public are fickle. A lot of them will be thinking that cops are corrupt and probably a lot more won't give a shit if evidence was planted against criminals. In fact, I think most cops say that was an awful deed in public, but privately think 'good on you for getting the son of a bitch'."

"Yeah; I guess you are right. I guess I have to thank you for taking all this flack on account of me."

"Don't mention it, Big Al."

"Why did you do it?"

"Which part?"

"Well when I approached you and asked to plant the evidence against me, you should have known that it may damage your reputation."

"Well actually I didn't think that part through. I really didn't think any of it would get out. Whenever you gave me the laundered money, I was just worried that I may be caught with the money in my possession. Leaving it in your car was the easy bit."

"Yeah, the detectives, especially that senior moron Detective McCartney, thought he had caught me red-handed. He thought I would be stupid enough to leave two hundred thousand dollars in my car. I thought when the pressure came on you when you were seen on CCTV with a bag near my car you would have squealed."

"What do you take me for, Big Al?"

"No, I had read you right in the first place, I knew you could take the pressure."

"Well the NYPD also didn't want extra heat on the force and were just happy to get you. I just got a blot against my name, which on retrospection has not done my reputation much harm."

Big Al laughed, "Yeah, you cops stick together."

Jim nodded.

"But I noticed, Jim, you didn't answer my question."

"Shit, I was hoping you wouldn't notice."

Jim leant back on his seat. He looked at the camera and came forward again. "I wish I could say it was for some philanthropic reason to save the New York Public from a gangster like you, or for altruism to help your family. But no, the reason was simple. You helped my pops once."

Big Al looked puzzled. "Now I am baffled. Why the fuck would I help anybody?"

"My pops told me the story. About two years previous to your arrest my pops was walking in the pouring rain. He was carrying a heavy shopping load, he stepped off the kerb and twisted and fractured his ankle. You were driving a car. You swerved and avoided hitting him. You got out of the car and saw his foot at an angle from his lower leg. You helped him into your car and drove him to ER. He refused to go in for treatment as his insurance had lapsed and he said he would have to use up all his savings. He was going to take a taxi to a community hospital. You walked to the desk and left your card with the receptionist and told her to charge everything to your account and that someone would be there to pick up the card the next day. By this stage my dad was in too much pain to argue and had in fact nearly fainted due to the pain. He never saw you again. But he recognized you from the news on TV the previous day."

"My God!" Big Al exclaimed. "You know, outside of my family I have never done anything for anyone. One time I help someone, and it pays back years later!"

"And why did you pick me, Big Al? You were very brave asking a police detective for help. I could have nailed you."

"Well I was not that stupid. First of all, I was discrete in asking you about it. Also, I had heard about your reputation of doing deals with criminals. You were known amongst us as being tough and straight, but also always looked at the bigger picture and not interested in peripheral matters getting in the way of the big picture."

"So why did you offer me a million dollars?"

"Well it was simple. If you had said yes to the million dollars I would have never gone through the deal. I would have known that you couldn't be trusted."

"Clever fellow, Big Al."

"Thank you. I was very meticulous. My solicitor cleverly made sure I went to prison without being too obvious. This saved my life and I thought my family's too. Didn't quite work out that way."

Jim hesitated. "Big Al, I was very sorry to hear about your family. It must have been difficult for you."

"Yeah. I was happy in here knowing they were safe. Once they both perished, I have made this my home."

"In another ten years you will be out, won't you?"

Big Al nodded. "Yeah, maybe five. But I am only just beginning to think about that. To be honest I feel so comfortable in here. Anyway, I have some time to think about this. Perhaps I may make some moves for getting out. I'll see."

Jim reached out his hand. "Well Big Al, don't know if our paths will cross again, but if you are out, give me a shout. If you get involved in criminal activities don't expect me to go easy on you."

Big Al shook his hand. "I wouldn't expect anything less from you, Jim. Pleasure to have known you."

"I'm surprised to say likewise."

CHAPTER 55

Stick or Twist?

Gabby came out of the back door of the restaurant and stood in the rain. "Where the hell is the taxi?" she said out loud as she put her handbag over her head. Suddenly she became aware that there was a cover over her head. She looked up and saw a leather jacket. She followed the hands and saw Geno standing there in a short-sleeve shirt.

"What the hell are you doing here?"

"That's a very nice welcome for someone who is getting soaked to the bone to keep you dry."

"You can keep your chivalry; I am getting a taxi home."

"I will give you a lift."

"No thanks, I am happy with my taxi. I have had a busy day and am in no mood."

"No mood for what, Gabby?"

"For … well, no mood for you!"

"Okay, but you may have a long wait."

"No, I won't. In fact, my taxi is a little late and he should know never to be late for me."

"He wasn't late, Gabby. He made twenty dollars just by turning around and going back."

"What? How dare you cancel my taxi? I'll call another one now, you can clear off!"

Geno put his leather jacket on top of Gabby's hair and took a step back.

"That's okay. But I will have to wait here until the taxi gets here in case someone sees your breasts through you wet shirt and then won't be able to keep their hands off you."

Gabby looked at her chest. The rain had soaked her white shirt and her white bra and left little to the imagination. "Oh my God." She used the jacket to cover her chest and her hair started to get soaked. She shrugged her shoulders and lifted the jacket. "What the hell, here's your jacket, no point trying to stay dry now."

Geno put the jacket back in front on her chest. "At least it will keep you a bit dry."

"Thank you," said Gabby in a slightly softer tone. "What brings you here anyway?"

"Are you going to use my name?"

"What?"

"Well you haven't used my name once. Are you angry with me?"

"No, I'm not angry. I am fuming with you!"

Geno didn't say anything.

Gabby carried on, "I had the best night of my life with you, why did it all have to get ruined?"

"And I suppose I am to blame, that's why you are angry with me?"

Gabby took a couple of steps back and leant on the wall, now oblivious to the rain. "No, Geno. I am angry with myself for doing something I had never done before or thought I would ever do, have a one-night stand. And it has ruined my chance of …"

"Chance of what?"

"Well, chance of … YOU!"

"Well Gabby, that is why I am here. Firstly, I have a confession to make. After that night when we had dinner together, when I went to bed, I could only think of you all night. Didn't sleep a wink!"

"Me too, Geno."

"But now when I think of kissing you, I can only picture you and Paolo."

"I hate to say it too, but I can't get Paolo out of my mind when I think of kissing you. But then why are you here?"

"Well, this is the other thing. Since my sister got married, I am quite alone, and apart from Paolo I have never felt so close to anyone in my life. In fact, I would find it easier talking to you than anybody in my life. And I have hardly known you."

"So, what are you saying. Geno?"

"Gabby, I don't know if we can be romantic together. But I would like you to be a close part of my life until the day I die."

Gabby was silent.

"Well, maybe I have been a bit forward. I am sorry I don't know what has come over me. Perhaps relationships like this don't exist. Just ignore what I said."

Gabby put her hand on his chest. "Geno, I think whoever my husband is will be very jealous."

"What do you mean?"

"He will be jealous of how close you and I will be for the rest of our lives, but he better get used to it." She kissed him on the cheek. "Now come on before we both get pneumonia." She pointed to his chest which was soaked, revealing his hairy chest. "Or some girls may be queuing to see you."

Geno laughed out loud.

They walked toward the car. Gabby said, "Hold on, you are going to the wrong side of the car!"

"No I'm not," said Geno. "No best friend of mine is not going to be able to drive."

"But it's dark and raining, Geno!"

"I've heard it all before, Gabby, get behind the wheel. The rain has nearly stopped. Now get in the driver's seat. YOU are driving!"

CHAPTER 56

Jake Thanks Lucy

Jake knocked at Lucy's door.

"Come in," said Lucy.

Jake walked in. For a few seconds they were both silent, gazing straight into each other's eyes.

"I …" said Lucy, whilst Jake said, "I …" at exactly the same time.

"You first," said Jake.

Lucy paused before she spoke. "I feel terrible, really bad."

Jake reached out and held Lucy's wrist very lightly. "Please don't apologise."

"I would like you to hear me out. Please Jake."

"You have nothing to apologise for, Lucy."

"Please Jake, I would like you to hear me out."

"Okay if it makes you feel better."

"It does." She hesitated. "Now I am not sure where to start."

"Well if you–" Jake began to say.

But Lucy interjected, "Please don't interrupt, this is hard enough." She paused again. "Let me put it this way; I am sorry for ever doubting you." She paused again. "I guess that says it all!"

"Can I speak now?" Jake asked timidly.

"Only if you promise to be gentle with me."

"Well, actually, I want to ask you something."

"Go ahead, what is it?"

"Well Lucy, I want to know if deep inside you always felt that I was innocent."

"Oh? You mean like what was my first impression."

"Yes exactly. Whether you felt right at the start that I might have been telling the truth."

"The honest truth?"

"Yes, the honest truth."

"Well actually at first I thought you were full of shit, a drunkard bum, and guilty as sin. And you smelled like a wet ash tray!"

Jake laughed out loud. "Lucy if we are going to get to know each other you have to learn not to hide your feelings and be a bit more honest."

"I am sorry, but you did ask!"

"And has that opinion changed?"

"What do you think?"

"I would have hoped so. But perhaps we can have a cup of coffee and you can elaborate on that." Jake paused. "I am sorry, maybe I was presumptuous, I suppose you don't usually have coffee with your clients?"

"The answer is no to both your questions. I don't usually have coffee with my clients, but if you remember I invited you for coffee first. And Jake, you are anything but usual!"

Jake laughed, "I take that as a compliment."

"There is a pre-condition though."

"What is that, Lucy?"

"We have to have coffee tonight. I don't want to be on my own tonight and Amanda has just abandoned me again."

"Okay, but in that case, I also have a pre-condition?"

"And what would that be?"

"We have to have some food before the coffee."

Lucy reached out her hand and they shook hands. "It's a deal," she said. "And, I would like to know a bit more about Tracey."

"That would be nice," said Jake.

Lucy wrote her number on a piece of paper and handed it to Jake. "Give me a call later on for the arrangements."

"I will, surely!" Jake was walking out and he stopped and turned around, "I would like to say something."

"Go ahead, I'm all ears."

"Well this is rather difficult …" He hesitated.

Lucy sat on the edge of the table and was silent.

Jake looked down. "Well. What I am trying to say and struggling is …" He looked at Lucy. He then sat beside her and looked at the ceiling. "You know Lucy, there is not a day that goes by that I don't think of Tracey and how I could have, maybe should have, prevented her death."

"But surely, Jake, that is not your fault."

"I know, I know. But anyway, that is not my point. What I am trying to say is that I think of her every day, and sometimes I close my eyes and remember what it was like to hold her in my arms. But in a way, it is as if with her murderer being found, there is a release, a closure, in that justice was done for Tracey. You know that I will always have her close to my heart."

Lucy nodded. "I understand, Jake, I really do. I admire that in you. I would one day like to meet a man that … Anyway, I'm sorry, I am talking without thinking again."

Jake turned to Lucy. "Lucy, what I am trying to say is that I am not having dinner with you just to thank you. I have no idea where this is going, but I would like to say at the outset that I think you are a pretty special person and I know that I would like to get to know you better."

Lucy reached out with her hand and gently stroked the back of Jake's hand. "Jake, I was hoping that is what you had in mind, because I find you such a deep and interesting person and I would like to get to know you too."

"You know, Lucy. I cannot make any promises and don't know how things will turn out."

Lucy smiled. "Let me put it this way to you. If a man was married and he wanted to date me, my first thought would be; why would I trust a man that cheats on the person he loves most? If I was with a man that forgot me as soon as I was gone and didn't miss me, I would be very disappointed. So, listen. I admire the feelings and the love that is in the centre of your heart for Tracey. I would honestly love to get to know more about her. What happens after that, let's wait and see. Okay?"

Jake held the tip of her fingers. "Wow, that is beautiful, Lucy. So, does that mean that you don't think I am a wet ashtray anymore and you are going out on a date with me?"

Lucy kissed him on his cheek. "Yes, we have a date."

Jake put the piece of paper safely in his top pocket. "I'll call you later."

"Looking forward to it!"

Jake hesitated, "There is one more thing I feel I need to say, it's been on my mind for a while."

Lucy looked intrigued, "What is it?"

Jake again seemed to be struggling to find the right words. He eventually spoke, "You know when you visited me once and asked me what I thought of you when I first met you?"

Lucy blushed a bit, "A girl can hardly forget when that is not answered. I sort of assumed that you didn't respond because you didn't want to hurt me, that you didn't like me."

Jake looked her in the eye, "Well, Lucy it was just the opposite."

"Not sure what that means Jake."

"Well... Actually, my heart skipped a beat when I saw you. For a second I got lost in your eyes."

'Oh gosh, I'm flattered."

Jake smiled, "Well I'm glad you don't think of me as a bum anymore, what was it you said, a wet ashtray."

"Well Jake, it took a while for you to grow on me, to realise what a wonderful person you area. The truth is *indeed* a mirage."

The End

ABOUT THE AUTHOR

Born and raised in Iran, over the years I have travelled across five continents and lived in four of them. By a twist of fate, I ended up living in Northern Ireland, where I have been since 1979. Perhaps meeting a red-haired beautiful Irish girl had something to do with this.

I have wanted to be a doctor for as long as I can remember and medical practice, to me, is the best job in the world, but it can be like a vacuum, it sucks in a large part of your life. It took me some eight years of writing and another year of preparation before I got this book to the publishing stage.

Now that I am working part-time, I plan to write a whole lot more.